CLOSER and CLOSER

JENNA BARTON

OMNIFIC PUBLISHING
LOS ANGELES

Omnific Publishing
1901 Avenue of the Stars, 2nd floor
Los Angeles, CA 90067
www.omnificpublishing.com

First Omnific eBook edition, February 2015
First Omnific trade paperback edition, February 2015

The characters and events in this book are fictitious.
Any similarity to real persons, living or dead,
is coincidental and not intended by the author.

Library of Congress Cataloguing-in-Publication Data

Barton, Jenna.
  Closer and Closer / Jenna Barton – 1st ed.
  ISBN: 978-1-623420-70-3
  1. Love — Fiction. 2. Power Exchange — Fiction.
  3. BDSM — Fiction. 4. Dominance and submission — Fiction. I. Title

10 9 8 7 6 5 4 3 2 1

Cover Design by Micha Stone and Amy Brokaw
Interior Book Design by Coreen Montagna

Printed in the United States of America

For my Old Man,
who has always known love is a journey, not a destination.

CHAPTER ONE

For nearly six months, my dental hygienist fascinated me. Actually, it was her neck. Or, rather, it was what she wore around her neck. I knew what it was, because I've seen people in collars that looked like they weren't really collars. Before I moved to North Carolina, I saw the full range of human coupling—*everything*—in San Francisco. I'd watched, safe and distant, all the years I'd lived there.

Claire Saldino's torso hovered over mine as she clasped a blue paper bib in place. "So, think you're settled in now that you've been here awhile?"

This afternoon, her nearness, my interest and something about the two mixing, made her smooth actions…They were too smooth, bordering on a façade.

I couldn't respond. After thirty-four years of side-stepping the everyday intimacies most people found simple, I knew too well the sound of my voice skipping and stuttering as I searched for the right thing to say. Instead I held my breath, crimping my lips closed.

Claire pulled away, leaving a faint wash of something spiced and exotic in the air she'd just occupied. Patchouli. Just like my sister Dani. Specifically, Dani, version 3.7, when we were twenty-three and she decided she would move downstate to a place called the Peaceful Valley collective. Version 3.8 followed, four months later, when

Dani left the collective and began bartending at the latest in a long succession of restaurants where our mother, Kathy, waited tables.

Claire's gaze met mine again and before I could prevent it, my eyes skipped away, betraying me. The sight of the thin, woven black leather band around her neck was a siren's song. It called me to gaze at the creamy skin around it like a malnourished succubus. And I was too clumsy with my fascination to hide it.

Claire cleared her throat.

She knew. She knew I was drawn to that thin woven-leather band. And she knew why I couldn't distract myself from it.

"I am so relieved to see the end of winter. Aren't you, Erin?"

A polite question about the weather? She knew. Of course she did. Of course.

Probably, she'd started to wonder during my last visit, when she prepped me for the temporary crown. Today, though, I stumbled right into confirmation when I yanked my eyes back to hers a sliver of a second too late.

She knew *I knew* that delicate strip of braided leather was more than a trendy artifact she might have picked up on a Saturday afternoon trip to one of those artsy shops in Asheville. Our eyes met for a second longer than necessary. And she knew I knew that she knew.

After three visits to the office of Dr. Paul Saldino, DDS, Claire Saldino and I had been silently taking each other's accounts. There was an unspoken curiosity, but no words confirmed it. Yet.

I met Claire when I came to her husband's practice, nearly whimpering with pain, for an emergency repair to the broken molar I'd given myself somewhere between Oklahoma City and Maumelle, Arkansas as I tried to simultaneously open a bottle of water and maneuver a fully-loaded U-Haul. That stretch of Interstate 40 was particularly jagged, and apparently I'd worn that tooth into fragility. By the time I reached the tidy two-bedroom house I'd rented via Skype with a Callahan-based Realtor, I could hardly move my jaw. TMJ was as much an occupational hazard for system engineers as carpal tunnel.

That was in November, two days before Thanksgiving. I'd moved myself across the country to direct a team of system engineers at the new East Coast data center for ThinkMine, an Internet giant that spawned its own verb. Web browsers "mined" for information now, thanks to the company—and culture—where I'd spent all of my post-MBA years pushing myself to work longer and harder, making two steps to every male engineer's one. One of two female engineers in my management acceleration group. Two out of sixty-five selected from ThinkMine's sites—called *houses* in our organization's unique jargon—scattered from Finland to India to New Zealand.

And now, at a new data center in Callahan, North Carolina, too. In California, the final destination on my mother's long and dogged trek to the West Coast with her twin girls in tow, I was a sober set of legs, a source of extra cash to make Mom and Dani's PG&E bill. Someone had to be more sane, more sensible, more grounded. Kathy had never moved Dani and me south, sticking to New York and the Midwest before she got enough traction to get us to northern California, where she'd always intended to land, even before Dani and me. The opportunity—and my move east—was about more than my profession. It was my chance, finally, to arrange my life with the comfort of enough distance between me and them.

After five months, spring arrived. April. I'd spent my first winter in North Carolina. Survived? Acclimated? Nothing much about the everyday mechanisms of me had actually changed. But, even without a notable shift, I was still *here*. On my own. In a town I chose for myself, a house I picked because I liked the clean hominess of it.

Beside me, Claire inhaled minutely. I swallowed at my own telltale gasp, blinking to cover how I forced my line of sight from the braid circling her neck. I smiled evenly at her.

Question…she was asking—ah, right. *Nice weather; tired of winter.*

When in the throes of awkward, mention the weather.

"A few of the locals at work keep telling me this winter was unusually warm, but those two storms were enough for me," I said.

"Just wait for summer. Hot and humid around here."

Mercifully, her husband appeared behind her and Claire rose without further comment. As he settled in, checking the progress of his repairs, I sank a little against the chair, relieved to be not a person with a voice, available for conversation, but a silenced, open-mouthed observer. Dr. Saldino—never something more friendly like Dr. Paul or Dr. S—hardly spoke to his wife, but she orchestrated every step of his examination. Glancing between the curve of her cheek above me and her green-flecked hazel eyes, I turned my studies to watching her watch him.

She anticipated each movement. It was mesmerizing, a dance of sorts. Their breath settled, in concert. She was ready with an answer for each of his needs a half beat before she was required.

And she was aware I was watching them work together, how these mundane actions from each of them were part of a much deeper sense of tandem. I *felt* it. As irrational as I knew it was, I felt a warmed current of energy radiating from Claire.

"Suction, Claire."

She blinked, heavy. Were her pupils really as dilated as they seemed?

"Claire?"

"Sir?"

Sir.

My face flamed. A bloom of pink rose around that thin leather band on her neck.

She called him Sir.

Claire recovered quickly, and what she said didn't really give anything away. Given the environment, it wouldn't be unimaginable to answer her employer so. But he was also her husband. She dodged the instrument at my gums and I played passive, the good patient allowing her to do her work.

For the rest of the my appointment, reclining in Dr. Saldino's dental chair, I counted my breaths, clenched my toes, and told myself—repeatedly—that a surprised, breathy voice answering *Sir* did not turn the gusset of my sensible white cotton panties sodden, that my thighs weren't aching-tight from controlling this quick and ferocious arousal.

Over a word. *Sir.* Not him, Dr. Paul Saldino, DDS or Claire, but a word. Over what it meant to say it.

That word, and those slim strips of leather. All that it implied and how long I'd hung around the edges of it all, too curious and too fearful in turns to commit. I did little more than lurk in the anonymous safety of the Internet. When I was still in California, the closest I came to gathering my courage was spending four separate evenings parked outside of a restaurant, watching people go in and out and berating myself because I knew I'd never follow them inside and join the group meet-up there.

This *something*. It had a name. I had known the name, but now I had relatively familiar faces to attach to it.

Dr. Paul Saldino, DDS and his dental hygienist, his black leather necklace-wearing wife Claire, were Dominant and submissive. Or Top and bottom. Maybe Master and slave. But *they* did that something.

After Dr. Saldino declared my tooth in good order, he left without another word. As I tucked the generic toothbrush and mouthwash sample into my purse, Claire lingered. She offered an extra toothbrush. A little hesitant, she kept a respectable but available distance. Something—yes, *something* again—told me this was unusual, not up to form of how *they* did things. I was supposed to find them, or people like them, on my own. But Claire and I had chatted pleasantly since my broken molar and I arrived in Callahan, even after I noticed what she wore around her neck. It seemed like our conversation was based on real ease—more than geniality between dentist's assistant and patient.

"I'm glad you're doing so well, Erin." She smiled. Her round cheeks lifted. There was encouragement there.

"Me too." I had to do it. I knew enough from playing sidekick to my adventuresome sister that the requestee was responsible for starting the dialogue in underground conversations like the one I was about to open. Claire's shoulder lifted, beginning her turn away from me. "Oh, um…Claire, I've been meaning to tell you. I—I like your necklace."

Her hand rose to it, her index finger tracing lightly over the strands. Something, a taut awareness of each other that had been growing between us during my exam, eased.

"Necklace?" Claire's smile broadened a little as she nodded, a soft laugh rising from her throat. "Oh. Thanks. It's a favorite. I never really take it off unless we're going somewhere special."

I wondered where that somewhere special might be. A rush of disjointed images snapped to life in my mind's eye. Did he gather her auburn hair in his fist and pull? Were there orders? Threats? Promises? Hard metallic clamps, sharp stings from leather? The scald of his gloved hand on her bare skin? His voice in her ear, telling her in careful, succinct detail, how he planned to use her and how she would feel when it happened? That he was the one in control?

Did she know who she really was for so long—for years, like me—before she found herself on her knees before him? Was it all new? Her latest fad?

The melodrama of my imagination hit me, full and without warning, and suddenly I giggled. I kept giggling too, even as I raised my hand, still clutching the extra toothbrush, to my mouth and fought at the anxious laughter that was as pedestrian and obvious as a discussion of the warmer-than-usual western North Carolina winter just gone.

I rousted my sensible adult and hoped I could muster a semi-intelligent observation. "Um, well…it's really pretty. It looks so intricate. And…pretty."

"You know, my friend who makes them lives in Charlotte. I—" she glanced over her shoulder, then slanted her head toward me "—I could introduce you if you're interested in this style of jewelry."

I didn't consider how unusual, how much of a risk this was for her, offering a more personal connection than my broken right molar. I didn't think about how accepting the dentistry practice's appointment card with her personal email address and cell number might alter the landscape of my life in a month, or a number of months.

She did know. And she was offering to show me.

I'm not the only Proctor sister who's tenacious. And, I swore to myself, I wasn't the only one who could be brave. I was making a new, different life on my own, a coast away from anyone who knew me.

"I'd like that." I took the card from her and promised to call soon.

"Come."

"Beg your pardon, Madame?" Settling back into the gimpy government-issue office chair, Walt stretched his legs past the corner of his desk, chinned his phone, and started to work at his muddy boot-laces. After a full workday that began at seven in the morning, Lucy's exquisite diva-Domme act was the very last thing he wanted to hear.

"You heard me, Wanda," she all but snarled. "You are coming with me."

Lucy Johns had no patience for excess when dealing with the simple bitching and moaning of mere mortals. Lucy, Lu, Doma Lucia—or Walt's own special nickname for her, Louis—all were facets of the same very complicated, very intense woman. Doma Lucia consumed all of her excess-related resources. The single-mindedness of her in Dominant headspace made understanding her easy. *Do what Doma Lucia says and do it now.* Simple. Unless she was trying to order Walt around and calling him Wanda, which she usually was. That could get complicated.

"Busy." Walt nudged one mud-caked boot from his foot, groaning. Both a second boot and happy grunt followed. "Damn, that's better."

"Not better and not busy. You're acting like a fucking old lady." She huffed. "Damn it to hell. Hang on, I need both of my arms for this dress."

From the dull *thunk* in his ear, Walt figured she'd tossed her phone aside, relieving him, for a moment at least, of her own skewed version of heartfelt encouragement. He'd never been able to reconcile the sound of Lu's molasses-dipped purr growling her suspicions about his work ethic, his intellect, or his manhood. That low and raspy voice of hers — it was hot. Everything about his best friend, from her death-trap stiletto heels to her sleek, tricked-out Range Rover, would make a man break his neck to get a second look at her, and as the nameplate at one of Charlotte's most successful boutique architecture practices, she brought more than a spoonful of brains to the table. But all of Lucinda Johns' charms were intended for the ladies. Hapless males need not — and should not — apply.

"There," she said, announcing her return over the swish of a zipper. "Damn, I'm hot. And you're acting like such an old woman, you won't be there to appreciate it."

"I've been *working* all day. Laboring. Outside, like a man with thirty-eight hundred acres to look after."

"Waaah-waah."

"Tonight I'll be writing up an incident report, which my job requires, because I relocated a milk snake from a stall in the women's showers it was sharing with one of our campers, who hopefully won't sue the state parks for having too much nature in our nature. After that eye-opener, I led three hikes — and not the granny-walks, either, so don't start with me. And if you didn't notice, it was ninety-four degrees this afternoon. I stopped five times to wring sweat out of my shirt — polyester, your tax dollars at work, thank you — oh, and I redirected three separate groups of crunchies from Asheville back to the campground because their new REI gear was going to get a bit muddy if they stayed off-trail." Walt's stomach growled at the mention of crunchy, reminding him he'd spent his lunch hour away from civilization.

"Okay, okay. Quit your whining, Wanda. Speaking of snake, I'm wearing the red snakeskin Louboutins…"

Rustling through a pile of invoices and budget requests scattered across his ancient metal desk, Walt located a protein bar stashed there within recent memory. He could say no all he wanted; Lucy would catalog each piece of her ensemble for him anyway.

Walt tucked his phone under his chin again, buying conversational time with a grunt or two so he could rustle with the protein bar's noncompliant metallic wrapper. It refused to budge. Maybe Lu was right—if his fingers, as battered as they were, were unable to grasp a protein bar wrapper and wrench it open, *damn old* might just be right on the money.

"…and the last time Tate spilled lube all over my python Daffodilles—Hello? Are you even paying attention to me?"

"No. Don't need to hear any more about your outfits. I'm trying to eat dinner," he grumbled, tugging at the compressed foil ends between his fingers.

"Predigested whey protein isn't a meal, Wanda." Behind her voice, a bass-heavy techno song blared from the premium speakers she'd installed in her SUV.

"It's doing a fine imitation of one right now." The wrapper wrenched open, revealing one long, pale, unappetizing piece of apple cinnamon-flavored meal replacement bar. "Ha! Hell yes, victory is mine."

Grunting, Walt bit into lunch…dinner, whatever. This was nourishment. A hot meal, maybe an actual meat and two vegetables, along with a soft, pretty face smiling back at him from across the table were not dietary requirements. They were set dressing…fantasies. Not his reality. Which was fine. The personalities behind most of the soft, pretty faces he ran into lately were some variety or other of bat-shit crazy anyway. CPEP was wall-to-rafters packed with it.

"Walt, seriously."

"*Luuuuu*…no. I've got paperwork to do, and after that I've got to clean up." He crossed the small front room of his forestry service cabin, tugging the hem of his damp green polo shirt from his pants. "I'm tired. I'm definitely sunburned and probably dehydrated. The last thing I want to do is follow you around CPEP all night, playing good-boy-go-fetch-pretty-bottom for you."

"Hmmmm…pretty bottoms. Oh! Speaking of hydrating—Paul's having his first hot tub soiree of the year after the club closes." Lu's purr did its intended job of communicating the possibility of carnal delights in a suburban hot tub.

Same people, different night. Same kinks, different backdrop, and more of Paul Saldino's one true way to kink. The thought was nearly as unappetizing as a beige slab of apple cinnamon flavored, predigested whey protein.

"Hey, I think my phone's running out of steam, darlin'. I gotta run."

Toeing his dirt-smeared olive pants from his ankles, Walt tossed the rest of the protein bar atop a heavy text, *Invaded Ecosystems: Discovery and Management*, splayed open on his nightstand, and a stack of unopened mail. A dip in the Saldinos' overpopulated hot tub wasn't the way he wanted to spend his Saturday evenings these days, and a fake dinner was more than he could stomach.

"I'm not letting this go, Walt. You're going down to Charlotte tonight. I don't want to spend my night DMing alone. And you told TK you'd do a Florentine demo, don't you remember?"

"Gonna take a shower, Lu. Careful goin' down to town, okay?"

"The charming and concerned country boy act doesn't work on me," she sneered. "I'll see you in—"

Before Lucy could tear into him again, Walt checked out of the conversation, his hand falling away from his ear. He tossed his phone to the bed. Hot water—and a good quantity of it—spilling over his dusty, dry head was the best idea Lucy'd had in months. Then he would sleep for twelve hours or so, alone and by the grace of his own sanity, then another Saturday night would be done.

"Wake the hell up, Wanda."

An unholy clatter followed, making the rusted hinges on the front door screech in protest. And grumbling. Not the yawls of a hungry four-legged park resident, either.

"You'd better be dressed."

What was this with the snapping orders and the damn attitude?

Walt exhaled heavily and rubbed at his eyes. After his shower, he'd jacked up the window unit air conditioner to high, turned on his ceiling fan and fallen asleep, sprawled across his unmade bed with no more than a towel looped around his hips. In the meantime, the remains of day had faded to night, and apparently Lucy had driven the twenty miles that separated her glass and steel house overlooking Lake Arden from Walt's cabin, tucked at a respectable distance from the Poplar Branch Visitor Center.

From somewhere under the rumpled sheets, Walt's phone buzzed. Once he managed to fish it from beneath him, he brought it to his mouth, licking at dry lips. "Waaa-hell, Lu?"

"You're mouth-breathing in my ear and it's not doing a thing for me. Open the door."

On the tail of her voice, another sharp rap on the cabin door pierced the Saturday evening stillness. The visitor center staff had gone, and the overnight guard came on down at the campground an hour before.

Oh, hell no.

Walt staggered from his bed, smoothing down the tails of the soggy towel tangled around him. His hair was pressed in a damp mat along his temple, and if that taut stretch of skin was a reliable indicator, he'd drooled all over his cheek as he slept.

Damn stubborn woman.

He shuffled to the front room, his phone tucked into his chin, scratching at a new mosquito bite right behind his knee as he moved. May was too early for a mosquito bloom, especially this close to his front door.

At the moment, a bigger bloodthirsty female was taking up residency on his front porch. In the night shadows, at least six-foot-three — if you counted those sky-high red heels she was perched on — of corseted, expertly made-up, fine-smelling blonde stalked toward him and pushed her way through his front door.

"Aw, Louis, you look a bit put out. What's wrong?"

"You're coming with me."

Lu strutted inside, scowling at him as she passed. No way to deny it, the effect of Lucinda Johns nearly meeting him eye-to-eye, and in full-out Domina plumage was impressive. But it didn't intimidate Walt. Leaning against the front door, he watched her first performance of the evening, stretching along with his deep yawn. The towel slithered down his hips.

Doma Lucia wasn't the only Top who knew how to put on a show.

"Well, hello, Miss Johns. I don't seem to have you on my engagement calendar this evening." Eyeing her, he folded his arms over his chest and grinned. "If you'll just step back to the veranda, I'll pull out my appointment book and see when my next opening—"

"Shut it with that 'Miss Johns' shit, or the toe of these pretty, pretty pumps will find your next opening." Before he could catch her, she snatched the towel away, slapping it against Walt's stomach. "Now climb into your party dress and let's go. After your demo, you're working the atrium and entrance hallway. You can play welcome wagon to all that hot housewife ass that keeps showing up at the club these days."

Walt shrugged and pushed at the screen door with his knee, standing aside for Lucy to exit, hopefully in a minute or less. He wasn't in the mood for a social call. The refusal to head down to Charlotte was non-negotiable too. Absolutely non-negotiable.

"I'm beat, Lu. Tell TK I'm sorry."

Lucy perched on the edge of his desk. She wasn't going anywhere, damn her.

They stared, neither moving, nothing but the night sounds and their breath huffing at each other breaking their obstinate silence.

"You'd better close that door before you let every bug in your wilderness wonderland inside, stupid."

Walt stepped away from the screen door. It banged closed, stuttering against the worn doorjamb until it settled.

Lucy turned her sultriest, doe-eyed, come-hither look on him. She even fucking fluttered her eyelashes, just like she had when they were sophomores at Clemson. Like an idiot nineteen-year-old with too much testosterone, he'd actually tried to get her to go out with him, only to be set in his place in front of their entire calculus class.

"C'mon. I'll even get you a cookie," she said.

Outside, crickets sang.

"Fuck you, Louis." Walt growled and crossed the room, flinging his wet towel toward Lucy as he passed. She crossed her legs with a self-satisfied smirk and smiled after him.

"Not if my life depended on it, Wanda."

CHAPTER TWO

I wasn't surprised in the least. The soundtrack for the Charlotte Power Exchange Party, LLC, held at an outwardly nondescript club known as Area 51, included Nine Inch Nails.

Certainly, I didn't expect a sound system blasting James Taylor warbling about his imminent arrival within the North Carolina state boundaries, but the twenty-year-old, wailing, bass-accented electronica was an obvious, if outdated, choice. And the black vinyl sofas and steel gridwork suspended between the lobby and more intimate rooms of CPEP did nothing to alleviate the realization that this was exactly what I'd expected a fetish club would look like.

Bad decorating choices or not, Area 51 was the end of my path. Or the beginning of a new one. It was spread out before me, lined in matte-black cinderblock walls and lit with rows of recessed lighting.

Happy laughter rose around several clusters of arrivals, and numerous sets of arms opened and closed in warm, familiar hugs. I glanced over my shoulder again, looking for Claire. My attempt at easy nonchalance probably translated as skittish anxiety to the number of people who milled around the club's vestibule. A younger woman, one who had been introduced to me as Powderpuff at the group's monthly meet-up — or, as they called it, "munch" — I'd attended two weeks ago, squealed as she flung herself into the leather-vested torso of a grandfatherly-looking man. He chuckled, patting her fuchsia hot-pants-clad behind as she draped her arms around his neck.

Powderpuff was Dr. Paul Saldino, DDS's, girlfriend. Her real name was Tracy. Or was it Tricia? Or Tessa? It was a T-name, one I always associated with the very sort of woman — *girl?* — who might select Powderpuff as an Internet handle. I'd missed most of Powderpuff's particulars because I was struggling to swallow the anemic Applebee's iced tea I'd just sipped when Claire introduced her to me as her husband's girlfriend.

Who lived in their guest bedroom.

Until she *worked a few things out.*

I felt movement behind me and turned from the scene in the vestibule back to the front desk where I waited for the club owner, a woman known by the much simpler nickname of TK.

"All right, there's your six-month club pass, still nice and warm from the laminator. Now, if you'll just put your arm out for me I'll get you tagged and numbered…" TK raised a randy smile toward me, shaking an electric blue plastic band. "Can't have a newbie wandering off unaccounted for, can I?"

Newbie.

Clenching my molars together, I forced a soft giggle. She was making another small joke, I reminded myself. Probably attempting to jostle my surely obvious anxiety. She'd been the same during my repeated phone calls, using a gentle tease to help me progress through my questions and concerns.

Claire insisted she had introduced me to Area 51's owner the same evening I'd met Powderpuff, but most of the evening — my first munch — was a blur. TK's spiky, chartreuse flattop and black skull-and-crossbones bowling shirt were a temporary disconnect when she reminded me we'd shared spinach *queso* dip as we discussed the merits of latex body paint. The same smoky-warm drawl I'd heard over the phone was familiar, though, and it soothed my flaring nerves.

After all, I *was* a newbie.

"Thank you." I returned her smile as I tested the span of vinyl encasing my wrist, and snapped it lightly against my skin. "Do you know where I can find Clai — um, I mean clover?"

"Clai-clover?"

God, such a newbie. Already forgetting rules, breaking their protocols, and I was barely inside, still standing by the front door. Claire was nicknamed — or her scene name, as she called it — clover. Short for HisLuckyclover. Emphasis on the lowercase c, as dictated by the conventions of her *Sir*, Master Lucky — who still resided in my mind as Dr. Paul Saldino, DDS.

TK chuckled at me and, after a conspiratorial wink, rose over the counter on her toes, indicating a doorway across the congested lobby. "She's in the dressing room getting ready to do a demo. Told me to send you her way. Over there, past the slave cages."

"I see."

"Oh you will, sweetie. You surely will," she drawled, offering her hand with a chuckle. "Nice to see you in person again, Reboot. You go have fun, now."

Reboot. I had to choose a scene name when TK added me to the guest list. I couldn't really dream up any fluffy-fuzzy ethereal adjectives to describe myself while I ground my teeth that afternoon. Waiting for the test servers at ThinkMine's Los Altos headquarters to recognize a new software install script I'd written had already stretched my patience to its limit. Since I was sitting in my cubicle at the time, watching a line of code hanging there for what felt like hours, Reboot seemed like the most obvious choice.

And unfortunately, BlueScreenofDeath was taken.

"Oh, Wally, you came!"

On the heels of her quick, bright smile, Claire stilled. She turned to Paul, lowering her gaze, waiting for his notice or dismissal or permission. Inhaling deeply, Walt stuffed his hands in the pockets of his jeans and scanned the toes of his boots instead of watching her wait for her husband to give her leave.

Seconds went by. Nothing but silence. Claire's ever-patient waiting and silence.

Walt ground his teeth. *Asshole.* When did it get like this between them? When did he decide she had to worry about every move she made? That was what pleased him as her Master? Fucking bullshit.

Finally Claire cleared her throat. It was a soft, dainty sound. So much like her.

"Sir?"

Paul had been a friend. Claire was still one—a very close one. Like Lu and a few others Walt considered family and thought of in his private moments as *my people.*

She was so decent and light-filled, so full of belief in the people she cared for, he couldn't help feel protective of her. Problematic when the biggest threat to Claire was her husband, the man she saw as Owner and Master.

"What is it, girl?"

"May I talk to Walt about his demo?"

"Demo?" For the first time in recent memory, Paul and Walt seemed to be on the same page about something, both clueless about the particulars of this demo that had been on the CPEP schedule for months, according to Lucy and TK and Claire. Turning away from the circle of newcomers still adjusting to their bright blue new member wristbands, Paul gave Walt a cool once-over. "You didn't mention any demo."

Behind him, a tall brunette with the long, tanned arms of a year-round tennis player stepped forward. "Demo? You mean a demonstration? What kind?"

Once again, Lu was right on the money. *Hot housewife ass,* indeed, and Walt was pretty sure it was firm and just itching to try out a couple of kinks before she moved on to her next new thing. Crossing his arms, Walt stepped back and looked away, reminded just why he'd been avoiding CPEP for months.

"I don't have time to do much with the education group," Paul said to the group clustered around him. "This is Ranger, ladies. He and a few others handle intros on toys and safety rules at the dungeon. Good stuff. For beginners."

Paul reached past Claire and placed a genial cuff on Walt's shoulder. His arm itched to sling the smaller man's hand from his body. Instead he turned a brisk nod to CPEP's newest.

Oh yeah, we're all Master Lucky's grateful subjects here.

"So, what, exactly, are you going to be showing off—" the brunette spoke again, all lazy vowels, thick with suburban-grade innuendo "—Ranger?"

The scene name rankled Walt in the best of times. It had been thrust on him without his consent and stuck because it was an argument he wasn't willing to have. Too many layers of explanation, too close to real and symbolic broken bone, would be required. The people who counted—his people—would never call him Ranger.

"Floggers. The big, big, mean leather ones," Walt said, letting his gaze sweep past the brunette's wide eyes and across the crowded room. "Paul, just want to go over a few things with Claire, if you're good with that."

"Sure. Of course." Paul turned to his audience. "Ranger is going to use my girl as a demo bottom. There's nothing between them."

"Oh, so is he one of the Doms too?"

It's a damn BDSM club, not Doms-R-Us, lady.

Walt turned, not particularly caring if Miss Tennis and Tan-lines caught his eyes rolling, and looked to Claire. "Ready?"

Claire paused. The silence stretched on, moving toward uncomfortable, as she waited, still tethered to Paul.

"Hm?" His eyes bounced between them and he blinked. "Oh, of course. They're going to discuss his demo scene." Paul smiled at the newcomers like he was sharing secret wisdom with them. He even paused to stroke thoughtfully at his scrawny salt and pepper goatee. "Go ahead, Ranger. I'll find you two before you begin."

Paul's last words dissolved in the chatter around them as he stepped aside, waiting for Claire to walk ahead of him.

"You've got to be fucking kidding me with this shit, *one of the Doms*," Walt grumbled.

"Oh come on, don't be so grumpy about the new people. They're not all bad."

He and Claire moved through the crowd, pausing to greet a few friends as they crossed. Claire reached through the throng for his hand.

"We'll have to go in The Palace."

Great. That pink monstrosity made him feel even bigger and more likely to break something than usual. Following Claire into the space decorated for gender and age play, Walt stuffed himself against the door and tried to find a surface not painted pink where he could let his eyes fall.

"Just for the record, Claire, I think you and Lu are full of shit."

"We talked about doing more demos at the April munch, Walt. Don't you remember?" Claire began unbuttoning her skirt. And did not look his way.

"I wasn't at the April munch. I haven't been to munch since last November."

"Really? I thought you were."

"You and Lu were giving me hell about it just a few weeks ago. Remember?"

"Oh?" Claire squatted beside her big shoulder bag, known to hold everything but a map to Atlantis, and began removing items, one by one.

The worst liar of them all.

"Should've let Lu tell your stories for you," Walt said. "What are you two up to?"

"Just trying to get you out more." Claire sniffed as she stood and hung her clothes in one of the gold-painted school lockers. "You're turning that park service cabin into a monk's cell."

"Monk?" He chuckled softly. "You know better."

"Okay, you might not be ready to take your holy orders and turn permanently celibate, but still…" She crossed to him, smiling softly. "You should come down and play once in a while. We don't bite."

"Don't bite? Then you're not doing kink right." Grinning at Claire's rolled eyes, he pushed off from the door and clapped his hands. "So. Floggers? Florentine demo?"

Claire considered it and then nodded. "Yeah, with the big ones. There's so many new people tonight. They like the showy stuff."

"Good deal," Walt said and reached behind him for the doorknob.

"Oh, and can we use that cross at the back of the main room? I'm a little stiff today."

Walt's fingers stilled on the metal under them. "You okay? I can find another bottom if you're really hurt, Claire. Or we can cancel."

"No, no. I'm okay, really." She glanced past him, shrugging, and turned a small smile toward him. "Sir is doing a trial week with Tessa."

"Trial week?"

"Yes, a trial week of 24/7 service to Sir. Wally, stop making that face. It's fine. He's probably going to collar her. They've had the main bedroom. I've been downstairs on the futon."

Plenty of the people they knew from CPEP and many among those that visited the Enclave had alliances within the community that made their relationships look more like a Venn diagram than the traditional one plus one. Since the most recent influx of newly curious people started appearing in the scene a couple of years earlier, Paul and Claire's relationship had shifted from two happy, overlapping circles to a pyramid. He sat at the apex, and a steady stream of new girls — younger, edgier girls — made up the layers beneath him.

And that was just how Claire said she liked it. Her Sir; his rules.

Walt pulled Claire to him for a quick hug. For now, Paul hadn't forbade anyone touching her without his oversight.

"I'll get things ready. See you in a bit." He left Claire to finish changing.

A new wave of arrivals were already coming in across the club's vestibule. More faces and voices he didn't recognize. Paul still stood by TK's desk preaching his version of the one true way to do kink. Now with his friend, Tommy, standing by as Paul's favorite gospel of BDSM yes-man, he'd managed to pull a pretty impressive audience.

Walt let out a long, slow breath. *Oh yeah. Amen, brother.*

Instead of looking for the few familiar faces he saw in the crowd, Walt turned for the rear exit, making his way to the narrow outside space where people took a breather from the press of bodies and attitude. He'd been back at Area 51 for less than thirty minutes and already needed one himself.

"Hey, you made it!" Claire's reflection beamed at me in the mirror, her smiling face topping a heavy, gleaming silver collar — and her bare breasts.

"Oh…um…hi." There was little I could do to cover the absolute discomfort of being in a small space, so close to another woman who was so completely unclothed — and who was apparently so completely unfazed by it.

She noticed me looking anywhere but at her very prominent nipples and winced with sympathy. "Here, hand me my shirt, I'll put it back on."

"No! No, there's no need unless…I mea — if you're more comfortable, it's really oka—"

"Erin, take a deep breath; your energy's all over the place," she said, stepping past me. I flinched as her breast brushed my arm. "You're going to see mostly naked people here. A lot of them."

"Okay." I sagged against the opposite wall. "I'll do that. Over here." Far, far away from any more accidental crossings of my appendages and her breasts.

"Do you need some water?" She studied me with concern, looking at the number of inches that separated us. "Did you have dinner? You look woozy."

Claire, I'd learned, looked after everyone, not just her husband. In the month since our friendship had developed beyond my dental woes, she'd decided I needed looking after too. I still hadn't found a way to dissuade her—or accept her attention, for that matter. Having someone care for me felt foreign. I'd been able to go about my business, generally unnoticed, for most of my nearly thirty-five years.

"Oh, fine. I just feel a little awkward dressed like this when almost everyone else really isn't so…um, dressed—and look like they belong here…just being new, not really knowing anyone." I shrugged with a rueful laugh over my litany of social woes.

"I understand," Claire said as she sat again and began to wind her long, burnished auburn curls into a thick braid. She'd forgotten her shirt and her breasts were still out there, rising and falling as she worked at her hair. "I was so young at my first play party. I'm naturally an introverted person—a lot like you, actually. But back then… very reserved. I only really knew how to relate to people through my art. Sir—erm, you know, Paul—was so poised and…well, his personality is just so big. He brings people together. He taught me how to come out of my shell and have some confidence in myself. And not have so many hang-ups. Like about *nudity*."

"Claire, it's fine. I'm really fine." If I heard myself telling it to her enough, then maybe I'd believe it. I needed so much to be fine, at the very least to show all of these people that I was fine. I liked Claire. I wanted her friends to like me; I wanted to know more about this half-shadowed world they played in.

And I very much wanted all of them to still be clothed while I did that.

"Sit." She pointed to another plush, oversized, pink velvet-covered ottoman beside the one she sat on and began coating her eyelashes with mascara. The ottoman was the same lurid pink of the walls and the puppet-fur pelt under my feet. Every surface that wasn't pink was burnished with thick gold paint.

I'd worn my black knee-length business-dress skirt and a tailored black silk blouse. What looked marginally edgy-elegant in my bathroom mirror suddenly felt very dowdy. I unbuttoned the blouse's top button, then another, and glanced at my reflection. The result barely approached sexy secretary.

"It's very…um…My Pretty Princess in here."

"It's the sissy-boy room." Claire's reflection nodded at me, and she continued to touch up a thin flare of black eyeliner on one closed eye. "I didn't plan on playing tonight since it's your first time, but a friend—um, he called a few minutes ago. He needed an emergency stunt-bottom, you know, and this is the only place I could change."

I caught my own stunned face behind hers in the mirror and snapped my mouth shut. She giggled and looked through her makeup bag.

"Which part didn't you understand?"

"Nearly all of it." I stood, shouldering my purse, and gave her a weak smile. "I think I'm going to go."

"Erin," she said, setting her bag aside. "Please. Don't leave before you give yourself a chance to see everything. Maybe say hi to a few of the people I introduced you to at munch?"

"Is the woman with the neon purple foxtail attached to her jeans going to be here?"

"Foxtail? Oh, you mean Lucy. Yes, she will definitely be here, but there's no telling what she'll be wearing tonight. That one always makes an entrance." Claire rolled her eyes, giggling. "Don't let her intimidate you. She's only scary if you allow her to be scary. Or, need her to be."

Women were never easy friends for me, Claire being an unexpected and surprisingly pleasant exception. Thanks to life spent as the *other twin* to my sister Danielle, flamboyant, attention-grabbing women like Lucy—and like Dani—set me on edge. I sank into the depths of the ottoman again.

"What are you demonstrating?" I assumed it wasn't Tupperware.

"Flogging. Well, the Top is—I'm just the target." Sliding a tissue over her lips, she pressed them together, blotting at her dusky plum lipstick. "You'll like it—the end's really showy—Florentine flogging. The Top uses two of them, swings them in circles like this." She moved her arms in arcs, creating a kind of infinity symbol in the air.

Before I could stop myself, I asked the obvious. "Two? Doesn't that hurt?"

Rising, Claire gathered her bag and placed it in one of the gilded metal lockers that lined the opposite wall. "It can. The big leather ones are like a smack with some force behind it — we call them 'thuddy.' If he was using thinner leather or plastic, there would be less force but much more sting."

She could have teased me, or even rolled her eyes, dismissing such an inane question. Reflexively, I'd braced myself for it. But Claire, as I had come to understand from her actions and words, didn't judge. It seemed beyond her.

"Oh." I wanted to hear more but didn't know how to ask.

"This demo probably won't hurt much — Walt's showing his technique to the guys in the new member group, not hitting me for play."

"Of course," I muttered, suddenly aware of my hair charged with static and clinging to my cheek. As I raised my arm to brush it away, the silk of my sleeve rippled over my skin. My hair floated away from my hand, live on the current in the air. *Play. Hitting. Hurting.* Play was hitting and hurting. I turned my eyes to her, ready for more.

"I wouldn't mind if it hurt, though." She was so close. How did she clear so much space without me noticing, and *what* was she noticing as she watched me? I was upended, in the middle of this absurd pink closet, and nearly begging Claire to describe every sensation, name each toy and what it did to her.

Behind me, a burst of cool air carried in the sound of distant other voices. And Nitzer Ebb. The club's playlist really wasn't helping me dismiss the specter of my sister and her club-kid life so many years ago.

"They're ready to get started, honeybuns," said a throaty female voice. I turned to it as Claire stepped by me, finding Lucy — minus the purple foxtail hanging from her belt — standing just inside the door. Her eyes flicked toward me. Cool appraisal, recognition, and nothing more. "Oh…hi. Karen?"

At least she recognized me.

My voice and breath were still tangled with the questions I wanted to ask Claire, leaving me unable to do more than make a genial sound and nod toward the golden-haired woman who, as Claire had predicted, was dressed to impress in deep ruby satin and high-sheen PVC — the complete antithesis of the black denim and leather that accompanied her purple foxtail at the meetup.

Munch. It's called a munch.

As the door swung closed behind Lucy, I managed to get out a garbled "No, um…it's Erin. I — I mean Reboot?"

Too late. Lucy had disappeared into the sea of bodies behind her.

Claire led me from the small room, making sure my scene name was repeated—correctly—and remembered as she navigated the knots of attendees. As we skirted the edges of the long, gallery-like room, she nodded to pairs of questioning eyes, their owners trying to place me. She told me the names of a succession of faces, all indistinct to me beyond the reach of the shafts of light scattered throughout the room.

And in the shadows of the space, tucked into corners and lined in short rows were broad, crossed widths of blackened wood, low tiered benches upholstered in bright yellow and purple, and higher, single spans, covered in the same yellow and purple urethane. There were medical exam tables, time warps from a mid-century doctor's office, wide ladders to nowhere braced into two adjoined walls, and a thick steel ring gleaming at the end of each step.

It was real.

As more people filled the space around me and the lights dimmed, my apprehension eased a little. Once I was sure there were nothing more than a few dim inches between the black-coated block wall and me, I took up residency behind one of the low benches. When the cool concrete blocks pressed into my shoulder blades, I was pinned in place.

"Hey, y'all, I'm going to get started."

The chatter drew in, ceasing except for a few stray comments that quickly died away. And thanks to a universe that was occasionally benevolent even to me, that voice kept talking. It was deep, so *male*, and his accent...I'd heard plenty of elongated Southern vowels since I'd been in North Carolina, but none of them had turned my ear toward them quite like this one.

Rising on my toes, I tried to peer between the sets of shoulders and outlines of heads that separated me from the owner of that voice. A shift in the crowd opened a narrow sight line, and I caught a glimpse of Claire as she passed under narrow bands of intense light, her pale skin gleaming in contrast to the coppery braid swishing around her shoulders. Her husband, who I reminded myself was now Paul, not Dr. Saldino, was before her, navigating the outskirts of the waiting crowd as she followed. He stopped in the middle of the room and Claire followed suit at his heel, her arms behind her back, her hands clasped.

From the cavernous space overhead, a mechanical hum whirred to life as a length of steel tubing descended. Paul made an adjustment or two, then motioned Claire to his side. When she lifted her arms from her back and held them—offered them—to Paul, I noticed, for the first time, the thick black leather cuffs enclosing her wrists. The gesture, maybe the sight of the cuffs themselves, winded me. As I watched Paul attach the leather bands to a bar suspended from some point in the darkened space above, tension coiled up my arms toward my ears. My pulse coursed heavy against my neck, so strong my sight bounced along with it. I was boxed in by shaded figures on both sides, and with no clear route to move past them.

Inhale.

Claire's arms rose over her head as the bar climbed back to the ceiling, bowing her back into a soft swath of bare skin. Even with the occasional rise of a shoulder or turning head obscuring her from my sight, I couldn't look away from her. With her wrists bound to this bar by someone else, someone who decided *that* was where she was to be, and handed over for the use of another person, Claire was everything I'd been curious about for so long.

Another figure stepped toward Claire, this one also male but much larger than her or her husband. Head turning to Paul as he spoke, he gestured to the points where her wrists were restrained. I shuffled along the wall, searching for a better vantage point. Two women, their backs turned toward the imminent scene, prevented me from moving any further.

"Oh God, I'm *so* tired of them," said a female voice. Young, I assumed from the high pitch, affected with a generous side of frustration and boredom. "All of those people who go up to that house are so into themselves and Paul's bullshit high protocol."

"*Do you accept what you are about to receive from me?*" another female voice chimed, emulating a masculine tone.

"Fuck that noise, all of them trying to act like they're so exclusive and it's some big mysterious thing that happens out there."

"Nic, don't let them get to you. Getting to go up to the house doesn't mean you're anything special. It's just another play party and getting there is a damn popularity contest. The lifestyle's no different than vanilla life. And, besides, Tommy said he can bring guests to that big party they have in June."

At the front of the room, the same deep male voice began talking, his words obscured by my neighbors.

"Whatever. I don't care anyways. Too bad Walt's mixed up with them. He didn't even seem like he would be their type, y'know?"

"I know. He's the last person I could see buying into that bullshit D/s protocol of Paul's."

"Ugh. *Sir* Paul."

"Please, a sadistic dentist. Now that's a fucking cliché, right?"

They snorted with suppressed laughter, and the taller of the two brushed her shoulder against mine as she swung her purse behind her in a dangerous arc. I tried to step away, in the opposite direction of the two faceless women, but the crowd had filled in the spot I'd just vacated. The concrete block wall behind me pressed twin points, cool and solid, into my shoulder blades.

"Paul's so sketchy, anyway. He hits on every new girl with all that *I'll be your Daddy-Dom, let me show you what the real, true lifestyle is* bull—"

"Did it to me."

"He did it to me too, girl. And poor clover—"

"*Poor clover*, my ass—like she doesn't know he's doing half the twenty-year-olds who show up around here. And she's just as bad as he is, with all of her new-agey crap about being a slave. *Nobody* fucking owns me." Despite the harsh whispers of the two women, a few heads turned their way, accompanied by the sound of a cleared throat.

"Hi, girls," another, much huskier female voice said over the distinct rap of stiletto heels on concrete. "Question time is after the demo."

As unobtrusively as possible, I dipped my head forward, glancing sideways. At the side of the women I'd overheard, Lucy Johns stared back at me with a tight, challenging smile.

"Yeah, thanks." The two whisked past her, leaving a scented wake of sugared-fruit perfume and hair spray.

"I wasn't—"

"Of course you weren't," Lucy said, nodding. Around us bodies shuffled, reorienting toward a far corner of the room. "Those two were just getting started, and they like to keep the pot stirred around here. If they'd kept talking, you would've missed the demo. And *that's* why you're here, right?" Her sculpted eyebrows rose over her pursed, glossy lips. I didn't know how to answer her, or even what to say if I could, only managing a weak nod in reply.

Saving me from any further attempt at conversation, Lucy pointed toward the opposite side of the dungeon. During the conversation of my neighbors, I'd missed a change of location. Claire was now attached to the wide planks of one of the wooden *X*s that occupied the opposite wall.

The group stilled as Paul stepped before Claire and displayed what was a simply brutal-looking flogger. With her head bowed and hands raised past her shoulders, Claire's chest thrust forward. A shaft of light fell from above her, highlighting the side of her breast and the slope of her back, clear even from our distance. Paul handed the flogger to the other man — the Top Claire called Walt, I assumed — who had removed the dark T-shirt he was wearing. A trail of heavy black lines accented with fiery patches of reds and oranges roped around his shoulder and ribcage, sprawling over the curved valley of smooth skin between his stomach and hipbone before disappearing inside a worn denim waistband.

"Inch-and-half, buffalo leather. Fifty falls or so, I think. Solid. It's a mean son of a bitch," Lucy whispered in my ear. "One of my favorites too, but…something that thick is usually for boys."

Boys? Thick?

My head whipped in her direction again, placing us almost nose to nose.

"It's okay, babysub. Some little girls can take it, too. Curious?"

A hiss of air punctuated by a thud jerked my line of sight from her to the front of the room. Walt had swung the flogger, but not at Claire, whose back was angled toward the crowd. He'd grasped the long bands of leather at midpoint and, judging by the angry, oddly hypnotic red marks on his forearm, he had applied the flogger with some force to his own skin. I watched with a suddenly arid throat and mouth as he held his arm before Paul, then Claire. Once Paul stepped aside, Walt crouched, speaking quietly and directly to her. After a glance in Paul's direction, Walt held the flogger before her.

Still aware I was under Lucy's scrutiny and losing the ability to defend against it by the second, I kept my eyes forward. Captivated, annoyed, envious — and unfortunately, again, utterly awkward. My attempt to shutter my interest was quickly losing ground against the sight of the bare skin of his back and arms and the enticing trail of his tattoo.

When Claire's gaze rose to his, her lips brushed the thick—and irritatingly phallic—handle of the flogger. In spite of my most determined effort at control, my breath hitched.

"You all right there, babysub?" Lucy was by my ear again, so near her torso and hip pressed against my arm. I forced my lips together in a hard line and nodded, refusing to meet her eyes.

"Fine, thanks," I murmured, shifting incrementally away from her.

"Interesting picture? Cat o' nine tails got your tongue?"

I couldn't look in her direction. Didn't dare respond to her. And I was far more interested in watching him.

He draped the long leather strips over Claire's shoulders, letting them splay across the round of her back, and slide down its length, a gentle, measured course. She shivered, apparent even across the room, as he allowed the thick leather to glide along her skin. There was a rhythm about his movements, even in this, the earliest stage of their scene. Or demo? *Was this a scene or a demonstration? Claire said "stunt bottom," so that must mean this is nothing but exactly what it looks like.*

What would it look like if what he was doing to her, or to someone else, meant much more?

Occasionally his voice registered; mostly I heard nothing more than the sound of my own breath in my ears. This was nothing like I'd imagined; the sight of him adjusting his hips, increasing the arc of his arm and the wide fan of the flogger's tails. As he discussed which areas on Claire's shoulders, backside, and thighs could withstand such attentions, I was confronted with my years of wondering—and concocting scenarios when I'd allow it. The times I'd given in to curiosity and opened files online, only to close them as revulsion and arousal choked me. None of it was the same as hearing the air stirred by the heavy leather opposite his bulky bicep and feeling the temperature in the room rise as the bodies around me drew closer.

What would it—what would he—feel like? That close, his breath on my neck as he dropped those leather ribbons over my shoulder, let them cascade down the curve of my neck, between my—

A resonant *slap-thump*, answered with a soft, female *oof* snagged the familiar lines of script running in my head. *They* were far more interesting. Watching in the same room, hearing the increased breathing of the others who observed, the scents of sweet perfumes and natural musks wafting into the air as bodies warmed with intense interest and probably arousal at the scene before me, was entirely different.

And again, real.

It was the first time—ever—I could recall having no encroaching memories of the past or questions of the future. I was bound to the moment, watching each movement of Walt's arm and wrist, the clench of his thighs as he moved with his swing and delivered another thudding blow across Claire's flushed skin.

Claire and Walt, and what little I knew of them as distinct people, faded away as the scene intensified, leaving me with the simplified impressions of maleness and power, and a femininity that wasn't made wholesale when it was offered.

For his use. For his whims. His guidance, his intentions, his will. Given up to him.

And on the heels of that revelation, as always, just like when I managed to actually watch one of those videos online instead of looking away, the logical and conflicted part of me sneered at my own romanticizing of what was happening before me.

He was hitting her, I reminded myself. What he was doing was no longer the sinuous stroke of leather, led on by gravity, across her flesh, all at the whim of someone who took control of her. Simply, her wrists were cuffed to two crossed planks of wood. A large, powerful man was hitting her with a hard, brutal tangle of black leather. And I couldn't look away.

He paused and took a second flogger, twin to the first, from the back pocket of his jeans. The strips of leather swung out, stretching from his wide fists and landing across her pale skin. As the black hide ribbons rose and fell again and again, the dimmed room and its inhabitants seemed to fade away.

My breath aligned with his arm as it swung away from his body. With each *thump-whack* as he turned and flicked his wrists, like the sound of a weightier, more determined ceiling fan, the leather made impact with her skin. I exhaled, long and silent, in reply.

Circling over her, the dark leather tails became swirling extensions of his forearms. The floggers arced and intersected. Light and shadow fell in rhythmic flickers over his face and shoulders. Each time he struck her back, the air rose and lifted a few dark curls from his forehead, his body's only answer to the slap of leather on skin.

It went on, and I know it did for some time. Vivid pink stripes began to emerge on her back. Once, I felt a body pass beside me. Music changed tempo, a thin gasp and wail rang out. His muscles shone, glazed with sweat, in the dim light streaking down the wall. That alone would have taken minutes.

Skin doesn't spontaneously glimmer with sweat. It's a physical reaction. It takes time.

I couldn't stop watching. I fought to not look. Impossible. Where else could I look but where he stood?

"That's my good girl."

The flogger's dance ended. They dropped abruptly, dangling at Walt's hips. Blinking heavily, punch-drunk from what I'd seen and felt, I glanced around me. In the hushed room, Paul's voice was a rude wrench back to reality. He stepped forward and stroked Claire's hair, her cheek, then unhooked her cuffs from the bar over her head. I peered behind them, searching for Walt.

Why did he stop? I realized, too late, I'd said it out loud.

"Paul handles his girls' aftercare."

Lucy. She was still there, watching. A cagey cat eyeing a dish of cream.

Squaring my shoulders, I turned to her, my "here for business" smile fixed firmly in place.

"Excuse me?"

"Walt's probably heading outside for a breath of fresh air. Paul does what he wants, and that means he does aftercare if he lends out one of his girls." She shrugged, her drawl plunging with each suggestive dip of her eyelashes as she spoke. "I think I'll take in the night breeze myself. Why don't you grab something cool to drink from TK? Claire's fine. She'll find you in a bit."

I watched her stride away. *Lends out?*

And Lucy was quite serious about it — Paul considered Claire his property to *lend* to Walt. Dread knotted in my throat. It was the same dread I'd experience in high school when Danielle brought boys home on the nights our mother closed whatever restaurant she was working at after a dinner shift. I swallowed at it, licking my dry lips. The easiest thing would be to occupy myself with the formalities of a drink, maybe finding another brief patch of conversation with TK before I left.

The process of gathering my purse against my body and edging through the crowd until I reached the entrance played out in my mind. And even though it was the best, most sensible, safest thing to do, I couldn't leave. Not without seeing him again.

"Wanda." Something cold and wet nudged against Walt's shoulder. Icy water trickled down his side and he shot to his feet, swatting with the T-shirt clenched in his hand.

"You wanna watch that, Louis?" He grumbled and pulled his T-shirt over his head. He accepted the bottle of water from Lucy with a nod and drank the bulk of it in heavy gulps. "Thanks."

Lucy settled herself into one of the numerous wrought iron deck chairs and crossed the length of her fishnet-clad legs. Her eyes didn't leave his once. Damn her.

"I'm not in the mood." He finished the water and tossed the bottle in one of the galvanized steel trashcans scattered around the small, enclosed deck.

"Aw thanks, babe. I had a headache anyway." Lucy's eyebrow arched at him. She turned her hands in front of her, admiring her glossy black manicure. "I'm just checking on you. No reason to snarl at me."

Walt nodded and walked across the empty concrete pad. His elbow and wrist twinged with warning after each step. Why the hell had he agreed to do a damn demo with that big-assed flogger after a long day at the park? He couldn't remember talking to anyone at CPEP about it, but Lucy and—after an odd, silent minute, TK—insisted the plan had been in place for months.

He swung his arms wide a few times, stopping when he felt a satisfying pop in his shoulder.

"I'm fine." Shaking his head, he stood and faced Lucy. "How's Claire?"

"Paul's with her. I'm sure she's okay. You barely rubbed her back, you pussy."

"Right. Why don't you ask her about her back, hound?"

Walt cracked a smile, in spite of himself. Luce was the only person who could kid him out of a funk with love disguised in unvarnished verbal abuse.

It was hard to walk away from any bottom after he'd played with them, though Paul would make sure Claire was okay physically. The way he'd just cut in and ended the demo—that was more than a bad example. Paul had little regard these days for the way things had always been done, both at the Charlotte club and up at Tate's house.

Walt knew he'd have to find Claire and check in with her, even if it was for only a few seconds. That moment was as important to him as any other. Aftercare was an open circle finding its way closed, the *I'm okay, you're okay, we're done here* of topping someone. If he didn't close that gap, the old demon—wondering if what he'd done *was* really okay—might start talking, questioning, condemning.

"When you're cooled off, come inside. There's someone I want you to meet."

"Oh no." Walt threw up his hands, laughing. "You stay away from me with that welcome wagon bullshit."

"I don't know what you could possibly mean. Claire brought a friend along." Lucy blinked at him and damned if she almost looked innocent. Almost. Until she smirked. "I'm just being a friendly-friend. All friendly to the new people."

"Come on, Luce. You're never friendly to the new shiny. You have 'em for dinner."

"I always have a sensible meal *before* CPEP." Her mouth drew together in a smirk. "New shiny is my midnight snack."

"All right, let's do this," Walt said, standing as he shook his head at her. "I'll be nice to the new people. Then you can hit the buffet and I'll head home."

They lingered as the door closed behind them, allowing their eyes to adjust to the dim interior light. The social aspect of attending CPEP was Lucy's playtime, saving her real kinky play for the Enclave parties and her own home on Lake Arden. Walt let her lead him through several group conversations, pausing only to greet a couple of people who came out to Tate's house regularly. Lucy trailed by the homeowner himself, mussing his hair mischievously and earning a swipe at her ass for her trouble. A couple of eyebrows rose at them, and Walt chuckled to himself over it.

Lucy was a kitten; you just had to know when she put her claws out for real.

"Hey, Ma, don't mess with the hair," Tate drawled, and offered his hand to Walt. As they shook, Lucy draped herself around Tate's shoulder and fussed with his hundred-dollar haircut. "I pay a girl good money to fix that shit up before I come to town."

"I'm not surprised. You know, Tatiana, you're the most tarted-up Southern girl in this room." Lucy tucked a couple of pieces of hair behind Tate's ear and kissed his cheek.

"The hell you say." Tate's grin was wide enough, but it hardened a bit and Walt couldn't blame him for it.

The guy fought the rumor mill all the time, thanks to the envious stories about him and his invitation-only house parties carried around the Charlotte and Atlanta communities. If Tate Jernigan did half of the people and a quarter of the things those stories insisted he did, the guy would either be dead or on a constant stream of antibiotics. And not many guys could handle Lucy's repeated swipes at their masculinity like Tate and Walt bore in mostly good humor.

"Louis, you're one to talk about tarted-up." Walt raised an eyebrow at her, hoping Tate would take the opportunity to dish it back to her with someone on his side. Sometimes he rolled over for Lucy just a little too quickly. And he didn't take the bait this time, either. Walt cleared his throat. "How've you been, man?"

"Good. Finished another bench last night."

Tate's latest hobby was designing and building dungeon furniture. Claire had worried over him using power tools up at the house by himself, but he swore it made him focus on keeping all of his fingers rather than worrying about the bottles of bourbon he wasn't drinking.

"Oooh, can't wait to break it in for you," Lucy purred.

"Hey, Walt, speaking of the furniture, I might head down to Atlanta later this summer. There's a new club opening in an old meatpacking plant downtown. I know the guy. Might be able to sell him a couple of pieces."

Tate always knew a guy. He knew most of the kinky East Coast, and a good bit of the left coasters too.

"Selling a couple of pieces? Why…" Walt stopped himself. It couldn't be for money. Tate didn't lord his family's wealth over his friends, but he also wasn't shy about making himself comfortable because of it. "That's great." He glanced at Lucy, who widened her eyes, as curious as he was.

"And I'm thinking we should do another mentor's class later in the summer."

"Okay, okay, princess." Lucy turned a wink toward Walt as she nudged Tate. "We might have coaxed the bear from hibernation, but let's not fill up his schedule too fast."

Instead of scrubbing at his face, Walt shoved his hands in his pockets. The entire evening was beginning to reek of setup.

"All right, Lucinda. I'm just hitting him up while he's in a good mood," Tate said. "So, you two interested?"

One of the few true stories about the happenings at Tate's house was about a sixteen-week private mentoring class held there once a year. Usually. The last group had finished in the early spring.

"I would *love* to!" Lucy threw her head back and rolled her eyes in outlandish ecstasy. Of course she'd love to—she bossed her mentees around like they were fraternity pledges. But they came out being among the best Tops in the southeast. "Love. To. Give me three of them!"

"One victim per Top, Lucinda." Tate took a swig of his ever-present Diet Sprite and nodded in Walt's direction. "How about you, man? I might have a couple of people interested in driving up from Atlanta and Birmingham for weekend intensives too. We can split the registration fees."

"I'll have to see what things look like at work."

"You count caterpillars, chase down lost hikers, and bust underage drinkers at the campground," Lucy said, huffing. "That's not really a tight schedule."

"I might have something going on then." Walt eyed Lucy, setting his jaw. He'd done the last four rounds of mentor groups. He was tired of it, tired of the hollow, soulless sound of things he caught himself saying to his assigned mentees in the last two rounds. "Uh…I'll let you know, okay?"

Tate had a sense about people, almost as good as Claire's, and thankfully, it appeared to kick in before Lu could come back at Walt with another jibe.

"No worries, man. Just let me know if the other thing doesn't pan out." He shook Walt's hand again, edging past Lucy with his hip. "Luce, why don't you come with me to talk to Paul and Tommy about it while they're here and not working over their bottoms of the hour yet?"

Walt drifted away from them, grateful to be released from Lucy's high-intensity focus for a few minutes. He wandered through the crowd, stopping to talk and exchange hugs with bottoms he still played with occasionally and kissing the upturned cheeks of the few other girls he'd done more than play with over the years.

By the narrow bar that stretched from TK's desk, Claire was perched on a barstool. She looked okay — subdued, but smiling happily and leaning in to speak to —

Someone he didn't recognize.

A blonde. Pale, her skin turned near pearly in the band of light falling over her. Most of her hair was piled into a tidy ponytail that swayed across her round shoulder as she leaned and nodded, listening to Claire. More than one Top in the room would be dying to give her hair a good yank, pulled up like it was. She turned a bit, so she could see someone Claire pointed to. He stopped hard, probably almost stepped on someone's toe or thrust one of his big arms out too far in the middle of so many people, but he had to take a breath and get his shit together and resist the urge to just stare like a damn kid at her.

Everything about her face was soft — the curve of her cheek, her full lips, and the wide, round eyes he saw behind her little silver-rimmed glasses. She'd covered up her body nearly as much as most of the women in the room had uncovered theirs, only showing a few long, pale-tipped fingers under the cuff of her black blouse, and a swath of milky skin at her neck.

She looked a little uncomfortable, a little overwhelmed. Right over the fold of her crisp black collar, flushed skin hinted at a climb toward her ear. *God, skin like that.* Before he could catch his libido and wrestle it down, she leaned across the bar to say something to TK, crossing her legs and showing off her round pillow of an ass. She'd hidden so much under her sensible black clothes. All the covered-up skin tempted, making him wonder what that ass would look like, pushed up and pink, her hair loose, spilled over his bed, her eyes turned toward him, waiting...

"Walt!"

Shit.

He waved and smiled in Claire's direction, discomfort and dread surging in his throat. There was no one around he could divert his attention to. He was going to have to walk their way, holding back the mental image of his hand resting on the curve of this unknown woman's bare ass with every step he took toward them.

Walt stole another quick glance at this new girl. He gave himself one last fraction of a second to take in her silvery-blond hair, her round cheeks, and even rounder lips. The dips and rises of breast and waist and hip. All of her was in a prim little package that looked like it belonged pressed against an ancient desk or card catalog, hips writhing against his…*what does she sound like when she whines for more?*

Out of nowhere, Lucy's glaring face replaced the distant scene of Claire and this new girl. He'd been standing there, watching like a damn stupid, drunken owl.

Nice one. Way to leer at the newbie.

"Wanda, excuse me. When you're finished eyefucking the babysub, *I* am speaking to you."

With a spike of regret he didn't care to admit to himself, Walt's head snapped away from the magnetic stretch of black nylon-clad leg he'd been admiring and refocused on Lu.

"Just…hang on." He silenced *Madame* with a hand and began to step around her. "I'm going to check in with Claire and then I'm going home."

"Claire and I wanted to—"

Walt shouldered past Lucy, focusing instead on Claire's familiar, warm face. Before he was within speaking distance, a hint of perfume hit him: something deep and…moody? It wasn't Claire; he would have noticed that warm, spicy-flower scent during the demo. Whatever it was, the blonde's scent and the sight of her looking slightly panicked as he and Luce came closer hit Walt in the gut.

"Hey, Wand—"

He grunted a halfhearted excuse about his arm, shrugging Lucy's hand from his shoulder. Before he could turn away, Claire eased herself from her stool and made her way to them.

"I thought you two left," she said and took Lucy's hand, leading her right toward Miss Pale and Pearly. Exactly *not* the direction Walt needed to head. "Come sit with me and have some lemonade."

Lemonade? Since when did Claire and Lucy treat TK's desk like a front veranda at the big house?

Oh.

Blond. Alone. New. And Walt, more interested in spending Saturday night with a couple of beers and his dark, cool bedroom, before he was conned into coming down to Charlotte.

"You'll get me a cookie, huh? Damn it, Lu."

Lucy smirked. "Now who's fetching the pretty bottoms for who?"

Walt cocked an eyebrow at Claire, muttering more to himself than his two friends. "Aren't you two a bit old for the matchmaker shit?" Lucy's head swiveled around to him first, Claire's right after.

"Aren't you a bit too old to act like a pouty widdle boy?"

"Oh come on, Wally," Claire added. She had the nerve to wink at him as she steered him toward the desk. "You'll like her."

Irritated, he let Claire take his hand and lead him, his legs jostling around her much shorter ones. She sidestepped at the last second, leaving him face-to-face with *her*.

The pale, pearly, pillowy woman had a name. Claire told him it was Erin. She had to say it twice. Or maybe three times.

Her real name, not some ridiculous, concocted scene name.

The last time Claire said it — "This is Erin" — Pale and Pearly offered her hand to him, like the right thing to do was shake hands, like it was Saturday evening at a country club or Sunday morning after church services. Not at all like what was really happening, where they were. At that moment, Walt didn't care. All he noticed was the satiny sweep of her palm against his, the tiny tremor rippling up her arm as his fingers closed around hers.

"Hi." Her cheeks rose when she smiled, so high they pushed the little silver rims of her glasses toward her forehead. Fighting the urge to raise his index finger to the bridge and ease them back into place, he shook her hand again, reminding himself how big he looked to most women, how he had to look harmless to them when they looked up at him so words like *hulk* didn't come to mind.

"This is Ranger," TK added, coughing — a sad, showy attempt to disguise her devious giggle. Damn her, she was in on it too. "He was the one who did the flogging demo. She saw the demo, right, Lucy?"

"I think she caught the high points. Right, babysub?" Lucy's voice sounded like it came from the rim of a well, high overhead.

The new girl didn't so much as flinch in Lu's direction. But she inhaled, deeply, and never took her gaze from his. Her lips circled around her escaping breath, sent as a faint draft of air skimming past his elbow. He tipped his head toward hers politely and forced his eyes away, turning to say something to Luce or look for Tate or at any damned thing but the soft salvation of the first woman he knew on sight he'd wanted—deep down in his bones—in years.

He'd not let her smooth hand go, which made a getaway a bit of a problem. And when he gave in and let his eyes trail back to hers, she was still looking up at him, flushed and smiling a prim little smile that seemed to surprise her nearly as much as it did him. Lost to his own best instincts, Walt leaned his head toward her ear, inhaling the very same flowered, spiced perfume that drew him to her. Something told him she'd go loose-limbed over it, and because he knew, instinctively and without question he was the only one in the room who could do it to her, he let his voice drop deep and spoke right beside her ear.

"Hi."

Her eyes drowsed at it, but she didn't move toward him. Instead, she breathed in again, gulping.

"Hello." One of them shivered. Both of them noticed, and they chuckled silently over it. "I'm Erin."

"So I've heard," he said, grinning down at her.

"Or…um, Reboot. That's what I'm supposed to say—Reboot."

"Reboot?" In addition to turning him slack-jawed, she'd intrigued him. Most of the girls he encountered these days used a kind of fairy-goddess, windchimes-and-dreamcatchers sort of scene name, or one that made her preferred kinks pretty damn clear. But this?

"It's ridiculous, right?" Her shoulders climbed toward her ears and she smiled up at him. "I know. It was the first thing that came to mind when TK asked me. I was at work at the time. I didn't know what to say and someone might have heard me because we just have cubicles and so…Reboot."

The babbling wasn't put on. That shit was real. She was as nervy over him as he was over her.

"I like it."

"Ranger? Are you an Army Ranger?"

"Hey," he said, cocking an eyebrow at her, just to raise the color on her cheeks again. "Don't you know you're not supposed to ask about the world beyond the front door?"

"I…oh, God…" She swallowed hard and looked up at him, wincing. The air of her own high expectations and embarrassment, maybe over not getting the scene-speak just right, wafted around her. "I'm sorry, I—"

Suddenly, it was the time to put on his harmless guy face after all. He held up his hands, shrugging.

"Don't worry about it. No harm, no foul." When the agitated expression didn't fade from her face, he leaned away from her, humming. "You look pretty trustworthy, anyway. I'm with the forestry service." And that was general enough if something with this girl went south quick.

"I'm going to go get some water," Claire broke in as she stood on her toes and placed a demure kiss on Walt's cheek. How long had she been there, watching? And Lucy too? *Fuck.* "Thanks for asking me to be your stunt ass, Wally. It was fun."

"Oh…hey—no, Claire, I'll get your water. Just sit here, talk to your, uh—to Reboot?"

Claire shook her head, smiling, and pulled away from him. "I'm fine. Really. You know me, Walt, I'm fine. And I will call you later this week," she told Erin with a quick parting hug.

He watched after Claire, shaking his head. When she disappeared from sight, he pulled over the stool she'd left and glanced around for the rest of his audience. In the meantime, Lucy, the rascal, had done a vanishing act of her own.

"So…"

"A park ranger?" Erin nodded toward him, wide-eyed. "Like Smokey the Bear?"

Huh? Oh, *Ranger.* Yeah, like Smokey the Bear. "You know, you look harmless, but you're a bit of a smart ass under there, aren't you?" He laughed, in spite of himself. It was the oldest joke in a park ranger's life, but in her voice, for some reason, that didn't matter. "I've never heard that one before."

She brightened, and the sassy little smirk said there might be a bit of back talk in her. Just enough to keep things interesting, not full-on bratty like the last girl he'd played with. "Oh, I doubt that. You've probably heard the ones about Yogi and Boo-Boo—oh, and Woodsy the Owl too?"

"Yeah, Luce just called me Ranger Rick tonight. But Woodsy the Owl? Now, that's an obscure one. Been at least six months since I've heard about him. Nice work there, Reboot."

"Erin's fine with me. I can't keep up with another name." Her eyelashes dropped to her cheeks when she laughed. All at once, Walt wanted to make that happen again, maybe as much as realizing the fantasy of her he'd worked up as he watched her talking to Claire.

"Um, should I call you Sir?"

The word was like a cold curtain of water dropped over his shoulders. Not welcome and soothing, like his earlier cool shower, but abrupt, a big root in the path she'd tripped over. Sir was the very last thing he wanted to hear from this girl. No, this woman. Lady? Not a girl, because he was sick of calling grown women girls and thinking of them as somebody's property or a friendly piece of ass.

"No. Not Sir." He knew he sounded gruff, and regretted it, but she was too new and obviously understood just enough to be dangerous to herself. Some other guy like Paul, preaching his one true path of kink, or a hardass Top like Tommy who'd push her too fast—or worse, one of those designer-suit posers from town—would jump all over her newness and break her because they were too stupid to see just what she was. A surge of protectiveness rose in him. "Don't say that to someone until he's earned it."

"Right." Head slanting away from him, Erin closed her eyes. "Right, I knew that."

Of course she knew that. Probably read it in four or five books, or worse, saw it on FetLife or some other kink web site. This woman was the eagerest of eager students, the one who memorized the textbook before the first day of class.

She clamped her eyes shut, raising a deep furrow between her eyes. Something told him self-judgment was this woman's frequent companion, and though he couldn't explain it, Walt didn't like seeing her suddenly consumed by it. He nudged at her knee with his own, grinning.

"Don't worry about it. Hey, what about you—what do you do when it's light outside?"

"I.T." Her shoulders squared as her chin rose. "Storage team manager at ThinkMine."

ThinkMine was one of the biggest names on the Internet. The company had bought up a big tract of land north of Callahan, not far from the park Walt managed, a couple of years ago. With little notice of the locals, ThinkMine erected a very sterile-looking, bleached-white concrete and glass box, set back from the state highway where it was located. Most of the employees — people like Erin — had been transferred in or brought to southwestern North Carolina for the purpose of running whatever it was that happened in that plain building.

Erin might have done her research — but she wasn't acting on it. Walt couldn't resist pushing her buttons one more time, just to make sure she got it. She'd given up way, way too many real-life details about herself. He just didn't want to think about why it mattered.

"Not trying to give you a hard time, but now I know exactly where your office is, and with a little Dick Tracy on my part, I could probably figure out your work number."

"You're right but…well, if I can't trust Woodsy the Owl, who can I trust?" She laughed, shrugging. "Besides, I know Claire and she speaks well of you, so…"

"All right, just don't do that again."

Her chin jutted toward him as she gave him the sly eye. "Are you telling me what to do?"

"No, not like that. But you should be careful." Even Walt had learned it — too well — after his years in the lifestyle. Clearing his throat, he pushed past another memory of Holly. "Common sense doesn't go away once you cross the threshold of a play party — or a club like this one."

"Hmmm." She went silent for a minute, her thigh jostling against his as she shifted and glanced around the room again. "Do you have a forest?"

"A forest? Do I *have* a forest?"

"Or a park? A monument you guard or something? Oh, that's personal," she said as she prodded her glasses back to the bridge of her nose. "Do you want lemonade? Claire said she made it from scratch. Is that even possible? I know it is, of course, but who actually makes lemonade from scratch? All those lemons." Her nose wrinkled, and once again her glasses slid down her nose.

"Claire," he said, chuckling as he accepted a red Solo cup of her latest concoction. This Reboot…or Erin — her brain hopped around like a frog on hot pavement. "Claire would make it from scratch. She's like one of those lifestyle mavens from TV — but kinkier."

"Or so you assume." She wagged her eyebrows and sipped from her cup. When she set it aside, her expression had turned thoughtful.

"We're sitting in a sex club and talking about lemonade. This is not how I expected this evening would go."

"You had a plan?"

"No, not at all," she said, shaking her head vigorously. He did the same as a tease, laughing when she made insistent noises. Finally, she gave in, giggling along with him. "Okay. I *may* have had a plan."

"Uh-huh, I'm not surprised. How'd that work out for you?"

Erin glanced up at him, her smile softening. "Okay, I suppose? Considering I hate it when things don't go as I've anticipated, I think I've handled things pretty well." Her eyes darted away. "But honestly, I also think I'm ready to go."

"I'll walk you out."

She shook her head again, swinging that tempting, glossy ponytail from side to side. "I'll be fine. There's no need to—"

"Hey, it's expected. Doing demos, being a DM…I'm one of the people who makes sure all of the other people have fun and head home in one piece."

"Even if the piece is bruised or has rope burn?" Her lips pursed as she watched him over the rims of her glasses. Resisting the urge to scrub at his face with his hand in frustration, Walt stood, gesturing to the front door.

"C'mon, we have bad guys in Charlotte too. Let me make sure you get to your car safe, all right?"

Her expression softened, so much he wondered if he'd said the wrong thing or even worse, the right thing. Without comment, she stepped past him. As they crossed the club's social area, both remained quiet, settling into their own thoughts. Even after her dodges and feints over being walked to her car, silence with her felt easy. There was no pressure to drum up more chatter just to fill the air between them.

"I manage a state forest," Walt said finally as they reached the door.

"Ah-ha." Tapping her temple, she nodded proudly. "So that's why 'Ranger.' You chose that name because it means guardian."

"Well…" He stared at her for a couple of extra seconds, not bothering to shut his mouth or hide his surprise. "Most people just think—"

"They think it's because of Ranger Rick and Smokey the Bear and Yogi and Boo-Boo. Because it's your job." She turned, looking up at him as she passed. "But it's because of more than the forest, isn't it? It's more than what you do, it's who you are."

"All of that's right in a way, I suppose, but—no. Not really. Someone started calling me that a few years back for another reason and it's sort of stuck."

"Hm. Easier to ignore it?"

"Easier than explaining it." He reached behind, pushing the door away from him. "Reboot is different. For a girl."

"Oh? What do you think is an acceptable woman's nickname?"

"Scene name," he said, grinning again over the lip of his red plastic cup. "Your scene name."

"Fine. Scene name. What is an acceptable woman's scene name?"

"You can call yourself hot butter on toast, doesn't matter to me. Around here a lot of girls seem to like the crunchy business, so there's fairies and dragonflies and all kinds of femmes and windy this and flowering that. Maybe a dragon if she's bratty. Every once in a while you'll run across a sl—um, something more colorful about the girl's kinks." *Slut? Nice one, dumbass.*

"Colorful?" She laughed, despite the checklist of misogynist horrors she was probably cruising through in her head. He knew his damn ears were reddening by the second, too. "You censored yourself for me, Ranger? Were you going to say slut?"

"Walt's fine."

"Okay. Walt." She smiled up at him. "And as I said earlier, Erin's fine, too."

"So, Erin it is."

She looked down, slanting her head a little, and went quiet for an extra second or two. "Did it hurt?"

"Huh?" He glanced around his body and then realization hit. She was looking at his forearm, still striped a bit from the demo. Turning his arm over, he held it out for her. "This?"

"Yes. From before you flo—before you and Claire? Did it?"

"Nah...not really. To be honest, I was so keyed up, I don't remember doing it. It's not something I'd do. I know how my toys feel before I put them to a bottom. But Paul...well, he likes things a certain way. Top to Top, I respect him letting me play with Claire for the demo, so I go by his rules."

"*Does* it hurt?"

"You mean floggers? Sure. It can." He leveled his gaze at her, an instinctive need to challenge her overriding good sense. "But it can be good when it does."

Walt eased back on the heavy steel door, suddenly interested in his cup of Claire's homemade lemonade again. No one stirred up so many disparate topics like Erin had done, within only minutes of meeting her.

"Did she put something besides lemons in here?"

"I think it's ginger." Erin swirled the contents of her own red plastic cup. "I'm sorry, that was odd. And too personal. And…just—I think Claire's rubbing off on me. Last Saturday she took me along to one of her galleries in Asheville so she could drop off some new bowls or coffee mugs or something. I bought a huge piece of amethyst quartz she swore called out to me across the store."

His shoulders dropping a bit, Walt nodded, the awkward moment clearing. This line of conversation was more comfortable than exploring his innermost feelings about trees and the older, more obscure meaning of the term ranger, and the balance of hurt and pleasure. Especially when Lucy or Tate, or even both of them, could be around the corner, hearing every mortifying word.

Besides, if he let Erin run on and on with that *the forest is who you are* business, next she'd be imagining him plucking a lute, naked, and skipping down the Sawtooth Overlook trail.

But wouldn't she fit in there? And it was exactly where Walt wanted to see her. Out there, in the deep woods. Naked would be a nice touch, too. But outside, in the daylight, with sun-scattered green leaves all around her, the sound of her voice mingling with the rush of Sawtooth Creek, and the songbirds arriving, back from wintering in South America as summer came on. This woman didn't belong in a place like Area 51.

Where she belonged…that really shouldn't be his business.

"Do you know why she said I couldn't put it—the crystal—near my desktop?"

"What?" He tossed his cup in a large trashcan by the club door and stepped aside so she could walk out. "No. I mean, I'm sorry but I don't know, ask Cla—Hey, do you hike?"

Shit. Made it my business, just like that.

She froze at his side, eyebrows shot high over the rims of her glasses. "Hike? In the mountains? Outdoors?"

"You should. You should come out tomorrow. My last hike leaves the visitor center at three fifteen." As they stepped from the protective span of the red awning-surrounded entrance, Erin looked across the parking lot, dubious.

"It's raining. You'll be soaked...and I can make it on my own."

"Couple of raindrops won't bother me. In fact, it's sort of nice." It fell against his cheeks, splashing across his eyelashes. Walt looked up, grinning for the fourth or fifth time since he'd sat beside her. He tucked his hands in his pockets and leaned toward her, closer than he should. "Y'know, I'm not gonna melt in a rainstorm, Erin."

"No. I..." She considered it, staring hard into the distance. "I guess it's okay."

"Why wouldn't it be?"

They started across the darkened parking lot.

"I know how to take care of myself." For the first time since Claire and Lucy hustled him toward her, Erin seemed chilly. They walked in silence for a minute, Walt pausing once as she adjusted the ankle strap on one of her shoes. When she spoke again, her voice was nearly too soft to hear. "Hiking isn't really...I don't go outside very often."

They stopped by a dark mid-sized sedan. Erin opened her door, preparing to step inside the car. Grasping the doorframe, Walt stepped toward her, then back a half step, suddenly aware again of his size relative to hers.

"Why?"

She looked up at the steadily increasing raindrops, blinking at the few that found their way past her glasses' lenses. "It's too chaotic."

"Come anyway." He stepped to her again, hoping his shoulders would block some of the rain coming down toward her face. He was toeing at the line between welcoming and creep who tracks new girls at their first play party. The balance in the need to act right but not let her go was never clear. Walt backtracked away from her car door. "I do know a few things about managing nature."

Not convinced, Erin sat behind the wheel and turned over the engine. "Can I drive you back to the front door?"

"No, my truck's over there. I'm gonna head home too." He reached out, catching her door before it closed. "Poplar Branch State Park.

North of Callahan. Can't be more than twenty minutes from your big mainframe or whatever ThinkMine's got in that building down on Highway 54."

"It's a server farm — or data center. Lots and lots of servers."

"It's still twenty minutes away."

"Okay." She sighed a little and smiled up at him. "I'll think about it."

"I'll see you tomorrow. Three fifteen."

"I'll think about it," she said, an almost-concealed note in her voice heavy. "Thank you, Walt. It was nice to have met you. Good night."

It was a promising end to a night he'd had no business participating in, but had found himself in the thick of anyway. Nothing more than Erin agreeing to crunch over the pros and cons of a simple afternoon walk on a moderate trail. Still, he liked her. He wanted to know more about what made her quirky mind tick. As Walt made his way through the rows of cars, humming contentedly at the warm rain falling around him, the taillights of Erin's sensible little car disappeared around the corner of Area 51.

Suddenly, he was absolutely sure he'd screwed up. A woman like Erin would try to think her way right out of coming over to the park, and maybe right out of the lifestyle before she'd had a chance to see what she'd come looking for.

When she'd said good night, it sounded like good-bye.

CHAPTER THREE

Every moment, and during each distraction of the day, I'd resolutely assured myself I was not thinking about him.

I spent my morning applying new drawer liners in the kitchen, sure I was home for the day. Determined to be focused, I finished the rest of the projects I'd scribbled out before I went to bed. By early afternoon, I sat beside an open window in my living room, fingers drumming across the spine of an open repair manual laid on my knee. It was barely May and already so hot here, the cooling unit in the rental house had labored until it gave over and clicked off.

But last night, and the third time I heard his "hi" in that lazy-afternoon accent, did make me think. Or think more, maybe differently. Diminishing waistbands and tropical humidity should have made me turn my Passat back on the winding access road and go home.

Thinking—what I did best—had failed me.

Action brought me to Poplar Branch State Park. To see Walt, and for no logical reason other than a few minutes of good tension-filled conversation and a pair of impressively sized biceps. I came to meet him. Outdoors. On a hiking trail.

I didn't pursue men. Especially men like Walt, the tattooed, leather implement swinging forest ranger. And why would I? Men like him never really saw women like me anyway.

I flung the car door open, suddenly indignant. Why wouldn't he? And why wouldn't I? This was why I'd uprooted myself, moved cross-country, and taken on the work of actually managing people instead of lines of code. I needed to *be* different. Or maybe more. But not anonymous, and not an observer.

It was 3:19. I was late, already sweaty, and in addition to wearing dusty six-year-old running shoes that still looked brand-new, my only pair of khaki shorts must have shrunk significantly during my cross-country move.

I bent over and retied the unruly right lace for the fourth time, sucking in at a sudden, sharp clench around my waist. At least I'd walked through damp grass on my way from the parking lot. The longish, wet blades dislodged most of the dust that had collected on my running shoes since they found their home, seven months ago, in the back of a closet in my spare bedroom.

Before I saw him, the baritone of his voice floated to me, landed in my solar plexus and radiated through my body.

"…does rise about three hundred and forty feet and is a three-and-a-half-mile round trip. There's a self-guided trail that starts past the visitor center. It's a nice, gentle pace and pretty flat. Y'can't miss it. Follow the signs to Hemlock Walk."

I pulled at one fraying lace, stopping to blow away escapee strands of hair from my ponytail. And definitely *not* listening to that voice.

"But I wanted to see the waterfalls. This trail goes to the waterfalls," came the petulant retort of one of the heavier and older-looking women. A veritable gaggle of them were clustered at an information kiosk around a tall, shadowed figure who could only be Walt.

When Dani and I were twelve, our mother moved us to Glens Falls, New York, for some boyfriend or another. I placed this woman as a Long Island native. Poor Walt, he had a battle on his hands.

"I understand, ma'am." Walt's nod and a sheepish shrug of his broad shoulders were clear, even across the field. "I just like for folks to know what to expect. A moderate walk on flat land is different than a hike on an uneven trail with a couple of big elevation changes."

"This is ridiculous. Why don't you people just pave over the walkway so everyone can see it?"

"Well, *ma'am*…this is first and foremost a wilderness. The state is trying to maintain Sawtooth Falls as a place where nature is left alone and hopefully allowed to recover to its natural state. Not paved over and sanitized."

Another woman from the group, apparently all vacationing together, took the spokeswoman by the elbow, gesturing dismissively. "Oh, let's go, Estelle. We saw a waterfall last year in Jamaica."

They moved as one like a gaggle of honking geese toward the parking lot, Estelle's complaints still reverberating across the grassy expanse.

According to the North Carolina state parks' web site, the entire trail was three-point-nine miles long, forking to either Sawtooth Falls, or one-point-seven miles when followed to an unnamed overlook. Both places seemed remote. A tall, muscular man with an impressive trail of ink spanning shoulder to groin might choose a place like that to hide a pale, lumpy, too-tight-khaki-shorts-clad body — and its dusty New Balances. But that man wouldn't also be pictured on the Poplar Branch State Park web page, showing a group of fascinated schoolchildren a newly molted butterfly and its spent chrysalis.

A pair of long, dark-green clad legs passed me, lifting the hair escaping my ponytail with their stride. Still bent over, I watched as the disarmingly large feet attached to the legs paused, then turned toward me. Of course it was him. Of course it was.

I pushed myself upright on tight thigh muscles, certain I'd hear a seam or two in my shorts give up the good fight as I rose.

He took off his hat, revealing damp, dark brown curls. "Well, it's Erin. Afternoon. You came."

I did, the night before. I never would have been able to sleep otherwise. I did not share this information with him.

"Surprised?" I said instead.

"Yeah, kind of." He held a peaked brown straw hat with an official-looking red crest, and there was a slim brass badge attached to his light-green dress shirt, stamped *Easton* in blocky letters. He really, really was Ranger Walt.

"Me too," I said.

He offered his wide-palmed hand, his long fingers just worn enough from work to speak *masculine* rather than *sandpaper*. The same sensation of them bumping over mine registered from the night before. We shook, slower and for a beat longer than could be considered purely social.

I released his hand and nodded toward the group he'd just dismissed. "Good thing they were in Jamaica last year."

Walt turned, hands planted on his hips, and watched them go. "Yeah. They would've been disappointed anyway," he said, and pivoted back to me, his eyes twinkling. "No gift shop."

Our laughter only lasted a few seconds before an inevitable silence fell down hard between us. I glanced back to the parking lot, looking for other hikers. Of course there wasn't a single figure crossing the grass toward us.

"Looks like we're it," he said.

"If you have to have a certain number of people you have to —"

"Nope. I'll lead this hike for one or twenty." His cool, crystalline-blue eyes suddenly tucked inside the same crinkling laugh lines I'd noticed last night, and two deep dimples appeared on his cheeks.

"I'm sorry if…there's no obligation."

"No need to say sorry, Erin. It's my job." The brim of his hat passed through his fingers. "And a pleasure too, to show you around."

"So —" we both began after a long moment, faltering and laughing, self-conscious.

He was recalling last night. I knew it, in another atypical flash of human-focused intuition. Felt it, really, as a plume of heat rolled down my neck.

I cleared my throat. "Thank you for inviting me. I'm sure it's unusual, asking someone to your workplace who's from…well, you know — there?"

He glanced away, turning the brim of his hat through his hand, then gestured toward me.

"I'm glad you came."

The timbre of his voice never changed, but the volume softened appreciably. Before I could stifle the thought, I wondered what his voice would sound like in the morning, across from me in my bed, or in my ear as his thick thighs rode between mine, behind me as he grasped my hair and drove into me again and again.

Warmth quite unlike anything I'd known spread, from that first shimmer across my neck, to my shoulders, and sparked a fuse traveling straight down my spine.

His mouth twitched slightly, then spread into a disarmingly sweet smile as his eyebrows lifted. A small rumbling chuckle escaped his chest, and then Walt the Park Ranger with matching floggers shocked the hell out of me. His eyes darted toward the parking lot, he looked down, and the tips of his ears flushed.

"I think it's just us," he said, still looking away, and put his ranger's hat on. "Want to get goin'?"

"Yes, of course." I bristled inwardly at the sound of my own voice: too efficient, mechanical, harsh.

As we walked across the wooden bridge at the trail's head, I settled into a pace a little slower than his. Practically, his legs were much longer and he would constantly trip over me if I lead. Letting him lead made sense.

An added benefit was a better view of the movement of his legs against his dark olive green pants, and the round, muscular backside that rippled in differing defined landscapes with each step. His pale green ranger's shirt stretched across his broad back as his arms swung, revealing even more refined muscles. They strained slightly against the short sleeves before continuing on to tanned forearms, scattered with brown hair.

I pushed a damp strand of hair from my neck. *Only May and it's this humid?*

"So what have you been up to today?" Walt asked, slowing his pace to match mine.

"The usual Sunday afternoon chores. I checked on a couple of projects I'm managing. My sister called to remind me it's our bir—" I snapped my mouth shut over the stupid, stupid admission of a day I didn't remotely care about. "She called to say hello."

"Erin." He leaned down to me a little, raising his eyebrows. "Are you a birthday girl today?"

"Yes." I felt my chin rise again. What was it with him this afternoon?

"Well then, happy birthday." He chuckled to himself in a way that was endearing—and infuriating—and ambled down the trail, his thigh muscles constricting under his uniform trousers.

Unmoved, I paused in the middle of a footbridge and looked back over my shoulder for another glimpse of the parking lot. Men didn't usually flirt with me. None like Walt. Since work had become my all-day-every-day, most men didn't really see *me* at all. Now that I'd admitted it was, indeed, my birthday, he likely assumed I was telling him to catch his attention, maybe cause him to obligate himself to me socially. Dani played with men in similar ways. I'd watched as she'd perfected the skill at my mother's elbow.

But even if my only remaining pair of khaki shorts were tighter than most of the corsets I saw last night, and I was winded from simply following him to the trailhead, I still had my pride. Or was it dignity? I couldn't remember the difference. His smoked-cedar and cinnamon scent, clinging to my hair and navy blue T-shirt, was too distracting to reason it through.

Walt pivoted back to me, still moving—and of course still snickering over his own little private joke.

"Coming?"

"Before I take another step I want to know what's so funny," I called back over the rush of the creek beneath me.

"Nothing funny *ha ha* but funny—hmmm—ironic." He kept walking. Backward. Up a leaf-strewn, bare root-stabbed, dirt-trailed hill.

"Yes? And?"

"It's your birthday, but looks like I got the present." His eyebrows lifted barely under his straw hat and he turned to face the trail again without a further glance my way. "Pick up your feet, now. This is a three-hour hike."

He loped up the trail, adjusting the weight of his daypack as he walked. With a small, exasperated burst of breath, I narrowed my eyes at him.

"Did you just tell me what to do?"

"Friendly suggestion." His broad back disappeared into the new spring foliage. "Park closes at dusk. Best get after it if you're coming."

The first thirty minutes were brisk, taking me up bumpy, root-cragged hills and through two narrow, wooded streams. Those thirty minutes seemed like a gentle amble through a spring meadow compared to the next hour and twelve minutes I spent gasping for air and clutching tree limbs to steady me as I scaled not one, but two rocky inclines. And Walt—he never paused once. He kept a reasonable but most likely restrained pace, stopping only to sip from a water bottle that hung from a mesh bag attached to his olive green park service backpack.

Occasionally he would just disappear into the bright green and muted gray of young springtime foliage, then reappear as he rounded another bend in the trail. As my heart pounded, my frustration began to beat the same tempo in my head. I forced myself to breathe — in through the nose, out through the mouth — and keep my own pace.

When I crested what I fervently hoped to be the final hill, he appeared again, down the trail a hundred feet or so, perched on a giant, lichen- and moss-covered boulder, his long legs dangling in front of him like a child's might. Smiling amiably when I reached his side, he pushed himself from his perch with an agility that, given his sheer size, was incongruous — and perfect. He was power and grace, waiting for me.

Reaching past his daypack, he drew something toward us. Lumpy and pale, a bar of some kind with a stumpy white something rising from it. *Oh.*

"Here, hold this," he instructed and drew a safety lighter from his pocket. As the stumpy white thing flickered and caught flame, he grinned down at me.

"It's a protein bar," I said, toneless. Disbelieving.

"Best I could do on short notice." He pointed toward my hand. "It's white fudge and peanut butter, though. Those are the best ones."

I glanced between the safety candle-topped protein bar and Walt. I did it again, just to be sure I'd rounded up the facts before me and arrived at the correct interpretation.

"You're resourceful."

"It's my job to be."

"Oh." I looked around the trees and rocks and brown earth of his forest. "I guess it is."

"Happy birthday, Erin."

The phrase was foreign to me. Once I was on my own, there was never a cause to inform others it was my birthday. Before, it was "Happy birthday, Dani! And Erin!"

"I...um, thank you."

I knew I was too quiet with all of it: what he'd done, the notion of the day being mine, exclusively — and under Walt's notice. Before I could let his gesture, one so kind I know any sane woman would have beamed over it, unravel my composure more, I blew out the candle and handed it back to him. No wishes from me. That was too much.

His eyes settled across the trail, just over a newly-leafed bush. It burst with conical white fronds, populated with tiny blooms that nearly shivered as a pair of pale blue and black butterflies darted in the air around them, between the shoots of green.

"We don't see many of those in the park anymore. *Cupido comyntas*. Eastern Tailed-Blue. Fairly sensitive species." The dusk-blue butterflies danced around each other, dipping together, then flitting away, always in mutual orbit, always flirting with a connection. Walt turned back to me, his eyebrows lifting with mischief. "Mating."

Nodding as any dutiful student would, my eyes made a hasty retreat to my wayward shoelace. As I crouched over the muddied strings, I tied them—and a few primitive notions of mating with Ranger Walt—into submission with a firm yank.

And he was chuckling to himself again.

"You gonna eat this?"

He swung his body up on the boulder once more, offering me a closeup view of his bicep at work. In my peripheral vision, his hand stretched toward me, offering a boost to his perch. I pretended not to notice, and pushed myself up on the gravelly granite, hoping my arms wouldn't wobble under me as I kicked myself and my too-tight khaki shorts up to Walt.

His hand was still outstretched when I got myself on top of the rock, holding out half of the protein bar for me once I'd settled beside him.

"So how long have you been in…um, known Cla—clover?"

"How long have I known Claire or how long have I been in the lifestyle?" He took a long drink from his water bottle. "Or how long have I been kinky?"

"I don't know." His directness pinned me down, with no easy route to a more comfortable means of discovering everything I wanted to know about him. I wanted to hear his version of this thing—a lifestyle, maybe—he shared with Claire. And I did want to know, not only because I should if what felt like our mutual attraction became something more, but because of him. Already, I liked him. I wanted to know Walt's story. Maybe all of them.

"Kinky. How long?"

Glancing over at me with a wry half-smile, he laughed softly. "Straight to the point, huh?"

I shrugged, pulled at a stray peanut and bit into it. "I suppose. I wonder about things, though."

"About?"

"About people. I'm curious about how people figure things out. Not just with—" I gestured toward the forest, like it was where I'd find the perfect example of the parts of BDSM I always was curious about "—that. Being into that."

"Hey, Erin," he said, tipping his shoulder toward mine like a conspirator. "If you have a hard time saying *it*, you might want to reconsider giving it a try."

"Into kink, okay?" I barked at him. My voice hung in the air, making me cringe at it echoing in my ears. "I'm sorry."

"It's okay," he said, more gently, and offered me his water bottle. "I was pushing you a little."

"It's fine."

"*I* wasn't apologizing." His eyes met mine over the clear orange plastic and I snatched the bottle away from my mouth, leaving a trail of water on my chin.

"What?"

"Didn't intend to be rude and I do apologize if you took it like I was, but not for what I said. Anyway, you should be asking yourself why you're sniffing around at the lifestyle. It's no kiddie ride."

"Oh, I see," I said and thrust his water bottle back at him as I prepared to push myself from the rock where we sat. "You have a list of criteria to be met just to get into your exclusive little culture? Tell me, does that apply to everyone you meet or just *girls*, as all of you say?"

"Hey," he said, catching my wrist in his hand. "Erin, you got me wrong here. I'm not threatening you with some imaginary yardstick, just telling you to take it slow…to be careful. With whatever you decide to do."

His thumb trailed rhythmic and slow on the inside of my wrist, washing away my irritation with each pass of his skin on mine. My body settled back to the rock beneath me and I stilled inside.

Finally, Walt's voice broke the silence between us. "I was seventeen."

"Seventeen?"

"The first time I did anything kinky I was seventeen." He nodded and eased back on his elbows. "My girlfriend at the time asked me to spank her, so I did."

I looked over my shoulder at him, waiting for more information, which didn't come. He watched me, clearly waiting for my reaction. Finally, I waved my hand toward him, encouraging him for more details.

"And? That's all?"

"Pretty much." He grinned at me and settled himself on his hip. "I don't spank and tell, even after twenty years."

"How did you know what to do?"

"A spanking is a pretty simple thing. Someone's hand is going to slap someone's ass," he said. "You can add some fancy-hands moves and mix up how you place the bottom you're playing with, but it's still pretty much my hand on a girl's ass."

There was no pretense from him. Walt's logic made sense — and made him seem sensible. But the languid confidence he exuded as he spoke was turning me incapable of much more than nodding and mindlessly pulling my shoelace apart so my fingers wouldn't shake with the urge to push the smattering of sun-flecked chocolate brown hair from his forehead. *My hand on a girl's ass* echoed in my ears. I dropped my shoelace.

"Hang on a minute. Why *girl?* Is there a linguistic problem with woman or even lady? Why girl?"

He leaned back on his elbows again, and flicked his eyes at me, huffing. "Girl. Girl…it's what you are, I'm pretty sure, since you've presented yourself that way. If you feel like a guy inside, that's your business. Girl…woman…guy…boy, boi with an I. It's all just words. Shit, I call Lu 'girl.'"

"Oh, I think it matters to the person."

He nodded and shrugged, sheepish. The thought of neon purple foxtail and leather vest-wearing Lucy being called a girl didn't bring to mind a good result. "You called Lucy 'girl'? Really? When?"

"Once." He thumped the heel of his hiking boot against the granite underneath us.

A strong, snorting laugh escaped before I could clench my wrist to my mouth and hold it back. Unable to resist, I turned his own words from the night before on him. "So how did that work for you?"

"Well, she didn't break my jaw like she wanted to, so it went fine, I guess." Unconscious or in an outright effort to prove his jaw did, in fact, still operate as intended, he shifted his chin and grinned up at me. "Tell me what you prefer and I'll say that, okay?"

"I…" And the truth hung in my throat. Walt didn't back away and so his question didn't either. After a few seconds, I swallowed and shrugged. "I don't really care. Woman, girl. Lady makes me think I should wear pearls and have doilies on my furniture. Erin?"

He shifted his torso to the arm closest to mine and poked my elbow with his free hand. "So why all the trouble about it?"

"I don't know." I looked past the trees to the overlook. Girl was a long time ago in my everyday frame of reference, but I liked how it sounded with Walt's way of turning it deep and sloping and a little rough on his voice. Questioning it was another one of those logical diversions, the same ones that kept me sitting outside of munches and lurking on web sites for years. "I thought I should care."

"But you don't?"

"No. I don't think so. Not really, right now."

He was watching me. Not merely looking on as I talked, but taking me in. The sense of it rode my spine, and made nerves and muscles I hadn't considered out of more than necessity go taut. My nipples pulsed at the lining of my bra, in time with the clench nesting into my thighs. I started to remind myself that pulsing and clenching weren't really me, and that was when Walt poked my arm again. This time his touch lingered, just enough to notice his fingertip was still on my skin.

"How do you like the woods so far?"

"I like it." I took in the rolling, hazy green mountains visible past the overlook. "It's different here. Not as chaotic as I thought."

We sat in silence for a few minutes, watching the afternoon sun stretch across the wooded valley below us when we weren't darting glances at each other. Every time Walt's eyes moved in my direction, I felt the same sense of openness settling into my chest.

Finally, Walt shifted and cleared his throat. "Hey, Birthday Erin?"

"Yes?" My voice hardly overpowered the sounds of wind and birds and forest all around us. As I turned my head toward him, Walt's body rose toward mine. He paused, balanced on his hand so we were eye to eye.

"I'd like to kiss you. That okay?"

His nose was scattered with freckles. A tiny mole rested between the crinkled laugh lines at his right eye. And his eyes—not just blue. There was amber circling his pupil, troughs of liquid aquamarines smattered between the wide deep-water blues.

His forearm brushed mine. My shoulder swept past his bicep.

"Okay."

I tensed my lips a little, waiting for his. They didn't meet mine. They brushed across my cheek, so close I felt my lashes touch his nose and the tips of his dark curls tickle my ear.

When he moved away, I knew my cheeks were flaming red, and I had to scuttle after the breath I'd forgotten to take. Once again, I had to glance toward the mountains to reorder my senses and was utterly, completely unable to disguise my surprise.

I'd watched him, not twenty-four hours before, swinging two heavy black floggers at a woman much smaller in both height and frame than me. It was entirely likely, given his size and apparent stamina, that Walt could have been a brute if he'd been so inclined—and without much to hinder him. But he'd asked for my permission to kiss me. And when he did, it was a soft, chaste kiss on my cheek.

I wanted to climb in his lap and inhale every broad, earthy, male bit of him.

"Should probably head back soon," he said.

"Do you know about air filters?" I dropped my eyelids twice. *Air filters? Of course I'm a seductive temptress. Of course I am.* Turning to him, still very close to his face, I blinked again.

"You mean for your car or for—"

"For the house I'm renting. Or the HVAC, not the house entirely. I mean, it cools the entire house but—"

"No, I get it. Sure, what do you need to know?"

"Where do I buy one?"

"Uh…" He scratched his earlobe and grinned. "Do you need one? There's a Home Outfitters in Shanesborro."

"Yes. I tried reading the manual…" I glanced down at my hands and smarted over my fingers twined together. Like a girl's. It was a small thing, asking for help. But asking for help from a man after watching so many of them fail Kathy and then Dani, too, was different. More. And Mr. Jensen, the elderly man next door, could barely understand me when I asked him about them. "I'm not sure how to fix it."

"Well," he said, hopping back to the ground, "how about we drive over to Shanesborro and see if we can figure it out."

"Yes, okay." And as I nodded to confirm it, a small voice sounded in my mind, adding one syllable not yet ready to be put to air.

Sir.

CHAPTER FOUR

The walk back to the visitor center was downhill and went quicker, both of them in silence as their feet fell on the hard-packed trail.

Inside Walt's head, a cadence of *what the fuck was that* thrummed for the entire hour it took to reach the parking lot. The tips of his ears felt like they were near singed, and his fists curled with the urge to punch something big and hard, a sensation he hadn't known since he was thirteen and his voice started to change.

It was a ridiculous question anyway. He knew exactly what the fuck *that* was because he'd been thinking *it* about Erin damn near constantly since he watched the red tail lights of her car disappear into the night. All day long. Through a couple of nature walks and a stalled RV in the south campground loop, and restocking the supply of area attraction maps in the visitor center. He couldn't get her out of his head. And then he caught a glimpse of her walking across the grass in front of the visitor center that afternoon, wearing those just-perfectly snug, ass-cupping khaki shorts that nearly caused him to embarrass himself with an unruly erection like some damn teenaged kid.

Tommy, another of the regular Tops in the mentor program, always said everybody in the lifestyle got at least one date with crazy if they stuck around long enough. Holly, the last woman in the lifestyle Walt had dated, surely fulfilled his quota for a couple of lifetimes. After a bad run with a couple of fucked-up, ego-driven SirMasterlyDom-types, she wasn't set up to handle more of it. Any of it: submission, pain and sex, a relationship. And so she broke. Into messy, hurt-filled pieces he tried—and failed—to put right.

As he'd driven away from Holly's parents' house that last night and, for all purposes, out of her life, Walt had considered all of the internal landmines he usually avoided: his undefined relationship with Holly, his mom, the way he'd left home at seventeen. It made sense that he'd tried to fix her. It made sense why he kept things just past casual but not too far down the road of commitments and collars. And even though he stayed in an undefined valley between Holly's boyfriend and her Dominant, it was his job to protect her. Even from herself. Hell, he wasn't a two-hundred-dollar-an-hour shrink like the ones Holly's parents hired for her, but he could damn well recognize a couple of themes.

After he'd left Holly with her family, Walt didn't wait to call home. He got Lucy on the phone, excited to tell her he'd managed to cobble the whole shitty eight months of Holly's slow decline into a story that fit together. He had made some damn sense of what he'd been through, wanted someone to agree with him, maybe, so it didn't seem so simple to blame himself for Holly's breakdown.

"Jesus, Walt, do you think you're some great mystery?" She'd snorted a laugh as she always did when someone offered up the obvious to her. *"I mean, no man is a mystery, but it's so clear you're one of those 'scratch my belly, keep me fed and comfortable and tell me no lies' guys."*

It was the only time Luce had let him down. She was hardly surprised.

"As a professional observer of the pussy, not to mention an owner of one, let me give you a piece of advice. There are women who know that's who you are and will run all over you with it because you're too damn gentlemanly to call them out on that shit the first time. But then there are women who naturally want to be like that for you, even if they've just—what is it you say—uh…'slayed a dragon'…some shit like that, and you need to find one of those girls. Hopefully she'll have a nice rack and let you pink up her ass. Anyway, choose door number two."

The enthusiasm of his insight had deflated.

Was he that transparent? That easy to play?

He'd never tell Lu, since he knew she had no intention of hurting him. It was well-intentioned advice wrapped in her usual sarcasm, but her words ate at him as he lay awake all night. By the time he returned his rental car and boarded a flight back to North Carolina, he was convinced he should sit out anything but the most superficial of interactions with women.

Never again.

And too soon after Holly, watching the aftermath of his best friend Brady's death and being no comfort to his widow, Hailey, why would he? Two years later, after a very successful run at keeping a relationship on shutdown, there was Erin sitting at the bar inside Area 51, turning to see whom Claire was motioning their way.

Untested and raw, obviously, and utterly impossible to ignore.

Door number two.

Not a tourist. Not a kid looking for attention. And not another housewife, scrabbling after her fantasies instead of taking up yoga or poetry-writing, or some other shit that would do her a lot more good. And he'd brought her up here to one of his few peaceful places, already shown her how to get deeper under his skin than she already had, if she was as observant as she seemed.

Shit.

Walt listened to his feet pounding on the ground beneath him. As he walked, old words in voices belonging to his grandfather, Lucy, Holly, Brady, and Hailey replayed in his head. For a good while, he let them talk, until finally he admitted he shouldn't work over his whole scarred inner self in one afternoon, no matter how tempting it was to dredge up reason after reason to let this thing with Erin alone.

He'd figure it out later. Anyway, her ass in those shorts would make a saint tell himself lies.

After a quick tour of the visitor center and its facilities, Erin told him she'd stay behind at her car. She needed to check on a couple of things for work and would wait for him to lock up and change out of his uniform. Thirty minutes later, he pulled up alongside her car. She was moving her fingers over the glass screen on her smartphone, chewing on the corner of her bottom lip with a frustrated scowl as she typed.

He cut the engine, reached over and rolled down the passenger-side window of his truck.

"Erin?"

She continued to type, oblivious.

Walt cleared his throat and called to her again without acknowledgment. After two more tries, he tapped his horn. "Hey, Erin? I think Home Outfitters closes at eight on Sundays. We should probably head out if we're gonna make it before closing time."

Her head snapped up and she looked across her car's half-open window toward him. Disoriented, she pushed her glasses up the bridge of her nose and blinked.

"I'm just…" She offered up her phone as evidence and shrugged. "Work. I'm sorry. How long have you been there?"

He couldn't help chuckling at her a little and waved his hand over the back of his seat. "Just got here, don't need to be sorry about it. You ready?"

"Yes. I'll be right behind you."

She followed him over to Shanesborro. Watching Erin in the rearview and the traffic in front of him was a welcome diversion from the occasional wheeze coming out of his fourteen-year-old Tacoma's engine. As she pulled in beside him in the home store's parking lot, Walt gritted his teeth over his truck's clutch shuddering when he shifted into first and pulled up the emergency brake, hoping she didn't notice. But Erin's head was bowed over her phone again, the glow from the screen bouncing from the lenses of her glasses and easing the dim around her. She waved at him, pointed to her phone and held up her index finger, signaling for a bit of time.

Leaning against the dusty, scratched rear panel of his truck, Walt watched her for a few minutes, aware in a distant way that the Erin show was better than anything he'd seen on TV or movies for a while. As she continued to type and flip through screens, her head shook, she gestured to the air in front of her and even smacked the top of her steering wheel once. Finally she stepped from her car, pulling a small black bag with her. She pressed down on her key-fob once, then again as she walked toward him.

"I'm sorry about that. Work. Again. Do we still have time?"

She paused and shot her hand back toward her car, nearly catching Walt's arm with her key ring. Was she locking it for the third time? There was a fine line between detail-oriented and a bit obsessive. Where was Erin on that line? Same side Holly had been on?

"Yeah, we've still got a couple of minutes before the store closes. Hope everything's okay," he said. "And you don't need to apologize over doing your job."

"Actually I shouldn't have had to pitch in on that call." She shook her head and slipped her keys into her bag. "You have direct reports, correct?"

Direct reports? He had Sam Cross, who covered every other weekend and sat, half-asleep, behind the desk in the visitor center most weekdays, a couple of part-timers for overnight security and the big cleanup jobs at the campground during the summer, and a few volunteers who helped him lead nature walks when school kids came up from Shanesborro or Callahan on their field trips. Passing out park guides to rambunctious first-graders and sticking a Band-Aid or two on a skinned knee, parts of the job he'd loved for years, suddenly felt pretty paltry compared to running millions of dollars' worth of computer equipment he didn't even know the names for.

Walt cleared his throat. "Yeah, I got a couple of people I'm over."

"I..." She gestured from the center of her chest and gave him a weak smile. "Details—I remember, no personal details so soon. But I *have* visited you at work now and spent the afternoon in your forest with you. At this point we've crossed the potential danger threshold, right?"

Not really. This open and this personal, this soon, was not what he'd advise to another woman. But Erin wasn't another woman. He thought of her, earlier, up at the Sawtooth overlook, holding the protein bar he'd made into her birthday cake. As she looked up at him, she'd tried so hard to cover a sore spot he'd touched by accident.

A woman who obeyed that many traffic laws and triple-checked her car alarm wasn't going to go off the deep end on him. At least a deep end he couldn't handle in the air filter aisle at Home Outfitters.

Fuck slow steps—and fuck sensible and sane. He didn't really care about her details and obsessions, anyway.

"Suppose so." He grinned at her and stuck his hands in his jeans pockets to still the sudden urge to put his arm around her shoulder. "So what's the big emergency?"

"I have this new sys-admin—um, a system administrator—just assigned to me from another team," she said and closed her eyes for a second, pulling in a slow, steady breath. "He's one of those me—er, *people...* He's certain he knows the answer to everything, only follows my direction when it's for a task he thinks he can attribute to his own skill set and always, always does what he wants to do when he's unsupervised."

"So the guy's an asshole."

"He's challenging," she said and rolled her eyes. "He has *opportunities for growth*, as they say in HR. They also say it's my job to help him navigate those opportunities."

"Uh-huh?"

"Frankly, I think he's an entitled, arrogant...douchebag."

Walt laughed in spite of her scowl. "Whoa, there. Tell me how you really feel." Her shoulders drew in and before she could speak, he threw up a hand. "No, no apologies. The guy sounds like a douchebag. So call him a douchebag."

Erin laughed along with him. "I know. And he really *is* a—what I said. It's exactly what any other Miner would say, so I can say it, too. Right?"

"Sure. If that's what you'd prefer, why not?"

Her nose wrinkled as she shook her head. "But I hear myself say things like that and immediately remember nearly every Women's Studies lecture I had in college. You know, the ones where you realize half of the words we use to brand a person or their behavior as objectionable is also slang for a vagina—or something to do with a woman's body?"

"Um, I didn't take that as an elective."

He'd cruised through a couple of history classes while doing his forestry degree on an Army ROTC scholarship down at Clemson. *Women's Studies?* At twenty years old he wouldn't have been equipped to listen to lectures like those anyway.

They entered through the store's sliding doors. Erin paused by a display of soft drinks and candy, designed to entice hungry contractors and befuddled homeowners alike.

"Hey, how about dirtbag instead?"

"That sounds...um, do you like Sno-Caps?"

"Excuse me?" Walt turned to her, and didn't bother to hide his surprise at this new round of mental hopscotch. "From dou—er dirtbags to feminist academics to candy?"

She faced him, blinking and wide-eyed. "How about popcorn? With butter? Payment for installing the filter?"

"Yeah, I think that would be a fair trade." Since he'd caught up to her brain and was prepared to spend his last thirty bucks in cash on air filters and chalky candy just to keep her around for a few more minutes, fake-butter popcorn would do instead of the nice dinner date she deserved. "I believe we want aisle fourteen."

"You seem to know your way around the store," she said, grinning up at him.

"Uh…" He chuckled and fought the urge to scratch at his earlobe. "Yeah, well, most people in the lifestyle call Home Outfitters 'Kink Outfitters.'"

A new flush bloomed on her cheeks. "So I've heard. Sno-Caps it is, then." Erin dropped a couple of boxes of the candy in her cart and pulled a technical-looking manual from her purse. "This was in the home information the Realtor gave me when I moved in."

"You live in that new apartment complex east of town?"

"No, I live in Callahan. Three blocks from Main, on Sycamore."

There were few stands of old-growth trees left in the southeast, one being the stretch of land between the park and Tate's property, seven over-mountain miles from the visitor center. For years, most of what had made up the town of Callahan was constructed by Callahan Paper Mills, a company founded a hundred years ago with the intention of taking down as many of the Blue Ridge's trees as possible. A couple of new subdivisions and a small apartment complex had gone up in the past few years, but the town had stayed the same. Until ThinkMine turned up.

"It's always been funny to me, how they named all the streets in town after trees," he said before he could think better of it.

She glanced up at him, over the rims over her glasses. "After trees? I thought the same thing when I moved in. Memorializing the thing they came to consume."

"Yeah." He nodded. "Irony, huh?"

"It's beautiful here. I didn't expect that, but I like seeing so much green."

"Just don't want to be out in it, right?"

Her lips pursed into that little, saucy smile he was starting to like a lot. "It wasn't so bad today."

"What brought you here? Oh, pardon," he said and stepped aside for a shopper pushing an overloaded cart. "I know it was your job, but coming across country had to be a hell of a change."

"It was. It has been and still is sometimes."

"You're from San Francisco, right?"

"The Bay Area, I suppose. We—my mom and sister and I—we lived lots of places. Mom wanted to live there before she had Dani and me, so she kept moving west as we grew up. I finished my undergrad at San Jose State and then my MBA from Cal-Berkley while I was an admin at ThinkMine. And you? I assume you're from this area?"

"What was it that made you think that?"

"The accent? The naturalist job?"

"I'm not—local, that is. I'm from Sweetwater, Tennessee. Over the mountains."

She peered up at him. "That can't be more than a hundred and fifty miles west."

"Different place. My grandparents raised me. My grandfather was the county sheriff for years."

Erin considered it and finally nodded. They paused in front of shelves of air filters. "Oh, these?"

"Yeah, the book says twenty-one by—"

"*Waaaa-lllt?*" a nasally voice rang out behind him, and immediately he clenched his teeth. "Hey, you!"

Arms and long, square purple nails snaked around his waist from behind, followed by an artificial, powdery scent. He pulled the hands from him and turned toward the voice in disbelief.

Couldn't be.

Nicole.

Great.

She had that sneaky friend of hers, one of Tommy's regular bottoms, with her too. Her name—and much about the woman herself—had failed to make enough of an impression on Walt to cause specifics about her stick. But he did know she liked to carry stories—real or created.

"Hi." He stepped back, blocking Erin from their sight.

"Look at you, all cleaned up like you went home for Sunday dinner." Nicole pressed against him, flipping the collar of his shirt, and looked up at him like he'd terrified half of Grayson County by wearing a plaid button-down.

"It's just a shirt, Nicole."

"I know it is, but you look like some suburban vanilla dad. I mean — plaid?" Her hand crawled toward the waistband of his jeans. "I bet you're still going commando in those jeans, though."

Behind him — and of course, right at the moment Nicole decided to look and sound her trashiest — Erin sneezed. Walt turned in time to see her push her glasses into place and shrug up at him.

"Excuse me," she said quietly.

"Who's that? Lucy?" Nicole pressed herself toward him again, with her sneaky friend on her heels, and pitched her hands on his hips. She dropped her voice low as she pushed her body against his. "Why don't you let Kelsi take her home and you can finally show me around that cabin of yours?"

"That's not Lucy," muttered her friend.

"Nope." Erin stepped to Walt's side. "I'm not Lucy."

Everything about Nicole reminded him of a kid's flimsy toy, the gaudy plastic as thin as the attention span it was made to amuse. Playing with her was fun — the first few times. After the new and exciting part of her wore off, and he began paying attention to what was beneath the bratty attitude and skimpy clothes, he'd noticed how flat he felt after they'd scened.

It took two, maybe three more times of disengaged observation, like he was floating above their two figures as he fucked her, to see why. There was nothing more driving Nicole's responses than Nicole, and he could have been the next Top in line. She put on the right expressions, made the right noises — the ones that brought interested people around to watch them when they played at the club in Charlotte — and she was never shy about asking for sex in some very imaginative positions. But for Walt, there was no more intimacy with her than watching a couple of figures on a computer screen.

"Weren't you at the club last night?" Her friend — named Kelsi, apparently — who always set off Walt's alarm bells for a shit-stirrer, looked up and down Erin like she was beneath her. "You were way in the back, by yourself, watching the demo."

He stepped closer to Erin, let his shoulders spread a little so their bodies nearly touched, and looked down at the woman.

"I think we're running late." His hand hovered at Erin's elbow, brushing against her. Beneath his fingers, her skin was chilled — and shook, just barely.

"You're together?" Nicole looked from Erin, to him, and back to Erin, seconds from letting out the condescending laugh rising in her voice. "Right, a new girl. Of course you're together. You sure are running late this time, Walt. Took you more than an hour to warm up this one."

He fought with the urge to step in front of Erin and take the brunt of Nicole's pettiness. "Go on home, Nicole. Jealous doesn't look real good on you." Tension hung heavy around Erin, and he could feel her hand clenching at the hem of her T-shirt.

Nicole's eyes glinted and she brushed the flat, dull strands of plum-red hair from her shoulder as she leaned toward him.

"I looked a hell of a lot better on you than that ever will." She gave Erin a final, sneering once-over and turned for the parking lot, barely missing Walt's chin with the wide arc she achieved with her fake cow-print vinyl purse as it cleared her shoulder.

He watched them saunter away. Once again, Tommy Blackwell was right. Crazy caught up with everybody sooner or later.

Erin was probably putting together the last pieces of the picture the two had sketched out for her. An urge to clean himself, not just physically, but of the memory of being with Nicole, nearly overloaded him.

Finally Erin broke the silence. "I'm sorry."

"Why are you sorry? For them? Hell, I'm sorry she insulted you like that."

Walt looked after the two distant figures again, wishing for a strong gust of wind to blow away the sugary scent of Nicole's perfume, still sucking the air from around him. He wished he could undo the past five minutes of what had been a pretty damn decent day spent with someone he'd never seen naked before. And he wished he knew what the hell had possessed him to play with Nicole, not to mention sleep with her, in the first place.

"Here's the right size. Sixteen by twenty-five." He handed her a package of filters and they moved toward the front of the store in silence.

"That was…"

"Small town, right? Everywhere you go, there's someone you know. Or who knows about you." She looked past him and past the cashier, into the darkened parking lot. She shivered a little and tucked her hands deeper into her pockets.

"Where's your coat?"

"I didn't wear one. It was warm today." Her voice was more distant than it had been all day, even when he'd questioned her about her birthday.

"I've probably got a jacket or sweatshirt stashed in the truck." The cashier gave them the price for her purchases. Walt pulled out his wallet. "Here, let me get that for you."

"It's okay." She moved around him, leaning in to swipe a credit card. "Don't worry about the jacket. I can survive — and I couldn't take it from you."

"You can give it back once we've got that air filter installed." *What the hell was going on with this woman?*

"Maybe we can do this another time?"

"Yeah, of course. Sure," he said, and stepped aside so Erin could pass him. They walked to their cars, silent again. He followed her to her door, opening it for her as the alarm disarmed.

"I'm not really certain where I am," she said, glancing across the parking lot at the slow, Sunday-evening traffic out on Shanesborro Highway. "Could I follow you back to your forest? It's close to work and I can find my way home from there."

"Sure." He could barely hear his own voice over the sounds of traffic and new spring crickets and the jingle of her car keys in her hand.

Twice now, in as many days, he'd felt the sensation of losing her attention claw up at his throat from deep in his gut.

"Okay. I'd appreciate that."

"No problem." He closed the door softly behind her and moved toward his own vehicle, dragging his keys from his pocket as he walked.

He got the Tacoma started, thank God, and gave the engine a couple long, slow revs before he backed out, balancing his clutch against the gas gingerly as he waited for Erin to pull out behind him.

He played every piece of what happened from the moment they got to the store over in his head. Lost for an answer to why a woman like Erin would turn and scatter when faced with someone like Nicole,

Walt considered everything he'd said, and every one of his actions again. He nearly had convinced himself admitting he'd like some Sno-Caps had turned Erin off when the red light at the Cider Fork Road intersection changed, catching him by surprise. Not only had he stalled out with Erin again, his truck had stalled too. And he couldn't get the damn thing to turn over.

CHAPTER FIVE

In front of me, the taillights on Walt's truck flickered erratically again, dimming almost to dark before his brake lights flared bright red. Squinting, I lowered my window and called out into the night.

"Walt?"

His arm shot from inside his vehicle, waving me on.

"I can't go around." Shifting my own car into park, I engaged my hazard lamps and pushed myself further out the window. "Walt, I don't know where I am and I can't leave you out here alone."

The driver's side door opened and Walt stepped from his truck. He walked toward me, jaw clenched, his face highlighted by my car's headlights.

"Hey," he said, crouching down to my level. "I've been having some trouble with the transmission lately."

"Is there anything I can do?"

"Nah, I've got it." He stood, and motioned past his disabled truck. "If you just stay on the highway another seven or eight—"

"Walt, I'm not going to leave you here."

"—miles. No, you head on home. I'll be—"

"No."

He stopped and shocked me by actually looking surprised I'd said no to him.

"No?" Drawing his hands back to his hips, he turned to me and tipped back on his heels so he could catch my line of vision.

"No," I said, and swallowed at my suddenly thick throat. "It's dark. I won't leave you alone."

"Erin," he said, chuckling, and gestured to his broad torso. "I'm not exactly worried about a big bad guy coming after me. I could probably take him."

I opened my door and pushed it toward him as I stood, sending him backtracking toward the flashing lights on his truck.

"The manly man act doesn't impress me." I marched toward his car, willing myself not to look back at him. I couldn't purr in his ear or say the right sort of provocative things about his lack of underwear, but I could be reliable. I could be helpful for him. Those things I knew how to do.

Suddenly, the dark beyond the jumble of newly-leafed trees lining the road loomed higher, and that dark within them, a deeper, blacker dark than anything I'd experienced in California. There were live things in there. With teeth and fangs and claws and possibly even venom.

Walt was close on my heels. And, without another thought about what lay beyond the reach of the traffic lights beyond Walt's truck and my own car, I was very glad for the safety I felt around him.

"Hey, be careful, just walking off down the road in the middle of the night like that," he said as he reached my side, taking my elbow and steering me away from the right traffic lane even though it was completely devoid of traffic.

"I'm not just walking off, I'm walking *to*." I swallowed at the surge of my own relief to be back beside something solid and tangible. When we arrived at the driver's door, I motioned to the interior. "I'll steer. You push."

As I pulled at the worn silver door handle, his hand reached toward mine.

"Wait a minute, there. What do you think you're doing?" Walt's fingers closed around my hand. The same span of chest he'd just suggested as invulnerable rose and fell with his breath, mere inches from my face.

"You have two options: one, you can get me rolling down that hill on the cross street and I'll pop the clutch." He scowled down at me, apparently not impressed with his first choice. "Or two, I can put the truck in neutral and you can push it through the intersection to the opposite side of the road, just over there. Then we'll call my auto club and have your truck towed to a mechanic."

"Three, you'll get back in your nice little car, put it in drive, and follow Shanesborro Highway about seven or eight miles, down to the intersection with highway 54, and—"

"Excuse me," I said and opened the door. Before he could catch me, I was inside, seated behind the wheel, although unable to completely touch the pedals.

"Erin, you don't know how to do something like this…"

"Of course I do." Scooting forward, I depressed the clutch and brake and shifted the truck into neutral. "Do you have any idea how many times my mother ran out of gas before I was old enough to drive the car to the gas station and fill the tank myself? Why would you assume otherwise?"

"You—uh…really?"

I pointed to the doorframe and took the wheel. "Push, Walt."

With the force of his considerable size, he leaned against the steel frame, grunting softly as the truck began to inch forward. Without the benefit of power steering, keeping the stalled truck under control as we crested the intersection's slight incline was difficult. Thankfully difficult. I had no choice but to look forward and not at Walt, glancing side to side for oncoming cars, as the truck gained momentum.

Once the truck had coasted safely, deep into the roadside gravel, I pulled the emergency brake taut and finally allowed myself to look up at him. Hands planted above him, his arms spanned the open door. I scanned his chest, following the line of his shirt's tiny white buttons to the waistband of his jeans. It pulled free there, exposing a narrow line of tanned skin at his hip.

Just to be sure, I tugged at the emergency brake again.

"Okay, Super Girl, let's get your car out of the middle of the road." He grunted and stepped aside. I handed him his keys and without a look his way, started for my car, the lone source of light on the remote stretch of road. Damn whatever was beyond those trees. "Erin. Wait."

"I'll be fine." I continued along the road. Behind me, Walt muttered a florid word or three and slammed his truck's door.

"Do you understand—" he snarled, feet falling heavy on the pavement behind me "—what *wait* means?"

"I can handle it myself." I forced myself to not look up at him as he reached my side.

"Hey, I told you the same thing, but you sure as hell didn't listen."

I stopped at the corner of the intersection and looked up at him, shrugging.

"I'm sorry."

"Stop apologizing to me." His hand cupped my elbow and he nodded toward my car. "C'mon now, hurry."

Once my car was parked, idling, in front of Walt's truck, he took out his flip phone and punched numbers into it. He listened, scowling, as the tinny sound of a female voice filled the car. After repeating the process with an answering male voice, he flipped the phone shut and rubbed his broad hand over his face.

"Will you let me call my auto club now?" I asked quietly.

"No, the truck'll be fine here overnight. Tommy Blackwe—Shadow…aw, fuck it, Tommy—from the club? He owns a wrecker service. I'll give him a call tomorrow morning." He sighed, his chest filling wide and falling as he sank into the passenger seat, rubbing at his eyes.

A wave of exhaustion, not unlike one that came from any one of my admins during the long build-out we'd executed to open the data center on time, flowed from him. Pushing the truck across the road wouldn't have exhausted Walt physically. Nonetheless, he seemed fatigued.

I paused to check the intersection and drove, sending silent good wishes to Walt's abandoned truck as we passed. After some minutes' quiet, he shifted his long legs, a little awkwardly, so he faced me.

"What're you doin', Erin?" His voice had turned a little hoarse and sounded more than tired. Weary.

"I'm driving," I said, shrugging and smiling as I watched him from the corner of my eye.

"You know what I mean. What's got you coming around the club like you did last night, when you can hardly bring yourself to say B and D, or S and M together."

"What?" I clenched my fingers hard around the steering wheel. "Don't patronize me."

"I'm not patronizing you."

"It sure sounded like it." I smirked and turned my voice to a deep drawl. "Aw, little darlin', y'all ain't the kind of girl who belongs in a corset and a collar."

"Hey, that's not what I meant," he said, his voice taking on a husky huff of its own. "You're assigning a hell of a lot of pompous damn intentions to me just asking you a valid question. And by the way, I'm not that much of a prick. *And* I'd never call you anything as condescending as *little darlin'*."

How could his voice dip that low?

"I didn't say you were. I just don't understand…" I focused on the swath of light in front of me. Not the time, place, or especially person to open that topic.

"Understand?" I felt his eyes on me, watching me in the faint gleam of the car's interior. Minutes passed. I drove, stubbornly silent, hardly aware of Callahan's now-familiar streets as they passed. But very aware of every movement of his body, so close to mine.

He still watched.

"I don't understand why it's so easy for women like them," I said finally.

"Like who? You mean Nicole and—uh, her friend?"

Blinking hard, I clenched my jaw, nodding. "Yes. They walk into any situation, every environment, and it's always so easy for them. How long have you known them?" I shifted the car into park and turned to him.

He considered it a moment. "I guess six months, maybe? Don't remember exactly when they turned—"

"So, to be generous, eight months. In eight months, women like her—like Nicole—can decide it's perfectly acceptable to go into a new situation, all alone—"

"Nope. Come to think of it, I believe those two showed up together," he said, considering, as he scratched his earlobe.

"Fine. Together. Arm in arm. Two comrades in kink, right? They turn up together and manage to ignore years of expectations and social bias and their own insecurities." I paused at the sound of Walt's voice. "Pardon me?"

"No, it's nothing. Was just saying neither one of those girls are what I'd call insecure."

"And that's wonderful!" I cried, throwing my hand into the air. "It's absolutely right and valid that those *girls* should be without a single drop of insecurity. In charge of their own sexuality. Making their own choices about how to enjoy their bodies. It's absolutely. Fine."

My voice reverberated through the car, still echoing in my ears. Finally, after a number of seconds, Walt scratched his earlobe again, eyebrows rising.

"Hey, Erin, you care if I ask you a question?"

"Um…no."

"What are we doing at your house?" He gestured toward the compact, pale green cottage that was, in fact, my house. "And of course, at the risk of sounding like a patronizing prick again, assuming this *is* your house."

I sighed, the heaviness of it much like his from earlier.

"It actually is my house." I shrugged, sheepish, and turned a hesitant smile to him. "I must have gone on autopilot when we started argu — um, talking. I need a jacket and to…um…Would you like to come in for a minute? I could make some tea. I might even have some popcorn, if you're still willing to help with the air filter?"

His left cheek rose, a half-smile in return. "Still want to share those Sno-Caps?"

"I can't make any promises," I said. "*But* if you're still willing to help me with the air filter?"

"Be glad to," he said, grinning, and opened his door. "And I'll take my chances on the Sno-Caps."

Inhaling hard, I looked away, giving myself a few beats to catch the diverse threads of words and emotion that had just passed between us. Before I could gather my bag and phone and open my door, it swung open. Walt waited in the space beyond, his hand extended toward me.

"Ready?"

CHAPTER SIX

Her house was neater than Lu's, which shocked the hell out of Walt, because if there was ever someone too uptight about housework, it was Ms. Lucinda Johns, of the Richmond Johns. Lucy was many years gone from her upper-class Virginia debutante roots, but she still insisted on having a housekeeper come around once a week, same as the mother who'd disowned her.

Erin was still puttering around in the kitchen when he finished with the air filter. Walt glanced around the living room. The light curtains, matching beige sofas, and big, square oak coffee table all looked off-the-truck new. Even the little kit of homeowner's tools she handed him when he took the cover off the heating and air unit looked brand-new. It was a simple thing, took thirty seconds to change.

Last time he and Lu were in Atlanta, she'd run him around a Pottery Barn store for a couple of hours, comparing do-dads for her guest bedroom. Eventually she gave up and dragged him clear to the opposite end of the mall into Neiman Marcus, a place the Johns women knew like their own homes.

Lu and her inherited money considered a store like Pottery Barn for furnishing a mostly vacant spare room, but Erin had bought the whole living room package—and kept it so it looked unused.

"The tea will be ready in a minute." Her voice shook him from his thoughts. He found her across the living room, watching him as she pulled a dark blue sweater around her shoulders. Walt lingered by one of the soft-looking sofas, unsure how to move or where to sit around things that surely meant a lot more than furniture to her.

"This is a nice place," he said instead, shoving his hands into his jeans pockets.

She glanced around the room, smiling. "Thank you. I like it a lot. It's the first time I've lived in a house." Motioning an invitation to the opposite side of the sofa, she sat down. "We—my mom and my sister and I—lived in apartments. Mostly. I think we might have lived in half of one house for a few months when we were in Wisconsin."

"Wisconsin?" Walt lowered his body carefully, hoping the wood wouldn't groan as it bore him. He turned his knees to accommodate the narrow space between the couch under him and the coffee table. "Hope it wasn't winter."

"It was." She laughed to herself, a little sad sound she turned into her shoulder. "I was fourteen, and had acne, braces, a bad perm, and was very, very chubby. And yes, it *was* horrible. After I finished my MBA, I turned down a very good offer from a company in Minnesota, much better financially than the one I had from ThinkMine. I don't like being cold."

"It snows here." Walt cocked his eyebrow at her. He liked her riled up and with her feathers ruffled much more than sad over a history she'd had no choice in living.

"True," she said, brightening. "But not like that. It melts here. There it…it just goes on and on for months." She stood suddenly and Walt followed, the long-ago lessons in manners his granny had taught him propelling him to his feet. Erin sauntered toward the back of the house, pausing once she was in the next room to glance over her shoulder at him.

To a lot of people this little house would probably be an inexpensive rental—an old millworker's house down one of Callahan's original tree-lined streets that someone had bothered to renovate with a little care so it looked good again. He looked at the room, at Erin, with new eyes.

The first house she'd ever lived in.

"I wasn't sure how you wanted it, so I brought some sweetener," she said, re-entering, carrying two teacups. With saucers. "I've got some popcorn going in the microwave."

She looked happy. Comfortable. Like he'd seen Claire look when he visited her and Paul at their home during the week, without the crowds of people turning up for one of Area 51's afterparties. Seeing Erin content and holding a delicate piece of something that looked like doll's china out to him stirred up feelings he'd rather stay put to rest.

Walt accepted the tea, the cup and saucer fumbling around a little in his big hand.

"Oh."

"Oh?" he parroted, and looked back to the steam rising off of his tea. "*Oh* what?"

"You thought I meant the other tea."

"I didn't know there was other—I mean there's different flavors, and there's that herbal stuff that Claire always drinks—"

"No, you meant iced tea." She reached for the cup and took it away from him. "Or sweet tea. That's what you say down here. In the South it's sweet tea, right? I'll get you something else." She turned, starting for the kitchen again.

How many times had she done this? Enough to understand living in different places meant learning the little differences, and knowing that learning them could help her fit in. The idea of her always trying so hard, and her little teacups and saucers, and the carefully ordered living room of her first house made Erin come into full bloom, right before his eyes.

Screw good behavior. He wanted her.

"I have apple juice…and mil—"

Before she could finish, Walt crossed the living room in three long strides. He had to have his hand under the full curve of her ass and get her against him as quick as possible. He needed to taste Erin, and all the flower- and spice-smelling, soft, clean space that belonged to her could only be made better with her lips and her scent and *her* pressed into him.

He held on to her arm as he leaned down, pulling her with him as he reached blind behind her, their kissing more important than finding a place to settle the cup sloshing hot tea over his hand. Erin's mouth opened, her tongue found Walt's, and a sweet girl's sigh rose from her throat just as the plate landed on something that sounded solid to his ear. His fingers just made it to the slope between her ear and shoulder when something crashed to the floor behind them.

"Damn," he growled, half out of frustration from the lost sensation of Erin's lips pressed against his as her body curved into him, and half-pissed at himself over causing something small and probably important to her to break. Looking over her shoulder to survey the damage, Walt guided her away from the shards of china surrounded by a puddle of tea. When he looked back to Erin, he expected a pair of knitted eyebrows and a heavy glare.

He found her almost as he'd left her: eyes half-lidded and round, lips still open.

"I'm sorry, Erin—your cup…"

"It's okay. I've got nineteen more tea cup and saucer sets," she said, completely sincere, and pulled Walt back into another kiss.

"Wait, you count your cups?" He couldn't help laughing against her lips.

"Tea cups."

"Tea cups? You *count* them?"

She lifted her head away, just a little, and turned wide, completely sincere eyes toward him.

"Well, yes. Doesn't everyone know how many tea cups they have?"

And that time he laughed out loud. He couldn't stop himself. It was so absurd, so much like the Erin he was already coming to know, and the idea of her counting little cups and saucers settled into a place inside Walt that had been closed off for a very long time.

"No, they don't." He worked his fingers into the elastic band holding her hair back and pulled it free. "Can we stop talking about cups?"

"Tea cups," she mumbled against his lips.

"Whatever." He couldn't stop grinning, even when her hands traveled up his chest and rested at the back of his neck. Her nose brushed against his, she giggled, and finally her body shook a little with her own laughter.

"You think I'm ridiculous," Erin said as her fingers traced over the outside of his ear. "I probably am."

"No." He kissed her again, harder, and cradled the back of her head in his palm. "Not ridiculous." Distantly, he heard a series of beeps.

"Popcorn," she whispered against his lips as her fingers tugged the hem of his shirt free from his jeans.

"No, thanks."

With a good bit of the important parts of Erin still pressed against him, Walt led her back to the living room, hoping his leg contacted with soft upholstery before it caught the stout corner of her oak coffee table. When he felt what he was reasonably sure to be a sofa arm press against his thigh, he sat, and found thick cushions waiting to meet him.

Erin stood between his knees, her hair falling in a pale and wild tangle over one eye. She pushed it away and smiled down at him, her breath hitching in and out as she swayed against his legs.

"Walt," she said, pushing at the lock of hair tumbling over her eye again. "I know why she did it."

Stretching his fingers around her hips, he tugged gently, causing her to tumble against him. Gasping, she caught herself on his shoulders as her hair slid forward, curtaining around them.

"Oops. Didn't mean to do that." He nipped at her earlobe, just so she was clear he wasn't sorry at all.

"No, why *Claire* did it. She thought you're..." The past two days were coming together like a good string of code I just *knew* would work, elegantly and efficiently. Unfortunately, Walt was touching me all over, with his hands at my waist and his thighs around my legs and his lips right in the little dip behind my ear, and I couldn't pull the final sequence together. "Oh, wow, that's just..."

"Thought I was what?" His teeth closed over my earlobe and my knees nearly buckled.

I managed to tell him part of my theory before I gave up and sagged against him. He didn't seem to mind, even guided my legs around him so we could see each other better.

"Safe?"

"Right, she—um...Claire? She asked you to sit with me last night because you're safe. Y'know—here. Or there, I mean. She probably thought you weren't going to try to scare me or something because of the...well, the atmosphere."

"Atmosphere?" There was that easy, half-smile of his again, but this time his eyes glinted, obvious even in my living room's low light. Walt's hand traveled, slowly, his fingers dragging hot points on the skin under my T-shirt. When he settled his palm under my breast, across my one side of my ribcage, my breath bundled up, more than it might if I'd cinched myself in a corset like so many of the women I'd seen the night before. Once again, I absolutely could not summon the will to look somewhere—anywhere—else but at him. "You got that wrong, Erin."

The something I'd ignored and attempted to rationalize and tried to placate with my own distant, anonymous investigation had a face, a body it lived in, and a voice pitched deep and low that found its resonator in me.

"Pardon me?"

"In the…well, in *the atmosphere?* I'm not safe. Not in the way you're thinking." He leaned back against the sofa, watching me. Walt's eyes never strayed from mine.

I fisted the plaid cotton of his collar in my hands and leaned into his neck. He smelled like wood and the mountain air we'd hiked in and the slight tang of his sweat. I couldn't wait to taste him there or at the hollow of his throat or along the long, thickly muscled ridge of his inner thigh. His fingers skimmed over the skin under my bra. He cupped my cheek with his other hand, trailing his thumb over my bottom lip. The strong salt drew my tongue toward it like a magnet and I pressed my teeth against his skin, tasting. The denim covering his legs rasped as his ankles crossed—*How did I hear that? But I did; he's the only thing I can hear*—shifting me further down his thighs. I drew away, pushing my hair behind my ear.

My God, what a beautiful man.

Walt still watched me, but there was a difference—he wasn't just looking or affecting some sort of heated male gaze. Suddenly, I was more than sure of his evaluation, I *knew* it, just like I'd known that day in the dentist's office with Claire. I felt his curiosity, but it was more than that. This was a second-by-second sizing-up and marking my accounts. But as the echo of my breath surged in my ears, an icy, blue-fire sensation spread through my torso. It twisted my nipples taut and chilled my spine.

Inside I scrambled, looking for a safe distance from the sudden, wide-open vulnerability I felt as he looked back at me, his hands holding me in place. And he knew. His head dipped, acknowledging—not even a single millimeter would have been apparent to anyone watching us—but I saw it. He looked on, appraising me, and completely aware of my body reacting to him.

He was pleased, too.

Mental pathways I relied on, the foundation of the logic I lived by, faltered, then shut down, so obvious it surged over my skin like the vacating, energized air of large engines powering down, a streetlight at the snap of an electrical blackout. A data center going quiet.

This was like a face-off between a predator and its cornered, dread-aware prey. One more move would break the current between us wide open.

Perfectly stock-still was the way to go. I couldn't begin to predict how this odd sensation might change, or even if I'd know the same circumstances—being nowhere, knowing nothing more than seeing him seeing me—again. And I wanted to. It was a decision of odds—either move with the possibility of escape, move and bring the watchtowers of logic and propriety back online, or move and end the seductive, cool hum radiating through my body. It was a dilemma of should, must, and want.

I swallowed at the dry knot in my throat. And I stayed still.

Being so close to him, being the only thing he saw, was too luxurious to give up so soon. Everything about Walt felt too good to push back from, he was an exotic banquet laid out on a perfectly set table.

How long had I been starving?

My body gave in, moved two inches—maybe three—toward him.

Air rushed from my lungs in a long, steady sigh.

"See, I'm not safe. But I'm not reckless either, Erin." His thumb crested over my lip again.

"No. I don't think you're reckless." I squared my shoulders, forced myself to smile and damn sure to remain steady. I couldn't let him see my teeth close to chattering with the adrenaline flooding my nerves. And before I could stop myself, I prattled on. "Maybe you're too good at being careful."

"You think so?" The tanned skin beside his left eye crinkled, barely, and Walt's head dipped closer to mine. His voice came in low, husky enough to draw me in to him, just to be certain he was still speaking. "Well, then, I could fill up a book with all the careful I see in you."

His jaw jutted forward a little under his unwavering smile. He was thinking about it. *In front of me*, he was savoring me. Considering unraveling me. The sight of it was comfort and condemnation.

He wasn't too genial to back down from me and wasn't pretending for the access to a receptive, submissive woman.

This man — all contrast in big biceps and bigger dimples, swinging leather falls and mating butterflies — well, it seemed he was interested. In me. And no one's interest had ever turned me inside out like this Walt Easton, man of the forest, already had done.

I nudged closer to him. Under the faded denim stretching across his hips, he was hard. So hard. Over me. My hand dropped between us and I stroked the curve of his erection under my fingertips.

"God damn," he said, guttural and grunting. His hand pressed up, palming my breast, and closing, in agonizing, slow, steady increments, around it. When his fingertips scaled over the edge of my bra and sank further into my flesh, I whined, my head swaying against my shoulder. His eyebrows rose. "You like that, don't you?"

"Yes." I meant to say it. But even as I gathered the necessary sounds for such a commonplace word, Walt's fingers compressed more. I don't know if I managed to convert that single, simple word from thought to speech. My T-shirt fluttered past my face, catching around the tanned skin at his elbow.

"More?"

I nodded heavily, licking at my lips, and let my head fall into his shoulder. Pushing the nylon and lace cup aside, he lifted me free of it. His thumb and forefinger closed around my nipple, coaxing it to an aching point.

"Walt," I sighed into the warmed skin behind his jaw. "Oh God, Walt…"

"More," he said, his hushed voice rasping across my earlobe.

"Yes. Please."

I wanted to say it. *Sir.* I wanted the release of using that word, of falling under his control. I hardly knew Walt, but I knew my own instincts, and some still unidentifiable thing about him felt safe and right and brave and terrifying.

Walt's head slanted away from mine again, his eyes narrowed.

"Erin." He said my name with purpose, so it took on a different intention I couldn't quite grasp. "If I keep going, I'm gonna bruise you." But his touch never wavered. His fingers still clenched, turning my ghost-pale skin into taut, round rises between each of them.

"Please." *Please, Sir.*

For now, asking—saying please—would have to suffice.

The pressure of his fingertips increased as he drew my breast closer to him. He dipped his head, still watching me, and flicked his tongue across my nipple. His teeth followed, scraping the tight, pebbled skin, and his tongue touched me again. Orgasm hovered, so close. I rocked against his hips, whining.

"Shhhhh," he said, withdrawing his mouth enough to speak, still so close his hot breath skated over the wet skin he'd left behind. With a quick lift of his eyebrow, he licked again, grinning to himself as I whimpered from his mouth so near the single part of me he'd claimed. "No, not yet. Keep your hips still."

I needed to touch more of him. Shirt buttons fumbled under my shaky fingers and then fell loose. Another, and another, and still Walt's hands and teeth and tongue played hard and heavy with my breast, wrenching frustrated, groaning calls from me. The final button hung, refusing to slide free. Walt's other hand closed over mine and pulled, hard, sending that last stubborn button pinging across the wood floor under us.

"Oh...crap, I'm sor..." I said, pushing against his shoulder as I stood. "Your button."

"I've got more damn buttons—get back down here," he growled as he grabbed my hips and tugged me back to his legs. As I pushed the dark cotton from his chest, he leaned away from me so I could pull his shirt free of his arms.

Without his shirt covering his bicep, I noticed his tattoo, the head of the big, Celtic-looking creature that had been hidden in shadow last night at the club. Under the bird ascending from stylized flames were words in another language. Gaelic or Breton, maybe. *Agus fós titeann sé liom.* It was a phoenix, rising from its own ashes. I nearly wept at the jagged, black edges and long swirls of red and orange ink circling his shoulder, disappearing down his back until it peeked from under his ribcage. Here was every marker, every cataloged desire and secret whim I'd collected since I noticed a man could call my body and mind to recognition.

A fine thatch of dark hair covered his chest, curving around the hardened nubs of his nipples, narrowing to a single line that disappeared behind the faded denim circling his waist.

"Walt," I said, swallowing hard to control my voice. "If we're going to—"

"We're going to." He touched his thumb to my bottom lip again and a beat skipped against it. His or mine? I wasn't sure and couldn't have diverted the mental capacity to separate my pulse from his. "Aren't we?"

"Yes," I said, nearly saying the new *it*—Sir—as I answered. But his mouth was on mine again, lips and tongue pulling against mine as his hand slid under my jaw. Once more held just where and how he wanted me. I shivered against him. "W-Walt…then I need to…"

I tugged at the buttons holding his jeans together. Walt hissed through his teeth and pushed both of us off the sofa, sending me teetering away from his body. Before I could stumble, his arms were around me.

"You okay?"

"Yeah, fine." Inhaling, shaky and shallow, I steadied myself against him. "We need a condom."

"We do." He grinned, cupping my cheek as he leaned down to kiss me. "You have thirty seconds to find one."

"Um…okay," I mumbled as his lips skated over mine again.

"Hurry."

I set off down the darkened hallway, pinballing from wall to doorframe to wall, nearly a stranger in my own home. And condoms? When was the last time I needed those on a regular basis?

Condoms…Weekend in Cabo with Danielle. Unused because she met that lifeguard and spent the weekend in the room, and I read all day under one of those straw umbrellas…palapas…they call them palapas…

I bounded down the hall, hoping Walt wasn't keeping time, but if he was, he might be a disciplinarian about a few extra seconds spent scuttling around my house. Heart pounding and stumbling in the dark, I felt my way across the bed in my spare bedroom, wondering if my suitcase was where I last saw it.

Behind my running shoes, this afternoon…

I couldn't really think about what was happening, or I'd stop banging through doorjambs and actually have to stop and consider *it*. The other, not hard to say *it*—that was sex. I'd met Walt the night before, barely twenty-four hours earlier. And now—sex, which was something I understood. Though I hadn't done it recently, I was certain the basics hadn't changed.

But would there be more? Would he expect to tie me up or make me hit my knees in front of him or even turn me over *his* knees and take the broad, just-right-rough palm of his hand to my backside?

"Erin?" he said as he ducked his head into the hallway. "You okay?"

Plastic bag in hand, I collided headfirst with his shirt-free chest. It was still broad and muscled and heated, all woodsy-smelling skin and springy dark curls. His jeans hung at his hips, a line of silver buttons open and revealing more dark, springy curls—and a hint of the smooth, flushed cap of his penis, tucked beside his hipbone. No underwear.

I fumbled and nearly dropped the condoms.

"I'm fine," I managed to say as his arms crossed around my waist. Skin to skin again, our lips followed. Just as I began to fall back into the haze of feeling Walt's mouth and hands on me, he stepped away. His fingers linked through mine, and he led me back to the living room sofa.

"This is quick. Are you really sure?" He looked so…concerned. Not stern or demanding or even mildly miffed.

I glanced at the bag of assorted condoms in my hand, idly wondering if condoms had expiration dates. "No. It is quick, but I'm okay." Straddling his legs again, I handed him the bag. His eyebrows rose and he chuckled softly as he turned it over in his hands.

"All of these? Looks ambitious for nine o'clock on a Sunday night."

"It's a selection. There's latex and ribbed. Large? Oh, and non-latex, and some with spermicide and—" Before I could finish, his mouth was on mine again. From the corner of my eye, I saw the zipper bag of condoms fly over the back of the sofa, followed by a single wrapper.

Walt pushed my hair from my shoulder and nestled his head against me, his teeth grazing over the curve where my shoulder met my neck. After a few seconds he shifted his body toward mine again and caught my earlobe between his teeth, flicking his tongue over the tiny aquamarine studs I always wore.

"You smell good," he said in a husky voice so soft it could only be just for me, and his lips skated over the contours of my ear. "I noticed it last night. Before Claire told me your name, I knew what your skin smelled like."

I nodded, and my temple nudged at his. "I watched you with her."

"I know."

"I wanted to be her," I said, and flinched as soon as I'd confessed it. In the weeks prior to going to Area 51 with Claire, I'd never given her a true and complete account of what my interests were. I'd never said them out loud.

Walt's eyes came in line with mine as his head turned. He slid my glasses off and set them on the small table beside us.

"I know."

"I don't know how to…" I didn't even know the right words. Maybe he was right. If I couldn't tell Walt I wanted him to hurt me and tease me with it, needed him to show me how to say and do the things I'd been watching and reading about for years, how ready was I? "The other things, I—"

Leaning back on his knees, I turned, reaching for my glasses. Walt's hand went around my wrist before I could find them, his fingers steady, but not confining.

"Shhh. Let's do this now." His thumb stroked over the inside of my wrist again, just as he'd done earlier when I'd been overwhelmed. "The other stuff—we can figure it out later."

"Okay." I relaxed my arm and he took my hand again. "Let's do *this* now."

A raspy, concurring purr rumbled through him. We stood simultaneously, as if a starter's pistol had fired, tugging at the remains of our clothes. I sent my fingernails skimming down his chest and found the shock of hair under his navel. Walt's hands responded, moving from their already natural resting place across my backside to the top of my thighs. His fingers curled and he stroked the length of skin inside my legs with his knuckles, to my knees and up again, just fluttering his index fingers across me where thigh gave over to coarse hair and wet warmth. I allowed my voice and body to react to him, let myself return his blatant stare. I even reacted with a similar trailing, teasing touch, watching as my fingertips skimmed across the heavy lines of inked knotwork on his hipbone, black hair, and a tiny freckle that caused me to pause and smile at him over discovering it.

Someday that freckle and how I like to kiss it will be a secret between us, Walt.

When his fingers delved deeper, the idea was gone like flashpaper dipped over a flame. I closed my hand around him in response, and we groaned together, finding need and want again and turning them to stroking, circling, raking, plunging.

"Have wanted this…mmmm…*fuck*…" His hand circled my hips once more and grasped the fleshiest part of my rear. "*This* delectable ass in my hands since I saw you."

I was too gone, drunk on the sound and feel of his words beside my ear as they reverberated through my torso, to argue delectable and *my ass* were not meant to meet in thought or speech. Instead, my body opened further for him. I let out a moan in response to the sight of his much larger hand closing mine around his erection.

When he angled my hip and guided himself inside me, he hissed a round of delicious, erotic expletives that made my throat open with panted responses. Our foreheads fell together as Walt lay back on the sofa pillows behind him, taking me with him. My arms circled his neck and I sank against him, giving over direction of my body to him.

He used his muscled thighs to lift me higher. His hands guided me against him, rocking my hips in slow, deliberate undulations that brought him inside me at perfect cadence. Our breath came heavier, the humid warmth of his tickling the beads of perspiration at my hairline. The sounds and feel, even the scent of us together, engaged part of me that refused to keep careful watch over my own speech. I found my lips at his earlobe, nipping at the swell of smoky-spiced skin.

"Mmmmm…" I purred in his ear. The voice—it was mine, but completely unrecognizable. "Fuck *yes*…Walt. *Harder.*"

He responded with a gravelly moan in my ear, and his body arched toward mine, answering with *much harder*. The hums and gasps we made mingled, climbing in proportion, until he pushed deep into me, his body rigid as his muscles quaked between my legs.

"God…*damn.*"

A final thrust dragged me into my own orgasm, a bright surge that made me whine, clawing at his shoulders when a second, much more forceful tremor flared much deeper inside me. As the shocks faded, his hand glided along my back, resting at the base of my skull as his fingers trembled against my spine.

Stilled against each other, we kissed. Again and again. We panted out heavy breaths and returned to each other, lips on lips.

His kiss was divine.

"Damn," he said. His unoccupied hand found another stretch of skin on my backside and he pushed, urging me against his broad, sweat-damp chest.

"Wow." I nodded, still shaking. A drop of sweat rolled across my eyelid, forcing me to blink it away. When I opened my eyes, Walt was studying a ring of oblong, purpling marks circling my breast.

The contrast of color against my skin was startling, but the memory—what he'd done to put those fingerprints on my skin—made me want him all over again. I smiled and drew my finger across the marks he'd left on me.

"You okay about that?" He watched me warily. "Those are going to be pretty heavy."

"Yeah," I said, nodding. "Thank you."

"Thank me?" He laughed and drew his palm across my arm. "And you've never played—anything?"

I hushed a yawn. "No. Nothing." His shoulder looked warm and solid. I leaned against it. "Stay?"

His fingers paused then resumed their path across my skin. "Yeah. Okay." I felt him nod against my cheek. "Yeah, I'd like to."

CHAPTER SEVEN

I woke up the next morning with a man in my bed.

He wasn't simply in my bed; he'd taken up a good portion of it, including my preferred side. But I couldn't find the will to be annoyed about the loss of space. Walt looked very...well, it seemed a little odd, thinking of a man so tall and so muscular as adorable, but when he slept, he made soft, snuffling sounds as he burrowed his head under my pillow. His body had stayed close, facing mine, all night. We'd fallen asleep holding hands. Talking.

The last thing he'd told me, between deep yawns, made me stare at him, squinting across the pillows in the dark.

"Lu's pretty much my sister. And Tate and Claire, but me an' Luce and Bra—well, we've all been together since we were pretty much still kids. They're my people," he said, the last words drifting into steady, slow breath. "My family."

I untucked my thumb from his, brushing over the imprints of his fingers on my skin. He'd had the fortitude to keep going, leaving evidence on my body of how hard he could be with me, and still vulnerable enough to fall asleep claiming three friends as his only family. He knew the names of butterflies. He walked me across dark highways, watching for any threat in the distance. He made my birthday my own day, not shared with the sister who had always claimed everything first.

Returning my thumb to his, I closed my eyes and said, "Good night, Walt."

His fingers had squeezed mine. Just a little. Enough to know he was there.

Erin brought him home before eight. She woke him after she was freshly showered and scrubbed, wearing a starched white shirt tucked into a gray skirt that made her ass look even better than those little shorts she'd worn the day before. Painful as they were to ignore, Walt tucked away hazy impressions of the warmth her body had left on the sheets beside him, the sway of her ponytail as she walked around her bedroom dressing, her voice in his ear telling him it was time to go, and promised to revisit them once he was home and in his own shower.

He had called Tommy about his truck, dodging questions about how he'd managed to make it home. Once dressed in his clothes—which Erin had gathered and placed, folded, on an old steamer trunk at the end of the hallway—he had found her in the kitchen. Her perfume, mixed with fresh coffee, washed over him.

"I don't have any milk—I'm out—but I do have some hazelnut creamer."

Okay, so she wasn't perfect. *Creamer? Hazelnuts?*

"I'm okay. Just some water, thanks." He accepted a bottle from her and drained it in four long swallows. "Let's talk tonight, okay?"

"Um...okay," she said. The little stubborn crease between her eyes said otherwise.

"What's that?" He smoothed at it with the pad of his thumb. "No '*Um...okay.*' That was intense, last night. We probably should probably talk a little bit. Make sure we're on the same page about a few things."

The crease deepened. "Like?"

"Like, me doing what I did to you—or anything close to the rough stuff—it's not going to happen again until we talk about you. About your limits. About going slow."

"Limits. Okay." She had looked up at him, through the top rim of her glasses. He'd never cared for innocent-acting bottoms, but

Erin, with her pale cheeks and wide blue eyes looking back at him made him wonder if he might still have a few unexplored kinks too.

"Stop," he said, leaning down to her ear. Fuck it, he couldn't resist. "Pout and you'll get spanked."

She flushed, deeply. Walt had added the knowledge she pinked up easily to his list of things to remember later.

He couldn't *stop* remembering any of it, though. All morning, even after he roared out as he came hard against the tile in his shower, he kept seeing the near-translucent skin on her wrist and hearing her mutter to herself over some work email she read while they waited out a red light. By the time Sam trundled away from the visitor center's front desk for his lunch break, Walt was so wound up he was ready to cuss and stomp on something until it broke. Or sneak back to his cabin before lunch and jerk off again. He stalked across the honed bluestone floor and busied himself with one of the local attraction displays.

"Wanda, you're mouthbreathing again."

Ah, perfect.

"Where the hell did you come from?" Walt looked out to the parking lot, empty just seconds before.

"You answered your own question, precious." Lucy was dressed for work. A high-end, sexed-up version of the conservative office attire Erin wore, but unlike Erin, Lucy was carrying a wicker picnic basket, not an overstuffed black messenger bag. "I brought you a present from the pit. Shouldn't have too much sulfur on it."

"Lunch?" He was so busy with his morning activities, he'd missed breakfast.

"Lunch—and other treats." Lucy adjusted the wide gold cuff on her wrist. "Come with me."

As they crossed to the cabin, Walt noticed a gleaming black luxury sedan. "Who's the suit?"

"Client. Sandy Cutshill." She rolled her eyes. "Can you believe it? A guy trying to butch up for his family in the South wears that much bronzer and still goes by Sandy? Gold link bracelet and a pinkie ring too, Lord help us. I'm putting together some plans for a renovation to a few of his daddy's time-share properties near Asheville. Barely half-sold. Daddy's very disappointed."

"Aren't you supposed to be the one chauffeuring him around, sweetening him up?"

"No, honey. He needs *me*."

They stopped in the driveway. Walt turned on his heel and started for the visitor center.

"I'm not taking Roxanne," he said over his shoulder.

"Of course you will," she replied, linking her arm around his as she caught up with him.

Roxanne was Lucy's baby. A 1979 Mercedes Benz 450SL Roadster, left to her by her grandmother Percelle Estes. After the cold shoulders and colder stares he and Lu got at Percy's funeral, Walt figured the final connection to her family was severed forever. Then, six weeks later, the car was delivered to Lucy, right on campus at Clemson. A cashier's check with more zeros than Walt had ever seen on one check was tucked inside the owner's manual, a single piece of paper under it with the words *Show 'em* scrawled in heavy, black ink.

"No. Lucy. I thank you, but no."

"You need a way to get around, and don't tell me you'll take the state truck, because you know as well as I do you're risking your ass if some uptight local sees you driving it outside the park." Lu followed him across the parking lot, her heels clicking against the asphalt. "Stupid politicians and their stupid budget bullshit—don't they know state employees can't pay their bills with IOUs?"

"Careful, you're startin' to sound like me," he said as he stopped to scuff at a wad of chewing gum molded to the new sidewalk he'd finally gotten funding for the previous winter.

"Peanut butter works better." Lucy folded her arms across her chest, rolling her eyes.

"And invites the six-legged locals to come for supper." He covered the remains with a few stray leaves and deposited the mess in one of the bear-proof trash cans. "Lucy, I appreciate it, but I can't drive that car around. It would cost more than I make in five years, *before* I pay the tax man, to replace it. And it's not replaceable, anyway. If something happened—"

"If something happens to it, it's insured." She shoved the key fob in his work pants. "And I added you to the policy, so don't argue with me."

Walt looked back to the dark red coupe parked in front of his cabin, its tan top tucked inside a matching cover. Behind his on-site quarters was the park vehicle, a leaf-dusted Chevy Blazer that was, at best, a much older brother to his own truck. His own currently inoperable truck. He buried the heavy sigh he wanted to let out. Instead, he reminded himself he was lucky to have friends with enough money to not give a shit he had very little of it. He swore it was just until the bill for his granddad's care was settled for the quarter.

"Thanks, darlin'." He wrapped an arm around Lucy. "See you tomorrow night?"

"Wait, you." She thumped the picnic basket against his leg. "We still have our lunch to eat, and you have some beans to spill." She looked much hungrier for the story than the lunch.

"Don't you need to catch up with your copilot over there?" Sandy Cutshill was still waiting in his new Lexus, adjusting his tie in the rearview mirror as the engine idled away.

"Stupid boy. He can wait."

"I can't. Time rolls fast in the high-stakes world of park management."

"Oh? Need to lead a family of raccoons to their spring accommodations?"

"I got a walk to lead in twenty minutes. Why don't we catch up tomorrow night at Tate's?"

He leaned down for a quick kiss on the cheek and, grinning, snatched the picnic basket from Lucy's hand.

"You know what I'm talking about, Yogi," she drawled, walking after him. "I heard where you slept last night."

"And how did you hear about that? Thought Miss Percy taught you not to pay attention to gossip."

Lu pulled him from the doorway. "So? How was she?"

"Lu. Stop." He huffed at her rolling eyes. "Okay, I like her. You and Claire called that one right. Damn the both of you."

"Of course we were right. That was obvious Saturday night. You followed her around like a little puppy, right out the front door." She swatted at his ass with a throaty giggle. "Glad you're back on the horse, Wanda. I've missed having you around."

"Wait a minute. I want to date this gir—woman. Maybe figure out if I like her before we play."

"You already said you like her, Sport." She flipped back the collar of his uniform shirt. "And it looks like she figured out she's not opposed to your presence, either. God help her."

"She's nice. Easy to like."

"But is she kinky?"

"Probably. Whatever that means." He remembered Erin the night before, swaying over him, the noises she made and the sweet, carried-away look on her face when his fingers sank harder into her body. Walt tipped his head toward Lu, mindful of where he was. "I don't care much about who passes the kink litmus test. It's not enough anymore."

Lu looked up at him, a small, stiff smile at her lips. "You really are getting old."

He shrugged. "I don't think I mind."

"You leave the playpen and you'll get bored, quick."

"Thanks for the lunch, Louis. Y'all have a safe drive back to town." He waved, answering her raised middle finger, as the visitor center door swooshed closed behind him.

How the hell did she know already?

"Have a minute?"

My back was turned to him, thank goodness. I sat my bags beside my desk, one by one. It gave me enough time to take a deep breath and remind myself that I was paid—and expected—to manage him. No matter what.

"Alan. Good morning. Of course. Let me boot up. I'll give you a call when I'm settled." I turned to him, reminding myself to use the neutral smile, the one that didn't say *I'd rather suck rocks/eat dirt/ stick my tongue in a blender, or any combination of them, than speak to you, Alan.*

He ignored me. Of course. Instead, he made a bit of show out of taking in my appearance. I clenched my teeth, still smiling.

Neutral. Neutral.

"Whoa, Erin." On a slow beat, he nodded, crossing the width of my triple-sized cubicle, and sat at the round table I often used for impromptu informal discussions. ThinkMine's culture encouraged "pick-up talks." This kind of interaction was one of the skills I'd had to work hardest to learn. Alan Richardson, my newest admin, made me wonder if I'd learned anything about handling people. "Skirt and jacket? You're dressed up today," he said. His voice and manner indicated I normally looked to him like an unkempt charwoman rather than a hippopotamus in charcoal gray gabardine, as I apparently did this morning.

"Alan, I want to go over that patch you installed last night so we can talk about what happened. There are a couple of lines of code I don't recognize. Let's talk around ten—"

"Can't. Steve Gomez and I are going to lunch."

The site director. My mentor in the management training program. How did he manage that? "Steve's not an early lunch guy. I think we can work in a ten to fifteen—"

"Gonna take a run first." Alan clasped his hands behind his neck and stretched his legs well into the center of my cubicle. I imagined him slipping right out of the chair, thump-thumping to the carpet under him as his head bounced from his seat to the floor. "That rec trail we put in is great. Did you know about it? Stretches a couple of miles into the woods. Even runs along this river—"

"It's called Sawtooth Creek." I smiled. Neutrally.

"Is it? You sure? Never heard that, and I'm local."

The jerk didn't believe me. And I knew he was imported from a small research start-up that went under when it lost a government contract that comprised nearly all of its business. In Cary. Over one hundred miles to the east, where he had moved when recruited out of Michigan State. Hardly local. I wasn't, and I'd learned the Southern stance on how specific local could mean—and how important locality was to this tradition-focused region.

Jerk.

Walt's voice rang in my ears from the night before. *No, no apologies. The guy sounds like a dirtbag. So call him a dirtbag.*

Dirtbag.

"I'll ping Steve. I need to take a look at what happened last night with you." I sat at my desk and began logging in to our intraoffice messaging system.

"I'll go grab him," Alan said, scuttling to his feet. "We can look at our schedules together."

"I've got your schedule right here." I tapped the screen in front of me. Each of my eleven team members and my lead admin filed weekly activity projections with me. I clicked on Alan's name. "I see you've got a conference call with the Main House at eleven. Asset management project? Isn't this a regular call-in? I thought we're getting close to satellite site start-up phase. I need numbers from that census so I can estimate capacity needs for the virtualization project."

"Yeah, it's pretty regular at this point. But I have my end under control, anyway. Those guys in the Main are all FNGs, trying to keep up, there's nothing going on that I need to cover from my team's angle."

"*Our* team."

"Of course. Our team."

"So I need your presence there. Thanks. I'll let Steve know." I looked at him, once again smiling. Patient. Neutral. *You've only worked here eight months, Dirtbag.*

His chin rose, giving me a clear view of his flared nostrils. "Thanks, Erin. You take care of that for me. Appreciate it."

Damn. I didn't move, didn't let my expression falter, didn't allow my mind to register anything past the wide, beige mental firewall I imagined descending when he did this. Across the surface, in white, sans serif: neutral.

"Oh, Alan?" I glanced toward the opening of my cube, where he would hopefully depart in seconds. "By the way, *fucking new guy*—FNG? It's derogatory. I realize you're still acclimating to Think-Mine culture, but we really stress that every team member has something to offer, even if it's day one with us. And even if they're not a *guy*. It's a core value. Important."

So there. Dirtbag.

"Rah rah," he said. As he rounded the twill-wrapped wall divider I heard him cough. And under it, "Fucking cunt."

It was going to be a long week.

"Don't forget to hop on that call for me, okay, Alan?" I said to the wall. Another longer burst of coughing was my only answer. A few seconds after, whispers and a trio of hearty laughs. Biting the inside of my cheek, I focused hard on the monitor I connected to my laptop in the office.

Some people never left the back of the school bus.

The day continued in the same pattern: Alan evading the responsibilities he deemed beneath him, me devoting too much of my time checking after him instead of working with my other team members. And because it was Monday, and because I'd been eye-shamed by

Alan for daring to wear a pencil skirt, and because I had left a gorgeous, tall, warm man on the front steps of his cabin—a cabin: a real mountain *cabin*—before I drove myself and my pencil skirt to work, my personal cell chimed at three, interrupting me as I got to a critical line of code that would fix the final hiccoughs from last night's errors.

And of course it was Danielle.

"You never called me back yesterday," she said over a stiff wind and music I couldn't name. But I could see her easily—hair blowing around her face, big sunglasses perched on her nose as she chatted. She was probably on her way through downtown Yountville with the top of Mom's ancient yellow VW Bug pulled down, headed toward the restaurant where she was currently apprenticing as a sommelier—this year's dream job.

She was so different from me. Everything about Danielle was always in motion, swift, erratic.

"I was busy. I'm sorry."

"You never blow me off. Where were you?"

"Nowhere," I said, purposely and slowly. I regretted it immediately.

"Don't lie to me, Pudge," she squealed, her voice reverberated in my ears. "Have a birthday hookup with that Iranian guy?"

"Indian. Ardhi's *Indian*, Dani." I went quiet and purposely left her with her assumptions. It was too soon to talk about Walt. And once she started asking questions, my sister didn't stop until she exhausted her curiosity, something I couldn't risk at work. But she also loved to talk about herself. "Did you go out Saturday night?"

"Why do you think I didn't call you until *last* night?" Once she laughed, the dread of discovery faded, relaxing my throat enough to carry on a conversation. I listened to her for the next half-hour and clicked around the net, looking at low-carb diets. And Danielle, in usual form, was distracted with her own story.

The secluded bends and curves of Lake Arden Way saw more than its fair share of sedate European sedans, but a classic convertible like Roxanne, screaming red with a top in a rich tan the color of a show-jumper's saddle, got attention Walt didn't care for. He looked like a tourist, or worse, one of the half-timers who kept buying up big stretches of the Blue Ridge to park their cabin-castles on. And, because Roxanne the Mercedes was all of those things — and Lu's grandmother's favorite car, left to her favorite, black sheep grand-daughter — he was too nervy to drive like the regular residents of Grayson County.

Signaling with many extra yards of fair warning to the stealthy black BMW coupe prowling behind him, Walt swung Roxanne between the riverstone pillars that marked the private drive to Tate's house. A sprawling lodge with deep porches and thick leaded glass windows, the place was set a half-mile from Lake Arden Way, through a meandering drive landscaped over a hundred years ago to look like nature intended each long-branched hemlock and lichen-spotted granite boulder to be exactly where they were.

The road was lit with weathered copper lamps, long rectangles composed of the same leaded glass squares that topped each window of the house. Ten years before, when he and Lu had driven up for the first time to visit Tate simply as friends, she fawned in a very un-Lu way over those lamps, gawping and babbling about a Scottish guy by the name of Mackintosh. It was an actual architect fangirl moment.

He got it. It was a nice house. Nice land, nice access to one of the prettiest, most unspoiled lakes in the Blue Ridge. All held by Tate and a few other private homeowners. No water-skiers or jet-skis, please. Very rich folk gone rustic. Which, to Walt, was always the only real selfish perk of being one of Tate's best friends — a single, secret thrill.

Wouldn't some of these snobs fall over and shit themselves if they found out about the kinky clubhouse right under their noses?

Thanks to Tate's ingenuity and his long-gone bachelor uncle's wise investments, the house and most of its original landhold had stayed in the Jernigan family. The Enclave was an unknown gem from the gilded age that had seen another of the East Coast industrial barons, this one called Vanderbilt, come down to western North Carolina to build a mountain home. The Jernigans' lakeside home was noth-ing like Biltmore in scale, but the heels of both owners' families had crossed the floors of their respective owners' houses during their summer retreats to the Blue Ridge.

A century later, once or twice a month, on Saturday afternoon, a number of cars with license plates from North Carolina, Virginia,

Tennessee, South Carolina, and even Georgia came down Lake Arden Way, causing no trouble and raising no reason for suspicion. They turned between those same riverstone and copper-lanterned pillars. Between seventy-five and a hundred and fifty might arrive, depending on the guest list, and park their cars in a few discreet alleys tucked into the landscape. They would come up the stone path to Tate's house and enjoy a nice dinner and maybe a walk on the paths of the disheveled but comfortable old gardens before heading downstairs to be tied to a piece of custom dungeon furniture and spending the rest of the evening in luxurious, carnal torment.

Or doing the tormenting.

Walt smiled to himself for a half-second over what he knew went on in the lodge's former basement kitchen and old servants' quarters tucked under the Enclave house main floors. Then the thought of Erin collided with his lazy inventorying. In the smaller, back playroom. Past the whip lane and the primal-play pit. The smooth, natural cherry Saint Andrew's cross—one of Walt's favorite pieces of equipment—with Erin's pale wrists and ankles roped to it. Her hair twisted on top of her head and messy because he'd made it that way. A few escapee silvery-blond pieces falling around the white silk covering her eyes. The tension and release he gave to her, playing her body with his hands, making her squirm against the crossed rails as her lips curved in the same lush O she made when she came hard above him. Whining and digging her nails into his shoulders as he pushed deeper into her and made her come again.

Slowing the Mercedes, Walt cranked the anemic late-seventies a/c. He'd masturbated more in the past three days than he had in the past two months. His own hand was a damn poor substitute for the feel of Erin's long, nimble fingers stroking his cock.

When he rounded the final curve to the house, he caught sight of Lu's Range Rover parked beside Tommy Blackwell's well-maintained but modest black truck. A few more vehicles belonging to other local members were parked around the drive. And right under the covered side entrance was Paul's giant white SUV, nearly blocking the entire span of orchard stone steps. It was just the thing Walt needed to kill his latest, Erin-inspired hard-on.

Paul never showed up on time, sending Claire ahead to help Tate organize the house. On nights like this, the two could handle things. For parties, they often worked with a core group of service-oriented slaves and submissives under her guidance. When Walt passed Paul's Escalade, the engine was ticking down, still cooling from the drive up from Callahan.

Good. They probably had already started.

He came in through the side entrance, a set of double doors that opened into a mudroom and wide corridor that ended in the kitchen — one of the house's few modern renovations.

"Oh hey, Ranger." Paul's most recent secondary partner, a girl called Powderpuff who had no fondness for vanilla clothes, was perched on the long, granite-topped island. She was actually working a shiny, red Blow Pop around her equally red and shiny lips. Her teeth had been stained pink for her efforts.

"Hey there," he said. As she started to snake down from the island, Walt waved to her. "I'm late, aren't I? Shit. Hey, see you later."

Before her platform boots could hit the floor, Walt turned the corner and crossed the central hallway. He slid into the big front room and parked himself behind Tommy and his wife, Alex. Before his eyes connected completely with Lu's, he looked down and made a show of shuffling around, reaching between his legs to adjust the dining chair where he sat. From the corner of his eye, he still caught her sticking her tongue out at him.

"Sir?" Eyes down, Claire's head tilted toward Paul, waiting. He grunted his consent, never one to waste his words on his wife, and she went on. "Thank you, Sir. I've met someone I'd like to put forward. She came to CPEP last week and I've known her for a few months. Her name is Er—"

"That computer girl wants to be a sub?"

Walt's head bobbed up in time to see Paul watching his girl with little interest. He looked like a damn gray-headed vulture, sneering down at her with his bushy eyebrows and puffed-up professor attitude.

She's interested in submission, not becoming a sandwich, asshole.

Lately, Claire's shoulders climbed to her ears every time Paul opened his mouth, a contrast to the soft smile she still gave the man she called her Master. The hope and desperation in it made Walt clench his jaw, which was probably smarter than punching Paul's.

"Yes, Sir." Claire paused, waiting for Paul's input, tethered to his whims. This wasn't about their dynamic; it was his damn show for the others.

"Het fem submissive, right? Reboot? Erin?" Lucy suddenly looked more interested than she had in six months of guardian meetings. The cocky smile she tossed in Walt's direction was a bit overdone, even for Lu. "You know her, Wanda?"

"Know who? Erin?" He remembered her long legs, her upturned, round ass as she untied and retied her shoelace. The surprise whiff of her perfume on his shirt Monday morning when he undressed after she dropped him at home. "Yeah, I've met her once or twice."

"Oh have you, now? After Saturday night at the club?" Lu chuckled to herself and stood, blowing a kiss at Walt in response to his raised middle finger. "Your ears are turning red as a fox's ass, Wanda."

"Oh, Wally!" Claire shifted on her knees so Lucy could pass by, beaming up at him.

Rubbing his hand over his face, Walt groaned. Now Claire was going to fuss over him like he was her little pet. He eyed the door, grunting to himself when he saw Tate was between him and a clean exit.

"So that's three votes in favor, yes?" When Tate wanted to, he could pull out the child of privilege routine and cast attitude around better than a Park Avenue heiress. Walt thanked him silently, swearing he'd buy the man a twelve-pack of Diet Sprite. It was the least he could do, since Tate had stopped drinking bourbon two years ago. "Paul, your girl available for mentoring a new *submissive?*"

Claire's head inclined toward her Master, waiting.

"Sure." Paul shrugged without a glance in Claire's direction. "I've hardly interacted with her, but they seem to know each other already."

"Great." Tate nodded toward Claire with a reserved smile. "Thank you, Claire."

And that was that. Erin would be invited up to The Enclave. *Barely* as a guest of Paul's, but under his slave's guidance. The rest of the meeting was unremarkable, and finished minutes later. Walt moved around a few clusters of people, heading for the kitchen.

He poured himself a glass of tea and pretended to study the contents of Tate's fridge as Paul and Tommy passed through. Times like this were the worst for missing Brady. And his girl Hailey. Even Holly, before her demons turned on her. If she accepted the invitation, Erin, simply by virtue of her newness, made the balance of personalities and power dynamics change well before she would arrive at Tate's house. Really, before she even knew she'd been invited.

There were stories she would want to hear, maybe a few he'd want to tell her too. Burying his best friend Brady. Standing beside his wife Hailey as she took the flag from the honor guard, how her hands shook around the deep blue edges, even though she wore her own Dress Blues and still kept her chin high as her tears spilled down her cheeks. And Holly. And the dark winter last year, after he'd returned from seeing Hailey in San Diego.

He'd made that trip at his best friend's request—his last request. It was supposed to bring closure to Hailey, and to Walt too. Instead, he came back to North Carolina after New Year's Day more edgy and bitter than ever, struggling with the realities of his life and age, his lifestyle.

Walt stared into the bright light glaring directly into his eyes from the back of the fridge.

Bright light. *Sun.*

Glaring into his eyes as Lu chatted his ear off about her New Year's trip to Atlanta with Tate, the enormous dungeon just opened there in an old meatpacking factory. His body a concert of muscle aches and stiff joints after making himself into a damn contortionist, flying coach all the way home from California to see to Hailey. His last duty to Brady, his best friend, his brother, and one-time savior, too.

Lucy glared at him. "Wanda, are you even listening—" The Rover's wheels screamed as they locked, sending the big SUV fishtailing across the highway. The vehicle came to a hard stop, throwing Lucy into Walt's aching body. "The hell?"

In front of them, a huge flatbed had swung from a clearing in Callahan Paper's woodland management area. A few miles back into the forest, it adjoined a backcountry area of the park. There was talk the Callahan family had sold off a big parcel of their land, but apparently the sale was no rumor. In the week Walt had been gone, trees had been cleared. A gravel drive was put down. And a high, razor wire-topped fence spanned the clearing.

CONSTRUCTION SITE
SEE FOREMAN FOR ADMITTANCE
THINKMINE INC.

ThinkMine, her work—a server farm, she called it. Before he knew Erin was coming, there she was.

"I'll be damned." Walt muttered to the ever-present case of Diet Sprite, and the remains of cold cut trays and jars of fancy condiments

Claire put together for the social hour before the meeting. He stood up, fast. Too fast to clear the stainless steel edge above his head. Behind him, Lu, Tate and Claire howled.

Damned, indeed. He scowled at the three, rubbing his head.

"Oooh, sweetie, that looked bad," Claire said, crossing to him. "Bend down. Let me see if you broke the skin."

"Like you could crack that thick skull." Lucy snorted. "So, Wanda... you have something to tell us?"

Claire huffed. "Oh, leave him alone, Lucy."

Assured he'd not damaged himself—or Tate's high-end refrigerator—Claire helped herself to a bottle of water and brought out cans of soda for Tate and Lu. She and Lu opened their beverages and drank.

Walt leaned into the cool granite countertop behind him and did the same with his tea.

Silence.

"Damn, would somebody say something?" Tate crumpled the aluminum can in his hand and cracked open another one. "Why the hell are we all standing around, watchin' each other breathe?"

"Wanda got lucky." Lucy's eyes never moved. She watched him closely, smirking as she lifted the can to her lips.

"Well, thank God. That grumpy-bear bullshit of his was hell on my mood." Tate folded his arms across his chest and looked between Walt and Lu and Claire. "What? So Walt got laid. Walt used to get laid a lot, if y'all remember."

"No, Tate...he met a *girl*." Claire smiled—no, hell, she was *beaming* at him like he'd just walked on his hind legs for her.

"I've got to get out of here before this one tries to teach me to sit up and beg." Walt stepped around Claire, still grinning up at him like he was her new puppy, and shook Tate's outstretched hand as he passed him. "See you, man. And Louis, thanks for the loaner. I'll have it back to you by next weekend."

"Just keep Roxanne until you can get a new truck. That one you've had since we graduated from college is headed for the junkyard. If it was a kid, you'd be buying it a prom dress."

"I'll have it back to you next weekend. Tommy's already ordered the clutch." The screen door closed behind him with a heavy crack. He wasn't surprised when he heard the hinges squeak again.

"Wally?" Claire jogged after him, alone, it sounded, from the soft slap of her bare feet on the old orchard stone path. "Walt?"

He couldn't walk away from Claire. Tate, probably. Lucy, definitely. But Claire wasn't following him to ride his ass about Erin. She probably wanted to talk, which was worse. He shoved his hands in his pockets and paused by one of the old rose arbors.

"Sorry about that," he said, nudging his boot against the gray, split wood.

"It's okay." She brushed her hand across the bench, scattering spent rose petals to the ground. "Bet Lucy's not let up on you since Monday morning."

"Not since." Walt sat beside her, careful of the overloaded vines twisting over above their heads. "You know Lu."

Claire was quiet for a minute, watching him in that way of hers that made him feel too big and clumsy to be near her. "She's not Holly."

"Erin? No." So *this* talk was already happening. Walt settled back, stretching his arm along the creaky wood, ready for a long one. "It would be a hell of a trick if she was, since I don't believe in ghosts."

"So stop acting like a haunted man."

"Claire…" He knew about his blind spots and the old, gimpy places in his head. "I know. Can y'all take it down a notch? I just met the girl."

Claire raised her shoulders, conceding. "You're right. I'm sorry. Lucy and I got a little excited," she said. "It's been so long…"

She had him there. "Has been. But a new girl…hell, I probably should've been more careful. I was staying away from new girls, remember?"

"Maybe. Maybe not. Erin's very smart. She's been watching for a long time."

He looked out over the garden's tangle of overgrown hedges and rosebushes, wishing he'd thought to bring a can of Tate's beverage of choice along so he'd have something to do with his hands. Instead he studied them, remembering the sound she made when he pulled at her nipple, the way she asked for more. Someone like Erin asking for harder, heavier sensation from him could get very close to those old, gimpy places he'd kept blocked off since he was a kid, getting his first tastes of playing and doing it with someone he had feelings for.

"Watching isn't the same as doing. You know that, Claire."

"Reading and learning about the lifestyle and then getting into things is smarter than jumping in blind." She tucked her arm through his. "I've spent some time with her, Walt. She's smart. I thought you'd like her."

He couldn't stop himself from chuckling a little at her. "Soon as I saw her, I knew you and Lu had something cooked up."

"We've been concerned."

"About me? Since when? I'm fine." His voice sounded rushed, false to his own ears.

"Since you got back from seeing Hailey last Christmas." Her hand smoothed over the fist he'd made against his hip. "You've had a lot happen in the past two years, Wally. I think you needed a break after losing so much so fast."

Walt slumped a little against the wooden slats behind him. The feel of something solid behind him was good. He let out a long breath.

"I was done, you know?"

"I know," she said, smoothing over his knuckles again.

"Holly—after her, I said 'nope, just going to keep it casual, nothing serious anymore.' That was when I figured I wasn't up for any more."

"Walt, even if Erin doesn't become a long-term part of your life, you can't just tell yourself you're writing off relationships because you've lost people who were important to you."

"It's not that." Gritting his teeth, he looked around the garden, nearly dark in advance of nighttime. "I was starting to think I'd never have someone want me to stick around." Claire made a small sound, but he coughed out a tired, disbelieving laugh at her. "You know, she said that to me Sunday night. She asked me to stay. It—I know she didn't mean it like that, but it still got me a little." He laughed again, easier and softer this time.

"Just go slow," Claire said, her voice a soft whisper over the night sounds coming on around them. "You know that, but I'm going to tell you anyway."

"Trying to. It's going real fast."

Smiling a little, she sighed and tucked herself into his arm. "The only thing I miss about being actively poly is that first spark. The way you feel when you've just met someone and the sex is really hot and you could just talk for hours and then you want to do it again and it's even hotter the next time." He couldn't stop the understanding nod—or the need to shift his legs. "Enjoy it. Enjoy her."

"Yeah," he said, kissing the top of Claire's deep red curls. "I'm gonna."

CHAPTER EIGHT

My phone chirped, showing a short text from Walt.

I'm out front. -W

"I'm going to wrap up for tonight, Alan. We can pick up tomorrow morning. Seven thirty?"

"Fine. Fine with me, Erin."

I hated the sound of my own name on his voice. Mercifully, he was gone without another word. I gathered my things, resolutely reciting *neutral…neutral…neutral.* Alan wouldn't spoil my date.

Date. Dinner. Or date for dinner?

It was more than a *thanks for the sex* dinner, because he'd called more than once, and Claire also called, sounding so smug in a kind way but definitely smug over something, and when Walt called, he asked about my day and how Dirtbag was behaving, and…

"Okay, enough." I forced myself to sit. Walt would wait an extra sixty seconds. I, however, needed to catch my racing, panicky pulse. He wouldn't go away over an extra minute. "And," I said, whispering, "if he does, he does."

Around me, the data center had stilled to the even, smooth hum that took over when most of our people had gone home. This was often my favorite time at the Callahan House, when I did my most concentrated work. I caught my reflection in the dark screen of my monitor, and then the scene beyond me. Past my shoulder, the late spring afternoon light threaded through the trees, throwing bright shafts of sun across the stretch of new grass, reflecting its deep green at the old forest beyond. There was so much random and unpredictable out there. No even gradients of gray paint and carpet and temporary walls in easily manageable right angles.

There was something more interesting than the rigid, methodical environment I controlled, after all. Walt was out there too.

I gathered my things and headed to the front entrance.

I didn't see him right away. Not sure what sort of car to look for, my eyes glided past the red convertible. But then the door opened, drawing back in time to see Walt's broad shoulders clearing the windshield. His hand came up as he smiled, hovering for a moment until it went to his pocket.

He met me at the end of the front walk, his fingers under my elbow as I stepped from concrete to asphalt, lingering as he walked beside me to the passenger side of the car.

"This is your loaner?" I smiled at it, a little disbelieving and charmed. "Who keeps a vintage Mercedes as their spare car?"

"Luce, who else?" Stepping aside, he opened the door for me. "Feel like I hear the *Miami Vice* soundtrack playing every time I get in it."

I set my messenger bag and purse inside, turning so I could follow. "I like it. It's…well, it's nearly summer and it's a convertible. But it's…"

"It's what?" His hand still hadn't left my elbow.

"It's not very…*you*. No offense, just—"

"No offense taken. You're right," he said, laughing. "I feel like a bear on a tightrope driving it."

"I haven't been in a convertible in years."

"You're kidding me. Re—" His face shifted, drew in tight around his eyes. "Come here," he said, suddenly gruff, fingers sliding down my waist.

I stumbled into him, graceless and more than a little shocked at his change. Before I could steady myself, Walt kissed me. His mouth was surprising again after four days, making me reach for his arm as his tongue passed over my lips. One long, muscled thigh nudged over mine and my hips settled against his. In the distance, I heard voices, then a round of male laughter, and I stumbled over Walt's foot as my head canted toward them.

And of course, Alan passed us, clapping his hand to Steve Gomez's shoulder as they passed. He turned his head, over his shoulder, toward me, with a smile that didn't reach his eyes.

"Oh God."

Walt's arm circled my waist as he chuckled. "Whoa. All right there?"

"Fine," I said, shuddering. The wave of horror was instant and hard. *No, no, no…* That laughter, they weren't…*no, not they, just Alan,* because Steve was my management mentor, and he was looking away, pointing his key fob toward his waiting car. "I'm fine. Can I just get in, please?"

The seatbelt fumbled through my fingers, catching across my breasts. I lost it, and it slid back, tightening over my neck. Under me, hot leather scorched my legs and I pushed myself up, hissing.

Walt was back at my side. "Hey, you okay?"

Huffing and blinded by the late afternoon sun, I pointed at the seatbelt, now dug hard into the crevice between my neck and shoulder. I was pinned, struggling to shimmy from the webbing. Intent on helping, Walt touched my arm, and my eyes clenched with humiliated frustration. "No, thank you. No, just…oh, darn it—no, let me!"

"Okay." The sense of him beside me evaporated, and a moment later the driver's door opened.

"I'm sorry." Freed, finally, I adjusted the seatbelt and clicked it into place.

Walt started the car. We drove in silence across the parking lot. Finally, when we had cleared sight of the building, he pulled into the deep shade of a tall evergreen.

"That was Alan," I said. "Um, Dirtbag?"

"Yeah, I know." He shrugged casually.

"How—"

"I saw him watching us. Well, *you.* When you said you were working late with him, I had a feeling he'd be around about the same time you left. And wouldn't you know it? There he was."

"Watching us—me? He hates me."

"No, he hates himself because he can't have you," he said. "Guys like him, they're used to women falling all over themselves to get his attention. He's used to it, and he uses it. I'd imagine you treat him like you treat everybody else on your team."

I looked over at him, my throat tightening. "Well, yes, of course. I give everyone I work with the same respect and…"

"*And* he thinks he's better than pretty much everyone, except the guys he thinks will give him power. And he probably thinks they're nothing but a stepping stone anyway."

"I don't think he's interested in me," I said, giving the seat belt a tug away from my neck. "Not sexually."

"You're kidding me." Walt cocked his head toward me. "You're beautiful, Erin. And smart, and a decent gir— woman. *And* you have power over him, and doesn't it just piss him off that he can't fuck you out of your power?"

"Beautiful?" I winced a little, but turned back to him, slanting my head in his direction. I smiled. "That's some speech. How do you know all of this?"

"One, I've got eyes and you are beautiful." He shifted, looping his arm over my seat. His other hand wrapped around mine. "Two, I'm a man who was raised by an old-fashioned granddad, played sports, was a military cadet for three years, and have been in the lifestyle for near-eighteen."

I pursed my lips, stunting a giggle. "Oh, the man's man thing. That's why you kissed me?"

"No, not really. I've seen my share of pissing contests. But I was going to kiss you anyway." His thumb swept over my wrist as he'd taken to doing, and my shoulders dropped a little as I exhaled. "You sure you're okay?"

"Yes." *Yes, Sir.* Beside my head on the headrest, his fingertips skimmed my cheek. It hummed between us, this unnamed thing that happened when I was aware of him like that. Like what I was beginning to understand as Dominant. Distantly, I noted a car pass. And another. Walt didn't look away either. "You are too, you know."

"Am what?" His thumb tipped across my bottom lip.

"Beautiful." He rolled his eyes, laughing toward the heavy green branches over us. "No, you are. Walt, stop laughing." I dug my fingers into his exposed side, tickling. He laughed harder, but growled and caught my arm, stilling it against his ribs.

"No tickling," he said, eyebrow rising. I opened my mouth to protest, but he shook his head. "I said no tickling. Okay?"

I let out a long breath and nodded, unable to look away. "Okay."

After a silent second, he let my hand go. "You like Italian, right?"

"Sure." I resisted the urge to compile low-carb alternatives to pasta in my head. "Love it."

"Let's go eat," he said, leaning against my forehead for a quick kiss.

I watched him for a few minutes as he guided the car along the road into Callahan. It was about power: Alan's sudden interest in our site director, questioning my solutions. Going his own way when he installed the upgrades I wrote for our servers' operating system. And his territory: a manager's seat by the windows, his because he thought he was entitled to it.

Without a second thought, Walt made it clear, in a male language I now had no doubt was real, that I was under his protection. I should have bristled over it or dismissed it. The surprise, though, was I liked being someone Walt concerned himself about. I liked that the problem of how to handle Alan seemed smaller, and how much less villainous he'd become.

"Does it always break down to that?"

"To what?"

"Power. Is that how men always relate to each other?"

He glanced at me as the car hummed forward. "Women do it too."

"No, not...okay, they do." I watched the suburb of Callahan passing us. All those new homes, possibly one of them belonging to Alan or another one of my team members. Their wives at home? Working too? Settled into traditional expectations or bucking them, like his friend Lucy, or even Claire and Dr. Paul Saldino, DDS. Or Walt. "Do you think you're always a Dominant?"

His eyebrows rose over his sunglasses. "Dominant? No. And no, I don't think about playing all the time."

"That's not what I meant."

"I know," he said, grinning. "I'm a Top. I don't call myself a Dominant, Erin."

I pushed my hair away from my face. "But you are. I mean, that's how it feels." There was so much more in me and seemingly between us, feelings and instincts so base and chemical I didn't know how to name them. I hushed myself. *Too much.*

"It does." His hand left the gearshift and picked up mine. "Let's take this a step at a time, okay?"

Silently I nodded, and focused on the road.

"Don't," he said as we braked for a couple in the crosswalk.

I shook my head. "Not doing anything."

He parked the car along a row of refurbished brick storefronts, evidence that Callahan's center was coming back to life.

"It's not a little thing, Erin. Not the way it feels like it could be with you. The way I think about us together. That's a lot to say for me, but it seems like this—" He moved his hand in the air between us. "*We're* moving pretty fast."

"Yeah," I said. This wasn't going to fall apart. I liked him. I should hold it together, and just not need him so soon, even though there was so much about Walt that felt good. Right. "I'm having pasta."

"Excuse me?"

Pointing to the restaurant, Trattoria Stella, I repeated, "Pasta. I'm going to have pasta."

He gave me his half-grin, the one mimicked in the crescent lines around his eyes. "All right, then. Me too. Hope they've got enough. I skipped lunch again."

He had pasta. Spaghettini tossed with tomato, crispy, glistening pancetta, and peppers. A big salad of arugula, roasted beets, and goat cheese. When he held out a bite for me, I leaned forward for it without question, humming over the balsamic-sage dressing. And I ate. Chicken piccata. With the fettuccine.

"I'm glad you like your dinner." He chuckled as I sighed at another forkful of lemony-bright chicken. "You skip lunch too?"

"Um…no. I brought my lunch. Salad." I sat my fork aside and sipped at the glass of Sauvignon Blanc suggested by our waiter. "I don't think I've been out to dinner since I've been here. A sit-down dinner, with wine." I certainly knew more than a couple of the evening crews at Crusts, a local sandwich shop.

"You haven't dated since you've been here?"

"No."

Walt swirled the Malbec in his glass, his eyes narrowing a little. "You're kidding."

"No. Not for a while." I cut a triangle of chicken. "Do you want to try this?"

"No, thanks. I can't believe that."

"I can't believe it either. This is the best chicken piccata I've ever had. You should have a bite."

His eyes skipped to my plate and back to me. "I don't care for capers, and I don't mean the chicken."

I popped the chicken I'd cut for him into my mouth. "'S really good," I said behind my hand, nodding.

"How long?" He was on the scent of it now, and wouldn't stop.

"Close to five years. Regularly." I swirled my wine and drank again. "I've…there was a guy in California, but it was convenience for both of us, I think. We're really just good friends. He transferred back to our data center in Mumbai last spring. Since then, no one."

"Huh." He shrugged and looked at me with considered silence for a moment. "You like tiramisu, right?"

"Tiramisu?" I cleared my throat with a sound that, again, was not mine but was mine. It was coming from my mouth and the words were coming from my brain. It was impossible to follow him when he spoke in that voice, and he made it so difficult to draw together what I needed and wanted to tell him, when he was so close and smiling at me like I was an appealing, amusing girl. Who would never lose twenty-five pounds if she kept eating cream and fettuccine and tiramisu. But why lie? "Yes."

"Good. So, you have anything against dating?"

"Um, no. As a concept, no."

The corner of his mouth lifted. "But in practice?"

"It's never seemed to be an important part of the logic chain."

"Why don't you give it a try? Do something different." He sipped from his wine, eyes leveled toward me over the rim of his glass.

We watched each other for a span of seconds, the edge of what I had to accept and commit to creating such a big, yawning gap between what I knew and what he'd challenged me to be. Different. And more. "I don't know how, Walt," I admitted, probably too quietly for him to hear.

"Then let's figure it out. One *thing* at a time." He chuckled softly, already wise to my aversion of naming what it was I wanted.

I knew, without any doubt. I liked him. I wanted him to like me too. Behaving like a silly, babbling girl fifteen years younger than myself was not the right way to communicate this. I'd look like someone who was emotionally—and possibly mentally—incapable of doing BDSM things with him.

BDSM things? God, I even think in awkward to myself.

"What?" He looked at me closely, grinning. "That thought—right there. What's going on in there?"

"I—I'm—ahh…"

A corner of his mouth twitched, then lifted. "Go ahead, spit it out."

"Walt—" Glancing around us, I took a deep breath, because that's what people usually did when they needed courage, and leaned forward "—I'd like to play with you."

"I know."

"Oh?"

"Well, considering where we met, and Sunday night, and you and Claire—"

"Claire?" I sat back, unsure of the appropriate response, because I didn't care about it, but if he meant *together*, because she wasn't—

"No, back up. Not like that. You two are friends. You came to the club with her, right?"

"Yes. Well, no. I drove myself, but—"

"So what are you looking for?"

"Looking for?" He was asking me this during dinner? I must have gaped at him a little because he chuckled softly.

"Yes, you're interested in what, when it comes to play?" He waited, suddenly the amused and patient professor. An errant thought of him wearing round glasses and a tweed blazer flashed through my stuttering brain, turning my thighs tense.

Well, *that* was one. An easy one.

"I'd like to try a spanking."

A lazy smile spread across his features. He twirled his fork through his pasta. "Would you?"

"I would. Yes. That…it seems like a simple thing." I nodded, taking a deep breath. "Right?"

"Sure," he said. He bit into the curl of pasta and sauce, leaving me in edgy silence as he chewed and considered. "Simple thing.

Like I said, it's hand and ass, no matter how fancy you get about it. Over the knee?"

My spine went rigid, sending me into the seat back. "Excuse me?"

"Do you want me to turn you over my knee when I spank you?" Maybe it was his accent, or the veneer of ease he laid over this interrogation, but there was more than challenge in his question. Every word had a particular weight as he spoke.

"You're thinking about it, aren't you?"

"Yeah." His expression didn't change. He didn't move. "I am."

Tension whirred across my back and coiled through the muscles in my hips. The twin currents bolted, crashing together deep under my stomach. I had no way to understand, in my own experience, what the act of submission to Walt would be like, but I already recognized the exchange between us. It was a straight, simple causeway.

Yes, Sir.

"So am I," I said, reaching forward, blind, for something to put my fingers on.

"I know you are."

"I haven't…you know." I emptied my wineglass. "I haven't been. Before."

"I know. You said so the other night." He slid his water glass toward me. "What else?"

"Um…I'd like to be tied up."

"May want to work up to that," he said and broke off a piece of his bread. Pushing back from the table, he wiped his fingers across his napkin and returned it to his lap. "People think it's BDSM 101, but being restrained can fuck with your head a little."

The swim of my wine and his attention made me flushed, bold. "The way you'd do it to me?"

"Yes." He nodded, unblinking. "Your head needs a little fucking with."

"How would you do it? How are you thinking about it right now?"

"I'd tie your wrists to your ankles, ankles to knees. Keep you opened up, even though you'd worry over it, but not so much you'd talk yourself out of it. And that would be enough the first time. Just letting me see you and touch you like that would be enough."

The space around our table receded, nearly went dark beyond. In the brief distance between us, there was a zinging, phosphorescent line of attention and intention. The electricity of it tingled over my lips and unfurled across my chest, taking my chin higher, and with it, my torso stretched, open as he'd just said.

Open. Open for him, by his hand, and for his use. The word and its meaning relaxed my hold on everything around me. Those *other things* — the events and expectations I was so determined to manage, all of it outside myself and what Walt wanted from me — paled just enough to not be overwhelming. My ambition and expectation and desire for stability would be waiting. But I understood, without removing a stitch of clothing and surrounded by other people, that he could — and would — lift that control from me when we chose the time.

"You heard of The Enclave?"

"Enclave?" I searched through conversations I'd had with Claire, even Walt. Nothing. I shook my head.

"It's a house. You've not met him, but a good friend of Claire's and mine owns this house over on Lake Arden, where Lu lives. He has a private play party there every few weeks."

The words of the women we'd met at Home Outfitters came back to me. She *did* see me the night I went to Area 51.

All of those people who go up to that house are so into themselves…all of them trying to act like they're so exclusive, and it's some big mysterious thing that happens out there…another damn popularity contest, like everything else in the lifestyle.

"And?" Even though their opinion of this private party was apparently low, in my mind, the two women were attached to the place because they were the first people I'd heard mention it. And considering how I felt about them…

"It's just a nice house on some property. A place to play without worrying about people's neighbors or someone inviting the police."

"Po — ?!" I lowered my voice. "Police?"

"Erin, you do realize you're not in California? Half the states in the South still have sodomy laws."

"What are you talking about?" My stomach clenched. The chicken piccata with the pasta *was* a bad idea.

"They're not really enforced but — look, not everyone is so easygoing about the things we do." He nodded slowly, like he was talking to a child. "There's still prejudice out there. People can lose their jobs, their families, their kids."

The waiter appeared at Walt's side. While they spoke of to-go boxes and the dessert menu, I glanced around the restaurant. We were at a comfortable distance from the last few occupied tables, but we weren't alone. If someone heard…it didn't matter to me, but that was from the relative safety of consideration, not experiencing the actual event.

In San Francisco, I'd bounced down Folsom Street, through a throng of people, always peering around Danielle's shoulder. Any and all manner of relationship was on display, celebrated during the annual street fair. But I lived in North Carolina. And I did notice some attitudes, the focus of everyday life — it was *different* here.

"Erin?" Walt's palm rested, warm and solid, on the back of my hand. "You okay?"

"Of course, yes," I said, hushed.

"You've been invited to The Enclave."

"Okay…" I glanced around us again. "Is this a big deal?"

"It…" He shook his head, laughing. "It's a nice place. But no, I guess it's not really a big deal."

"Is she there? That woman — Nicole?"

"Uh, no." He scratched his earlobe as his brows drew together and he looked away. "No, Nicole hasn't been there."

"How long did you see her?"

"I played with her a few times but it was casual."

"And you slept with her?"

"No, we didn't sleep."

"Oh." I looked away, unsure how to ask questions I knew I should ask. And, logically, I shouldn't worry about asking Walt for too much information about his…things. Even if the answers changed how I saw him. "Did you date her?"

"Date? No, she's —" He leaned toward me, his forearm resting across the table. "Erin, there are people who are play partners who never see each other in the daylight."

His expression, his nearness, and the tone of his voice reminded me of the afternoon we'd spent together.

"You've seen me in the daylight," I said.

"I have. I'd like to see you like that again."

"You mean sweaty and out of breath in your forest, or how I was later?"

"Both." He moved forward a little more, still studying my face. "I want to date you, Erin. And play with you, after we get to know each other a little better. Maybe see what else happens."

I suspected a combination of the two, playing and dating, was not something Walt did regularly. But never had someone just set out their intentions toward me so I could question and discuss them.

"I'd like that too," I said, watching his reaction for some sign I'd followed the process of negotiation correctly. When it came, it was in the shape of the considering half-smile I was coming to know well. I wanted to reach across the space between us and touch the turned-up furrows by his eyes, let the dark coffee-colored hair just behind his ear curl around my finger. When I dodged my tongue across my lips, I tasted wine and lemons and garlic. Not him. I wanted to kiss him, so much. "Um…Walt?"

I didn't have to ask. His mouth was on mine before I could say it. The business of people arriving and placing orders and holding their own conversations continued around us. Walt's hand rested on my knee, his fingers splayed lightly along the outside of my thigh. Everything around us didn't matter. His touch, especially his kissing, was a first-order function.

Finally he pulled away, tongue nudging at the curve of his lower lip.

"Good," he said quietly.

"Good."

I let my hand trail after him and touched the single curl behind his ear I'd spied before. The stubble on his cheek rasped across my arm as he turned his head. Under my fingers, his hair rippled and curved. His lips brushed across the inside of my wrist. Beside us, there was the clatter of a glass against a table, a chair thunking across the worn wood floor. Walt sat back, giving our server a brief nod. He kept possession of my hand, lacing his fingers through mine.

"You wanna get out of here?"

"Yes." At that moment I wanted to go anywhere he'd lead me. He stood and tugged me to my feet.

"Got this for you," he said, placing a cardboard box in my other hand. "Somethin' sweet. For later."

CHAPTER NINE

His cock was so hard he could barely drive. The only thing that saved him was remembering that he was driving Lu's grandmother's mint-condition Mercedes with a hard-on that would choke a catfish. When Roxanne's headlights arced across the park entrance and lit the spur road leading to his cabin, Walt congratulated himself. He'd made the twenty-minute drive from Erin's place down in Callahan to his house without turning around, driving back, and dragging her across the arm of her couch to give her the spanking she'd asked for.

For as long as he could, Walt distracted himself from the white cardboard box with the day's mail, a load of laundry, a glass of milk. The milk broke him. Its icy cold creaminess damn near demanded he get what he wanted.

Erin's voice was creaky and far away when she answered her phone.

"Hi," she said over the muffled sounds of movement. "Was just thinking about you."

Her voice hit his ear at the same time the first bite touched his tongue. He wasn't ready for sweet, silky, and spicy and Erin hitting him all at once, turning his bones to liquid fire.

"Hey," he said, setting the box of tiramisu aside. "What were you thinking?"

"You first. I answered all the questions at dinner." She was a little bit saucy over the phone, when she had a little distance, and that made his fingers ache for a handful of her hair, and to turn her face to his so he could watch her eyes light up with it. "What have *you* been thinking about?"

"Nothing." He laughed along with her. "No, really. Nothing important, just about my dessert."

"You got one too?"

"Are you kidding me? You saw that dessert case when we walked in." He huffed, a broad, overblown sound that made him proud when she laughed at it. "Crazy woman."

"Shhh, Walt. Stop talking about it." Behind her words, fabric rustled over a distinct squeak he remembered from late Sunday night.

She was in bed, damn it. His cock pulsed against the seam of his boxers. He threw the sheets from his legs and sat up against the headboard, reaching for the take-out box.

"Go get it."

"Excuse me?"

"Go get it. Your cake."

"No. I can't eat it now. I've already brushed my teeth."

"You always follow the rules, don't you?"

"So if I eat dessert after I've brushed my teeth, that suddenly makes me edgy?"

"This isn't a psychological assessment, Erin." He took a bite of the espresso-soaked cake. "Shit…"

"Excuse me?"

"Nothing. I just dropped a bunch of this whipped cream stuff on my sheets."

This time when she laughed it was full and free, so much more musical and way less self-aware. "I've already changed my sheets once this week, thanks to you. And now you're tempting me to get my mouth dirty. Um—I mean—"

"Dirty?" He stopped wiping the splotch of sweetened mascarpone from his chest. "Don't say 'get my mouth dirty' to me, Erin. I need to sleep tonight."

"I…" The catch in her breath was obvious, and underlined by a long stretch of quiet. "Well, okay, but you're the one so desperate to get your beauty rest."

"But I don't *have* to sleep tonight," he offered. "I'd rather talk to you about tiramisu."

The line was quiet again, for so long he nearly asked her if she was still there. His answer came with another telltale squeak.

"Okay," Erin said, hushed.

"Bring it back to your bed."

"You're not going to ask me what I'm wearing?"

He could see her cheek rounding, the way she pursed her lips when she challenged him. Already it was a temptation, that evasive move of hers. She had so many of those emotional feints, each one asking him to catch her chin in his hand and make her stop trying to distract him.

"I don't really care what you're wearing now. When you get back to your bedroom, it better be nothing but your glasses. Wait on those till you're back in bed. Can't have you tripping over that rug in your hallway. Might have to drive over and rescue you or something."

"I don't do this," she said after a few seconds.

"You can brush your teeth again, Erin."

"You know what I mean." Something metallic clanked and rattled. She didn't *do this*, but she sure as hell was rattling through what sounded like her silverware drawer. "This isn't me."

"Sure it is," he said. "Someone just forgot to show you."

"Walt, I —" she started. Once again, the line went quiet, and longer this time. And then…squeak.

"Now your glasses."

"Done." There was a tiny giggle in her voice, and his apprehension dissolved. She just needed permission. He'd suspected it all along.

"Have some," he said and followed his own instructions. He imagined her mouth opening, lips poised over a spoon so full, near dripping with cake and cream.

"Mmmm…oh my God, that's good," she said with a sigh, setting off a torrent of pointed shocks traveling over his stomach, aimed for his balls. He cupped them in time, barely concealing the hiss of his breath over his teeth. Fucking killing him. The woman was fucking killing him, and she seemed to bounce along her merry way without a single idea of it.

Walt glanced at the dull red digital numbers shining 11:09 in the dim corner of his nightstand. He was too old for this shit. Too old to be teasing himself with a woman, too old to be considering what he suddenly was doing.

"Erin, go get another fork."

As he turned over Roxanne's motor, he hoped he wasn't so old he'd forgotten the way to Erin's house.

I knew he was on his way, so it wasn't a complete surprise when I opened the door and found Walt standing before me, dressed in sweatpants and a T-shirt, breathing a little heavily. The heavy breathing was a little unusual, actually, but the way Walt pulled me into his chest and tugged at the base of my ponytail as he kissed me was the revelation I wasn't expecting.

"Hi. Where's your tiramisu?"

"We're doing this too fast," he said against the base of my throat, tugging at my robe. I swallowed hard, whining when his mouth closed over the skin beneath my ear. That would bloom purple and plum. It was May. I lived in the South.

Instead of heeding those very sensible thoughts, I hailed him on, twisting my hips against his. "A turtleneck or scarf, maybe—"

He broke away, panting, his eyes level with mine. "What're you... *scarf?*"

"I'll wear one." Threading my fingers through his hair, I pulled his lips to mine. "I'll wear one around my neck, so just don't stop that biting."

"Don't tell me what to do," he said, grinning as he tilted his head away from mine. He chuckled softly when I trailed after him. "That's my job."

"Oh yes, sir." I added a mock salute before I realized what I'd said. It caught between us, a quick drumbeat underlining this thing that kept us circling each other, so fast we kept reminding each other of it, and so delirious from it we couldn't be responsible, risk-managing adults and step back to avoid it.

I shook a little. My teeth vibrated against my lips, pressed together tight so I wouldn't say it again. I'd dropped this thing between us into the open while we were too close for any more rational discussion, and not entirely sure we'd remembered to close my front door. And I could see it in his eyes. He was deciding.

"You ready for that spanking?" His breath fell in short, soft bursts against my cheek.

I forced myself to look past his shoulder, promising myself it was the last logical decision I'd make for the rest of the night, and checked the front door. Closed. Locked. As my eyes inched back to his, the wire-swung, slow motion feeling greeted me, and dangled me before him. I took a shallow, silent breath, and nodded, watching his mouth for my next direction.

"Yes…I am."

His hands skimmed over my arms, connecting my wrists behind me. One of his closed tidily around both of mine. Leaning down, Walt whispered, his lips skimming my ear, "Let's go." It ran over my spine like icy water. My hips wagged against his, so close behind me, and his hand wrenched my wrists against my back. "Do that again and you'll get fucked, not spanked."

My house's familiar, dim rooms ticked by us as he guided me toward my bedroom. Some distant Monday morning I might pass the short passage to the kitchen and remember Walt like this, a ravaging force behind me, made of solid bone and heavy muscle, directing me to my once-solitary bedroom. So he could. So we could. "I want both," I heard myself say into the turn of his jaw. "Please."

"Stay here," he said. His hand didn't leave my hip as he pulled a couple of pillows to the middle of my bed then nodded toward them.

It was happening. Right there, on my bed. Not attached to a wobbly, wooden bench with *Head Like a Hole* screaming in my ears and not with an angry, diffident pseudo-Dom doing me a favor.

I swallowed at a swell of panic in my throat. *Fettuccine. Cream sauce. Tiramisu.* This was happening *now*.

"IT ass" was something I once overheard at work, and in the years since, I was certain I'd developed it. He expected me to lie on those pillows. My backside would be pushed—thrust, really—up with every extra inch exposed to him.

Not my best angle.

"You're…this has to be with all of the lights on, right?"

His cheek twitched and rose with his smile, and he snorted a little. "I have to see what I'm spanking." He swept the pad of his thumb over my nipple. "No, I don't have to have all of them on. But I sure as hell want to watch you."

Walt brought her in for another kiss. The little clench of breath in her throat didn't help his straining cock, but damn sure cemented his idea of just what to do with Miss Reboot. If she squirmed while she was laid over his lap, it would all be over. Not over the knee tonight, but next time…that ass, that close. So close he could lean over and bite and suck and taste her as much as he wanted.

He tugged at the waistband of her pink gingham pajama pants. Gingham? Damn-near killing him, this woman with her sharp brains and inexperience and curving body made for dirty, drawn-out fucking.

"Get rid of these. Now." Before his mouth could go rogue and bark another order at her, Walt passed his tongue over his lip so he'd occupy it with something besides making words.

She was a little rattled. It was there in her wide eyes and underneath the authoritative lift in her chin. And behind those fucking glasses, which were cute five minutes ago when she'd answered the front door but now just looked like another barrier between him and the gasping, whimpering, dozy-eyed Erin he needed to get to.

He stretched his thumb, then his index finger along her jawline, and clasped the cool, thin metal between his fingers.

"These too." Walt swallowed hard over the hitch in her breath, and dropped his head toward her cheek. This was the first critical moment. Too much and she'd bolt. He'd never see the uncovered Erin again, never have her past the first wall, have her a little off-kilter and still hot and willing for him to take over. That one little break, the uncertain but willing reaction she had to him, made a bloom of purpose and control fire up from Walt's guts. "Be still, Erin."

She flicked a quick glance at him. Hardness threatened, her body tensed up right along with her eyes. A few wisps of her pale hair fell over her cheek as he lifted her glasses away. Before he could reason with the urge to do it, Walt eased in to her temple and brushed his lips against the skin there. Her pulse thumped against his lip. She knew it too and flinched, locking down her shoulders just a bit more.

"I can't see w —"

"I know." Walt inched his head back, enough to catch her line of sight on him and nothing else around her. "You don't need to."

There was a little twitch at the corner of her mouth. "I guess I don't really need to see during this, right?"

"No," Walt said. "I'm here. I've got you, Erin."

Whatever that was, saying it didn't make much sense. Still, she inhaled, deep and long, and returned the gesture with a little brave-girl smile. "I'm fine."

The come-what-may set of her shoulders and that smile was the tipping point. The veneers of responsible Walt, friendly Walt, safe Walt, turned soft. The Dominant inside pushed forward, a long-caged beast who accepted captivity because it was safer that way. He couldn't stay a reluctant, distant observer when that part of him was too enticed with exactly what he craved.

Walt pressed his fingers into the taut white cotton at her hip again and let his thumb graze over the waistband of her panties. It was just enough to get her focus out of her head and back to him.

With a slow rise of her chin, Erin's eyes came up to his. She'd made her decision.

The robe dropped to the floor, near those ugly, too-big and too-dark pants she'd worn at dinner. Later, Walt promised himself, he'd put them in the trash where they belonged.

"Lay down across the bed."

"Erin?"

He was waiting for me to move. Some day he might expect more, or faster, or even in some predetermined configuration. Did he do that? Was he about lists of expectations and protocols and rituals I would come to know as surely as booting up my machine or typing *goto* when I started a new script?

Eyeing my bed, I traveled mentally to the causeway I'd imagined between us, not with the certainty of details, but the feeling — *what he expected, what he wanted, what pleased him* — I knew that, even if I didn't understand the hows and whats of a spanking.

A spanking. From Walt.

It thrummed against my ears as I clambered to my knees and stretched over the ridge of pillows Walt had set in the middle of my bed. He was going to spank me.

Cool, smooth cotton sheets met my hips seconds before my cheek. I sensed him moving behind me and felt the mattress depress with his body. When his hand came to me, it wasn't with the force I anticipated.

"Hey," he said. I opened my eyes and found him stretched beside me, his jaw resting over his folded hand. "You doing okay?"

I blinked heavily. The slow buzz in my bones made it hard to do much more than nod. He smiled a little and brushed his fingers over my skin again, trailing the tips over the fullest, fleshiest part of my behind. Tickling between my thighs. Like that, he touched me, for hours or seconds, likely minutes. And he watched me, giving me his slow half-grin when I shivered and gasped under his hand.

His palm made lazy circles, turning my skin warm under his. I shook over a hasty breath and took another one right after it.

"Shhhhhhh," he said, still circling, still kneading, still watching me. "Got you."

"Mmmmm." I nodded again. The causeway opened, clear. *His.*

His hand left and came back, before I'd completely realized it was gone. It cracked hard against my warmed skin, bowing my back with the force of it. I whimpered and hissed, gritting my teeth at the sting. Four more times—same intensity, same measured pace.

"Breathe, Erin."

I did, gasping for it.

"You're fine."

I was. My hips rose, tilted toward him.

Walt slanted himself toward me and brushed his lips over mine. He was behind me then, a solid presence I couldn't see, but was the monolith I was tethered to.

It hurt. His hands were hard and hot, and the force of them drove my cheek against the damp sheets underneath. I heard my breath turn throaty, my whines turn to hoarse grunts. There was an apparent cadence about what he did, but the throb and singe spreading across my backside distracted me from following it. I told myself I could catch the rhythm of his hands, and if I did, I could drag myself back to the surety I was synced with him. My thighs shook, my fists curled around the sheets. *How many times? Which side now?* But it hurt and I lost track of the count and the burn was so much, so good, even better than good when I reminded myself it was Walt's hand—*Sir's hand*—and this was what I gave him. What I took from him. For him.

I was obliterated with the two things I knew. His hand, my burn. I swung between them, tipping forward with his hand, rocking back to meet the next touch. And it went on that way, until there was no more connection. His hand was gone, and the swing ceased. My cheek was on something softer, warmer, more solid. His chest. Once more, his hand was on me, still hot, but not on my ass. Stroking over my shoulders, heaving and shaking with my breath. His fingers, not grasping the spread of my thigh but pushing wet strands of hair from my eyes.

"Erin," he whispered. "You're okay. It's over."

"No, not yet," I said and clenched his T-shirt in my hands. The old fabric groaned, wrenching apart as I tugged him toward me. "Fuck me."

Erin didn't hold back once she let go. Since they'd met, Walt had wondered more than once how it would turn out, their first time, and he'd considered she might fall apart so readily. It was still a huge wave to ride when it happened, right under his hands.

Her damp hair and cheeks pressed into his jaw set up the battle inside him. Protector or predator. Good, sensible Top rules told him to calm her, take her breath and endorphins down. But the thought of easing her back made Walt grind his teeth together at the countering impulse to push her harder, asking for more from her body. Both of them were sweat-slick and breathy, arms and legs wrapped together. It could have been enough. Could have been. Before she said it.

No, not yet. Fuck me.

So-fucking-much for sensible.

He fumbled and pulled at a condom stashed in the ragged waistband on his old sweats, grateful he'd lost the confines of his boxer briefs before he drove over. Erin was under him in seconds, whining as his hips ground against hers. When her legs fell open, offering a core warm and wet and waiting for him, he didn't need to guide himself into her. She was so damn ready, and Walt plunged in.

He heard himself moan into the delicate skin at her temple, felt her mussed, damp hair against his cheek. Pushing himself back on his hands, he looked down, found her wide-eyed and watching underneath him. He saw Mel there, and then Holly.

More, Walt, please.

Erin. That was Erin's voice, not poor Holly. Not lost Melissa. He shook his head slowly, so she wouldn't see the afterimages of the before-women in his eyes. *Don't spook her. Don't scare her.*

Easing back to his knees, he cupped her ass and brought her up with him. Gritted his teeth at the swish of her long thighs straddling his. His hand glided over her hip and found the right place to hold on, angling her around him as he thundered forward to meet her.

Damn, he was going to hate himself tomorrow by the third hike up to the falls.

Or not. Not if he distracted himself with the memory of Erin, balanced across his lap, her hair a wild, silvery snarl around her shoulders, swaying in time with her tits to distract him.

"Oh damn," he mumbled and lifted one to his mouth. "Can't forget these."

"Forgot wha—Ohhh." Her question answered, she shivered and clenched her thighs around his hips.

Over and over, her voice cracked on his name. Her fingers wound through his hair and her head bent to his, seeking his mouth. A low, raspy moan came from deep in her chest as her body caved forward, pushing him to his back. Erin kissed him again and came, spasming hard around his cock. A torrent of shudders deep inside her body took him along with her, flooding his senses with her sounds and her scent and the far-away, pleading tilt of her head. Walt planted his feet on her bed and thrust, a final time. He shouted, his eyes fixed on hers, and everything within him drew down to a single compressed point before it exploded, rushing out from his gut and driving his ass from the bed.

Above him, Erin wobbled. He caught her arms as she collapsed to his chest, shaking. A half-second more of silence than was comfortable followed.

Walt drew his hand along her spine. "Erin?"

She still shook, harder, and his throat went arid. Once more, he stroked her skin, fingers riding the long slope of her back. "Hey... Erin?"

He wasn't prepared to see her rising from his chest, her hair falling forward in a blond curtain around them. And giggling. Her cheeks were pink, damp blooms, ripe with the widest, most relaxed smile he'd seen from her. Heaving a heavy, relieved breath, Walt felt his own body begin to quake with hers, and heard his laugh mingling with Erin's.

"Oh...ohm," she gasped. "Oh my God." She tumbled to the sheets beside him, still nuzzling into his cheek. "Wow."

"Wow?" He chuckled, twisting to face her. "Wow?"

"Can't think. Just wow."

Walt swallowed hard, disbelief and wonder thick in his throat. She was still laughing, reaching to him as she pushed at the damp hair on his forehead, eyes turned up to his. Her chest rose and fell with her breath.

"Wow."

Door two.

Once she slept, he watched her for a couple of hours, dozing a little when he could, but too strung up over the realization to get comfortable in her bed. She was what he'd always thought of as a good sleeper. Curled into him, her body lined up at the right places, her pearly blond hair a tumble over his forearm. It didn't make him want to push it away or scratch at his skin.

Being a good sleeper had been one of Holly's sweetest attractions. She fit against him and liked being there, too. But right away, she needed to be there, all the time, and that seemed too quick. If he didn't know in his gut Holly was just a lost heart looking for a place to be, Walt might have suspected she worked her way in, planning to make him comfortable enough to give herself a hold on him to dig into and latch on. She always called him Sir, even though he never asked it from her.

Walt started to turn his back to Erin, but she mumbled another one of her meandering questions. Instead, he tucked her head under his chin and settled into her pillows.

Hurting over someone's hurt, wanting to make it better, wasn't the same thing as love. At least the kind you can rely on at four a.m., twenty years in the future, when a kid's in the hospital or the water heater's blown and a storm is dumping down two new inches of snow an hour...*My only and forever*, like Hailey'd said the day at Coronado, when she turned down his lame-handed proposal. Like Brady and Hailey. That was where Walt figured he really wanted to end up, even though he'd never admitted it to himself, and even though he'd never found the right mix of partner and bottom to make him go after it.

His heart, a heavy, sure beat, drummed in his ears. Walt listened to it and the sound of Erin's breath passing over her lips. Together, the sounds lulled him. His eyelids drooped heavily, and he forced them open again and again, blinking at scratchy, sleep-hazed eyes so he could look at her face as she slept. Erin was more interesting than kink, more comfortable and sexier than it, too. She was the possibility of more than a friend with kinky benefits.

Walt's last thought before the heavy nothing of sleep took him away was Erin.

I'll be her boyfriend. Haven't been that in years.

"How hard?"

Mel's jaw jutted forward, just like it did when she got into one of those nasty scraps on the basketball court. And her eyes, a soft brown that always reminded him of a doe, narrowed over tears, threatening to spill.

"I don't know, Walt. Hard. Just...I really, um...care about you. I don't want you to treat me like I'm breakable. I want to feel it. How you...y'know...feel. About me."

His hand slipping into her messy, tempting ponytail and pulling, just a little more than he normally would when they horsed around during the dull part of a movie or when one of their friends got too serious. The second her eyes darkened and her breath caught, he knew she knew too. Hard and sweaty and dirty and rough wasn't so bad, maybe. If Mel said okay, then it was okay.

"More?" he asked, not even sure if it his own voice.

"Yeah, more. Please, Walt, harder."

Can't be a bad thing, making a girl come like that, make those sounds, raise her hips and claw at your skin...

"Melissa will be right down," he said. "Come out here for a minute, son."

Following, bile surging in his throat. No excuses, never would turn the blame on Mel. If her parents knew...

"Have a seat over there."

Look expectant, unaware, serious. "Yes, sir?"

"Walt, Missy's mama and I like you an awful lot. You treat her good, don't keep her out all night, and she cares for you more than any other of these boys she's brung home."

"Thank you, sir." Picking at a hangnail. Couldn't look in the man's eyes.

"Now you and Missy are both big kids, and I know when you're playin' around at your age..." He cleared his throat. "Well, I remember wrasslin' Missy's mama, tickle fights, all of them things you do..."

Oh. God.

"The two of you are big, strong kids."

"Um...yes, sir?"

"Son, I saw a handprint on Missy's leg. Ain't many kids with hands that big. Now she's told me you two got a little wound up playfightin', and you gave her a little pop on the rear and she gave you that scratch there on your arm and that was that."

"Yes, sir. I'm sorry, sir."

"Whatever it was, it looks like she got her licks in, too. Now, I talked to your granddad this afternoon. This won't happen again. But if you're dumber than I think you are, I'm gonna make it real clear to you right now. You just turned eighteen, son. If I see one more thing even lookin' like a mark on my baby girl, I'll take you out in the backyard and beat the hell out of you, and then I'll drop your ass in front of the jailhouse so Ron Carter don't have to bother himself to drive out from the Sheriff's department to pick you up. You got me?"

He came awake coughing. His throat hurt, and he wondered if he might have not have been coughing at all, but talking. Walt hadn't given serious thought to Missy's father in years. He rolled away from Erin, fighting his notice of her soft, mumbled protest, and focused on making himself alert as possible.

"Hey," he said, shaking her arm gently. "I need to get back before sunrise. Erin?"

After a long, reluctant breath, her eyelids tensed, and then body turned toward his. "Hmmm?"

"I gotta go. Have to make sure the park gate is open by seven."

She'd gone back to sleep. And it wasn't making leaving her any easier, especially on the heels of that old dream. Walt pushed her hair away from her cheek and leaned to her, taking in the warmth and scent of her cheek.

"Erin, wake up."

She sat up quick, blinking, her eyes wider every time they opening. "Oh no, Walt — I'm — what? I — I — sorry," she said, too fast. At the sight of her, disoriented and scared, he wrapped his arms around her.

"Shhh. It's okay." Kissing her head, Walt tucked her under his chin, gritting his teeth at the residuals of his subconscious and pissed at himself for scaring Erin. "Don't want to just go without saying good-bye, and you need to come lock up behind me anyway."

"Where are you going?" Her voice, still slurred with sleep, was muffled into his chest. "Was going to make you breakfast."

"Make me breakfast when I don't have to sell fishing licenses in half an hour, okay?" Reluctantly, Walt pushed himself away. "Now, come lock the door after I go, all right?"

Erin followed him down the darkened hallway, mussed and naked and probably mostly asleep too. He paused at the front door for one more kiss and started down the porch steps.

"Okay. Bye, Sir," she said after him, so sleepy and quiet he barely caught it and immediately doubted he'd heard her right.

Walt swung toward her, nearly tripping himself in the dewy grass under his feet. But Erin had closed the door, leaving him with nothing but the sounds of frogs and early morning birds, and the snick of a lock tumbling into place.

We spent the next month, after our first feverish week, *dating*. It seemed better that way. We said so to each other, assuring ourselves we should be sensible and slow about what we called *that other stuff*. Dinners, movies, an outdoor concert in Asheville. And visits to his forest.

When Walt could stay all night, we woke up together in my bed. We made each other breakfast. And often, Walt made me his first breakfast.

No more spankings or those other, still shadowy activities he called playing. Not even in the heat of *rather* heated moments. We learned the skinscapes of each other, the timbre and rhythm of each other's sighs and moans. I took him in to my life. He had the proverbial drawer in my bathroom, a favorite little this or that in my kitchen.

After sex, we fell asleep holding hands. Not just on weekends; unplanned weekdays, too. Waking up on a Thursday morning, skin-to-skin, with a shock of cocoa-brown curls nestled against my ear was somehow better, more intimate than Saturday morning.

Everything about Walt was rooting into me. I curled into him, twining, budding.

We talked about *it*, anyway. Decided it would happen. When I was ready. When we were ready. But *things*, they still happened. The *other stuff* we agreed to ignore refused to stay under the rug.

There was already an easy shorthand, even some simple routines beginning to take shape between us. Silently handing him the pepper at dinner, a cup of coffee in his hands as I exited the shower in the morning, the sweetener and milk just right after he'd convinced me my favorite hazelnut creamer tasted like chalk. Often, Walt kissed the top of my head when I sat curled into my sofa, writing shell script for my part of the storage virtualization project, a level of responsibility no female engineer had ever been given at ThinkMine. I couldn't resist touching the broad slope of his shoulder as I passed behind him and frequently his hand was waiting for mine as I made my way to the opposite shoulder.

Occasionally the hand would grasp and pull. I'd find myself in his lap, find his kisses hard on my mouth.

And that's what happened. It was more intense from the start, neither of us seemed playful about it: his jaw was set, grinding, and his eyes...well, frankly, they did seem to blaze.

This was not warm, careful, ardent Walt. I responded immediately, gratefully.

As our sex had become more familiar, I began fantasizing while we were together, imagining him finally doing those things to me the way we both wanted. I was hardly dissatisfied with him, just the opposite. Knowing he was this attentive, responsive to me, and appreciative afterward cemented him in my mind as the person I could really try *the other stuff* with.

Each time his touch or a word spoken tipped the power scales I responded — probably overzealously. When I was with him, I felt more open and sensual than I ever had in my life. I couldn't give him enough of me and, most certainly, couldn't be satisfied with single, vanilla servings of Walt.

I toed at the subject again, one Saturday in early June.

"Do you want to come over tonight? We still need to have that talk."

His laugh filled my ear, making me shuffle lazily as I smiled to myself. Walt had an unnerving ease with distracting me from simple tasks, like finding my keys, which I would need to do before I could lock the front door and get out to Claire before she —

A horn sounded, announcing Claire's early arrival. Wincing, I swung my front door open and waved to her, parked in the gravel and packed-dirt driveway.

"You might want to come out here this afternoon during my break. I think the only way I'm going to keep you in your clothes long enough to talk is with the threat of Sam walking in on us."

"Can't. I'm going to Asheville with Claire again. She's delivering an order to one of her galleries and then we're having lunch." I opened the front door and waved to her, parked outside. "Do you know what she means by mentoring? We're discussing it during lunch."

"Really? Huh. I guess Claire's taking it seriously. Don't let her talk you into her service brigade." He went quiet for a moment, then cleared his throat. "Unless you like that sort of thing."

"You mean actual service?" I shouldered my purse and closed the door behind me, pausing to check the deadbolt. "Volunteering?"

"No. It's not really…Hey, that was a jackassed thing to say. Claire likes to do things for people. It makes her happy to help out around Tate's house before people come for the night. And it pleases Paul, I guess."

I glanced across the front yard, snorting softly at the guilty knot in my stomach. "It's what makes them happy."

"Right." Walt's voice was leaden with resignation. "'S their dynamic."

Blindly, we both had strayed to an uncomfortable and unspeakable topic: Claire and Paul. Their relationship—their *dynamic,* as Walt and Lucy called it—didn't shine as brightly to me as it did to Claire. But what was I to say about it? Claire had been Paul's slave for fourteen years—since she was barely in her twenties.

I checked the deadbolt again and waved to Claire. "Is it everyone's?"

"No," he said hurriedly. "Nope, not at all. For them, Paul's always the boss. Claire always says so, too."

"Right."

"Hey, how about we go back to that Italian place for dinner tonight? The one with the tiramisu?"

"Yes, actually, that reminds me—" A burst of static and garbled voices from the mike attached to Walt's ever-present park walkie-talkie interrupted me.

"Shit, I gotta…Sam needs me down at the campground. I'll call you later, sweetheart." The call dropped and Walt was gone. But he'd called me sweetheart. And that was new.

As Claire drove, she chatted to me about the new gallery's quick sale of the pieces she'd taken them a month before. In the past, her pieces had sat on consignment for more than a few months, waiting for a tourist or new local's hands to take them home.

"I guess they're a little different, the new cups I've been doing." She pointed over her shoulder to a deep plastic bin taking up most of the back seat. "Have a look if you want."

I took a newspaper-wrapped bundle and brought it to the front seat. Under the layers of paper and bubble wrap was a wide-mouthed conical piece of pottery. Though it was heavy, with thick walls and a sturdy base, the cup felt natural in my hand. My wrist curled around it perfectly, and I tucked it to my chest without a second thought as I smoothed my palm around the undulating surface.

"Oooh," I said and laughed, surprised at how touchy-feely her pottery had made me. "This might sound odd, but it feels good, like a comfort, almost. It's like this cup wants hot tea in it and wants me on my front porch."

"Oh? Oh, that's really nice," she said, nodding with a pleased smile. "That's what I've been thinking about with the new pieces. Solitude and comfort. Common objects that are meaningful because they're useful."

I considered it all, letting my fingertip bump along the emerald and forest green-mottled glaze. "Claire, may I ask you something?"

"Sure, of course." She said it so readily, with so much enthusiasm, I had to sit back in the seat. My curiosities about the dissonances I saw in her relationship with Paul would be a sharp slap across the cheek. It was *their* relationship. It was them: their agreements regarding Dominance and submission. Things I didn't know and wouldn't understand about D/s, as a...well, a newbie.

I geared back, for easier topics. "Can you tell me more about Walt and Nicole?"

"Nicole? Who's—" Her brows crinkled as her eyes scanned the road before us. "I don't...wait, do you mean FiestyFelineFemme?"

Another outlandish scene name. I turned a laugh into my chest, forcing myself to inspect the cup I still clenched. "Um...I guess?"

After we cross-checked a couple of details, we decided we were, in fact, speaking of the same kitty.

"She's just...I hate to say she's no one, because everybody's somebody," Claire said, nodding. I agreed with a quiet noise, dismissing thoughts of several of my mother's boyfriends, a coworker or two, and people who hurt animals, children, and the elderly. All deserving of *nobody at all* status, in my estimation. "But in Walt's life, she was a play partner. And not even a long-term one." She glanced at me, shrugging apologetically. "Sometimes Walt and Tate are into their flavors of the month. Well, really most of the time. Except you and—I think *you're* different."

I waved away a second, hesitant shrug from her. Walt had, during a conversation we'd had over popcorn and wine the previous evening, referred to himself as *a little bit more hound than I'd like to admit to you* and gave me a very similar shift of his shoulders.

"I'm starting to understand the difference between play partners and people you see in the daylight." I smiled a little over using one of Walt's phrases. It felt intimate somehow. "Has he had a lot of...partners?"

"Walt?" Claire laughed a little as she turned into a small parking lot behind a brick building, painted in vivid blue and purple swirls. Over the back door hung a sign: *Gallerie Nerita*. "He's one of a kind. People like to play with him, you know. He's one of those people who makes everyone around them feel good."

"Understandably so," I said, turning a secret smile toward my window. Popcorn and wine made Walt pretty ardent. And that had certainly made me feel good, in several ways, the night before.

Claire pointed to her latest delivery, still inside her Jeep. "Lady Nerita will send out her boys for that. C'mon in. You'll love her."

I stopped inside the raw-brick vestibule, blinking at the difference in light.

"Well, look. It's the babysub."

Lucy. Minus her purple foxtail. She was seated on a blocky wooden stool at a high rusted-steel table, the only furnishings in the long expanse of gleaming gallery lights and polished concrete floors. A woman with a wide bundle of steely-silver dreadlocks clasped away from her face turned in my direction, nodding a cool smile to me before it thawed to a gentle welcome for Claire.

"This is Lady Nerita," Claire said, taking my hand. "She owns the gallery and is also a corsetière. Come say hello."

It was an invitation to an audience with the Lady. Claire—or Lucy, for that matter, wouldn't have had to tell me as much. Lady Nerita didn't simply own her own gallery and corset-making shop. She held court here.

"This Walt's girl?"

"Seems to be," Lucy told her and swung her golden hair over her shoulder. "Cute, huh?"

Correction. This wasn't a gallery. It was a coliseum.

"Hello," I said, offering my hand as I stepped past Claire. "I'm Erin Proctor."

"So you are."

For a second, I held my breath, waiting. I was in a surreal, out-of-my-experience world, in the middle of a sultry, early summer Saturday afternoon in Asheville. Tourists in their sensible earthy sandals and backpacks passed the long windows flanking us. Synthesizer music hummed, nearly indistinct, through the brick walls.

And I waited.

Finally, another nod. This time with a small but gracious smile.

"And I am Nerita," she said. As her cool, caramel skin slid past mine, there was a single, sharp electric charge in its wake. Her presence was vast, and not because of her tall, powerful body. Even Lucy seemed subdued beside Nerita. "So dear clover has brought me more of her beautiful heart-cups, and you, Erin, have brought me your body."

I sneaked a glance at Lucy, who, as usual, was watching the proceedings with the interested disinterest of a panther in a tree.

Claire's voice, behind my shoulder, came with a nearly dreamy sigh. "Heart-cup? That's beautiful. Thank you, ma'am."

Her new pieces were a tangible, real-world topic. Easier than even considering I'd been carted along with them as an offering. Quickly I checked for a memory of where I'd stashed my phone once I'd finished talking to Walt, immediately sneering at myself for doing it. Claire was beside me. Lucy, even though she still looked over me with a predator's eye, was Walt's best friend. They were safe. Nerita and her as-yet-faceless boys would be safe, too.

Of course she would.

"I came to help with the cups," I mumbled.

Nerita stood, followed by Lucy. "I understand you'll need something for Solstice?"

"Solstice?" I turned to Claire, still at my shoulder. She seemed like the appropriate translator. "Like summer solstice?"

She went to Lucy's side, nearly bouncing. "At the house. We have a Solstice weekend every year. Everyone comes. We all dress up for it and—"

"And you're not wearing a crappy costume-store corset to Solstice," Lucy added, barely concealing her smirk. "Time to step up your game, babysub."

"I assume this isn't about astronomy." More mumbling, on cue from my sulky inner adolescent.

Nerita's head fell back as she laughed, full and deep, and walked to me. "No, baby. No head trips to Mars, unless that's your kink—but I've known Walt since he wasn't nothin' more than a big boy with a singletail, and I don't remember him liking to play spaceman." She paused, eyeing me. "You want a real corset or not?"

Corset. On display and unable to breathe and looking like... not me. I nearly mumbled, once again sounding more like a sixteen-year-old me refusing my mother's help choosing school clothes than was comfortable to hear on my own adult voice. Walt was used to seeing women dressed for these house parties. It was an expectation.

"Sure," I said, with my most agreeable smile. "Sounds great."

Lady Nerita, I learned, was a recent transplant from New Orleans, hence the Franco-centric twist that leaped out occasionally in her midst. She made corsets in her *atelier*, located over her *gallerie*, served by her two *matous*. The tomcats in question were a pair of early-twen-tyish-looking men who appeared silently, just as she called for them.

For the next hour, Claire and Lucy chatted with Nerita about the upcoming party. The boys prepared vanilla Matevana and shortbread. I stood alone at the end of the long table, silent and horrified, as I tried to concentrate on swatches of velvets and brocades while repeatedly refusing the smaller sample card of supple leathers.

"That purple leather's hot," Lucy advised from her perch. Instead of suggesting she match it to her furry purple tail, I dabbed at the sweat turning my neck cold and refocused.

Finally, I placed an order for two. A simple black silk one, be-cause black was…well, it was sensible black. One in a claret-colored embroidered velvet I cleaved to like a favorite old secret I'd forgotten and found again. After paying for expedited delivery the following Thursday, and swallowing against bile as I signed a credit card receipt that exceeded my Passat's monthly payment by several hundred dol-lars, the boys showed us upstairs to a bright, high-ceilinged room resembling part dance studio and part fortune teller's retreat. Claire waited for Lucy and Nerita to choose their seats and I paused, assum-ing this was the right thing to do. Once they were seated at opposite ends of the deep violet velvet covered sofa, Claire sat gracefully at the edge of a matching armchair. I was free to take my own seat, sip my own lukewarm tea and swish shortbread crumbs from my own apparently *generous*—according to one of the boys—bustline.

As the boys served tea, Lady Nerita turned her attentions to me again, my measurements and fabric preferences having been settled. "So, Erin, you're new to the lifestyle or were you in it out in California?"

"Um…no. I'm new." Again, the newbie. Would it ever end? "I tried, but—"

"Big scene." Lucy, surprising me, nodded. "The first time I went out to San Francisco I felt lost."

"Lu? No." Nerita laughed. "Child, you haven't been intimidated since you came kicking and screaming onto this earth. Please, *intimidated.*"

"Did I say intimidated or did I say lost?"

"Anyway, *Erin*," Claire said, turning a narrowed eye at Lucy. "But you tried a couple of munches, right?"

The truth of it—and telling it to Lady Nerita and Lucy, not to mention those sleek, almond-skinned boys—made my stomach knot. "I never went inside. It was difficult, for a lot of reasons. But I suppose I never found the right place to insert myself. Meeting Claire was fortunate."

Lucy snorted, relaxing into the sofa again. "She's excellent at finding places to insert things, aren't you, Claire?"

"Lucy, stop!" Claire blushed—actually blushed—and giggled.

"You're what I call the educational gatekeeper for a lot of new submissives. Between her tips and tricks, and Tate and Wa—" Lips turned to a thin line, Lucy fell silent.

Then the room fell silent. Even the boys came to rest, as though settling on show benches at Nerita's flank. Walt's voice, again, telling me he had been *More hound than I'd like to admit to you* just the night before echoed in my ears. Lucy and Walt said that word a lot, hound, in reference to suspect males in the scene. A wayward dog under the direction of his basest instincts, their implication always was that a hound made his home on the driest, most accommodating porch within his range.

Claire turned her own cup of tea in her hand.

"I don't have a problem with that," I blurted. Lucy's eyebrow shot high and she grinned at me from her perch. "If that's why you stopped, Lucy. I know Walt has…done things—played—with a lot of people. He told me."

"Ah. Okay," Lucy said mildly.

The female ritual of discussing their dates never made sense to me. I never had the opportunity, honestly. Dani was far better at interrogation than me, but I also kept my interests obscured, safe from her questions. This circle was different, though. A country's distance, I reminded myself, from the commentary of my mother and sister. The trio of women clustered before me presented an opportunity.

"There was someone before Nicole. Someone else, right?"

Lucy craned her neck past one of Nerita's boys, who was assembling a small plate of shortbread for her, jutting her chin toward Claire. "Who's Nicole?"

"You know, the one with the red hair. FiestyFelineFemme."

"Who?" Nerita accepted her shortbread and immediately lifted one to her lips.

"The one with the big tits who played with Tate at the winter party. Remember? He hogtied her on the dining room table with those Christmas tree lights." Lucy made an exaggerated purring sound and shimmied her shoulders.

"No, that's Gala Apples. Lucy, you know, the other redhead. Tommy's new girl's friend. The tall one?"

"I know that girl." Nerita looked like she'd tasted too much lemon in her tea. "Walt played with that girl?"

"She was new," Claire said, shrugging. "It didn't last long."

New. No history, always unproven. I busied myself with an important pill at the seam of my linen dress.

Mercifully it was my turn for shortbread. "I thought you might prefer a cool drink to Lady's tea." A boy, the one I'd started calling Boy 1 in my head, stood before me, offering a tall, frosted glass full of iced water, cucumber, and mint. He spoke soft and swishy, much like the black silk I'd just chosen for my sensible corset, and turned sad doe eyes back toward the two Dominants on the sofa. "It does get quite warm up here in the afternoons. Lot hotter when Miss Lucinda come around."

I smiled up at him and took the plate. The glaze matched the one on the cup Claire had shown me earlier during our drive to Asheville. "Thank you."

"clover makes them tea sets too. Makes them for everybody. You just ask her, clover'll make you whatever you like to have."

"Never mind," Lucy said. I glanced toward her, and the boy turned to vapor, the plate of cookies my only evidence he'd been there. "Some girl."

"A play partner, that's all." Claire smiled at me. "Nothing serious."

"Wanda's been prone to whoring, the hound." Lucy winked with a lazy wave of her hand. "Don't worry, babysub. He's seen you in daylight. Different dynamic entirely."

Nerita turned to me, and again my neck prickled. "I think Erin is asking about Holly."

"Oh."

"Oh, yeah." Claire's silence matched Lucy's uncharacteristic reticence.

"Holly?" This name was new to me. I'd heard about Hailey, his best friend Brady's wife, and Melissa, his lost high school girlfriend. Most other women were *this girl in Atlanta* or *a bottom I know from Mid-Dixie LeatherFest*. They never had names, just places or...well, places in play.

Which I still didn't have.

"Holly was around for what, Lu? Two or three years?" Nerita waved over her shoulder, and the other boy appeared. "I'd like some of that cucumber water, boy."

"Yes, Ma'am."

"Poor thing," she continued. "Sweet girl."

"Yes. So sweet."

Lucy stood, her jaw hard. "Sweet. Real sweet, pulling crap like that on Walt. Pardon me, please."

Once she'd reached the bottom of the stairs, I looked at Claire. "I'm sorry. Should I have not asked about Holly?" The name was beginning to take on an ominous life of its own. "I should ask Walt."

"If you ask Walt you won't understand about Holly, though." Claire sat her tea aside. "Walt made a lot of mistakes—"

"But it wasn't his *fault*," Nerita added, beginning to look as agitated as Lucy had become. "Erin, I think you've been fortunate to find Claire. Not all new submissives are so blessed."

"Oh, Ma'am." Claire beamed.

"No, girl, you accept that as true." She waved her hand in my direction. "Claire, you ask this girl if you've not blessed her life since you've been friendly."

Inside, I turned nearly as squirmy as Claire appeared to be. How to say something like this to another person? And a woman who was my friend? "I do. I feel really lucky to know you."

Claire's lashes fluttered at her suddenly wet eyes, and she reached for my hand. "Me too. I'm glad you gave me a chance." She set her cup aside. "I think to Walt, Holly was one of those people who is never one thing. And they're not enough of one thing to make who they are definite, you know?"

I shrugged. "Not really."

"They dated some, but mostly played. She adored him."

"She did indeed." Nerita nodded. "I think he did care for her, too."

"Oh, definitely. We all did. But after everything Walt's been through—and those are things you should talk about—he's...well..."

"Claire doesn't want to tell you Walt tends to white knight, Erin. Not in a bad way. He's a good man with a good heart, who has been hurt and recognizes it in others. And that goodness makes him want to save people from their own hurts."

"Oh," I muttered. I didn't like the heavy slosh of cucumber-mint flavored bile climbing toward my throat.

"Holly had been around for a long time. But she had been in some very scary situations..."

"Ugly business," Nerita said. "She had been a slave in a very bad situation for years. Alex knew her—can't remember where they met."

"At a trade show," Claire offered. "Alex was selling her whips and—"

"Oh, that's right. Yes, down in Orlando?"

"Or Ft. Lauderdale, maybe?"

"Florida," Nerita concluded. "At any rate, you know Tommy's girl?"

"Hawkshadow?" Claire added. "He's one of Sir's mentees."

Their history was so long, had so much depth and spanned so many people. Not only did I have to learn all of these affiliations and tangential relationships, I had to remember who played on what side of the fence, and when. "I'm not sure..."

"What they're not telling you is Alex mailed Holly a bus ticket so she could leave her owner, a real charming guy who messed her head and body up—permanently. A lot." Lucy's voice echoed across the room. "So she came up here and moved in with Tommy and Alex. She had nothing of her own but what she could stuff in a backpack. She was fine at first."

"She was." Claire held her hand out to Lucy, who joined her on the arm of the club chair. She'd been crying. I could tell from the fresh powder and eyeliner she wore. It was evidence of how concerned she'd been for Walt then—and the depth of their friendship.

"*But* she wasn't, not really. And Walt wanted to make it better for her." Lucy huffed. "The dumbass."

"It wasn't to be helped," Nerita said and sipped her water. "The girl was broken."

"Yes. She was." Lucy took a deep breath and continued. "She wanted and needed a lot more from Walt than he wanted to give her. She wasn't the one for him, and he knew it. But he sold—"

Claire turned a sad smile toward Lucy and finished for her. "He soldiered on. Because she needed him."

Nerita made a soft, compassionate sound. "That's what he wouldn't tell you, Erin."

"Do you think he blames himself for what happened?" Claire looked at Nerita. "He did get her home, after all."

"Wait, Erin is missing a few details," Lucy said. "Holly got clingier and more weepy and needy."

"She was hurting, Lucy."

"Okay, Claire, we get it, she was hurt and broken and sad. That doesn't justify slitting her wrists in Walt's bathroom, okay?"

The room went silent, except for the sound of my pulse thudding in my ears. "Oh," I said dully. "Did she…"

"No. Walt got her fixed up and then found her family. He took her up to them in New Hampshire…Vermont…somewhere up north." Lucy flipped her hair over her shoulder. "And she became their problem, pulled the same trick in their bathroom a couple of months later."

"Oh no." I couldn't think of anything better to say about this poor, sad woman who apparently had loved Walt in the only way she knew how, but I felt very sorry for her. After a long moment, I took a deep breath. "I think sometimes loving someone new is like rubbing over a scar that's numb underneath. Instead of healing it, it just reminds you it hurts there."

Nerita nodded and smiled at me. "Yes, indeed, Erin. That is very true, indeed."

Refusing the temptation of more tea and cookies, we exchanged good-byes with the other ladies after a bit more, lighter-toned, conversation. We left Nerita's *gallerie* and crossed Asheville's busy main street. After a surprisingly good lunch of fried green tomato sandwiches and tea, this time, cold and sweet, Claire cleared her throat. Time to talk business.

"I'll be helping Tate set up, so you can drive over with Lucy. When you come up to the house, you might notice it's a bit different than the club in Charlotte."

"House?" I glanced at her over my glass. "Oh, you mean your friend's lake house? He lives near Lucy, right?"

"Yes. The Enclave is on Lake Arden. Lucy lives there but on the other side of the lake. The east side is Tate's side." She prodded the remains of her sandwich, considering something. "It's formal, you know. Up there—at the house."

I couldn't help laughing a little. "I hope it's formal. Otherwise, I never would have spent that much money on a piece of underwear I might never wear again."

"I think you'll have more than one opportunity to wear them," she said with a sly smile. "And anyway, corsets aren't underwear. Not in the lifestyle, anyway."

More pushing at her plate. Another prolonged sip of tea.

"Claire, is there something else? Does—should I not be there?"

"No, no…not at all. I think you'll find it interesting. I think you'll like it."

I couldn't help wonder who she was trying to convince. "Is there more?"

"There is."

I sat back against my chair. "Okay. What else?"

"Sir and I, we do formal protocol. Most of the couples, we do a sort of enhanced D/s. It's not a requirement, but when we voted to offer your invitation, I was asked to mentor you."

"Wait a minute." My head swam a little and I reached for a sip of tea. Living in the South was starting to seep into my bones, propelling me to reach toward a cool drink at the first whiff of disturbance. "I was *voted*—you mean people talked about me?"

"It sounds much worse than it actually is, Erin. Sir said I could propose you for an invitation, so I did. Then Lucy and Walt agreed. So three Tops agreed to put you forward. And me."

"And who sacrificed the goat?"

"Oh, Erin, it's not like that." She scowled at me playfully and pulled her spangled green patchwork tote to her lap. "I've been working on something for a while, and I thought you could read it. Maybe work through it? The big letter people have a mentoring class, one or two groups of ten a year. Walt is one of the mentors, actually."

"So why isn't Walt—if I need a teacher, why…I mean that assumes there's something he thinks I should learn." Suddenly the remains of my own lunch seemed to need inspection. I pushed at a sliver of cornmeal-dusted tomato with my fork.

"Most of the time couples join the Enclave. We have a few unpartnered Tops. Well, Lucy and Walt and Tate are the only regular ones now, but it's been a while since we had an unpartnered submissive. So even though you're seeing Walt, you're not together. Not collared to him, you know?"

"Sure," I said, nodding as though the pulse radiating into my throat was a small, hardly noticeable thing.

"I would have asked you to the house anyway, because I think you'll feel more comfortable somewhere private than at a public dungeon. But then, with Walt…"

"But you said we're—or I'm not attached to him."

"Just have a look." Her face was lit with excitement and expectation and so much hope. "You'll be the first person to see it. I've journaled for years, but last winter, when I was moving things around and clearing out our second bedroom for Sir's girl, I found some of my old ones." She tucked a stray auburn curl behind her ear. "And I decided to pull it all together."

"Oh…" I nodded, hoping I looked encouraging, even though Claire had gone far past my depth. "That's a great idea."

"The small letter people—oh, I mean submissive types, you know—we don't have any kind of organized mentorship in this area. There are in other communities, but it's usually just for Big Letters around here." She shrugged away a stormy look, and her face brightened again. "I try, but it seems like all the new people at CPEP pair off so fast, or they're already in a relationship, so they're not interested in really taking the time to work through this."

I laughed in spite of the earnest turn of our conversation. "So I'm your QA test?"

"No—well, I suppose. It sounded better when I asked Sir about it."

"Oh," I said, Paul's presence suddenly thudding dully into our conversation. "I'm very interested. Is this a class or a group of some kind?"

"No. Well, not right now." Claire placed a thin binder in my hands and her voice softened. "It's a notebook. A workbook, I suppose? And since I was asked to mentor you, I'd like to really mentor you. I think I could teach you, Erin."

I felt my brows crinkling before I could stop them. "Teach me?"

"How to be submissive—a good submissive."

I opened the binder and smoothed the cover back, reading the first page.

SUBMISSIVE.

Willing to submit to the orders of others. Voluntary yielding to the will of another. Deferential. Obedient. One who gives power to another.

My eyebrows shot high over wide eyes, and I looked instinctively over my shoulder.

These are some of the words and phrases you might find when searching the Internet for a definition of the word submissive.

Even if we listed each one, you, the person holding this book, would have a slightly different answer. Your identity as a submissive, your own submissive nature, is uniquely your own. With your consent, a Dominant, a Top, a Master enters into a pact — an exchange — with you. But note, the action, the intention all rest within you. Voluntary, willing, giving. Many a Dominant will claim your submission to be a "gift"; it's a popular catchphrase in the D/s lifestyle these days.

I say it is a decision.

You are on a journey that very much includes the way your body responds to your emotional need for submission. Try it on your own first, even if you already have a partner...

"Claire...I'm not sure," I said. "The physical things...those are good. And, um, interesting." I tucked my bangs behind my ears, very intent on thumbing over beads of condensation on my glass as I arranged words in my head. Claire was becoming a good friend, and I sensed she felt the same about me. "But I don't think I want to always be in submission or however it's termed. I haven't said much about it, but my mother constantly made concessions in her relationships. All of them. I don't think I can do that, and I'm not sure I'd want to."

I felt Claire's quiet first, before I'd taken note she was silent. And hurt?

"But submissives aren't taken advantage of, unless they let themselves." Her voice was a soft, but pointed, accusation.

Dreading the worst from my clumsiness, I rushed back at her, imploring as best I could without looking panicky. "Please understand, Claire. I don't judge anyone's choi—"

Paul was everything to Claire in many ways, her submission to him spanning the physical, mental, and emotional. It was close to being her personal spirituality. Even though I questioned it, seeing that kind of devotion and sensing how much of a locus it was for her made me feel incredibly alone.

"I didn't think you were being judgy toward me." She smiled at me serenely. "I thought you were judging yourself, Erin."

"I'm not." I needed to convince someone—Claire? Myself? Instead, I looked down at Claire's notebook again, reading over the words under my fingers.

> Do you remember the first time you felt a submissive need? Was it mental domination? Pain? A little of both? Restraint? Were words attached to the fantasy? If so, were they sensual, flirtatious, hard, demanding?
> Take the time to recall the tiny seed of your submissive nature...

Submissive nature. Was it natural for me to be this way? And the two words I'd fixed to Walt, without his welcome or cause. *Yes, Sir.* Those were words meant for bedroom voices. And being like Claire in Paul's presence? The notion of scurrying after Walt, hoping for his approval and attention left me cold. The possibility he could turn distant and high-handed about his supposed territory made a nerve behind my eyebrows flare with anger.

But I remembered him lying beside me before the spanking, watching me, the lazy smile, and his voice crossing the inches between us. *"Got you."* And suddenly I felt very brave.

"Okay," I said, sliding the notebook into my lap. "I'll take a look."

Claire left me on my front porch a few hours later, clutching her notebook and one of her new mugs. I realized, as I padded in silence from room to room, I had become accustomed to Walt's presence. I missed him.

I rinsed the mug Claire gave me, probably more than it needed. Nearly eight hundred dollars for two custom pieces of underwear and now this notebook. Walt called himself a Top and after his surprise admission — *it's not a little thing, Erin. Not the way I want it to be with you* — our first evening at Trattoria Stella, the topic of Dominance and submission had sat untouched. Since I had the opportunity to observe the difference, I'd started considering I might be a bottom, the complementary yin to his yang, no power, just play. But those *yes, Sirs* still echoed in my head.

Walt, minutes after we met.

Don't call anyone that unless he's earned it.

It was ridiculous and distracting, and every day those two words made me stare into those woods beyond my desk more than I cared to admit. Without any doubt, I wanted physical play. I wanted it to be attached to someone stronger, more willful and willing than me. I wanted to give provenance to someone else who could handle the task and adore me for it.

I wanted it to be Walt. All of it.

It…no, not it. Dominant. Sir.

I wanted Walt to be Sir. But there was an equal and opposite side to Sir, one I'd hardly considered.

Willing. Deferential. Yielding. Obedient.

Claire's notebook sat, benign, under my bag and the thin cotton cardigan I'd been stupid enough to wear to Asheville in the middle of a June heat wave. This place always seemed to demand more exposure than I anticipated.

> In this guide, I hope you'll find your own path to recognizing and understanding your own submissive nature. Just as each human is different, this facet of you is unique to your own experience. For some of us, submission is completely in the mind, others find their place accepting physical sensation from another, many of us find a place between both mental and physical.

Sensory Exploration

> I consider this journey one of the senses. Part of every section in this notebook will contain suggestions for sensory exploration of the topic I've written about.

As with everything I've included here, it is merely a guidepost and completely optional.

Do you remember the first time you felt a submissive need? Was it domination? Pain? A little of both? Restraint? Were words attached to the fantasy? If so, were they sensual, flirtatious, hard, exacting?

Take the time to recall the tiny seed of your submissive nature. Write about it, meditate on it. If it asks you, explore your body with it.

I set the notebook aside and walked from room to room, directionless.

Walt beside me. Deep-ocean blue eyes and slow-falling lashes. His hand on my hip. *Got you.*

Sensory exploration? I *sensed* that my kitchen work turned the house humid, thanks to all the repeated washings I had given my new coffee mug.

Walt was on surprise duty at Poplar Branch, filling in for his assistant ranger, Sam, and watching over his forest for the evening instead of occupying a good portion of my sofa. With a dismissive sniff, I sloughed my wrinkled linen dress away from my damp skin.

Cool drinks, cool showers. If I stayed in the South much longer, I'd need to start monogramming everything and buy a deviled egg plate.

As I showered, I was hardly relieved and actually adding to my own frustration. Instead of rushing to finish, I lathered a bath mitt as I thought about the words in Claire's notebook. *Submissive. Willing. Obedient.*

I soaped my legs, closed my eyes and let my mind run an old, familiar reel. The one I rarely allowed myself to think about. It was a fantasy. An indulgent one, and thoughts that made me wince over them as often as they turned me taut-limbed and aroused.

Yes, Sir.

Lips beside my ear whispering explicit instructions. The same lips brushing my forehead as a long, obviously masculine finger rested under my chin. My hands clenched behind my back. My head bowed. Face down and ass thrust high, waiting patiently. And I looked content, happy even. I was as soft and flouncy as the bed clothing around me. I could hear my own mind looping a cadence: *for Sir...for Sir...for Sir...*

A hand cracked across my bare skin, then a wisp of fur, then a springy cane. There was no discernible pattern: no start, no stop. I remained perfectly still and looked nearly euphoric. The man's lips descended to my pinked flesh, kissing and soothing, patting and stroking. I saw the same mouth, smiling beside my ear again, whispering as the long, gloved finger stroked my cheek and then bounced lightly against the tip of my nose. He withdrew his hand from my face and slid it between the mattress and my torso, and I saw my own nipples pinched and pulled taut over and over.

My thighs shook, trembling from the heavier attention. A thin, sinister-looking silver chain configured in a lengthy Y and finished at each end with small clamps was placed before my face. My eyes opened, seemingly commanded to do so, and focused on him as I pressed my lips against the metal. My nipples, now dusky and hardened, were caught up in the little clamps. The final clamp disappeared between my legs and snugged behind my clitoris.

His mouth was beside my ear again, whispering something that made me beam rapturously. He kissed my forehead and was gone, returning his attention to the skin on my thighs and ass, now readied for his more stern attentions. Again there was no pattern to the march of items assaulting my now reddened skin. Paddles covered in leather were replaced with bits of soft suede, then stinging, nibbed plastic strings. Without warning, his hand dipped between my legs, pulling at the chain or dancing lightly over the slick layers of skin. The hardest blows fell on my upturned backside, now a vivid, purple-splotched red. Another increase in speed and intensity.

I was seduced by my own obvious bliss as he struck me again and again. Sweaty, lost within my own reactions to the sensory overload. The chain went cruelly taut as his fingers dipped deep inside me, collecting the wetness pooled there as a leather-clad thumb stroked at my pinched clitoris. The effort I had to exert to stay completely still, even though I appeared to be inhabiting another type of consciousness, was extreme.

He nudged at my knees with his own legs, opening me further, and began again, this time slapping my bare labia as his fingers plunged inside me.

He was directly behind me, his skin and muscle pressed tight against my reddened thighs. The coarse dark hair on his legs and groin tickled and tormented my heated skin as his erection pressed against one heated red cheek. The weight of him fell along my body, making me feel engulfed with his solid and imposing presence. Once again he whispered in my ear as he slid inside me. Without warning his lips moved, and I finally heard his voice, deep, masculine, and even in this moment, dripping with a sort of lightheartedness.

"Let me have it, girl," he said, nuzzling his face against mine. Seeing me like this pleased him. "Come for me."

I did. Hard.

His hands were on my hips, pulling me against him as I panted and moaned through several waves of intense orgasm that swelled and spilled over as I heard him groan with his own climax. I constricted around him, pulling him deeper into me and into his own release. His hand slid around the crease of my thigh, settling on my bare mound, his fingers stroking again at my clitoris. Suddenly, he gave the chain imprisoning my nipples a rough tug.

"Come again. Now."

My body obeyed him and washed over into a deep wave, clenching from deep in my thighs and burning through my pelvis.

"Whose are you?" he asked as I submerged and rolled under again. When my answer wasn't rapid enough, the chain yanked again. "Whose are you?"

"Yours, S — Sir," I gasped.

"Whose?" His fingers flitted lightly at my still-tight clit as his voice slipped over my disoriented senses.

"Yours, Sir," I said in a small, breathy voice. It wasn't to his liking.

"Again."

"Yours, Sir." I repeated it with more focus through the shudders starting to take over my body.

"Good girl. One more time. Come for me again."

A low whine escaped from my throat and I was lost, battered by flashing colors and the sound of his breath in my ear. I collected the last vestiges of energy in my chest and screamed, flinging my head back against his shoulder.

Suddenly the screaming in my head was replaced by the sound of flesh slipping against porcelain. Unable to discern the heavy rub of lost footing and useless clutching of my own hands on the wet tile from the last wave of the most intense orgasm I'd ever experienced, alone or otherwise, I managed to catch myself just before I toppled over. I leaned heavily against the cool ceramic, my breath coming in ragged and shallow snatches.

My skin chilled, an evening breeze drifting through the open window.

Reality crashed in, and I was mortified. I wasn't even aware of what I was doing, and…the window. Open.

Oh my God. The realization of what I'd just done, the nature of the fantasy and my body's almost cataclysmic reaction to it, overwhelmed me.

That was *me.*

That was no fantasy, it's what I want and probably have for so long… Oh, the next door neighbors. Did they hear?

I am like that. I am.

I am a submissive.

I'd never felt so directionless and alone. Stiff, as though I really had borne the weight and sheer size of my fantasy Dominant, I leaned down to turn off the water and stepped from the shower. My trembling hands tucked a thick towel around me and wound another around my hair. As I dressed I avoided my own reflection in the mirror. I wasn't sure who would be looking back at me.

CHAPTER TEN

"Push harder, babysub."

"I'm pushing as hard as I can, *Madam*."

"Here, let me…just…Erin! Will you just let me do it?"

"Fine. I can't breathe in this thing, you know. It's too tight."

"God, you are almost — no, come to think of it, you are as whiny as Walt. You two belong together."

With a grunt, the hands on my backside shoved me forward. I managed to catch myself and sit without any damage to my ankles, wrists, or my *attire*. I lowered my eyes with the task of tamping down to rights the yards of black tulle I wore around my waist, but was impeded by my own breasts. *Heaving* breasts seemed like the right term, considering I was utterly out of breath, and they were spilling out of the corset I was bound into like some sort of theme park Scarlett O'Hara.

Lucy hopped in the driver's side of her oversized SUV. With the grace of a gazelle, of course. She snorted, not gracefully.

"Excuse me?"

"It's cute, how you're sulking like that. You sure you aren't into age play?"

"If I say yes can I take off this contraption?" I looked down again, fascinated with the flesh that overflowed past the black silk and satin binding, and poked dubiously at one of the mounds with my finger. Lucy watched with the sort of amused indulgence I'd usually associate as that given to children and the elderly.

"They're supposed to do that. Why do you think they're called 'merry widows'?"

"I don't know," I mumbled, still poking at my own breast as if it were a fully risen ball of dough, expecting the entire architecture to deflate. "I can't breathe."

"*I can't breathe,*" Lucy whined as she put her Range Rover into drive. "You're not supposed to breathe. You're supposed to go along quietly to Tate's, stand there, wait for Wand—er, *Walt,* and look irresistible and stop making me want to strangle you."

"I wasn't aware you had an agenda."

"God, you're mouthy." She turned from her driveway, too fast, and I slid into the door.

"I'm not afraid of you." I was lying. Lucy scared me witless, especially without Claire to water down her nonstop sarcasm. Lucy slanted her head toward me, smiling.

"Of course you're not, babysub. Of course you're not."

I settled into my seat as much as the ensemble she'd literally tied me into would allow. As we wound through the deep woods circling Lake Arden, I brought up and dismissed neutral topic after neutral topic. Every time I tried to open a line of conversation with Lucy, she introduced me to another new, naïve facet of my personality.

"Do you…are you going to do, or, um…"

"That's adorable, really. The stuttery, no-confidence newb thing is hot."

"Lucy, why don't you like me?"

She glanced at me again, her brows furrowing. "What? Don't like you?"

"You seem to not like me very much."

"I like you. You're in my car, aren't you?"

"Glad I passed your car test," I said, snatching at the poof of tulle threatening to spread to her seat. Once my skirt was under control, I turned a syrupy-sweet smile on her. "Okay, you like me. So who are you planning on beating tonight, Lucy?"

"Why? Want to see if my dance card's full?" She grinned at me, wagging her eyebrows.

"No, I was feigning interest."

The Range Rover glided to a stop and Lucy turned to me, laughing. "Okay, truce."

"Exc—are you sure?" I shifted, as much as I could, to face her.

"Yes, yes, of course." She waved her hand across the expanse between us. "This is me. I'm not cuddly. I give people a hard time. You might have heard your Sir refer to me as Lucifer a time or two? He didn't make that up merely to amuse people."

"No, Walt always calls you Lucy when he says something about you." I turned back to the road as we drove forward. "And he's not—I don't know if he's my Sir."

"No? You two fuck enough. Are you sure?"

"How do you know—?"

"Hey, you two have to decide what kind of relationship you're having." She directed another look my way. "So. What kind is it?"

"I thought Walt and I were deciding this."

"Wanda would never do or say anything without you asking. He's too polite to just throw you over his shoulder and turn caveman on you."

"Oh."

She chuckled. The sound was too ominous for comfort. "Okay, then. So you're one of those."

"Those?"

"You want him to be a caveman." The woman actually snorted as she laughed. "Oh damn, are you in trouble, Wanda."

"Trouble? Why?" I gaped at her.

"Because Walt's favorite game is *Ugg fetch woman*." She laughed harder. I didn't join her. "Oh, lighten up, Erin. You two need to stop thinking so much and just do some depraved shit and then go pick out some kitchen curtains or something domestic like that, and go back for more of the depraved shit. Make it all normal and about what you both want. But stop being polite and get dirty. It's the only way you'll get past this reasonable, nice…thing." She said *nice* with the same distaste she probably turned toward fast food and scratch and dent sales. The vehicle pitched again, almost sending me into Lucy's lap. "Heads up, babysub. We're here."

After passing a pair of lantern-topped stone pillars, Lucy stopped to key a series of numbers into a security monitor. Two wide, wrought-iron gates pulled apart smoothly, revealing a short drive that disappeared into a cluster of tall evergreens. As we wound through the landscape, the elevation rose slightly with each turn, offering views of spotted granite boulders nestled among more of the same long-limbed evergreens, deep patches of moss under bushes covered in bright white and pink flowers, and broad-trunked hardwood trees.

It was nature perfected, like a forest assembled for enchanted sprites and fairies instead of plodding, indifferent humans. I pushed myself forward in my seat, angling for a glimpse of the treetops overhead.

"Impressive," Lucy said. I nodded, wordless. "I've been coming up to Tate's for at least twelve years. Never stops blowing my mind, something like this place existing for one family."

"This is his? Just *his?*"

"Yep." Lucy swung the Range Rover through a deep turn, revealing a trio of long, pitched rooflines spiked with a matching number of chimney stacks. "All Tate's. It was his great-grandparents', maybe great-great." She shook her head with a wry smile. "Not sure. Turn of the last century, anyway. Sugar. Texas, Louisiana, and Haiti. Maybe the Grenadines too, somewhere else in the Caribbean? This was their summer cottage."

More than once Walt had hinted at Lucy's estranged family with words like "debutante" and "old money." And she was still impressed, after twelve years of visits. "A summer house? I can't imagine."

"Who could, coming to a lake house like this? Well, Tate, maybe."

At the crest of a final hill, there was a second, older set of pillars. A matching pair of weathered rectangular lanterns hung from a thick iron rod suspended in a patchwork of riverstone and mortar. Beyond them, atop the crest of another, smaller hill, was a house that looked like it had always been there, and couldn't have made sense anywhere else. Under the ridges of the three steep rooflines I saw from the drive were a series of smaller peaks topping wide, lead-glass windows. A deep porch wrapped around the house, shaded by a slope of cedar shingles.

"What did their winter cottage look like?" I muttered.

Lucy snickered. "You should ask Tate. I think it's on an island."

"Island. Of course. All the fine people have islands for winter."

"Well, thank your lucky stars, babysub. You know the wicked people now, and we have a mountain."

The wicked people also had terraced gardens and something Lucy called a *porte-cochère*, as though everyone had one outside their elegantly rustic, one-hundred-twenty-year-old lake house that was really the size of a small hotel. I followed her across a cobblestone pathway toward a set of burnished wood French doors bigger than any I'd seen at Home Outfitters. Behind her, I paused in silence as she stopped to greet several couples whose state of undress rose as we got closer to the house.

"See Wanda?" I scanned past a cluster of people just inside the doors, craning my neck for a glimpse of him. "No, over there." Lucy pointed to a stretch of gravel—and Walt, walking toward us.

It was ridiculous, it shouldn't have happened, but my breath did catch and my heart did sound in my ears.

I saw Walt frequently, at least three times a week. He was familiar to me at this point, both in and out of clothes. But he was different here. There seemed to be more of him—if that was possible—taller, and not just because of the black-laced boots he wore or the way he ducked under a weathered arbor spanning the path.

He stopped a few feet from me, leaving the last echoes of gravel crunching beneath his boots in the soft early evening air. I wanted to be still and look irresistible, just as Lucy had commanded. The sudden chill skating over my shoulders made me fight hard for it, even though I'd stopped in a narrow shaft of slanting sunlight. And I desperately needed to look, down at my skirt or over my shoulder at the old-fashioned rose arbor or anywhere but at Walt, saying something to himself as he moved toward me again. He was so…much. Too much gorgeous and earthy and powerful to be believed. And this place—what was I doing at a kinky lake house party? The urge for fight or flight prickled at my neck, and I couldn't look away from him—or anywhere but him.

"Thought Lu was gonna hide you away at her lair," he said as he came to my side. He pulled me into his chest, his voice dropping low, and the sudden questions evaporated as quickly as they arose. "There you are. Hey."

"Here I am. Hi," I managed to say before his lips were on mine. After a long kiss, he drew away enough to nuzzle into my neck. I found the spot on his scalp that made him grumble contentedly when I grazed my nails over it and turned to his ear, whispering. "You know, your skirt is shorter than mine."

"Not a skirt."

"It's a skirt if you're wearing bloomers under there, Wanda."

Walt's head rose as he chuckled. "Hey, hands off, Lucifer. It's a kilt."

Lucy was relentless, quickly beside him so he couldn't step away, and raising the yards of mottled brown, green, and deep blue plaid before he could tuck the hem away from her. Still snugged around my waist, Walt's arm carried me along. I inserted myself between him and Lucy, taking the fabric from her hand before either of them realized I was there.

"Oh yeah," I said, and razed my nails over the bare, muscular curve of Walt's hip. "It's definitely a kilt."

Lucy's eyebrow hovered, and finally her lips drew into a sly grin. "Well, I'll take your word for it, Erin." With a sweep of her gold hair, she turned for the house, calling back to us in sing-song. "See you two later, maybe."

Walt's deep laugh rumbled through his chest again. The sound of it, and the heavy, sure weight of his arm around my waist as his hand stroked my hip made me proud.

Erin. Not babysub.

Walt called in every favor and *owe you* and *thanks, man* he'd built up over the years to get rid of his DM shifts. Everyone wanted to experience Tate's Solstice party without the yoke of watching over the other Enclave guests. Usually Walt was happy to sit on the sidelines so others could enjoy themselves at Tate's parties, and lately he'd been grateful for the distance his responsibilities as a dungeon monitor gave him. But "usually" was before Erin.

She walked out of the shadow of a hemlock, looking like a puff of cream wrapped in black satin. Before he got to her, he knew from the pink flush rising on Erin's neck her heart was racing. He could see from the shallow breath making her chest rise and fall that Lucy had bound her up in that corset a hairsbreadth away from too tight. Good thing Luce knew when to stop. Erin's tits looked spectacular.

Erin's everything looked spectacular. *She* was spectacular, as quiet and graceful as the big house towering behind her.

"So this is The House, hmmm? 'In Xanadu did Kubla Khan a *stately* pleasure dome decree'? It really is like a hidden world."

Walt watched, too stupid with the sight and feel of her to make his mouth work. Her eyes darted around, taking in the people and the gardens, and even twinkled a little when she spotted a couple of members putting the last touches on a temporary rope frame rising in the center of the rose garden.

Smiling, she nudged him with her elbow. "What's that? A gallows?"

"It's for rope suspensions. Tate invited a couple of riggers from Atlanta. They've got some kind of show planned for sunset. Lit-up hula hoops and fire jugglers, too." Erin didn't answer. He looked down and caught her making a very determined effort to not notice an older couple passing by. Once they passed, her shoulders dropped.

"Part of the show?"

"No, they just do pony play when they come up. It takes a lot for him to get into his gear these days, so I think they save it for special occasions."

"That sounded really horrible, didn't it?"

He pulled her close again and kissed the top of her head, hoping it would distract her before the self-criticism rooted in. "You're just a little edgy. I won't tell."

She'd been edgy for the past week. Erin blamed work, and from what she told Walt, the guy she managed continued to test her, almost every day. It was hard to hear her blame herself for not having the right *soft communication skills*—whatever the hell that was. Nearly as hard as it was to keep convincing himself Erin wouldn't appreciate it if he took care of the situation with the hard kind of communication this Alan guy would understand.

Erin still watched the rope people from Atlanta setting up. "Do you—is that one of your things?" She tipped her head toward the span of wood and steel bolts.

"Rope? Not really. Between Scouts and the military, I know enough knots to keep a girl in one place. That's all I care to know."

"Hm. Really?"

"Yes, really. Why would I mess around tying fancy knots when I've got a real, live girl to play with?"

"Um, yes…why, indeed." She ducked her chin away from him, exposing the color rising on her neck again. He brushed his knuckle over the pink skin and was rewarded with one of her little shivers.

He cleared his throat, taking his hand away. "I should probably show you around, introduce you to a couple of people."

"Okay." The little crevices between her eyebrows said it wasn't. He couldn't resist sweeping his hand over the taut silk covering her back as he leaned close to her ear.

"Luce'll kill me if I have you out of that thing this early. She just got you into it."

She was quiet for an extra second. Considering. "That's between you two. I'm going to behave myself," she said finally, turning to him. That damn coy little smile she gave him when they teased like this was bait he should ignore.

He took her hand. "Claire's been asking where you are. We'd better show her Lu actually brought you before she spins her harmonies into another vibration or whatever it is she talks about."

Walt held the door open for Erin and stood aside so she could enter the house. Across the mudroom, Tommy Blackwell didn't bother to hide his surprise—or his interest, blatantly giving Erin a long, appraising once-over. Along with Tate, both of them had probably earned their reputations as the welcoming committee down at the club in Charlotte and occasionally with the odd guest at the Enclave.

"Hey," Walt said, sliding his arm around Erin's waist. Her head rose to his, and Walt drew her in for a kiss. He let himself take an extra second's slow, deep taste of her and drew away. "Need to check a bag, buddy?" He cast a flat stare across the space to Tommy.

Do we understand each other?

Tommy hefted his toybag and turned for the kitchen without a second glance at Erin. "Nah, man. I'm headed downstairs."

Once his lanky frame faded into the far end of the kitchen, Erin looked up at Walt over the rims of her glasses, barely keeping back a laugh.

"Does that happen often?"

"Damn," he said, wincing, and shook his head at himself. "That obvious?"

"Walt, I'm around men all the time. I might be new to this—" she gestured around the mudroom, smirking "—but I'm not entirely oblivious to testosterone asserting itself. I appreciate the gesture."

"It's no gesture."

Her features softened. "Okay."

"Okay, then." He reached for her hand.

Walking through the main floor rooms, Erin's shoulders eased down with each fact he gave her to file away. Every introduction that came and went made her falter less over her words, made her hand let go of a little more of the filmy black material from her skirt she'd tucked into her fist.

Claire called to them from across the kitchen, waving from the door of the butler's pantry, promising to find them once the final adjustments to the evening's dinner were complete. Behind her, Tate emerged from the dim room, carrying a wooden crate full of glassware.

"Hell, I was beginning to wonder if you were going to turn up sometime this afternoon, Walt. So who is this poor lady you've attached yourself to?" Tate slid the box to the wide kitchen island and turned back to them.

"Erin," she said, offering her hand. "Erin's fine. I'm...um..."

Walt linked his fingers through hers. "She's with me."

"Oh is she? Well, it's *poor lady* for sure, then." He offered his hand to Erin. "It's nice to meet you, Erin. You might hear me called Tango among other things around here, but I generally answer quicker to Tate."

Walt stepped aside as Tate rattled off more about the Enclave's history to Erin. Claire motioned him over.

"Can you give me a hand, Wally?" Glancing past his shoulder, she drew him into the butler's pantry. "Well? How's she doing?"

"Okay. Settling down. Lu had wound her up pretty good before they got here."

"That snot." Claire rolled her eyes indulgently. "I told her to behave herself. What happened?"

"Just Lu being Lu from what I could tell. Probably poking her, mostly, about us, and then poking me a little to wind Erin up more."

Across the kitchen, Erin gestured over her head, unaware she was giving Tate a glimpse down her corset as she pointed to the original handcarved woodwork above them. Snickering, Tate glanced in Walt and Claire's direction, lifting his eyebrows. *Nice tits,* he mouthed before gliding his attention — and well-bred host's gameface — back to Erin.

"Looks like Lucy's not the only one doing some poking," Claire said as Walt huffed over her giggles.

"You too, Claire? All right, everybody's had a piece of my ass this afternoon. Before I have to bust Tate's, why don't you find me something heavy to move? You're too sweet to be mad at, and Lu took off for downstairs before I could deal with her."

Laughing, Claire took his hand and led him toward the butler's pantry. "Relax, grumpy bear, nobody's going to steal your honey. Come on, I need someone to carry plates for me."

Tate was magnetic. Everything about him commanded attention, from his artfully disheveled hair and wrinkled, yet beautifully made linen shirt, to his broad, booming voice. Burnished, I told myself, as he answered another question I made up just to distract him so I could watch him talk. His hair and tanned skin looked like gradients of gold. His body was muscled in the lean, narrow-waisted way of a swimmer, and he was nearly as tall as Walt.

Walt. Who was wearing a kilt and flexing his arms around two wooden crates and scowling at us from across the giant kitchen in the most adorably annoyed way. He caught my eye as he slid the crates on the wide marble-topped island, and it started. That…something. The new something that made my cheeks heat as the sensation of being seen by him zinged over and under my skin. His eyebrow quirked a little and he turned, chuckling to himself as he moved across the kitchen.

"Well, aren't you two like a basket of puppies?"

"I'm sorry?"

"No, I am. That was good to see. I like seeing my friends happy." Tate leaned against the big marble-topped island, grinning. "I forget sometimes what it must be like to show up the first time and be shoved in the deep end with us, treating each other like we're at summer camp instead of acting like grown people at a play party."

I began to tell him it was fine, because it was, and how much I appreciated being part of the cast for once, instead of trying to figure out who to deliver my lines to. As I opened my mouth, a bluster of satin and tulle passed me, paused in front of Tate, and then continued toward the mudroom.

"Pardon me one second, please, Erin," he said. His words were still on the air between us and he was already gone, following a woman of nearly cartoon-proportion curves, outfitted in a searing hot pink corset and tulle skirt that barely reached the top of her thighs. Under perfectly applied, doll-like makeup, her porcelain skin looked like creamy velvet. It was the first time I'd actually seen a mouth worthy of being called a Cupid's bow, and she'd dressed it in the deep claret of a pomegranate's flesh.

Adjusting a set of black kitten ears behind her sculpted bangs, she rolled her eyes under a thick fringe of sooty lashes when Tate's arms went around the deep curve of her corseted waist.

"Don't come near me, Tate. I do *not* have patience for your bullshit today."

If my corset had pushed my breasts into pillows, hers were tuffets. And Tate—since he was, as Lucy and Walt had said, lord of the manor—apparently took his pleasure from their comforts. His broad shoulders hid just what those attentions actually were, but her scowl was melting by the second. Head rising, he spoke in a private voice just for her, saying something that made her giggle and squeal a little. Finally, her arms tucked over his shoulders, and she wound the strands of sandy hair falling at his neck through her black-tipped nails.

And Walt was nowhere to be seen. Claire, too. Standing by idly and waiting for people to finish kissing was not unfamiliar to me, but my sister had put me in that situation enough for the rest of my life. I cleared my throat.

"I can *not* believe you. God, Tate, you have no manners at all," she said, a little breathy, and adjusted her kitten ears. Pressing her round shoulder past Tate's arm, she offered her hand to me. "I am so very sorry. I'm Gala Apples, Tate's current pick of the crop." And she winked, so much the living embodiment of a vintage pinup, a Castro diva would have applauded.

Stepping forward, I reached for her hand. "I'm—"

Gala squealed again, this time a little louder, as Tate's hand connected—hard, judging from the sharp slap echoing through the room—with her backside.

"Tate," Walt called. His head appeared around a doorway. "Watch your han—Oh, hey, Gala."

"*Oh hey*, Ranger," she cooed, wiggling her fingers in his direction. "This your little muffin?"

"I'm Erin."

"She's Erin," Walt said, lifting his eyebrows twice. "I'm the muffin—the stud muffin."

"Damn, Walt, that's tired, even for you." Leaning over Gala's shoulder, Tate sank his mouth into her ample cleavage again. With a toss of her cherry-red hair, she pushed him away.

"You be sweet, hound. And you, Erin, how very nice to meet you." When her hand extended toward me, I stammered, shocked to still be a participant in the conversation. "If you need a break from these two boys and Doma Lucia and all their constant one-ups, you come find me."

"You'll be occupied." Tate hooked his arm around her waist, nearly purring into her ear. "Very, very occupied."

"We'll see." She blew Walt a kiss and wriggled out from Tate's arm.

Once Gala sashayed away from us, Tate steered me through the kitchen, so frustratingly close to Walt I caught a whiff of his warmed skin.

"No, no. You two leave each other alone for three-and-a-half seconds. Claire needs the brute squad if all these guests are going to have dishes for their supper, and I'm going to show you my reading room."

Shrugging after Walt's grumbled *bastard*, I followed Tate back to the wide foyer. "This isn't anything like showing me your etchings, right?"

"Entirely honorable." Tate covered his heart with his hand and then grinned. "Unless, of course, you ask otherwise."

Usually blatant flirtation like this sent me scattering. From someone like Tate, I should have been lost. I had no reference point of my own, only years of watching Danielle lob innuendo after innuendo at receptive boys — and then at men. But oddly, I felt at ease around him. Maybe even more so than Walt, in the early moments of our relationship. There was no sense of evaluation, and his actions didn't prickle my skin, making me aware of his nearness.

Tate turned down a corridor where the recessed lights were noticeably dimmer. That and a gorgeous, heavy wooden chair in the center of the hall said clearly — but elegantly — *keep out.* He noticed me gazing down at the chair's thick, curved arms.

"Do you like arts and crafts furniture?"

"I don't know." I smiled up at him. "I've never seen this style before, but it's beautiful. Different."

"It's a spindle chair. Black walnut, from the property. Carved onsite." He passed long fingers over it, rippling the sheen of polished, dark wood. "This is from one of the original dining room suites.

Found it in a back corner of the storage shed when I took over the house. Lucky to have a couple of them left. My uncle detested everything about his grandmother's taste in decorating. I'm surprised he didn't turn it all into firewood and replace the whole house with chrome and leather."

"So he passed all of this down to you?" I followed him, skirting around the large chair.

"*All of this*, indeed." He chuckled. "He did. For some reason, old Jackson approved of me. He was a blacker sheep than I am, as far as the family's concerned, anyway. Probably raised nearly as many eyebrows in his day as Luce did with her people. Of course, we're from Houston, so things are a little more relaxed so far south."

"Oh?" I said with a weak shrug. Texas was Texas to me, a nebulous idea based on old TV shows and cartoons starring oversized roosters. "What did he do?"

"He did as I do—invested his money and indulged his interests," Tate drawled easily. "What he *was* was the problem, as far as some of the Houston Jernigans were concerned. Uncle Jack was gay. And a Leatherman. And he was out, back when being gay like him was discussed in whispers as being a confirmed bachelor with a certain military bearing."

He talked of his uncle—in truth his great-uncle—with a gentle pride as we climbed a less-ornate rear staircase. Once World War II began, Jackson Jernigan ran away from the most recent boarding school where the family had managed to place him. He joined the Navy at seventeen, lying about his age and entering as a seaman.

"Old Jack could have waited it out, I'd imagine, and if the call of the sea was really what it was about, I guess the family would have sent him up to the Naval Academy."

"But he didn't."

"No. He didn't. I didn't get it until I was an adult and putting my own story together, but I think my family must have more than a few nonconformist genes. We've got a decent number of pirates, lawyers, and tropical land speculators swinging from the family tree."

We passed a long window seat tucked under a row of the leaded-glass windows I recognized from my drive up to the house with Lucy. Before I could stop myself, I sank my hand into the olive velvet tufted cushion, sighing.

"It's perfect." I looked up and found Tate smiling down at me.

"Looks like your kind of spot."

"Yes. I think it probably is."

"Then consider it your spot at the Enclave, any time you visit," he said, the picture of a gracious civility I'd only read about in old novels. "If you're more comfortable here now, I can bring up your bag, maybe some tea or a snack?"

"No, it's…I'm fine, thank you." I gazed out the windows to the gardens below us. Stretching around the entire house, the terraces were filled with rambling flower beds spilling blooms of every color. Each level sloped down toward a grove of tall hardwoods. Past the house and the lush green treetops, a deep blue lake shimmered in the late afternoon sun. "It's really beautiful here."

Tate had also turned to the broad view of his home. He seemed contemplative as he scanned over the scene below us — and, when I looked more closely at him, a little sad.

"Yes, it is. A beautiful place, indeed," he said. "I never seem to make it to this part of the house. Sometimes, all this space —" He looked to me, brightening. "Well, it's hard to keep up with all the panoramas, isn't it?"

I nodded, not quite able to dismiss the glimpse of resignation I'd seen a moment before.

"Erin, it's a pleasure to have you with us." Tate extended his hand to mine and pressed it sincerely between his. "I should find that kitten of mine before she turns hostile. Stay and enjoy the view as long as you like."

He turned, hands in pockets, and sauntered down the hall.

I settled into "my spot" — no small undertaking, considering the Medieval contraption I still wore — and turned to the gardens again. The sun's last rays lit the massive hardwood trees in fiery oranges and reds rivaling the scene on the lawn. Four women, their skin bare except for swaths of abstract body paint, danced in the grove below them, twirling hoops in the same shades of the sunset overhead. The "rope people," as Walt had called them, had been at work too. Under each of the wooden scaffolds I'd noticed earlier, a lithe woman had been bound into exaggerated contortions. An approximation of a winged victory here; Eros bound there, and Psyche swaying gently from a third wooden beam. They too wore little more than body paint, shimmering in silvers and the cool, deep colors of the North Carolina night sky.

Inhaling, I stood and pressed the folds of my body back into some kind of order inside my corset. The wicked people really did have a mountain. And since I had finally found them, it was time to go look at what wicked meant at The Enclave.

I was directed to the rear of the house and a long set of terracotta-tiled stairs. As I cleared the second landing, I heard voices below me.

"—another new girl. She makes web sites or something."

"It's always a new girl. Those two are here for the pussy, and all you new girls make it very available, so everyone is part of that game. If you thought it was about something different, you need to grow up, Nicole."

I stepped back, slowly, squinting between the iron railings.

"I think they're nice." Voices, both I recognized. From the home store in Shanesborro: *It's not Lucy.*

"Nice? Okay, sure. Nice. Thanks to *all* of these nice people, turning my kink into a fucking tea party." Another, unfamiliar voice huffed. "There, it's fixed. Next time don't rely on a satin ribbon to keep your boobs in your corset, Kelsi."

Footsteps echoed through the stairwell, the clatter of high heels ringing over the tile steps. I froze, stunted by a thready racing memory of another new school and a new set of girls appraising me without bothering to conceal it. Like then, I couldn't move without looking like they'd made me run away, so I started down the stairs, only taking each step once I was sure my foot was surely under me. Chin high, eyes forward. As I crossed the small vestibule and passed them, the three women stopped, the unfamiliar one at the front of their line.

"Hi, I'm Hawk's Chalice." She shifted a sheet of inky black hair from her shoulder and turned to me, offering her hand. "And you're the new girl with Ranger."

It was no inquiry; we all knew who I was. And there was no challenge from her, just a statement of fact. I accepted her hand. "Hello. I'm Erin."

"Erin," she repeated, nodding. "Alex. You've met Nicole and Kelsi? At the club in Charlotte, I heard."

I nodded, too interested by her to glance toward the shuffling and twittering I heard going on behind her. "They saw me, yes. And I saw them. In Shanesborro, the next day."

The twittering intensified. Would they start singing about being a Jet next?

"Good," Alex said, smiling efficiently. "So we all know who each other is now, right?" She glanced over her shoulder. "See, girls, not that hard. This is Erin."

Kelsi rose on her toes, peering over Alex's shoulder. "Hey."

Nicole, no surprise, remained silent, studying the bare white wall opposite us with serious determination.

"Nice to meet you."

"There. Nice. We're all nice and pleasant and have good manners." Alex wheeled up a black nylon carry-on behind her. She stepped by me, turning as she passed. "Have a good *visit*."

"I will. Thank you." I remained in place as they walked past me, expecting Nicole to shove her shoulder against mine in a final flourish appropriate to teenage drama. Her skyscraper heels clicked as she navigated the small space.

I watched them go, gritting my teeth. And though I hated myself for playing that old game of female one-upsmanship, I played over Walt's dismissal of Nicole in my mind. Her footing at the Enclave was much more precarious than mine. If she pushed, this time I'd push back. I could. I was wanted here. With that small measure of certainty, I moved on to find him.

Once Walt lashed the cross into place and dropped a few of bags of sand over the flat base rails to steady it, he stepped back, huffing. Next time Paul came to order him or another DM around, Walt half-expected him to be snapping his fingers like a damn third-world despot.

Behind him voices and the sound of ladies' shoes on the tile floor moved closer to the brick-topped alcove Paul had reserved. When Nicole was the first one through the curtain, it was a surprise that made complete sense after just a second's consideration. How many girls like her had he watched move through the ranks of Tops until she was done? He squashed the urge to roll his eyes and made a final pass over the cross to make sure it was secure.

"This is going to be great," she said, not bothering to disguise her glare at him. She made a show of putting her bag aside and sauntering over to the cross. Alex, Tommy, and Kelsi followed, block-ing Walt's exit.

He exchanged a quick hello with Tommy's wife, Alex, who he had played with off and on through the years, and moved toward the narrow gap in the black privacy curtains that turned the space from unused wine cellar to private room.

Nicole tracked him as he moved toward the curtains, and made a show of stretching over the long, polished planks of wood. "Nobody's ever hit me *real hard* with a singletail, Paul. Hey, can't we use that lane over by the couches?"

To his credit, Paul raised his eyebrows at her and gave her a cool stare. "No. I'm using that space with my girls in a few minutes." Standing, he stepped aside so Walt could pass. Instead of a clear exit, he caught himself just before colliding with Claire.

"Sir?" Flustered, she entered without acknowledging Walt.

Claire came to her knees beside Paul's feet. This was always part of them, the way they were together. In a gesture Walt had seen probably hundreds of times in the years he'd known them, Paul's hand went to Claire's head, passing over her hair and traveling to her chin. He unsnapped the thin everyday collar she always wore and tucked it into his back pocket, then bent to his bag, bringing out a shining silver ring.

Claire's formal collar.

He had been there, the day Claire bent her neck to Paul the first time — in this house and in front of many of the same people visiting for Solstice — and accepted his collar. The Saldinos had already been married in a nice ceremony over at Poplar Branch, in front of their families and vanilla friends, so the collaring a few weeks later seemed like another kind of partnership they agreed to, not something she gave up for him.

Everything around him was as familiar as the campground at Poplar Branch, or even the inside of his cabin, but Walt felt discon-nected from the scene and people in front of him. And it should have been private. They always went off for a moment, just the two of them, and came back to the party after he'd put on her formal collar. Claire beaming, Paul looking down at his wife with pride, and no question this was a union — not just a woman executing his commands. When did she turn into an accessory for his ego-trip?

Walt took a backward step through the narrow doorway and collided with another body. He glanced over his shoulder and found Erin rising on her toes so she could peer into the room. His head snapped back to Paul and Claire in time to see him hold her formal collar before her. Claire leaned forward and pressed her lips to the glimmering silver band. She bent forward, hidden under the fall of her thick, auburn hair, and extended her neck so Paul could click her formal collar into place and secure it with a tiny lock.

Once her collar was in place, she sat back on her heels, eyes cast to her Master's feet. Hands open, palms up, laid over her knees. And his hand came back to her chin, stroking the pale skin there in affirmation of her. Her eyes rose to his as she nestled her head into his hand, and fell shut again as she kissed his palm.

"Oh, I'm sorry. Was I…" a voice behind him said before gasping.

Erin.

Walt stepped back, blinking hard. The privacy curtain had looped over his shoulder and he was blocking the door. He turned to her, still trying to shake off the dozy-headed feeling that came from nowhere.

Nowhere. Because he'd been on the periphery of that ritual of Paul and Claire's hundreds of times.

He smiled at Erin, and hoped it didn't look nearly as false as he felt. "You ready for dinner?"

"Yes." She peered up at him over the top of her glasses, that expression that always made him feel closely observed—and a little undone in the bargain. Her face broke open in a wide smile. "Did you know there's women in body paint twirling flaming hoops in the rose garden?"

"Had no idea."

She looped her arm through his. "You have to see them, Walt. It's amazing. They might start singing about Mount Abora before it's finished."

"Yeah," he said, and blinked hard again. He needed air and light. Out of this dark dungeon of a basement. "Right behind you, sweetheart."

Some of the party guests were starting to make their way downstairs, looking for an open space. Erin paused by another open room.

"So this is the dungeon? Can you show it to me first?"

"Well, Tate calls it a playroom. He's not into that darkness and brooding bullshit."

Walt paused by a deep alcove where a wooden X similar to those I'd seen in Charlotte waited, his boots a few feet from long strips of orange and acid-yellow tape. His face hardened a little. "Now this is the whip lane. See how it's laid out? The edges of the tape are safe. Anything inside that isn't. When you see tape like this on the floor, be sure to look around you before you walk."

"What is it for?" We crossed the wider room and into a corridor with a bank of doors, each opening spanned with the same black privacy curtains.

"Tate and Tommy throw whips. Me too, sometimes."

"Whips? Like...in the movie?" I hummed a scrap of the theme music. "Whips like that?"

His face softened and he chuckled, scratching his earlobe. "Uh... well, kind of, but we're not swinging them at ninjas or whatever those guys in black turbans were. And not bullwhips usually."

"Saracens." I could see the scene and characters in my mind but the correct terms...out of reach. "I think — not Sufis because they were the mystics, but Saracens..."

"I think 'guys in black turbans' will work for a pop quiz, Professor." We stopped at the entrance to one of the last rooms. "Want to come inside?"

"Hm? Oh...sorry." I shook my head to dislodge the memory and smiled up at him.

"Don't. I never know what's gonna come out of there. I like that. A lot." He kissed me, settling me against his chest with more force than I expected. "You know, Tate made nearly every piece of equipment down here."

"Really?" I glanced around us at the frame Xs and two-tiered benches. They resembled what I'd seen at Area 51 — and in my occasional Internet research — only in shape and function. Each piece was much more substantial and elegantly finished from smooth, natural-stained wood. Before each piece and its possible uses could fully register, I turned away.

Walt looked down at me, smiling. "You can go look if you want to."

"Oh. Um…"

"Or not. Whatever you're comfortable with."

"I want to, I'm just not sure how to do or…" Wincing, I shut my eyes at this latest new thing I was expected to understand at first real-world glance. And why wouldn't he just show me?

"Hey," he said, taking my hand. "It's just some wood and bolts."

"The hell *some wood and bolts*," came a different voice—Tate, his linen shirt untucked and hanging open over his artfully distressed jeans. The woman Gala, now undressed except for a scrap of red lace panties and her kitten ears, padded behind him. "Pardon, by the way. The curtain was open and I didn't see y'all come in here."

"Hey, no problem. Just showing Erin around."

Gala slid Tate's shirt from his shoulders. "I'll get your bags," she whispered as she trailed her nails across his back.

I turned to Tate, deliberately not seeing Gala's very round backside sashaying from the room. "Walt said you made these?"

"I did." He passed a hand over the glossy wood. "The first six months after I got sober, I took up woodworking, which Lucy always said was evidence I'm a secret masochist."

"It's all really beautiful." Tucking my arms behind my back, I stepped closer to the bench he'd just admired. "It's um…well, it doesn't look like anything at Area 51."

"Indeed." Tate chuckled softly and turned to a weighty-looking X at the far end of the room, stepping in line behind Walt. As if on a string, I followed them. "No offense meant to TK, she's got a fine place, but I suppose my aesthetic is a little different." He stepped aside, opposite Walt. "Now I think this is your man's favorite thing down here."

Man? I looked around, gulping, and found Walt's hand beside mine.

"Oh?" I reached for him and followed as he stepped closer to the large X Tate indicated.

"It was one of the first things I made once I figured out how to mill my own wood. This is black walnut and cherry, just like that nice spindle chair you were looking at upstairs. Walt and I took the trees down a couple of winters ago and as a thank you, I made a St. Andrew's Cross that could even hold him. He is one of the best mentors we've got, after all."

I turned to Walt, not bothering to hide my surprise. "Hold you?"

"Yeah," he said, shrugging. "Mostly for the mentor group we do. We usually encourage new Tops to bottom with an experienced Top at first. Especially with the toys they're interested in learning. It's how I learned. And how the guys—er, people who work with me—are taught."

"Me too. Matter of fact, I believe Walt and I both learned to throw a singletail from your *corsetiere*, if I recognize Lady Nerita's handiwork correctly." Tate was still beside me. We'd all moved across the room, leaving me positioned directly in front of the crossed beams.

I raised my hand. "May I?"

For a few seconds there was silence.

"Go ahead," Walt said finally, his voice low.

Under my fingertips, the wood was satiny, cool. "What do I..." I looked to him. "Where do I put my hands?"

"Well," he said, catching my wrist lightly between his fingers. He extended my arm along the span rising toward him. "You could just stand here and hold on to it. Or you could be tied to it."

Behind me, Tate cleared his throat. "Or you could be cuffed. See those slots?" He reached past me and slid away a segment of the wooden beam. "There's bolts inside."

Walt glanced over my head to Tate. His eyes stayed there for a long second.

Suddenly, I was aware of Tate in a way similar to how I was nearly always aware of Walt.

The same certainty of his thought and intention as he looked at me caught me off guard, as it had done with Claire. Tate was thinking about me, maybe about Walt, too. About the three of us—together. Looking over my shoulder, I found him, all bare chest and broad, sardonic smile. Watching me.

The pressure from Walt's hand increased, a steady gradient, until my arm rested fully against the smooth beam. He reached behind me with his other hand and guided me to stretch above my head until I grasped the opposite rail, just beyond Tate's torso. I turned from Walt to Tate, and back again.

They could have me, together. Without an admission from either of them, instinct told me they'd shared women, played with them together, before. And right then, at the sudden insistence of a pulse thrumming between my legs, I would have allowed it. Even as the notion of it bloomed and came into focus in my mind, I shook my head, dismissing the thought. Gala was coming back. Walt hadn't touched me like that since the night of my first spanking.

But the most critical failure was my own lack of a script. I didn't know what to ask for—even if I was almost strung up from a wooden X three feet taller than me. I didn't know how to ask Walt and someone I assumed was his very close friend to take out their toybags and use each and every item within on me until I was a shuddering, sweaty mess. And the possibility of being with both of them, how was I to know if that was a real possibility or just a twist of my over-stimulated imagination? I was here, but didn't know *how to be* here.

A long stream of breath passed from me.

Walt leaned down to me, his lips hovering near my cheek. "You all right?"

"Yes." I nodded briskly and stepped away. "Yes, of course I am."

"Tate, I can't find that big paddle," Gala said behind us. The moment between Walt, Tate, and me snapped closed, and I felt Tate's attention whirring away as he turned for the door.

"Did you check the other bag?" He glanced over his shoulder. "Excuse me, y'all. I need to find this girl's favorite toy."

They disappeared into the far corners of the room, Gala's voice echoing back snatches of her own thoughts about the toy in question and their obvious miscommunication about whether or not it was, in fact, her favorite.

I sensed Walt turning for the entrance, but stilled behind him. Across the room, Tate was lining up a succession of items on a long table. Beside the wooden bench he showed us earlier, was Gala. A paradox of her earlier self, she waited, silent and unmoving, on her knees, posed as Claire had been earlier.

"Walt," I whispered. "Wait, please."

He turned to me but before he could speak, Lucy came through the black privacy curtains, pausing to tuck them over the metal rod they hung from. She had, effectively, opened the door for everyone—and for me—to see.

Lu rarely co-topped at parties. But she liked all of the attention—her bottom's and any observers who might happen by the scene. And though they'd been playing in the lifestyle for better than fifteen years, Walt couldn't remember more than a handful of times she'd done a scene where a man was her co-Top. She'd lost her corset and the brief excuse for a mini-skirt she'd been wearing, leaving her in nothing but her favorite pair of ass-high PVC boots. Reaching overhead, she twisted her long blond hair into a knot on top of her head and winked at Tate, who grinned like he knew he was the luckiest son-of-a-bitch in Grayson County.

Erin shifted at his side. *Well, the second-luckiest son-of-a-bitch in Grayson County.*

"All right, then," Lu purred. "Let's get this pretty little girl of yours dirty, Tatiana."

Gala stood and shed the white shirt she'd taken from Tate earlier, draping it across a chair. She rose on her bare toes, kissed his cheek, then did the same to Lu.

Erin leaned toward him, whispering, "Are they—um…?"

Walt shook his head. "No, just Tate and Gala. It's just them." He looked up in time to catch Gala stretching her generous hips over the back of Tate's newest spanking bench. Behind her, Lu adjusted a pair of long, latex gloves past her elbows. "Well, usually."

"The door was open. That means it's okay to stay, right?" Erin slanted her head away from the scene and glanced over the top of her glasses. "I'd like to…can we watch?"

Can we watch? Walt glanced in Lu's direction to be sure she hadn't heard. If she knew she had an audience, she'd try rattling Erin a little on purpose just to fuck with him. Still, the curtain was pulled back and looped over the rod it hung from, a clear sign the three of them didn't care about observers. He slid his hand under her arm and steered them away from a shaft of light. Tate glanced their way, nodding with a quick quirk of his eyebrows.

"Damn exhibitionists, all three of them." Walt shook his head, grinning at Tate, and leaned to Erin's ear. "Yeah, I think it's fine."

Lu had draped her long body over Gala, with one stiletto-booted foot still on the floor. She rocked her lean thigh slowly against the girl's round ass, pulling on her thick spill of red hair. Gala bowed back, away from the bench, and let out a sweet little moan.

Damn. Not the time to notice Gala's ass. Walt shifted his legs and risked a glance at Erin. As soon as he found her face in the dim room, a rapid series of *thwaks* across the room jerked his attention away.

Lu had turned and now rested on both knees, right over the sharp indention at Gala's waist. She was pinned—almost literally—in place by the sharp pointed heels of Lu's boots pressing into the soft mounds of flesh below her shoulder blades. With a throaty laugh, Lu threw her head back and landed another long series of smacks across the bright-red streaks already coming up on Gala's fair skin. Lu threw the final one hard, aimed for the sensitive crevice between the inside of Gala's thigh and pussy. She landed it at the right place, too, because the girl squealed, thrashing and flutter-kicking her feet. Lu's hand came down again, hard this time, across the crest of Gala's ass.

"You watch that kicking or I'll cuff your ankles to the bench, brat."

Tate came to their side, smoothing over his girl's scalded skin as he whispered in Lu's ear. As they talked, his hand dropped between Gala's legs. The little redhead shivered and gasped under his touch. Her thighs bounced against the bench, but she didn't kick again, not when Lu went back to smacking her ass, and not when Tate's hand thrust into her pussy.

Warm. This old basement was getting too damn warm. And beside him, Erin's arm felt like it was on fire. He heard her breath, so distinct she could have been draped over his shoulder and sighing in his ear. And she took a half-step closer to him. Their arms connected, and Erin threaded her fingers through his.

After an affectionate squeeze to one of the globes of her ass, Tate stepped away from Gala and offered his hand to Lu. She rose from the bench, patting the girl's reddened backside as she stood, and stepped aside.

"You are such a pretty girl," she purred and twisted Gala's hair in her fingers. She rose on her elbows, following the steady tension Lu exerted on her hair. Once the girl's torso was bowed back in a deep curve, Lu dipped her face to Gala's. "Did you know that big, juicy ass of yours is almost as red as your lips now?"

Lu didn't preen over a bottom unless she was going to break them into little bite-sized pieces. Anticipation of watching this luscious girl who, admittedly, Walt had looked over with appreciation more than once, come apart under two wicked Tops flared up his spine.

Reaching forward, Lu twisted one of Gala's nipples, drawing it out between her gloved fingers. Behind them, Tate skimmed the length of a paddle he'd crafted from oak and covered in ridged black rubber.

"Know what this is, girl?"

"I know what it is, Tate, and I hate that fucking thing," Gala sneered through a few sniffles.

Lu snorted and made a show of turning Gala's nipple between her fingers, plucking the nub with her other fingertip. "That's not what I heard. Tate says you call it The Brutal and every time he mentions it to you, you soak your panties like a trashy whore from the south side of Callahan."

Erin's hip connected with his thigh. Stayed there. Insisted he acknowledge her beside him. As unobtrusively as he could, he dipped his head to the side and kissed the top of her head. *Don't bolt. Don't bolt. Don't bolt.* Erin didn't know about Gala's love of humiliation or how it extended to the trailer park life she'd left behind. He wasn't even sure Erin knew about the mental side of some play, how plenty of bottoms like their feelings pushed as hard as their bodies. She didn't know this was how Tate and Gala—and now, it seemed, Lu—played together. And beside him, Erin was nearly fucking molding her body to his side, sending the coarse wool kilt nudging across his stiff, engorged cock.

Every time Tate connected that paddle to Gala's ass, every time she sniffled and sobbed against Lu's hip, Walt's hands and mouth and cock itched to have Erin against the rough wall behind them. He gritted his teeth at it, blew his breath out through his nose, but refused to move even an inch away from her. Watching and hearing the scene, feeling her beside him and not doing a damn thing was fucking torture, but it was better this way. Because even if she went from seduced to shocked in a second over what she saw in front of them and took off, never to be seen again, Walt would stay by Erin until the second she said "enough." He could take it.

Gala squirmed again, mewling and whimpering until Lu released her tit, then gasping when Lu caught her creamy pink flesh in her hand and slapped it. She said something, too low to hear, and Gala's body shook with a new round of silent tears.

The urge to indulge the inclinations he'd let play for so many years pushed hard, right at the knowledge Erin was beside him. The scent of her warmed perfume rose to him, and he felt the folds of her skirt drag across his calf. She was here, not watching a demo but an authentic—and very hot—scene going on before her. At his side, seeing how he and his closest friends really were when they played. He tugged his gaze down to her.

She wasn't wide-eyed, not shocked or even a little bewildered. Her eyes drooped a little, almost like they did when she was on top of him, rocking on his cock and so close to coming. Deep grunts, whines, a long, slow cry registered, distantly, but it was all secondary. Nothing mattered but seeing Erin watching them. Her eyes flicked up to his and she flushed as she looked back to them. A sleepy grin twitched at one side of her mouth. As soon as it appeared, she took a breath and pursed her lips, probably trying like hell to not to let him catch her reacting to them. Without taking her eyes from the scene, she turned her face toward his. Her eyes fell closed with long, drawn-out sweeps of her lashes against her cheeks.

He bent to her. "You okay?"

"Yes," she said and snapped her mouth shut. Her fingers tightened around his.

"I think she likes you, Lu," Tate said, motioning with the paddle. "Come have a look." When Lucy reached his side, he parted his girl's thighs, exposing her shiny-wet pussy. He parked the paddle over his girl's scalded ass and leaned into the handle. "Now you open up for Miss Lucinda, and show her how wet you are for her."

He could see it like that with her. Erin, on her knees before him, red and whimpering and wet. How he'd feel, seeing her body bent to his will and dripping from being on the receiving end of it. How her pearly skin would light up, scarlet and purple, and the sound of her voice in his ears, telling him she was his. Calling him Sir.

Lu didn't waste any more time with conversation. She thrust her fingers deep into the waiting cunt before her, working her hand against Gala's pussy as the girl struggled to stay in one place. When Lu withdrew from Gala's body, her gloved hand gleamed with the girl's arousal. She turned to Tate and drew her fingertips across his lips, then placed her index finger against his tongue. He drew it into his mouth and sucked, followed with each one of her fingers.

Beside him, Walt heard Erin's breath catch.

Lu leaned past Tate's hand, pursing her lips, and blew across Gala's glistening pussy. Gala squirmed, shimmying her hips toward Lu's hovering mouth.

"Easy, darlin'," Tate said, smoothing his hand over Gala's hip. Lu stood again and started for her toybag, then stopped suddenly. Turning for Tate, she trailed the tips of her fingers over Gala's skin.

"What does she taste like?" she asked, so soft Walt wasn't entirely sure she'd said it, or if he'd imagined it.

Tate sank his fingers into his girl. He offered his other hand to Lu and drew her against him. "Well, come on, then," he said, his voice rumbling low in his throat. Lifting his hand from Gala, he placed a finger at the corner of his mouth and slicked his girl's fluid over his lip. "Come taste."

Before Walt could summon the logic to explain what he knew was about to play out in front of him, Lu clasped Tate's neck and pulled his mouth to hers. Flame to tinder, the intensity burst between them, two people he never would've put together. Lu pulled Tate's bottom lip between her teeth and, with the advantage in height from her boots, leveraged him between Gala's legs. Cradling her thighs in his hands, he braced against her and scooped handfuls of his girl's creamy ass as Lu worked at his lips.

The absolute last fucking thing he'd expected. From the surprised but very satisfied grin Tate gave Lu when she broke away, he was in the same mental uncharted territory as Walt, but very pleased to be there. Tate, never one for subtleties when he played, swooped in for one more kiss from Lu, which she not only consented to, but damn-near dove into, even pressing one gloved hand to Tate's bare chest as she swayed into him.

When they broke apart again, Lu staggered for an instant. Her eyes narrowed immediately, though, and her body went taut. She rounded Gala's prone body again, raking her fingertips over the girl's welted ass as she left Tate's side.

"Cane?" she murmured to him. Gala began to shake her head vigorously. Lu chuckled, nodding to Tate. "Oh yeah. Time for the cane."

She crouched in front of the whimpering girl, pushing at the strands of lank red hair covering her face.

"Miss…" Gala pleaded.

Lu's face warmed with an intense, adoring smile. Placing one hand on the corner of the bench, she cupped Gala's chin and the lifted bottom's gaze to hers. "Yes. For me. For us. Yes. Now be a good girl for me and lift that ass so Tate can cane it for me."

"M-Miss…"

"Up on your elbows, pretty," Lu purred, still gazing into the girl's eyes mere inches from hers, and adjusted the little kitten ear headband that had disappeared under Gala's gone-wild hair. "Elbows and knees, like a good kitty over her bowl of cream."

Gala shifted her torso over her elbows, sending her tits swaying toward Lu's face. She leaned in, drawing one into her mouth and sucking so hard her cheeks hollowed. Gala whined again, wagging her ass in Tate's direction. He picked up a cane—what looked like a good, springy one from Walt's perspective—and took a hard swing at her ass.

"Ow! Fuck!"

Tate landed another strike, hard and just below the first one. "Didn't Miss tell you to be quiet?"

Lu tapped Gala's cheek with one finger. When the girl opened her eyes, Lu smiled sweetly and brushed her lips with her own. "Shhhh. I know gags are so hard for you. So we won't do that unless we have to. Hmmm?"

Gala replied, the words lost in the girl's shuddering voice.

"Look at me, cupcake."

Behind them, Tate softly tapped another, sturdier cane against Gala's ass.

"O-Okay."

"Good girl," Lucy said, nodding. "How's this girl's sloppy cunt now, Tate?"

Tate came in close to his girl's wide-open pussy and bit down on one of the wet folds.

"Dripping," he said, chuckling. "Didn't I tell you?"

Lu hummed, laughing quietly. "You did mention it."

Tate laid a lengthy succession of quick raps on his girl's skin. She froze in place, only flexing and squeezing her toes as the intensity increased, and finished with one sharp blow. Once a new, bright red stripe came up on her, he started another series of raps, hitting fast, again and again on the same spot, until he stepped back for a power swing. When he'd striped up a good portion of Gala's ass, Tate set the bamboo cane aside and took out a thin, gray rod. Starting at her knee, he trailed the narrow tip along her inner thighs. She whispered to Lu, something that made both women laugh. Lu leaned forward, still laughing, and kissed the girl's forehead as she mussed her hair.

Tate flexed his hand around the narrow carbon rod and dug the tip deep into one of the deep red stripes.

Lu's hand still steadying her, Gala made a soft little mewl, but nothing more.

Tate laid into every mark on his girl, crossing the wider red welt with a narrow stripe that bloomed vivid purple right away. The girl rocked over her knees, swaying, as her breath shuddered through her chest. Lu watched—no, *admired*—it all, still holding Gala's head in one place. The girl was a champ, too. Her ass had to be on fire but she didn't wince away from Lu's gaze.

"Yes, Miss, please," Gala moaned after a wicked swat to the sweet cleft between her ass and thigh.

"He was right," Lu whispered. "I didn't think a sweet little thing like you would be, but you are, aren't you? You *are* a pain slut, cupcake."

Gala smiled up at Lu, her face a sweaty smear of makeup and tears and who knew what all. "Yes, Miss."

A fucking beautiful mess, that's what she is.

Walt cleared his throat as quietly as possible, and bounced his legs. Erin's fingers were almost a vice around his and her arm had gone stiff. He glanced down and found her looking back, her eyes pinched.

I'd like to go now, please, she mouthed silently.

Nodding, Walt guided them toward the door.

"No, wait, please." Gala's voice echoed through the still room. Walt turned, half-expecting to see the girl's hand reached toward them. But she was reaching for Lu, who had left Tate to his aftercare with his girl and was starting to gather her things. Gala's fingers splayed wide toward Lu, hovering in the dimness around her and Tate. It was obvious Lu was at the point of a decision, and she froze before it, looking across the room at the couple for a long stretch of seconds.

This was too close, too much intimacy for a bystander.

"Let's go," Walt whispered to Erin.

He was behind me. He didn't reach for my hand or try to speak as we climbed the stairs, but he matched each step of mine.

We passed small groups and couples at each turn. The house was full now, dimmed to golden evening light and nearly pulsing with sexual energy. It pressed against my skin, taunting with a siren's crooked finger. I saw and understood the *something* all around me, but I was not allowed to do more than acknowledge its presence. And that gulf—my newness and inexperience—once again keeping me from being part of, rather than observing, made me fist my hands at my hips.

I had to get out of there.

Walt knew. Or felt. His hand came to my elbow, respectable and non-threatening, not possessive and most certainly not forceful. "Let's head down the hall there, toward Tate's study."

Once we were inside, he closed the door behind us. "What's going on?"

"I want to go ho—back to my house."

"Okay." He stared down at me. *Why* hung in the air around us, even though he gave me the consideration of not asking.

My skirt twisted under my fingers, the rough tulle digging into my palms. I forced it from my fingers, huffing.

"I don't know what to call this. I don't know who to be here."

"Huh? Erin, you don't have to be like anybody. It's okay if this isn't for—"

"No, it's not that. Walt, I think I'm more like all of this," I said, arcing my hand across an imaginary scene in front of us, "than some of these people think they are."

His chin dipped a little, and he grinned at me. "It's a lot to take in. I forget about that."

"No, they thought I don't belong here. And I wanted to be her," I stammered, tugging at the thing compressing my ribs. Thirty, maybe forty minutes of actual, real-life observation and words were failing me again. Finally I crossed my arms over my waist and huffed out a hard breath. "I know this is an important night, Walt, but I need to leave."

"Hey, it's just a party." His thumb went to my wrist as his fingers closed around mine. "Let's get you out of here."

I heard Walt speaking to a number of guests, and I went through the social pantomime of saying good-bye to some of them as well. I followed him down the quiet hallway toward the kitchen, waiting silently as he retrieved his own belongings. At the sound of footsteps behind me, I stepped aside instinctively. Tate passed me, his arm wrapped close around a very disheveled, very dazed Gala, who still clung to Lucy's hand. Without a word to me, or Walt as he approached, they climbed the same back staircase he and I had ascended earlier.

Outside, in the cooling night air, we walked to his truck in self-contained silence. Separate. And I needed to feel his skin on mine so much.

Once we were clear of the house and on the main road, Walt took my hand.

"What happened?"

Nothing formed on my lips, but I let it wither there. Even in the dim interior of his truck, the concern on Walt's face was apparent. I could have revived that airless *nothing* and let him glide away, and if it wasn't Walt, I might have done that. Something about the man made me tell the truth. Likely, he knew it anyway.

"I felt awkward," I said. My voice sounded small and too young, and it piled on another layer of frustration. "I didn't know what to do."

"Didn't look that way. Thought you did fine."

I watched the road turning before us for as he drove back to Callahan, replaying snatches of interactions with Alex and Nicole, the sight and sound of Gala as Tate caned her. Lucy's voice telling me I was lucky to know them, that *the wicked people have a mountain.* All of them part and participant in something that was still little more than a tidy list of concepts to me. I had little fact to base my presence on.

"Why haven't we done anything since the night you spanked me?"

Surprise radiated from him. Walt shifted his body and inhaled, deep into his chest. "For a lot of reasons. Some of them were probably bullshit."

"Such as?"

"Kept telling myself you weren't ready." Before I could speak he added, "That was one of the bullshit ones, by the way."

I couldn't help but laugh a little. "Thanks for admitting that."

"Can't let you take the heat for everything." He turned into my driveway and parked a few steps from the front walk. "Look, Erin. I don't believe all that mystical crap about being called to Dominance, like it's some kind of damn knight's quest."

I slid myself around, leaning against the cool glass behind me as I faced him. "What do you believe?"

"I'm not an owner, you know? I'm not one of these guys who wants you to question your every breath to jack up my own ego." He pulled his keys from the ignition and bounced them against his palm a few times. "What I do know is that the idea of you on your knees for me gets me hard. I know the thought of pushing your body and telling you to do things that fuck with your head hasn't left mine since I met you."

"I want you to," I said quietly. "Why worry so much about something I want too?"

"I'm worried about it because some of those thoughts aren't pretty and romantic, Erin, and I feel like that about you too. If we start down this road and I scare you, I lose you. I'm not ready to consider that happening."

"It won't."

"Sweetheart, you just asked me to take you out of one of the best-run private parties around because you said you didn't fit in there, but you think I won't scare you away."

I reached for him. Everything I knew about myself told me not to risk it, but I took Walt's hand in mine anyway and drew myself to him. "I'm not scared. I didn't belong there because I didn't..." I studied his hand in mine, the wide palm, and his long, thick fingers. His thumb rested, naturally, on my wrist, stroking across my thudding pulse. "Walt, I didn't belong there because I didn't know how to be there with you. And for you, too."

"What?"

"Everyone keeps referring to me as your *girl*, and Lucy seems to know more details of our sex life than I would tell my best girlfriend, if I had one. There's this assumption that I already belong to you, and I don't know what belonging to you really means." I took in as much air as I could and said the hardest part. "And I want to, Walt. I'm not scared about that."

"I know." He looked out into the darkness, shifting his jaw as he usually did when he turned serious. "I care about you, Erin. I haven't...

cared about someone I've played with — cared like this — in a while. And it's not easy. It doesn't work out well for me when I get serious and mix it with kink."

"Then we won't do it." I sounded stupidly optimistic and nearly shook my head at myself because of it. "There aren't many people who make me feel anything more than superficially for them, Walt. You do. I'll take that over…other things."

His hand rose from mine and cupped my cheek. "You are something," he said softly.

I shrugged. "I'm a near-sighted thirty-five-year-old woman who's reasonably good at telling servers what to do. I have squishy thighs and live in a rented house in a town where I only know four people beyond the most cursory details."

"No," he said as his palm settled closer to my skin. "You're a hell of a lot more than that."

I turned my lips into his hand, my eyes fluttering closed as I inhaled his scent at his wrist. I kissed him there, and as it happened, I remembered Claire seated at Paul's feet, hours before, doing the same thing. Walt's arm stiffened under me. He'd remembered too.

Sitting back, I raised my eyes to his. And the same crashing vacuum claimed the air between us.

"Can I…" he started, but caught himself and went quiet over something. Finally, he continued. "I'd like to stay here. Tonight. Not go back to Tate's."

"Okay — I mean, of course. Sure. I hoped you would, actually."

"I will then." His fingers trailed over my lip as they passed, moving down the length of my neck until they came, gently, to rest at the base of my throat. Around us the light was dim, but I still saw his smile. "Gonna stay here."

CHAPTER ELEVEN

The next morning, I woke up after him. Walt usually stretched himself over my share of the sheets once I surrendered them, taking up the expanse of my queen bed with six-and-a-half feet of dozing, snoring man. But the morning after we left the Enclave, he was up first—well before me. He was showered, dressed, and had made me breakfast.

"This was a huge mistake, you know," I said as I munched a piece of bacon. "Where did you learn to bake?"

He glanced over his shoulder at me, grinning, as he pulled a tray of blueberry muffins from the oven. "Damn, you really think I'm just a big, dumb guy, don't you?"

"I hoped so, but you keep surprising me." I wrinkled my nose at him and managed to scoot my legs away from the tea towel he snapped in my direction.

"I need to run around a little this morning. Want to come with me?" He took a seat beside me. "Gotta go check my traps."

Checking his traps was Walt-speak for sweating profusely and serving as a buffet for mosquitoes while walking many miles uphill. His traps, I'd learned soon after we met, weren't for a large and ferocious predator, but something far more dangerous.

As part of his ongoing studies—something he dismissed as *more of a hobby than what amounts to a real master's degree*—in conservation biology, Walt was tracking a dangerous moth's infiltration of the forest around Callahan. Without a natural predator, the harmless-looking gray moth could munch away, undeterred, at the old-growth hardwood trees in Walt's forest.

"Um…sure." I would happily sweat and bleed again, just for the view of his legs and shoulders as they moved in front of me. "Promise you'll take your shirt off again?"

His calf curled around my chair, drawing me into him. "Ask me nice and I'll take my shirt off right here," he said with lips that tasted of bacon and blueberries and the familiar mint of my toothpaste. "Could take yours off too."

Humming, I sank into him, rasping my fingertips over the spiny stubble on his jaw. His breath warmed my neck as his hands delved inside my T-shirt, pushing it toward my shoulders, his fingers skating over my skin. Before I could draw his bottom lip between my teeth, Walt cleared his throat and gently pushed himself away.

"But…"

"Traps," he warned, chuckling as his eyebrows rose. "I'll make us some lunch. Go on and get dressed."

After our third hike together, I realized the trend for what it was. I was going to be outdoorsy with a man. But the man was Walt, so I willingly accepted his influence. New, more accommodating shorts would probably be wise. When I returned to the kitchen, wearing them — simultaneously regretting the larger size in the same thought that I was grateful I'd purchased a sensible, streamlined black — Walt scowled.

"Where's the brown ones?"

"Do you mean the khaki ones? They're too tight."

"Too tight? They show off your legs. Looked just right to me." Swinging his daypack over his shoulder, he stuffed a lone surviving piece of our breakfast bacon in his mouth. "Ready?"

Nodding, I hoisted my own new bag, accepting a full water bottle from him. The contents of my daypack would feel like they weighed three times their actual weight by the time we reached the stand of hardwood trees Walt was observing for gypsy moth infestation. Opening the contents, though, would be worth the burden.

Introduced species, I'd learned, didn't follow wide, well-maintained trails like those at Walt's park. We climbed from the banks of Sawtooth Creek, passing a primitive trail marker, and headed into the many acres of land still owned by the family who once ran Callahan Paper.

The trail we followed was little more than tamped-down grass, decaying leaves and mud, spotted with what he identified as deer tracks and the occasional offering of scat. Once we were on the trail, I twisted my hair into a top-knot again, huffing at the already damp strands escaping around my neck.

"Now that was bear," he said as I skirted stepped around one particularly impressive piece of evidence.

"Bear?" I froze, and looked up at him stupidly. "You mean real bears?"

"Yeah, and now you know why I'm carrying the real shotgun." He glanced away from me, slanting his head toward the firearm hung from his opposite shoulder.

"Hope you brought the real bullets too." I followed him, once more adjusting the weight of my daypack.

"Shells. I got them." He pushed a sapling aside for me. "To be honest, we'd be more likely to have trouble with humans than bears. A wild animal would smell us and take off before we knew they were there. Stupid humans, though…"

"Really? Why so far from the main roads?"

"Seclusion." He scanned the elevation before us warily. "This far back from the state road, on private property, you can bet most of the folks you meet aren't up this way for a picnic."

We were quiet for a time as we continued along the path meandering diagonally to the top of a ridge. He poked a mossy rock, a little heavily, with his age-smoothed walking stick as we passed.

"So what's in the book?"

"Book?" Quelling my hand before it could race to my backpack strap, I made a fist and tucked it in my shorts pocket instead.

"Seemed a little heavy when I got it out of the truck for you. Either you've got a book in that bag or you're carrying a couple of bricks."

I had planned to discuss Claire's notebook with him over lunch. When I wasn't winded and smacking at gnats and sniffing at sweat plinking from the end of my nose.

"You're too observant for my own good, you know."

His eyebrows wagged toward the brim of his faded blue baseball cap. "Gotta stay sharp when you're around, Miss Reboot."

"It's something Claire gave me," I said, accepting his hand to steady me as I stepped over a fallen log. "And a couple of notes I made."

"Notes?"

"Okay, a checklist."

After a moment's silence, he said, "I assume it's one of those Internet checklists."

"Yes." I sniffed defensively. "Claire suggested it. And I've looked at them before. Why? Does that bother you?"

"It doesn't." He passed his hand over my arm, squeezing gently as it came to rest above my elbow. "Just didn't realize you were so far into this. What's the thing of Claire's?"

"It's a workbook, journal kind of thing." I looked ahead, even though I felt him peering down at me. "About being a submissive."

"Hm. Well, Claire would know about that."

We crossed a dry stream bed. "Walt, why don't you call yourself a Dominant?"

"Well, there's more to it than just calling yourself Dominant, for one thing."

"But we...I mean, you said the first night we had dinner at Trattoria Stella, and again, after—you said it felt that way. Between us?"

"It does." After a second of too-long silence, he reached for my hand. I ignored it, walking forward and enjoying a bit of petulance. Walt's footsteps stopped. "Erin, come back here."

I stepped back to him.

"I think you have this idea of what a Dominant and submissive situation is, and that seems good to you, but do you know what you really want out of it?"

"You." The quiet in my voice surprised me, nearly as much as the surge of tension rippling over my shoulders. "I want to...I don't know—please you? And be guided? I admire the way you live, so relaxed about things. I want that too. And I did like it that time when you...er..."

He leaned away from me, carefully propping his rifle against a tree. When he beckoned me closer, his hand came to rest on my jaw.

"Y'know, that relaxed disposition you speak of is what some people like to call selfish and lazy."

"Surely you don't believe that about yourself."

Walt's eyes, startling blue under the faint shadow of his hat, watched me. "For a long time I've told myself just because something feels good or looks appealing doesn't mean I should get into it. That's not selfish, from where I'm looking at it. It is probably a bit of self-preservation, but for the better part of it, I've chosen not to get involved in D/s. Mostly because it's not felt right with the girl, and eventually that would cause a problem."

"But…?"

His thumb passed over my cheek, the weight of his touch dissolving the importance of everything around me but him. Finally he said, "So what's on your checklist?"

I couldn't help but smile. "Shouldn't you do one too?"

He stepped aside, pausing to check some mechanism on his gun before he slid the webbing strap over his shoulder again, and chuckled, deep in his chest. "Sweetheart, I know what's on mine. You want me to take charge, let's work on yours first."

"Um…well, I didn't think about submission other than sexually."

"So you're figuring out it can be more than kinky sex, huh?"

"Yes, I think so." I glanced at him and was surprised to find him watching intently. "I like the possibility of knowing what's expected of me."

"Yeah well, you don't like to draw outside the lines much, so that makes sense."

"And there's something about you that's solid. Pragmatic." I looked up at him again. "I like that too. A lot."

He nodded, eyes fixed ahead on the trail. Finally, he spoke again. "How many times did your mom move you and your sister around?"

I laughed. "Okay. That question's valid, I guess." He joined me, holding up a hand in protest. "No, it is. I've wondered about it too. But…growing up with Kathy, and then Dani following in her footsteps, seems more like a cautionary tale against being captive to the whims of a man rather than a reason to eroticize them. And why are you changing the subject?"

"Maybe I'm still getting to know you and they're part of who you are."

"Maybe I don't want to talk about them."

"Maybe it's my prerogative to ask you about them."

"You're as hesitant to dig out the family history books as I am, Walt."

His head inclined toward me and he shrugged. "Okay. Fair enough. One for one then."

"You first," we said together.

"All right, ladies first."

Since Walt had brought it up, I stayed on the same topic. "What happened to your mom?"

"Damn." He winced theatrically, clutching a make-believe wound. "C'mon, Erin, you know this."

"I know your grandparents raised you. That's different."

"Yeah, I suppose." He scratched his earlobe, as he often did when disarmed. "She had me young, with a guy from high school who never came home again once he joined the Air Force. I don't know how hard he really tried to find him. And once she got sick…From what my grandparents would say, she kept to herself a lot, and you know, back in the seventies…in a small town…"

I made a small noise and nodded. I knew very well how small towns could be.

"Do you remember her?"

He turned a small, sad smile toward me. "Not really. There's a few pictures. I've got most of them, since we cleaned out the house and my granddad's moved to senior care." He brightened a little and added, "Y'know, I look like her."

For some reason this pleased me and I turned to him happily. "Do you?"

"Yeah." He seemed to like that too. "She was tall and had the same curly dark brown hair. Wore it long. She liked music. Played piano, and the French horn in her high school band."

The small detail suddenly swung the emotional scales too much toward him. He seemed too vulnerable to me, and I didn't want him to feel alone and exposed. I blurted out, "We moved four times when I was in elementary school, twice in middle school, and every year of high school."

"Ten times in twelve years? Can't imagine."

"Occasionally, it was for a job, but I think sometimes a relationship had gotten rocky, and maybe it ended badly. Sometimes, I think she was just bored. Kathy—I mean, my mother."

"I've lived in four places. My grandparents' house, college, barracks at Fort Campbell during the summer I did air assault school and…and, well, once I graduated, I started with the park service and moved into the cabin." He quieted, looking into the distance for a long stretch of seconds, finally clearing an unspoken thought with a slight shake of his head. "I wonder sometimes if I've seen enough of the world for thirty-seven years of living in it."

"That's jumping out of airplanes? Air assault?"

"No, helicopters. With a rope. It's called fast rope. But we hauled in big loads, too. Cargo, water, and fuel containers," he said, somewhat hardened.

"Why didn't you go on to the Army after finishing something like that? It sounds like intense training."

"Wasn't for me." He guided me over a fallen tree. "Brady was the soldier. Not me."

"But you said you and Brady…" He was too quiet, and his jaw was too tense. "Walt, if you'd rather not…"

"Hey, it's okay. You don't know this, and they're fair questions. Especially considering what you're carrying around in that backpack." He smiled down at me. "Brady and me hit it off, right from cadet orientation freshman year at Clemson. We roomed together, ran around together. I spent Christmases and school breaks with his family. Hell, we both even went after Lu when we saw her. Ever heard the saying 'brother from another mother'?"

I nodded, laughing softly. "I always wanted Dani to be *from* another mother. And another family entirely."

"Well, that was Brady and me. And once Lu shattered our illusions about who was going to bring her to the Homecoming game, she was our sister. Me and Lu were sort of orphans in our own way, and the whole Corbin family, not just Brady, took us in."

"I've never been that close to anyone." I'd always ached for distance from Mom and Dani, not more connection.

"I hadn't been," he said. "Not till I met Brady and Luce."

"But why did you leave cadets?"

"I had to. If I didn't leave, I would have been kicked out. Out of Clemson, too."

This was completely at odds with who I knew Walt to be. Expulsion from college seemed too serious—threatening—for him. "What? Why?"

"I was a discipline problem. Or our cadet bat commander said I was. The problem got worse and worse until one night there was an altercation."

I stopped, raising my eyebrows. "Altercation? This doesn't sound like you."

Walt came to a stop too, his hands on his hips. "Erin, it was a long time ago. I'm not proud of how I did it, but what I did was right. These guys, they weren't much more than kid bullies raised with too much money and too little sense about how to treat people. They pushed me too far one night. I pushed back. Brady got wind of it, jumped in and pushed some more. It was more than bumps and bruises, and that meant real disciplinary action from the school—not just something to be taken care of in the cadre. The other guys had broken bones, jaw, a concussion. I got a separated shoulder and broken arm. Someone had to take the heat for the fight, and the Corbins have four generations before Brady of service. If it hadn't been for Brady's dad, I would have been booted out of school too. Leaving cadets was a compromise to keep me and those guys away from each other."

"Walt," I muttered. The details were lost on me. I had little interaction with military people, only one man my mother had dated for a time. There was information missing, likely something difficult he didn't want to share. But what he was saying underneath was critical. He'd protected Brady, taking on the full weight of a loss—his friend's family's traditions—that would be too much to bear. Suddenly, I remembered the first night we'd met in Charlotte, his dismissal of the scene name someone else had given him. "That's why you don't like being called Ranger."

He nodded. "Holly started calling me that. She thought it would be some kind of memorial to Brady after he was killed in Afghanistan." When I looked up at him, confused, he shook his head. "Yeah. I know, I didn't get it either. But Holly...well..."

"She didn't understand?"

"No. But Holly romanticized the whole story—the fight, me taking the blame and saving his honor or some shit like that. Him going on to Ranger school and then deployed so many times and married to…to a marine who was also his slavegirl. Shit, it *is* a story, Brady and Hailey. And people do that, especially people like her. They fetishize sadness. I didn't encourage it, so the scene name didn't catch on much, and well…truth be told, you were right about that other stuff. The guardian, forest is who you are stuff, I mean. It didn't seem so bad after a while. Tolerable, I suppose." With red ears, he grinned down at me and squeezed my hand. "Just don't tell Lu. She'll laugh her ass off and I'll never hear the end of it."

I rose on my toes, looping my arms around his neck. "I promise. Our secret."

We walked on in easy quiet, up a narrow path that zig-zagged up to the top of a high ridge. After a final few steps, we crossed the ridgeline to the top of the hill. Below us stretched a verdant landscape of massive hardwood trees, punctuated with orange rectangles hung from a number of branches. Walt took several minutes on his own, setting up a digital camera and a hard plastic-covered clipboard in a smaller shoulder bag.

"Once I'm up, you care to hand me that?"

Reaching overhead, he swung himself parallel to the ground, twisting his body with a short, deep grunt. When he was upright and sitting on a thick tree branch, he balanced there and began threading a thick purple rope through a metal clip.

I glanced at the orange, open-sided boxes hanging high in the tree canopy and back to him, dubious. "How are you going to write and take pictures *and* hold on?"

"Like I always do," he called down. "By huggin' a tree."

"Why don't you let me help you?"

"It's okay. I do this twice a month, from March till November. I can handle it."

"I know you can. But I could make it a little easier for you."

He watched me for a few seconds, considering. "All right. You'll need to write the species, date, time of day, and coordinates from the GPS on my watch in that notebook, just like I did on the last page. Here, head's up." He passed his heavy black sports watch to me. "I'll call down and tell you the sample number to record everything with."

For two hours Walt let me help him. I followed from tree to tree, scribbling down notes for him and alternately clutching his backpack. I winced over his scaling the old hardwood trees with little more than a series of knots and a piece of fallible metal to care for him. Once he was back on the ground, he checked over everything I'd written, nodding with a silent smile when he finished.

"You're a good research assistant's assistant. I think I'll keep you," he said and tucked me into his arm for a kiss. "Can't pay you much, though."

"I'm very willing to barter."

Laughing, he settled me into his arm and directed us toward a cluster of giant hardwoods. "*Willing to barter*, you say? I like my odds. Why don't we have some lunch and I'll see what I can find for your dessert, then?"

"Not many people other than Tate and Claire, and Lucy—and a couple of other people who aren't around anymore—know something about me, Erin. But before we talk any more about playing, you need to."

"Okay," I said, swallowing hard. Walt often picked up conversations he'd left idle for hours or even days, something I was beginning to understand and follow like my own shifting planes of focus. He had already revealed so much. "What's this about?"

"When we first got together, you asked me when I knew I was kinky. And I told you I was seventeen."

"Yes?"

"It was my first serious girlfriend and me. We played quite a bit after we figured out we liked it."

Walt looked past me into the tree canopy, his eyes fierce. Unsure how much encouragement or silence he needed to continue, I gave his fingers a gentle squeeze.

"It was a mistake," he said, and shook his head at the conciliatory noise I made. "No, not what we did, but how I handled myself once her parents found out."

"Oh...God, Walt..."

"And that went about as well as you'd think it would." His eyebrows rose and he set his jaw. "I loved Melissa. I mean, we were kids, but as much as a kid could, I loved her. And she loved me too. Her friends—hell, even her mom, sometimes—they'd go on about us, how intense we seemed about each other. Before it all came out, they acted like it was a good thing."

"Oh, Walt," I muttered again, stupid with dread. We sat, quiet, for a minute. "There's more, isn't there?"

"Yeah." He considered stopping there. I saw a decision before him, and saw him debate it.

"Walt, you don't have to—"

"They said I forced her." He looked past me coolly. "And Mel agreed with it. It was bad enough to her parents, us having sex. But the kink? They didn't understand it. Hell, I didn't understand it either, and I was doing it. But I knew then I liked it. And I was not ready to explain that to my grandparents. Which is why I spent all of those Christmases and school breaks with Brady's family."

"Oh no." I winced. I knew about his upbringing with his grandparents in rural Tennessee, but not with many details about them. "Walt, I'm sor—I don't know how you'd…" I looked at his big hand in mine again, lost for the right thing to say.

"Hey," he said. "It's okay. Still here, aren't I?"

"Yes." I nodded and touched his arm. Under my fingers, a chilly sweat skimmed his skin. "You survived."

"When her father and my granddad sat me down and accused me of it, that was about the worst thing I'd been through. I didn't remember much about my mom or when she passed, never knew my dad. So having to look my granddad in the eye…"

"Walt…"

"It was pretty bad."

"Did they—were the police involved?"

"No," he laughed humorlessly. "And that's one of the biggest fucked-up parts of it, considering Granddad retired from the county sheriff's department. Because if I'd done what they said I'd done, and what Mel let them say I'd done…"

"But you didn't—" The word turned to putty in my mouth. "You didn't force her."

I wouldn't say it—*Did you?*—because he had never given me reason to think otherwise. But I wondered, not because of Walt. Because I saw it really happen to Danielle, and then watched as everyone in our lives, even our own mother, told her it didn't, not really, because Dani was always in the wrong clothes with the wrong boy at the wrong place and time.

"Erin, I didn't figure that out for three years. I know Mel asked me that first time, and every time after that there was some *thing* she did or said that made it seem okay. I didn't know better: that I should ask her outright every time. I didn't know what negotiation meant. It got bad for me after I left cadets. I figured I'd fucked up at that and fucked up with Mel. I was in pretty bad shape. Depressed. Thinking about ending it all. If Lu hadn't dragged me to the student counseling center, I don't know if I could have made it."

"I'm...Oh, Walt."

"But, I can tell you every single thing that happened that first time because I've been over it more times than I can count since then, and I believe we were on the same page."

"Of course you were," I said, much too quickly.

He glanced at me and shook his head. "But she changed her mind. If she'd just said something, we could have stopped. I loved her; that wouldn't have changed." His last words hung heavy on his voice. He sounded exhausted, and I wondered how many times he'd repeated the words to himself over the span of his adult life. "I don't want to be that guy again. I've come as close as I care to with you, back when we'd just met. I didn't do what I knew was right then."

"Walt," I said, leaning closer to him. "I'm not a seventeen-year-old girl who doesn't know how to stand up for her own decisions."

"No. I don't suppose you are."

For a while, we were quiet, nothing around us but forest sounds and wind in the leaves above us. Finally I sat back from him. Reaching behind me, I felt for my backpack, and took Claire's notebook from it, opening to my checklist. I took a quick breath and read. "Bondage by straight jacket. No. Hard limit."

He looked on, silent and unreadable.

"Bondage by scarves. Yes, very curious." I shifted the notebook in my hands, placing it on my bent knees. "Bondage by spreader bar. Yes, very curious. Bondage by rope. Yes, very curious. Bondage by rope with suspension. Yes, mildly curious." I shrugged and glanced at him. "I'm afraid of falling or breaking the rope."

"Rope's stronger than it looks." His voice was different. Deeper, without the accent I knew so well. "If rope can hang trees and pianos, it can hold up a person."

Walt hadn't moved at all. Still, the sensation of him so close I couldn't see or hear anything else was undeniable. "Bondage by tape. No, due to allergies."

"It would tear up your skin anyway. I wouldn't do it."

"Bondage by leather. Yes, very curious." I rifled through the pages. "That covers bondage, I guess. Um…okay, photography. Unsure."

"Unsure?"

I looked up from the notebook. "Unsure. I'm…" A surge of panic churned my stomach and I shook my head at it. Walt pushed himself forward, taking the notebook from my hands.

"Hey, what's that thought?"

"I don't know. I—"

"Yes, you do." He pushed at the limp strands of hair fanning around my glasses. "What's wrong with pictures?"

"I don't know *why*." Every word was lead on my tongue, barely pushing past my teeth. "I'm not sure why anyone would ask."

"Because they'd want to remember how beautiful you were when they didn't have you with them. Because they'd want to see your skin all warmed up and pink from their hands. Because they'd want to have proof for themselves they got you to make that face you make when you come."

He stopped me when I reached for the binder, catching my hand in his.

"But I need my notes—"

"No you don't," he said, settling my hands on my knees. "Is it okay if I ask the questions?"

I nodded, swallowing. "Sure."

"Sensation play with nails, teeth, and lips?"

"Yes. Very curious." The idea of Walt, doing things to me with his nails, teeth, and lips followed, making me shiver.

"Sensation play. Temperature."

"Temperature?"

"Ice cubes, hot wax."

"Oh," I said, considering. "Yes. Curious. But not burning."

"No, no burning." He grinned and moved closer. I tried to adjust my position, but he shook his head and steadied my legs as they were, against his. "Sensation play with needles, hair pulling, suction, pinching."

"Yes, very curious."

Walt's eyebrows rose a little. "Even needles?"

"I think so. But not those hooks."

"That's a different kind of play, and I don't know how to do it."

"Those yogis in India—"

Wincing, he threw up a hand. "Damn…no. Red."

"Really?" I was suddenly fascinated. "You've done this—"

"Sadomasochism, Erin, not *this*," he said, grinning.

"*Sadomasochism.* BDSM. You've done this for so long, I'm surprised."

"Sweetheart, everybody's got limits. That's one of mine. Don't want to see it, think about it, or especially do it. And I damn sure don't want to see my girl's skin all pulled out—" He made a particularly revolted grimace. We laughed together for a moment until what he said came clear.

"Your girl?"

"Yeah. My girl."

"Oh…" Unable to look from him, I twisted my fingers together.

"Don't," he said, separating my hands and returning them to my knees. "Sensation play, clamps on nipples?"

"Yes. Very curious," I said—*very* agreeably.

"Oh, I see. *Very curious.* Gonna have to remember that." He chuckled until he caught sight of my hands creeping from my knees. Then his eyebrow quirked. "Put your hands back on your knees, Erin."

Suddenly my perception of and participation in the conversation shifted. *Oh…*

"I'm sorry," I whispered, clutching my knees, my teeth nearly chattering at the tickling flush soaking the muscle and bone in my shoulders.

"No need to be sorry, you're doing good. Now turn your hands over, palms up."

I opened my hands, flexing them at the tension hemmed into my fingers.

"I just asked you about nipple clamps, didn't I?" I hummed my response to him, nodding. "I thought so. Sensation play, clamps on pussy?"

My knees twitched, and I pressed them into the pine needles under me. "You mean down—"

"I mean clamps on your clit and your lips." Again, my knees rose and Walt's hands covered them, solid but gentle. His voice dropped, so quiet I could have missed it had I not been bound to every sound he made. "Don't move, Erin. Are you curious about clamps on your pussy? Keeping you open and holding you still for me?"

"Yes." The memory of my surprising realization in the shower came into focus. "I had this fantasy…"

"And I put clamps on your pussy, didn't I?"

I nodded, my breath-sounds swelling in my ears. "Well, just one."

Walt's hands brushed over mine, settling beside them on my thighs. "Just one? I guess that would be enough if I wanted to keep a little pressure on your clit, remind you how swollen I made it."

"Yes." The weight of his hands never wavered, but my legs were slowly heating under them, curling the muscles taut, coaxing my knees to rise and grind together at the warmth building between them. Quickly, I pushed them back to the earth under me. Walt chuckled at me and I squirmed again as the vibrations of his laugh settled, stoking the ache.

"Bet it would keep you still too. What about impact?"

"Impact? Like hitting?"

"Well, I know you like your ass spanked. You looked pretty interested in that leather paddle of Tate's last night."

"I was," I said. I should have been struggling with myself, given the subject matter, forcing my eyes to stay open and focused on him. But staying with Walt, waiting and watching as he questioned me was the simplest, hardest thing I'd experienced. Being this open to him was so surprisingly easy, even as he lead me further into uncharted territory. "Yes, very curious."

"What else?"

"Floggers, those big ones of yours?"

"Really?" He looked pleasantly surprised and my pulse tumbled over itself. *I've pleased him.* "We can do that."

"And crops. Canes. And um…a belt." My eyes flitted to his waist. He was, sadly, missing one.

Walt leaned forward. "Not today, sweetheart." His palms lifted away, leaving his fingertips brushing along my thighs. I watched as he scaled higher but too late took notice of my shorts, bunched toward my hips. "Stay still."

Yes, Sir.

He shifted again, stretching my legs past his hips. "What about orgasm?"

I blinked stupidly at him. "I'm all for them?"

"Yeah, I do know that about you." He tugged my panties away, and suddenly his fingers were inside, twin points stroking over the tight, wet skin under them. "What if I told you no, you weren't allowed to come?"

He feathered his fingertips over me, drew me open with his palms. Gasping out his name, I clenched my knees. He stopped, though his hands didn't draw away.

"Erin, I told you not to move." Before I could open my mouth to apologize, he said, "Don't say you're sorry. Just don't do it again. All right?"

"Mmm…okay."

His fingers went to work again, teasing, dragging and circling, so maddeningly slow. "Answer the question."

"I'd hate it."

"You'd hate it if I teased you like this," he said as he stroked the slick channels around my clitoris, something he'd discovered sent me whining the first time we were together. "And made you walk back to the truck. Wet. Needing to come so bad."

"Oh God, Walt…"

"Don't." One blunt-tipped finger pushed, dipping inside me. "Look at me, Erin."

My breath rattled out in short gasps. I whined again, driving my palms hard into the ground. "I'm not looking anywhere else."

Another finger dodged inside me and still that fingertip stroking, edging around the throbbing nerves, lulling me, deeper and dazed over him.

"You want me to decide?"

I nodded, so much my wobbly glasses slid down the bridge of my nose. I gritted my teeth against the urge to right them, a motion more reflex than intention, I did it so often. I fought and kept my gaze on Walt.

"You look so beautiful right now." A momentary need to comment, maybe demur, or convince him otherwise fizzled with the thrust of his fingers. Harder. Deeper. I listed forward, nearly toppling into his chest, and Walt leaned closer, circling my hips between his strong thighs, his calves supporting my back. "Got you," he whispered.

"Okay." My nails bit into the pine needles and bits of gritty leaves under them. I held on. I stayed with him, still watching him, watching what he was doing to me.

"You want to come?"

"Yes," I said, so desperate and so elated, breathy and pleading, I shook at the sound of my own voice. "Walt, yes, please."

"Ask me."

"Walt, may I come?"

His hands stilled, and somehow I understood I should as well. Dangling, so close. "Who's in control, Erin?"

"You." I rushed to say it, smiling and certain I'd produced the right answer.

"No, baby. You are. You're the one giving me everything, letting me see you like this, with your hair all fallin' down crazy, and your glasses barely hanging on your nose." He smiled at me with something so close to adoration, I froze. The connection between us wasn't merely an open path, it blazed, a shimmering current snaring me and holding me so close, I almost felt truly blinded by it. "You're putting everything right here in the palm of my hand. You're submitting to me, but you're the one giving me control."

Submitting. This was submission. Not taking, but giving.

"Do you want it?" For a beat, he stayed quiet, his face full of placid fascination, watching as I struggled to stay still under his hands. And finally, I nearly keened out his name, so close to coming around his fingers merely from the warm fullness of them inside me. I would have given him any tangible thing to prove to him I was his to do with as he pleased. Like this, I was all I had to offer to him. My voice was a trembling, ragged whisper. "S—W-Walt, do you want me?"

"Yeah, Erin. I do. All of you. Now, you come for me."

And as he told me to, I was. His fingers twisted inside me, touching new nerves, and he pressed further, tugging my clitoris gently between his finger and thumb. Wailing, my eyes clenched shut as another, nearly unbearable wave turned me rigid and called my hips to bear down at it. My nose filled with the sharp scent of my body, mingling with the earthy tang of pine needles, and then the safe, familiar smell of Walt's skin.

Overhead, out there in the tree canopy a bird screamed, a counterpoint to my hard pants.

"Shhh…just an old crow. Give me one more, sweetheart."

I did, nearly sobbing over it, and clenched his forearms as it became too much.

His arms were around me. My legs were around him. And he was hard, pressing against me, making me tremble for him again. I reached for the waistband of his shorts.

He caught my hand. "It's okay —"

"No, please? I need to, Walt…please?" Scrambling to wobbly thighs, I knelt in front of him, fingers hovering and waiting to take him in my hands. "Please?"

Please, Sir?

His eyes bounced to his lap, then back to me. "All right," he muttered. Finally, his smile came, turning the tension and fear of asking for him to heated flirtation. Walt leaned back on his elbows. "I should make you ask me outright instead of talkin' around the subject of my cock in your mouth."

"I can't be perfect the first time." I giggled, punch-drunk, as I hovered over him, ready to slide him across my lips.

"Damn near close."

Later, I sat back on my heels, lips still buzzing with the feel of him skimming across them again and again, and the musky taste of him on my tongue. "So?"

"Okay," he said finally, pushing himself up to me.

"Okay?"

"What Claire can't teach you, I will." His fingers trailed over my lip as they passed, moving down the length of my neck until they came, gently, to rest at the base of my throat. "We'll get started next weekend."

CHAPTER TWELVE

Play

> The first time you encounter an item purposefully
> constructed for consensual BDSM play you might
> marvel at the idea anyone could call "that" a toy. Our
> toy boxes hold everything from the softest feathers
> to heavy braided leather floggers, silk scarves and
> electrical stimulation devices, not to mention the
> expected whips and chains. And some of the items you
> find would look suspiciously like something you'd find
> in the kitchen or home improvement aisles at your
> favorite big-box store.

Since they included me in their circle of intimate friends, I'd
heard Walt, Claire, and Lucy mention visiting "Home D-Perv," and
of course I'd visited Kinky Outfitters that first night with Walt. Lucy's
kitchen was commonly referred to as the kinky kitchen, though she
claimed to rarely use the space for cooking. Tate had apparently fitted
the long butcher's block island he built for her with hidden eyebolts,
whatever those were.

> If you've never seen some of the toys we play with, I
> suggest you make yourself familiar with them. Someday

a nice Dom/me might want to use one of them on you. For your safety and education, I'd recommend browsing a few online stores so you can look as long as you need to at large range of what you might find in a Dom/me's toybag.

Reaching past Claire's notebook, I found my glass of iced tea. How did Walt just know the right factors of tea bags, sugar, and ice? How was he good at so many unexpected, under-appreciated things?

What looks interesting to you? What have you seen before? What is completely new and intriguing and what is new and terrifying? It's okay to think some of these out-of-the-ordinary gadgets are frightening. Some of them, in fact, are meant to scare you. If you need and want that as part of your submission, great. Just know you don't have to like everything on offer out there.

There is no single definition of what a submissive is or of what she or he must enjoy. This investigation will eventually lead you, as an educated submissive, to understanding your limits. You'll know where you absolutely won't go, what you might consider, what you have to try immediately once you find a compatible and sane Dom/me to help you give them a whirl, and you'll even find a few things you think look like a bore. However, you need to know, before you enter into even discussing a BDSM relationship of any kind, just what you will not do and what is negotiable. These are called your hard and soft limits, and I feel it's imperative they are ingrained in you before you look for that first partner.

It is important that you're not so infatuated with the idea of finally being able to play with one of these interesting species we call Dominants that you'll be willing to do anything just so you can get to the fun parts! **Don't**. I've done it, have seen other subs do it.

Once again, as I say in every part of this workbook — it is your responsibility to take care of yourself. Any variety of submission to a Dominant does not give you a free pass from self-awareness, self-esteem, and self-nurture. And never, ever forget, aftercare is a Dom/me's responsibility. If a Dominant leaves you after a scene without any attention to your body, if they don't check in with you the next day regarding your physical and mental state, never give them that control over you again. They aren't worth it, and they are unsafe.

Sensory exploration

How would a scene involving the most intriguing thing you saw during your online shopping trip appear? Would your Dom/me be gentle, hard, connected to you, demanding, quiet, spinning a web of taunts, encouraging you to go further toward your limits? Try to imagine the kind of aftercare your body might need after using this toy.

Aftercare, so far, meant nothing more than orgasm-induced sleep, curled into Walt's shoulder, with his breath rustling my hair. Care meant I might need more than a nap or a few extra kisses. It meant the possibility of hurt and not of the variety that left memory-raising marks on my skin.

Condensation rolled from the lip of my glass, landing on my wrist. Shivering at it, I set my tea and Claire's notebook aside.

Down the narrow hallway that ran the length of my house, Walt was drilling…something. With a drill. He explained it all, and I had agreed to this drilling and installing of whatever it was over my bedroom door. Walt said things about headers and hard points and load bearing walls, and I just beamed up at him as we walked through Home Outfitters because after we were finished buying this thing called an eyebolt, there would be dinner. And then I would come home by myself, take off my clothes, and sit on my knees, waiting. For him.

After another week, and forced to fit it around another wave of patches to the data center operating system for me and two off-hours calls back to Poplar Branch for Walt, we finally sat down and talked about what the people at the Enclave called "playing"—doing an actual, formal scene—and about Walt and me, as Dominant and submissive.

I wanted him to tip me over into this deep end, finally, and let me go under a few times. We compromised. Agreed to sensory play, possibly another spanking, a deerskin flogger. More, if he felt I was ready. *Lightly.* But Walt's past was worth respect, as was my inexperience and my upcoming week-long trip back to Main House for project meetings and a wrap-up with my management prep group. So, all things considered, compromise was the word for us.

And Sir. This time, Sir and his girl.

They were simple, commonplace, one-syllable words but meant so much more to me. It felt different. Already, just the notion of truly, intentionally letting go, giving up, being his to control, made me feel different about this world I'd wondered about for so long. It wasn't merely what he might do to me, and I wanted him to be much harder with me than he seemed to feel comfortable about. It was because what would happen was between us, and how I was coming to see him. He was more than the promise of kinky sex and the exploration of my masochistic tendencies.

"All right," he said, ducking through the passage into the living room. "We're squared away. What are you up to, there?"

"Oh, ruminating. My favorite hobby."

He grinned, leaning down to me for a kiss. "How 'bout a new hobby?" He touched my lips with his. Once, then again. I giggled silently against his mouth. "Something involving less worrying and more of that."

I inhaled and smiled up toward him. "Okay."

We met at Trattoria Stella. Somehow the restaurant had become ours in four visits. Our place. The genial and perfectly stereotypical Italian owner — Isolde, who insisted on dubbing herself our *Fairy God-Nonni* — adopted us as her project, introducing us to her secret off-menu specialties. I said she paid attention to us because of Walt's smile. He disagreed, said it was because of how we looked at each other.

"Later," he whispered into my ear as his finger brushed against my neck.

The restaurant was dim, warmed with candles and the tiny lights strung above us. Nonni Isolde sat us in an alcove away from the main dining area, almost as if she knew something closer, more intimate was happening between us. And anyway, it was okay to shiver and let my cheeks heat over Walt. No one here would miss the obviousness of his affection, but no one would question it, either.

I glanced at my hands in my lap, let my eyes close at the heat from his finger and the chill cresting over me, bathing my skin and bone with my response to him. My lips parted, breath falling deep into my abdomen, and I heard him inhale similarly. We were quiet for a matter of seconds, connected by the rise and fall of our bodies taking in the air between us, then exhaled together, ragged…ready.

"Damn," he muttered.

After a meal of my favorite chicken piccata, we took my chocolate espresso cake and his *budino* to go. Separate cars, so I could drive home alone and have a few minutes to myself. To prepare for him.

We held hands, stopping only to gather phones and carry-out bags and shake hands with Isolde, who liked to pat our cheeks.

Walt grinned down at me as he opened my car door.

"Careful going home, sweetheart." He took my hand again, his thumb sliding over my knuckles. *Sweetheart* made me smile every time he said it, intoxicated over him. He knew it.

"I'll see you *soon*."

After a final pass of his lips over mine, he started down Main Street, then stopped.

"Hey, Erin? Brush your teeth." He chuckled and turned for his truck once more.

Oh, no, buddy.

Pursing my lips, I reached in my bag, following him as I turned the white tablet in my fingers.

"Walt?"

He stopped, grinning playfully, not seducing.

"Have an Altoid." I smirked and slid the little mint between his lips. He caught my retreating hand in his and leaned over it, tracing the rise of my thumb with his tongue, finishing with a tiny bite at my wrist.

"See you," Walt said, cocky and flirtatious and infuriating in the best way possible. I watched him walk from me, not caring that he most likely heard my whimpering after his broad shoulders fading into the early evening light.

At home, I brushed my teeth four times. Plus mouthwash. Then a final brush, just for insurance.

I arranged myself as he instructed, kneeling, palms open and upright on my knees. Hair pinned loosely with a few waves escaping—a deviation, but because he liked it that way. And not a single, scant item of clothing on my body.

Ready.

His key tumbled in the front door and he rustled in. Two heavy thumps. Bags, one with clothes for the next morning, most likely. And another one. The wheeled carry-on he called his toybag.

"Erin? I'm here, do you hear me?"

Not only were my eyes downcast, I realized, they were winched shut. I sat as I was supposed to, but my body was in revolt, shaking at the already soaring adrenaline in my veins. His voice, his presence and what they forecast spiked me close to overload.

"You can answer as I ask you questions, Erin."

"Y—" I paused, so ready to say it. A simple response to him. It felt like opening a gate to a long sought-for country. "Yes, S—" My eyes clouded a little and I furrowed my brow at the tears. *Not the time.*

So hyper-aware of everything around me, I felt the air change when he came into my bedroom. After a matter of seconds, I felt his hand on my cheek, tracing down my jawline. Once again, the little quakes took over my body, covering my skin and arcing toward him.

"Hey…Erin?" His voice resonated through my body, settling in my navel.

"H…h…"

Oh damn!

I tried again, swallowing at the thick lump in my throat.

"Hello," I replied, barely whispering a ragged whisper.

My adrenaline surged, and I tried to focus on the conversation I'd had with Claire, her advice for the first few minutes. I'd be overwhelmed, she reasoned, because I had so many ideas but little practical application of them. There were suggestions about breathing and staying *in the moment*—something Claire said frequently—and when I sniffed at her suggestion before I could censor myself, her soft laugh joined mine.

A mantra, she suggested. Something to keep me in the now, with Walt.

With Sir. For the next few hours: *Sir.*

Moment to moment…moment to moment…moment to moment.

My teeth began to chatter noisily and I wobbled, threatening to fall over in front of him.

Suddenly the comforter from my bed was floating around me; I felt him descend to the floor and sit in front of me. He took my hands, his thumbs brushing over my wrists.

"Hey, sweetheart, look at me."

I glanced up quickly, then looked down again.

"girl, look at me."

"I can't."

"I need you to tell me what's going on."

I twisted the ends of my comforter around me, still shivering, and buried my face in the deep folds. He would see me undone and useless to him. *Aftercare.* He would have to take care of me. I couldn't do it myself this time. And Walt had made sure I understood he wanted to take care of me afterward.

"Erin, we're going to be honest about this, remember? Above everything."

"I — *shit!* I'm terrified I'm going to do it wrong. I don't know what to do."

"You're okay, *Erin.* That's why I'm here. *You* don't have to know the answers now."

I looked up and found Walt sitting before me on the floor, legs crossed, in the same pair of battered jeans he'd worn the night we met and a navy T-shirt. No scary dungeon-wear, no weird alter-ego. Walt. Just like he promised.

Moment to moment…

I counted my breaths and felt my body still. With the absence of the high tension, my thoughts slowed as well, clearing to my mantra. Nothing more.

He slid forward, our knees barely touching.

"I'd like to try something."

"Yes, S—"

"Hey, let's just try yes and no, okay? This formal stuff's too much for you right now."

"I've attached so much meaning to it." The simple insight surprised me.

"That's understandable. You've waited a long time for this."

I glanced up at him, hardly containing a smirk that wouldn't be possible between couples at the Enclave. "You've made me wait long enough for this."

"I've waited long enough for this myself."

We stared at each other for a long moment. The balance of the evening could have gone either way in those minutes, but I sensed there would be no coming back if I let nervous giggles dilute the live current hovering between us. I sat back on my heels and nodded to him.

"All right, and we're going slow, no script, no expectations?"

"Okay."

He picked up a few strands of my hair and let it fall through his fingers.

"What is this, Erin?"

"Um…"

"Shhhh. Go with me." He drew my hair through his fingers again. "What is this?"

"My hair," I answered, wondering.

"Go with me, Erin. Don't question it."

"My hair," I repeated, more confident in him, dismissing my questions.

"It's beautiful." He glanced away, drawing his eyebrows together as he cleared his throat, then looked to me again. "The first time I saw you, I thought something crazy…it looked like you'd dripped moonlight over your head." A small smile transformed his face, highlighting dimples, smile lines, and traveling to his now bright eyes.

"No one has ever seen me like you have." I wanted to, needed to say it. My posture changed slightly and my shoulders squared. "Thank you, Sir."

Quiet, but clear and steady. I'd said it. I'd looked into the eyes of this man who had won over so many parts of me and given him the one thing I thought I would never truly wrest from myself. I felt it release from me—physically. Instead of a yawning nothing, a sense of stillness like I'd never known, a true sense of what for years I'd deluded myself into believing I existed in, settled into my bones. And I wasn't in control.

Sir has me.

His strong, sure hand moved from my hair to my cheek, his thumb gliding over the fragile skin at my temple. He smiled again.

"That's my girl."

The approval was apparent in every move of his body. It emanated from his direct, level gaze, the slight change in the pressure of his thumb on my skin, even the set of his jaw.

Pushing the comforter away from me, his hand hovered just above my shoulder, so close the heat pulsed into my skin.

"And this, Erin?"

"My shoulder, Sir."

Our eyes held the other's in an intense gaze, our breath finding the same rhythm.

"Erin, can I put my hands on your shoulders?"

"Yes, Sir."

His fingers traced the long muscles of my forearms, turned my palms over.

"My hands, Sir."

Reaching past us, he tugged and the sound of a zipper followed. I fought at the flare of warning and stayed with him, just as I'd done when we hiked up to the moth traps. He drew something out and sat it on my knees.

Rope. White, silky, and slim. A hank of it, twisted, lay on my legs, waiting for use. On me.

"Erin, I'm going to wrap this around your wrists. And then I'm going to put the rope through the hard point over the door. That okay with you?"

"Yes, Sir."

He gazed down at me, chuckling. "Couldn't get you to say 'Sir' five minutes ago. Now you won't quit."

"Sir. Sir. Sir. Sir." I looked up at him, dozy and grinning. His hand smoothed over my head, his laugh lingering around me as he passed, rising to his feet.

Suddenly, his hands were hard on my arms, pulling me up to stand. He looked down at me, still relaxed, still smiling. But sharper, a little wary. Watching me.

"Okay?"

"Yes, fine."

I looked on as he wound the rope, an infinity symbol containing my wrists and two of his fingers. Once he was satisfied with the placement of the bind, he removed his fingers and passed the opposite end through the bolt sunk into the doorframe and closed the door. My arms rose over my head, and suddenly my nipples twisted into hard points.

Vulnerable. Open. His.

"The door is here for you to lean against. Just hold the rope enough to stay steady, no gripping. I want you to face me." His hands were on my shoulders again, guiding me. "If your hands feel tingly, or you have any sudden pain, I want you to tell me."

"Okay—I mean, yes, Sir."

He smiled and leaned down to my lips for a short kiss. "Don't worry so much about saying the right thing. You just worry about steady, no grip, tingles, sharp pain, dizzy, no breath. Say it for me."

"Steady. No grip. Tingles. Sharp pain. Dizzy. No breath."

"Good girl."

Good girl. Approval. Affirmation. His.

I raised my chin and stared at him, unable look away. In my ears, my pulse sounded, a strong and steady thud playing against the half-time glide of air across my mouth. Distant sounds—a neighborhood dog barking, the nightly settling of the roof as the wood contracted in the night air—were there, clear, but nothings. Every present part of me hung, balanced before him and where he was taking me. I would have followed him anywhere, given him anything, so enormous was this feeling I'd only known before as gratitude for safety after being lost in an unfamiliar place.

After another touch of his lips to mine, he walked back to the duffel bag he'd brought in. Methodically, he took out each of his implements, laid each one on my bed. When the large flogger he'd used on Claire that first night came out, his gaze shifted to mine. The question was implicit.

I didn't look away, even though my cheeks flamed.

"We'll see," he said, grinning. The decision was his. Would it be reward or penance? "How are your arms? Open your fingers and wiggle them for me."

He stepped to me, sliding something into his back pocket as he crossed the room. I complied, turning my arms and fingers under his hand.

"They're okay."

"*You* look more than okay." He dropped a hand to my waist and trailed his thumb over my hipbone.

I shivered, sighing, and gasped a little under his hands. He touched me everywhere, with long, lingering passes of his palms on my skin. A small piece of my mind roused, objective and defiant, reminding me that I was naked, wrists tied, and nearly suspended from a piece of hardware bolted over my bedroom door, almost writhing as my boy-friend stroked my body. I ignored it, but the realization was too strong.

Moment to moment, Erin...c'mon...moment to moment...

His hand skimmed higher, rising to nestle under my ear, and this time the pad of his thumb traced my bottom lip. Nudging forward, I kissed his fingertip, parting my lips for him when he pressed against them. The shallow grooves skipped over my teeth, settling with his salty, warm skin on my tongue. I flooded there, and then between my thighs, at the pressure of his thumb in my open, waiting mouth.

It made me raise my chin, reacting like this, showing that dis-believing commentator inside me that I could take more. I wanted more—as much as he would give me. And I had no way to quantify it. There was no order to this sense of acceptance, being biddable under his hand, as a string of logic that started from what I thought was me. I wanted him—everywhere—but would wait, his hand the focus of his control over me, anchored at the single, sensitive point of his thumb against my tongue.

"God damn," he said, taking his hand from my mouth. "You know, you're something, Erin."

Protection. Possession. His.

"Sir." I looked down as the word crossed my lips, shutting my eyes hard at the cynical voice, suddenly louder and insisting I was attempting something I wasn't capable of.

He glanced over my head, turned my wrists gently. "Yeah? You okay?"

"I'm fine."

"Honesty, Erin, remember? What's happening?" His hands were back on the rope at my wrists.

"No. No, Wa—Sir, please don't. I was…No, it was you. You were everything." And I remembered her, the girl who had scarred him so much before he understood who he was and what he wanted. Honesty was imperative, no matter how much it hurt. I swallowed hard, frustrated at the words so inadequate to the overwhelmingness of Sir in front of me. "Like I looked in a mirror and I was so close to it, I saw you instead of me."

Sir's eyelashes fluttered a little as he smiled, and his fingers skated over the softer, more sensitive skin of my exposed inner arm. They came to rest, his big palm splayed across my neck, and he lifted my chin, bringing my eyes to his. I knew the sensation of him looking over me, his practiced ease with evaluating where my head was as much as he'd come to read my body's reaction to him.

"'S okay, sweetheart. I got you."

I smiled, nodding. Of course he did.

The weight of his hand fell heavier against my jaw, more possession than a gentle cradling, and his fingers slid deep into my hair at the nape of my neck. From there, steady tension kept my head lifted to him.

"You don't have to keep your eyes open, Erin. If you need to check out for a second, it's fine. But I want you to tell me if you need more time, all right?"

"Okay, Sir." I nuzzled into the warmth of his hand so I could stir the scent of his soap, and the leather from his steering wheel, and *him* around me.

"Gotta say, I do like hearing you call me Sir," he said and kissed me.

The pressure of his fingers wound again through my hair, a measured climb in intensity. Everything about him, his knowledge of physically and mentally dominating a partner, his size and strength, made me aware of the forces of power and surrender. It was laced into the foundations of who we were becoming as a couple. And that was when I understood something I'd never be able to forget about this man. He was in control of himself first. It was why he had always been able to inspire it from me.

My head sank against his hand and I let myself exhale.

His shoulder shifted and his other hand moved away from my hip. The air around it whispered over me and his fingertips returned to my skin.

"Well, all right, then," he said, chuckling softly. "Erin, this is the deer-suede flogger I showed you when we talked about tonight. Remember?"

It was small, compared to the dark buffalo-hide one he'd taken out earlier and left in full view on my bed. He wisped the velvety falls across my outer thigh, then dragged them along a slow course from knee to hip. A sound nearly as soft hummed over my lips, and my hips twisted after the lost sensation of suede on my skin.

"Erin? Remember?"

My spine shot straight behind me. "Hmm? Oh, yes. Sir. Yes, I remember."

"Shhh," he said easily. "Don't worry so much about the *Sirs*. Yes and no is fine."

"But you like it."

"I like watching you give yourself a little space to enjoy what you're feeling a lot more than worrying about the right honorific. Okay, Erin?"

I looked up to him and nodded.

He curved his left arm along mine and offset himself against the door behind me, leaving my skin chilled from the absence of his body. His hand rose and he held the flogger in front of me, inches from my breast.

"This is new. Did I tell you that when I showed it to you?"

"No. I don't remember."

His hip shifted, pressing more of his body beside me and into the door. In the scant space between the flogger and my nipple, the velvety tips came closer, hovering. So close, I felt my skin arc toward them. Above my head, his fingers closed, one by one, around my arm.

"I got this for you. I saw it a few weeks ago and thought about your skin, about how pale you are. Thought black wasn't right on you, but this light brown…it's the color of a fawn."

He dropped the strips of suede from above, like a waterfall, across the sloped skin under them. And beside me, his hand still firm around my arm, he watched. The falls came quicker, harder, skipped between my breasts with no way to predict where they would land. When the flogger snipped and stung, I gasped a little, and the sensation disappeared instantly, replaced by his fingers closing around my nipple, tugging.

"Oh, God." I danced to the tips of my toes again under tensed thighs.

"To God from Sir in one quick step. I like that." His mouth was by my ear, the flogger's falls compressed into a spiny circle in his palm. He released my nipple and dusted across it with the clench of suede. "You know, I can almost see what you're seeing, Erin. If I move my head just right—" his cheek pressed into my temple "—yeah, I can make out what it must look like to you, having your tits out and exposed for me. I can see the little chillbumps coming up on your stomach."

Swish-swish. Smack.

"Your skin is one of the first things that got me hard for you." He shifted his hips closer and proved he was no liar. "So damn pale."

In one smooth movement, he released my arm and was before me again. His arm rose and fell in an arc, skipping between each breast, then my stomach and thighs, never in the same place. But when I expected the bite and slap to fall on another stretch of skin, it stayed, fanning the burn. The lack of cadence frustrated me, and I turned my bottom lip under my teeth. This was how he'd decided I should be, and he'd told me so during our first real date.

Your head needs fucking with.

He knew, months before, how he would tumble me over while I stood before him. He knew the way inside. I gave so much away and probably looked needy and so naïve, while assuring him I knew what I was doing.

Moment to moment…moment to moment…

The flogger went whistling through the air, falling sharper and stinging more than I was prepared for. Once again he came to me, pulled at my nipple, and I whined at the sensation of sting followed by insistent pressure, bearing down on my lip as I rode out the crossing sensations.

"Don't bite your lip like that, girl. You could split it."

"So—" I caught myself in mid-apology. Since we met, he'd pointed out how often I apologized, often without realizing I'd said the words. He noticed so much, never attaching judgment to my quirks and failings. The impulse to say "sorry" again gurgled up from my throat, and I shook my head at it.

Instead I looked up to him and nodded. He returned the same, his cheek rising with a half grin. Stepping back, he reached behind himself, and his hand returned with that favorite leather flogger. The heavy black one he had used on Claire, the one Lucy called "mean."

"I'm going to use one this now."

His head dipped a little, so our gazes were level, and waited.

The pause wasn't persuasion. I was free to say yes or no. I knew that much about him after the time we'd been together, not doing *this*, but doing the other somethings people did when they spent time together. He was waiting for me to decide again. I'd read it in Claire's notebook, and it was true. Submission was a decision but not one. A series of them.

"Yes, Sir."

"Turn around and face the door."

I did, circling around the point my wrists were bound to. When he made a soft, grunted sound of approval, the hot pulse between my legs traveled deeper and higher between my hips, settling behind my navel. I clenched the rope under my fingertips, waiting.

There was no surprise about the physical side of a scene. It hurt. I'd learned before, when he spanked me, so there was no question the heavy strips of leather hurt. But this hurt came with the knowledge it was caused by that big, brutal-looking flogger he'd used on Claire, the same one he'd shown me before he turned me to face the door. Understanding it belonged to him, *to Sir*, reminded me of the bright line between us. That connection took me back to him, seeing and feeling more of him than of myself. It mingled hurt and need of him and want for him with the loose-limbed high that always flooded me after stress. The torrents of physical and emotional circled each other, conjuring my old, half-admitted fantasy, where I whispered *for him…for Sir* as the faceless man pressed his will on me.

The face of that well-known, well-used fantasy became *him*. Walt. And then it felt good.

Sir's soft grunts filled the air, a half-beat before my own higher, sharper gasp answered him. It intensified with each pass of the leather strips.

Every sense was answered. The sound of our voices, one trailing the other. The scent of my perfume warming on my skin and mingling with the soapy, herbal scent of leather that filled the air each time the flogger hit my backside. It swished in the air and I opened my eyes to scattered shadows over my head and around my shoulders. The salt of Sir's thumb was still on my bottom lip and in my mouth too. My head drooped, and I settled my cheek against the cool, glossy-painted wood.

The slap and thud on my shoulders and backside stopped, replaced with his broad hand stroking over the round of my hip, where it came to rest. He came closer, the hair on his chest ticking the heated, tingling skin he'd made.

"How are you doin', baby?"

A contented hum buzzed through my mouth, and I tucked my head into the hollow between his neck and shoulder. "Really good. I know why Claire likes that."

I felt his cheek curve and stretch against my temple. "*That?*"

"The flogger."

"Whose?"

"Yours, Sir."

He moved his hand to my chin and tipped my head back. "Yes, mine." His breath skated over my lips. "*Mine.* Good girl."

When he kissed me, it felt different. The first pass of his lips over mine made me wonder about the difference, if the change was a kind of mask he'd put on or if he had really changed because of what we were doing. But when he kissed me again, I stopped wondering. This was him. No persona, no shadow. It was something essential and determined, force and sureness and granite-deep strength. In part, the him I saw during the most intense parts of sex or hard work. When he swung his big body from the forest floor to a thick tree branch over his head. But this was not a glimpse.

His shoulders snugged around me, drawing me into his chest. And his mouth moved against mine, the slow slip of tongue and teeth rising with each pass of his lips over mine. He inhaled and pressed me against him, lifting me to my toes with his wide-palmed hands against my backside. I'd felt him consider having me, and felt it when he savored over me. And now he was consuming me.

"Gonna take you down," he said finally, pulling away.

No. Not yet. More.

"But, Sir…"

He grinned again, catching the rope in his hand. "Said take you down, not turn you loose." He tugged at my wrists and pulled me along with him, toward my bed. "How are your arms?"

"Fine, Sir."

"Sir, Sir, Sir." He chuckled as he led me across my bedroom. "There she goes again with the Sirs."

"I like saying it."

"On your knees. There." He pointed to my bed. After I'd managed it — with his hands under my bound wrists — he took the length of rope in his hands again. "Remember the first night we went to dinner?"

"Yes. Oh — I mean yes, S —"

He raised an eyebrow. "You're ahead for now, don't worry about *Sir*. Don't think that hard."

The bindings tumbled from my wrists, and he took my hands in his. There were light marks from the rope, but nothing that wouldn't fade in a few minutes' time. My skin tingled under the pink depressions, and I ached to run my fingertips over the little bumps the rope left behind.

He crouched before me and took one of my wrists in his hand.

"Remember when I told you your head needed fucking with?"

People think it's BDSM 101, but being tied can fuck with your head a little.

"Yes, Sir." As I looked on, he tightened my forearm along my backside and thigh, finishing with my wrist by my knee. "You're doing it, aren't you? What you told me over dinner."

He looked up at me with sharp, clear eyes as the rope hummed over my calf. "I am."

Another pass of rope drew my foot toward my backside. Rising, he circled his arm around my waist and steadied me against his chest as he pulled the rope taut. The long curve of his pectoral muscle tempted me, so close and brushing across my lips. I pushed forward and drew one of his blunt-tipped nipples across my teeth.

"Behave."

Leaning back, I gazed up to him. "You didn't tell me I had to stay still too."

"Then I'll tell you now," he said, cupping my chin. "Don't. Move."

The rope snaked over my other calf and went taut again. He'd balanced me on my knees, with no way of catching myself if I started to tip over. My pulse rose again, the sound of it joining the short breaths catching in my throat. My chin still rested in his hand, and I looked up to him again.

"I…um, this isn't what I imagined when you were talking that night at Trattoria Stella."

"Take a breath, Erin." After I complied, he nodded. "Good. So, it's a little bit of a surprise when things don't look like you'd planned, huh?"

My cheeks burned and though I wanted to fight it, everything about my body's position and his nearness, standing over me, insisted I tell him the truth.

"It's…" I swallowed hard and screwed my eyes tight. This simple, probably very obvious trait of mine was so hard to admit. I was so open and dependent on him to keep me steady.

"*It's…?*" His fingers tightened, very slightly, and my chin tipped up in a similar small increment.

I had to. And my reliance on linear and logical was no deep, dark secret. The first line of my own code, my personal *gotohome.*

"Yes, Sir. I don't like it."

"Yeah, I figured that." He stepped closer to my body and took his hand from my chin, trailing it down my neck as I settled again, hip-to-hip against him and still steadied on my knees. Once I was stable against his body, he reached behind him and brought the suede flogger from his back pocket again, leaving it looped over my shoulder. My head twisted toward it, and I inhaled. Above me, he shifted, pulled and kneaded at my nipple again, turning it to a hard point under his fingertips. "So how'd you think I'd do it?"

"Well…I—" I said, breathing deep again. The cool lemon and wood scent of suede washed over me. "I thought I'd be on my back. And, I guess, tied to something."

"Tied to something?" The timbre of his voice dropped again. I leaned forward, straining to hear him, as suede slid across my breast and into his open hand. "Like your bed?"

"Yeah. My bed."

As he dribbled the falls over my exposed breast again, his other hand left my shoulder, drifting down my back until the heat of it left my skin. Before I could parse out a logical path for that unseen hand, he slapped the flogger over the hard peak of my nipple. Hissing, I flinched away, nearly collapsing against his chest before my back arched and I bent, the tension on my arms pulling me backward.

"Now if you can't stay in one place when you're like this—" he tensed the rope again "—what makes you think I'd need to tie you to anything to keep you still?"

The flogger snapped again. Both thighs. One. Two. Then again. He moved away, clearing my body so I was arched before him, supported only on his arm underneath me. Again, and then back to my breasts, currents of air tufting toward my chin as the flogger fell quicker. Harder.

He chuckled. "Bet I could pick you up and carry you around like this."

"Please," I whispered, stifling a squeak in my throat as he swung hard at my splayed thighs. "You couldn't."

"Don't tell me what I can—" *smack* "—and can't do, girl."

"I'm sor—" The flogger snapped away from me, landing over his shoulder. His hand went between my legs before I could finish, shutting down my reflexive words.

"You know, I've heard enough of your *sorrys* to last me awhile. Make some other noises for me."

When his fingers plunged inside me, I did. I gasped and shuddered over the sudden sensation of fullness. He pressed his thumb to my clitoris, dragging slow circles that matched his stroking fingers. And I cried out over it with heavy breath and almost-words that sounded like pleas. Looking past the judgment and reality of what I'd consented to do and what he was doing to me—where I usually faltered—was a sense of him. A wary but capable sentry over himself first. I was giving the need deep within me I tried so often to deny to him. For him.

The sudden crest of an orgasm surprised me, so much my eyes flew open and I gaped up at him. His fingers went still.

"Don't."

"I...oh God, Sir, I can't help—"

"Yes, you can. Look at me. You can't come until I say you can. And you won't. Hear me?"

Under me the rope went taut again, pinching where I was bound as my body followed its pressure. As I began to collapse into the strain behind me, his hand drifted away. What was probably scant millimeters felt like miles. His hand and fingers that knew how to touch, where to stroke and flutter to make me come, so much harder than I'd ever known before, were going, and a well-deep part of me went livid at the loss of him. I'd have to struggle for him, and just seconds before I'd understood I adored him enough to do it.

I focused on the muscles in my stomach and thighs, grunting when they twisted and throbbed as I struggled to keep his hand between my legs. I gritted my teeth and found equilibrium again.

"Good girl."

Before I could smile up to him, he stepped aside, and I tumbled to the bed in a surprised, awkward clatter of limbs and rope. A wave of embarrassment rose in my throat, but before it could bore into my mind, he turned me to my back and crouched between my legs. On instinct, I tried to draw my knees together.

"Got you," he said softly and stroked the outside of my thigh. "Open."

I drew in a gulp of air I'd forgotten to take, swallowed at it, and looked to him for a sense of where I'd landed. "Sir, I…"

"Yes, you can. Open up for me."

It's a decision.

Panic threatened. And in front of him, on my back, exposed, and tied to stay so, I had to make the decision. He would stop. I knew *him*, the Walt part of him, and the other side…it couldn't negate Walt. I knew him well enough to believe in the consistency of his core identity. If I asked, I knew he'd end it all and take the rope away and soothe me and never push so far again.

But I could go further. I could take more. And I wanted to, for him.

I opened my eyes. When I found his, I let my legs fall open.

Looking down, he smiled and hummed with approval. "You wanted to show me your pussy all along, didn't you?"

I blinked hard at the word but nodded anyway. *He knew.* "Yes, Sir."

He moved forward, bracing my knees against his broad shoulders. I flinched again, but stayed still, even when he bent his head to my thigh and trailed his tongue over the tight, whip-reddened skin.

"I've got a question for you," he said. I twisted at the puffs of breath that came with each word. They flitted and teased. My knees tensed again, and then his shoulders flexed. Still open. Still pinned in place by his rope and his body. "Why don't you like it when I eat your pussy, Erin?"

"You have—I mean, I do. Sir."

"No. Takes a lot for you to do it," he said and curled his arms around my thighs. His hands rested easily in the juncture of my leg and hip, his thumbs met over my clitoris. "I think you get through it, but you don't like it. And I don't think it's the way I do it, either."

I knew where this was headed.

Maybe that was the allure and the threat of what we were doing. He was pressing against the most superficial, first line defenses and sensitive places. The logic in his actions made perfect, elegant sense. But where he'd decided I should go first still sent my instincts skittering. As much as I was primed for fight or flight, I also desperately wanted to move past the fear.

He brushed his thumbs, one following the other, over me, enough to guide me toward orgasm again. There wasn't the fast determination of someone who wanted me to just come so he could get on with his own release, though. He was settled in, ready to take a long time coaxing me from the watchtower where the true, brave me was hidden.

I wagged my hips toward him. If I showed him enough, maybe he'd just finish it. Instead, he laughed softly.

"Nice try." He leveled his shoulders toward me and lifted me toward his mouth.

"Wal—I mean, S...*please*," I squealed, thrashing.

Instead, he shook his head and pushed his mouth against me, and immediately I was at war. Of course it wasn't what he did that always made me go rigid. It felt good. *So good.* His mouth and tongue and lips and fingers were so right and found the places that distracted me from the horrified, indignant commentary gaining volume in my head. I didn't want to listen to her. I knew, intellectually I understood, that revulsion and discomfort at the notion of this man I'd come to care so much for—to trust more than I imagined I ever could—seeing me and using his mouth to bring pleasure to me alone, with no expectation of what I could, or should be doing for him was...just wrong. It was something inside of me, that damn narrator always telling me what I shouldn't want or do or have. Not him. *I* was holding myself back.

I always had.

In the moment, I knew I could decide about that too. I could put myself out there, completely vulnerable, and trust his hand was open and waiting for me.

"Okay," I said, hardly more than a skim of air across my lips. I barely heard my own voice.

His head rose and I saw *him*. Walt. Shiny-lipped from my arousal, smiling his half grin, and something—a new something I couldn't name—sparking in his eyes.

"You gonna let me, girl?"

"Yes, Sir."

There was nothing better than her, with her long legs draped over his thigh, all mussed and pink-cheeked—both sets—and dopey from good sex. That was, unless chocolate came into play.

"Mmmmmm," Erin sighed as he slid the spoon from her lips. "Oh my God, that's so good. How do Italians manage to turn even chocolate pudding into something that decadent?"

"I'd say a good bit of it is owing to heavy cream and some kind of liqueur, and a whole lot of butter." Walt swirled the spoon through his take-out carrier of Nonni Isolde's dark chocolate *budino* and offered Erin another bite.

"No, you should have some too. Don't feed it all to me."

"Isolde gave me enough for six people, sweetheart. I think I'll get my share."

She turned those big blue eyes up at him and shrugged. "Well, since you've put it that way…" Her mouth dropped open, waiting. He cocked an eyebrow at her and leaned down for a kiss instead.

But he still couldn't resist echoing the scene they'd just finished. Holding the spoon past her reach and swaying, he said, "Now open up for me again."

Erin's cheeks flushed. "I don't think I'll be able to hear that word without wanting you, Sir." She accepted another spoonful of pudding, humming the same low sounds she made when she'd started to let herself go and take pleasure from his mouth on her.

Lazy and naked Erin with a side of the world's best chocolate pudding. He had a new high-water mark for his best time. And then she called him Sir.

So much for my best time.

It didn't make sense at all, getting turned off at the word. Walt didn't object to titles, after all, and he'd been around all manner of them for nearly half of his life.

Still. It made him tense in a list of different places she'd just helped him ease tension from.

"You don't have to call me that now."

Erin smiled up at him and tucked herself into his chest. "It's okay. I'd like to." She sat up suddenly. "Is it odd that calling you Sir makes me feel so happy?"

"No. Not at all."

"So, can we keep going?"

"Going? You mean stay in D/s?" Damn. He tried to tell himself this was the last thing he'd expected from her, but it was a quick out. Of course she'd want to go 24/7 with it. She barely knew what that even meant.

Walt resisted the urge to scrub at his face, instead reaching across Erin and depositing the take-out container on her bedside table. Her hands skated over his back and down to his ass.

Much better. Keep thinking about moving that hand lower, not shit about 24/7 you don't get.

Erin sat up, pushing him away from her with shock and awe written all over her face. "Oh my God. Did I do that to you?" Her hand hovered by the shoulder she'd had her head on seconds before.

He glanced down at a line of four deep-red gouges stretching from his collarbone to well past his bicep. "Huh, what about that. Must've been you. I haven't had my nails done in ages," he finished with a drawn-out prissy voice, wiggling his fingers at her as he spoke. The giggle he wanted, hoped would come, never did.

"I'm serious, look at those. I hurt you." She wriggled away, shoving the sheets behind her.

"Erin, it's okay." He tugged at her hand and grinned, wide and with his best goofy crossed-eyed expression that always made her laugh.

She didn't laugh.

Instead she gnawed at her lip and reached toward her dresser.

"No, no, no. Not clothes. Put that away." He swatted at the T-shirt she held between them.

"We should talk about those marks. I didn't mean to hurt you. I'm not sure when *those*…happened, but I'm so sorry and —"

"Erin, I don't want to Monday morning quarterback this. We just played, and it was hot. C'mon, put down the shirt. Sit." When she did, her head fell into her hands. Walt rolled over and pushed himself upright, beside her. "Hey…don't."

Even muffled by her hands, her voice still sounded defeated. "I'm so sorry."

"I think it's not a couple of scratches you're worried about. And by the way, they're like badges of honor to guys, even from vanilla sex."

Her head turned toward him and she peeked out from behind her hands. "What's a Monday morning quarterback?"

"It's a football…analysis thing. Look, the point is that we don't need to pick over every second of your first scene just yet. Hell, I'm still buzzing a little off of it. Let's not beat it to death yet, okay?"

"Was I okay?"

Her voice was too cramped up and small. Walt hated seeing her this way, and hated the part of himself that was so quickly frustrated with her insecurities about kink.

"I suspect I'm going to have a matching set of your fingerprints on my back tomorrow. I like that, just like you do. Y'know, you don't just lie there, Erin."

"How could I, with you…" She dipped her chin with that pursed-lipped smile of hers as she took a long look at his body.

This was serious, not the time to show off for her, but he tensed his arm for her a little anyway. "Sounds like what you're worried about isn't doing something right or not knowing how to do whatever some book told you the right sub things are, but what you do — how you are with me. And just so you know, it's exactly right."

Her shoulders dropped a little and she turned to him with a little hopeful smile starting to ease her face again. Walt reached over and smoothed at the wrinkle between her eyes.

"I never forget I'm new. And you've done so much. I don't want to bore you."

"Bored? All of that experience you're so concerned about doesn't touch what happens when we're together, Erin." He lifted her legs across his lap, allowing himself a couple of passes over her skin. "You… shit, it's like night and day. You're with me, giving as much as you get."

Erin reached behind them, drawing the rumpled sheets around her. Her eyes skipped away and that damn line between her brows came back. He was going to have to talk more, which always made him more irritable, and his post-scene Top high had already washed out.

Fuck, Erin, don't do this.

Screwing on his nice guy face, he tipped his head toward his shoulder. "I told you when I took you up to the overlook the day after I met you that I don't spank and tell. I was trying to make you laugh, but there was a little truth in it, too. You know I'm no angel, and I've played and been around with a lot of people. I don't regret it. But I'll tell you something — in general — about new girls. By and large, they don't participate much. They think they should just lie there. It's like they see themselves as a target, nothing more. There's no connection with me, and half the time they're checked out from their own head, too."

And as soon as the words left his mouth, he knew he'd backed himself into a corner.

"I want to be like that for you all the time, Sir."

Fuck. She did it.

This moment, right after an amazing scene, with their bodies still raw from fucking and play was when the happy-endorphins painted the challenge of 24/7 over with a soft-focus brush, not showing the hard reality. With another girl, Walt would have gone there, and had had to, more than once. More so over the past couple of years with so many new people.

But not Erin. He couldn't shut her down. His damn feelings were in the way.

What was in that damn notebook of Claire's anyway? Had she told Erin the other side, the one where Paul could send his own wife downstairs into seclusion for a week while he hit it with a twenty-two-year-old in red pleather platform boots? *For a trial run*, whatever the hell that was.

Trial run.

"You should give it a try first," he said before he could think too much about it.

Her chin rose. "I know what and who I am, Walt."

"See," he said, grinning. She didn't. "Erin, take this a step at a time. Hell, look at me. Most of those male-led straight white guys think I'm barely a Dom, just more of a scene whore. And most of the people I know are pretty damn switchy by old school definitions."

"I don't care what they think. I do care what you think." Finally she smiled, a little sheepish and over her bare shoulder. *Ah, better. There's my girl.* "And maybe Claire. I think I'm afraid of what Lucy thinks."

"Yeah, you're probably not the only one." He settled against the headboard and held his arms open for her. Once she was beside him, he reached for his dessert again and tried to ignore a persistent notion that Lu would be laughing her ass off at him, lying there naked with Erin and a big Styrofoam pan of chocolate pudding, preaching the Way Kink Was like some old caveman.

"Okay, what was it like for you? How did you know what to do?"

"It was a lot different before the Internet and all of those books people treat like they're gospel. People aren't as simple as they're boiled down to be in a blog or some insider guide. After so long around the lifestyle, I've seen people do things I'd never have expected from them."

She looked up at him. "Like Melissa?"

"Yeah."

"I know who I am, Walt. And I'm not a girl."

That word. *Girl.* It was where they started this thing they were doing, and could be where it ended too. "Not a girl, no. But you're asking to be one."

"No, I'm asking to be yours." They stayed quiet for a long stretch of minutes, both of them too stubborn to give in. Finally, she picked up his hand and held it in both of hers. Her long, pale fingers curved around his, clean and tidy and never injured or rejected. "So, a trial?"

"Not what you're thinking, like it's gonna be the twelve labors. Just a step at a time."

"I can do that." She nodded, smiling.

"All right." He set the last of his dessert aside, uneaten. So much for riding Top space for the last few hours he had with her until she flew out to ThinkMine's headquarters in Silicon Valley for a week. "You get your packing finished up and I'll put together some things I want you to do."

CHAPTER THIRTEEN

When I came back to Los Altos for work, I rarely rented a car. There were at least five hotels within walking distance to the Main House, and if I ventured anywhere else, I had a small number of friendly coworkers I could depend on for a ride.

This time, though, I had rented a car. Because I would never subject a friend, especially one whose connection to me ended at the ThinkMine parking lot exit, to my mother and sister. Once I mentioned I'd be in town the first week of July for my annual review and a final meeting of my management skills class, the two of them had insisted I *drive up to their place* for a late brunch before I flew home.

In seven months, it seemed, they had managed to climb the ladder from hostess and apprentice sommelier to co-owners. I'd looked over the restaurant's web site, procrastinating about my drive up to Yountville by looking over the La Stanza Blu's extensive menu, and it still stated Dante Boriello was sole proprietor.

Danielle and Kathy were twenty minutes late after their "we're running behind" phone call, leaving me seated alone at the restaurant's bar for nearly an hour. I heard them before I saw them. Danielle first, of course, because this was her stage, and then on her heels my mother, her laughter fighting for dominance with Dani's. They both worked at La Stanza Blu, and likely had been there the evening before, but for the next twelve minutes, I listened to them greet everyone in the restaurant like dear, long-absent friends.

Finally I caught the bartender's eye, giving her a weak smile and nod toward my empty glass.

"Another Diet Coke?"

"Please."

Having spent more time parked at a dim back table with my school-books than most adults when I was an elementary-age child—and served an on-the-sly dinner of soup and complimentary bread or a basket of chips and salsa—I still felt more at home in a far corner of a lounge or bar than out for observation in the dining space. I liked my back against the wall.

Bartenders were a comfort and fascination when I was young—and still were. Their efficiency as they worked, managing so many details while maintaining friendliness without the imposition of too much familiarity, always impressed me.

"Didn't you say you're waiting on Dani and her mom?"

"Yes, I'm Danielle's sister. And Kathy's daughter," I said and tipped a few grains of salt over the new beverage napkin under my freshened drink.

"Oh, huh? Really?"

Before I could see the look on her face, I reached for my glass again, intent on twisting the salt grains into better contact with the soggy napkin and glass. Not looking at her, so we would have to make the unspoken agreement required to avoid the truth. No one, most likely not a single person with whom Danielle and my mother made such a display of effusive greetings within earshot of me, knew who I was.

My hand shook, and I realized it too late. The glass went tipping away from my fingers, dumping a full glass of Diet Coke and ice over the bar and into my lap.

Jesus. I spent two hundred dollars on a weekend car rental, drove two hours north of Los Altos, and waited for over an hour to be a nonentity.

"I'm so—"

"Hey, kid, you're cut off!"

Brushing ice and soda from my hands, I crouched into my mother's hug. "It slipped."

"God, Pudge, seriously?" Danielle was behind her, a new incarnation in discreet beiges and pale grays, her hair blown-out smooth. On a Sunday afternoon, the day she had always reserved for ponytails and ragged sweatpants.

The bartender, a nice woman named April—I learned this during my mother's forty-five-second, hugged-out greeting to her—stepped away to find some clean bar towels. Danielle watched the production at a distance.

"What?" She added an indulgent laugh after for good measure.

"You couldn't give me a hand? Maybe shove some bev naps at this mess or something?"

What was that hairstyle anyway? And a manicure? She kept petting the perfectly flat-ironed ends of her hair like it was a ferret laid across her shoulders.

And then I noticed. My sister was engaged.

Dani glowed and sparkled and shone as we were moved to a center four-top table with fresh drinks all around.

"It happened last weekend," Dani said as we sat. And my mother looked upon her like a racehorse she'd trained who'd just taken the grand prize. "Dante took me up in his investor's hot air balloon at dawn. Can you believe it?"

"Just like a television show." My mother's also newly manicured hands feathered over the ends of paper napkin under her wine glass. Apparently Kathy had developed a palate for Pinot Gris instead of Bud Light. "At dawn, isn't that romantic? They went right up over the valley where Dante's vineyard is, just as the sun rose and—"

"And he asked me." Danielle presented her left hand with its evidence of the asking, saluting me with white, glimmering light.

"Nice." I nodded.

Danielle fluttered her fingers. "Nice? Are you kidding me? I know marriage and love and happily-ever-after is all beneath you, Erin, but come on. Three carats."

"Flawless carats," my mother added.

Lucy's face, complete with rolling eyes, came to me and before I could stop her influence, she took over my voice. "Three flawless carats, huh? You got an appraisal that quickly?"

"Oh, envy," Danielle sneered over the sounds of Kathy's maternal tutting and shushing. "I know you're still bummed over that Iranian guy going home, Erin, but seriously, don't piss all over my happiness, okay?"

"You were dating an Iranian?" Kathy's eyes turned to wide, kohl-lined saucers. "Oh, Erin, those Arabic men can be so domineering and really don't treat women like we—"

"Indian." I fisted the scraps of napkin I'd been mindlessly shredding. "Ardhi was Indian. From Mumbai. Bombay?"

Two stilled, befuddled faces with the same blue eyes blinked back at me.

Kathy finally spoke. "Well…where did you meet someone from India?"

"At work, Mom. Ardhi and I worked together."

"Well, work's a fine place to meet a man." She patted the cream silk covering my sister's arm. "Dani met Dante here, of course. Executive chef and owner. Two restaurants, this one and Boriello's, here in the valley, and…" Her eyebrows rose over wide, excited eyes.

"He's talking to—" Danielle stopped short with a glance at our mother and snickered. She made a great display of composing herself and said, "Well, I can't really talk *le specifiche*, but there might be something happening in Vegas or Guatemala."

"Can you imagine?" Kathy clearly had.

"No. I can't." In English or in Italian. Suddenly I missed Trattoria Stella and Nonni Isolde, and the big, warm hand that usually held mine when we ate at the little restaurant in Callahan. I missed it all, very much. I swallowed hard at the swift, strong missing of Walt and kept it silenced in my throat. Instead, I glanced around the room, looking for a server. "I can't imagine at all."

After the prolonged buildup of Dani and Mom's arrival, dinner was a comparatively short event, consisting of nothing more than grilled octopus salads—with lemon instead of dressing. I winced with longing at the focaccia basket Danielle waved away. After the dinner plates disappeared and the wine glasses were replenished, Mom excused herself to the restaurant patio for a cigarette. My sister adjusted the cuff of her linen jacket and once again her flawless three-carat diamond flashed in my direction.

"So Erin," she began, then paused to swish her hair over her shoulder. "While Mom's gone, we should talk."

I glanced across the empty bar. Mom was out of sight and I was effectively trapped by her absence. Warning prickled across my skin.

"Talk? Okay, what about?"

"Mom. What are we going to do about her?"

"Do? I—is she okay? She seems fine."

"She's almost sixty." Danielle sighed heavily, blinking over our apparently mostly dead mother. "And I've taken care of her for a long time now."

"She's fifty-eight and you've been sharing an apartment." I nudged my glasses into place, biting back *that I help pay for*. "Dani, what is it? Has something happened? She hasn't mentioned—"

"Dante and I want to travel, you know? And entertain."

I watched her for a moment, waiting for another statement to tie together Kathy's apparent failing health, the hospice Danielle was convinced she had been running in their apartment, and her new fiancé's travel plans. "Okay. So travel. What does that have to do with Mom?"

"We just want to be newlyweds. Have fun and be spontaneous. And young."

Suddenly the real topic was clear as a wrinkle in my sister's recently acquired linen blazer. "So how does Dante get along with Kathy?"

"Oh, he loves her. Really. They get along so great."

"I bet."

"Everyone here just loves her. You know that, E."

I nodded again. She was really doing this. "Yes. I do."

"But she's going to be so lonely when we're away at the new sites. And our house at the vineyard won't be finished for months, maybe even a year. So I think—"

"Know what, Danielle? When it's really time to be concerned about Mom's care, I will be. Right now, I think Kathy's capable of deciding where she lives and how she spends her time and probably is relieved to finally have the opportunity to be on her own. She doesn't need either of us treating her like a something that has to be handled." I gathered my bag to me and stood, as calm and unfussed as I could manage. My sister followed, not calm and very fussed.

"I've had her for years," she said. "While you've gone off to college and grad school and done exactly what you wanted to do, with no thought of me stuck with her. I have a chance to have something—finally—and you're so—so fucking selfish. You won't even consider what life has been like for me, having to cart her around everywhere like she belongs with Dante's friends."

"Belongs with his friends? You're unbelievable." Turning, I shouldered my bag. Across the restaurant, Kathy was standing at the hostess desk with an older man and woman, chatting amiably. Danielle's fingers hooked around my elbow, twisting in the soft skin above it.

"No, *you* are unbelievable." Her breath hissed at my ear. "I will not let you fuck this up for me. You always lived for yourself and acted like you were so much better than me. You trot off across the country with your stupid job and leave me back here with Mom hanging from my neck."

"If you need some space from her, tell her. It's certainly time you realized she's your mother and not your partner in crime," I said, wrenching my arm from her grasp. "She's not an invalid and you're behaving as if she's completely dependent on you." Across the restaurant, our mother's laugh climbed, turning to a sharp cough.

"She's embarrassed Dante more than once." The pleading. I understood it, so much, this undertone in Dani's voice, because I'd been there too. Kathy was too much sometimes. Add a couple of beers or a few glasses of wine, and she could be much too much.

"I'm sor—" Walt's voice rang in my head from the day I'd first met him at Poplar Branch, and more than a few times since. *No need to be sorry, Erin.* "I know, Dani. I get it."

"She won't understand if we don't have her move in with us once the house is finished, E."

I looked from my sister to our mother, and back again. This was how Danielle always wanted her life to go. *A rich guy, good friends, a nice house in the valley.* I never looked forward to life defined by anything but space and the means to provide my own stability. With those things a relative certainty, I suddenly had Callahan and Claire and Lucy. And Walt.

Who refused to replace his dying truck so his aging grandfather could have a private room at his senior care home. Who, I knew, would make room in his life for my mother, if she appeared in my life.

A small Southern town, a rented house, my first two female friends, and a man who led hikes and flushed backed-up campsite toilets for his comparatively meager living. All of it mine, and not dependent on Danielle's or Mom's approval. Or open to their commentary.

"I've got to get back," I said, gathering her close for a quick hug. "I'll talk to you soon."

I drove back to Los Altos through the last, long shafts of afternoon light. Nearly two hours passed, but I barely noticed. Once I'd dropped the rental's keys at the concierge stand, I made my way to my room on leaden legs. After nine in California meant past midnight in North Carolina. Just a few hours until Walt would dress in his ranger's uniform, open the park gates, and begin his new day.

This wasn't missing. It was an ache for him. I didn't know how to say it out loud, especially to him. And, after Kathy and Danielle, I wasn't sure if I was equipped to withstand it alone.

I reached for my phone and dialed. "Hi."

"Is that you, Erin?"

"You sound surprised," I said. "I told you I'd call. Are you busy?"

"No, no. Not at all. I'm happy you've called. Shall I come by for a drink, then?" Ardhi cleared his throat. "Or, we could go downstairs to the bar."

I stood and began to shift files, my laptop, and several discarded changes of clothes from the small sitting area. "No, my room is fine. I have a couple of bottles of wine from my sister's…um…I'll call down for some glasses and a wine tool. Come over, I'm in seventeen-oh-three."

"I'll be right there."

The difference in him was profound. Ardhi's manner, his dress, even his glasses were completely different. He'd traded the small wire-rims I remembered for frameless, vaguely industrial-looking glasses that turned his features sleek and urbane. He'd shaved his goatee. And Bermuda shorts? A fresh, starched white dress shirt with the cuffs turned over a knife's edge. Someone had been grooming my formerly rumpled, Tim the Beaver T-shirt-wearing old bed buddy.

Most of all, after two and a half months of Walt, Ardhi seemed very short.

"And how is Mama and Sister?" He kissed me on each cheek as he stepped into my room. I rolled my eyes in response as the door closed behind us. "Oh dear. That well, eh?"

"Mama has switched to wine. Sister is engaged to a vineyard-owning chef." I pointed him toward the bottles of Boriello Blu's Merlot and Chenin Blanc Mom and Danielle gifted me as a belated birthday present. "Your pick."

"Ah, well, at least they sent you off with something to drink." He studied the labels for a moment and finally snorted. "I've no idea what this white is. The red will do, I suppose. So Sister has landed the big fish?"

"It would seem so." As the words came from my mouth, I winced. Ardhi and I had fallen into our familiar, snarky banter, but to my own ear, I sounded bitter instead of witty. "I'm…I'm glad for her. She seems happy."

Accepting a glass of wine from me, one of Ardhi's eyebrows climbed. "Romance, marriage. These things make people happy." He looked at me closely. "They've made me happy."

I sat in silence for a moment, waiting for him to complete the thought. And then I managed to follow his implications. "Oh! Ardhi, that's wonder…um, I wasn't—" I stammered, motioning at the wine and around my suddenly more-than-just-a-hotel-room hotel room. "I hope it didn't seem like I was inviting you—"

"No, of course not. But in the interest of preventing a misunder-standing, I thought I should make myself quite clear."

"You have, of course. And I don't…well, I wasn't seeking you out in that—when did you get engaged?"

"Officially, last month. A girl from home, family friends of ours, actually. Who would have expected me to become a traditionalist at the end of the day?" His disinterest in assimilating American-style social subtleties into his personality was something I'd liked about Ardhi immediately. He'd struggled with soft skills as a manager, as I did, but had done well with his data security team since returning to our Mumbai house.

"I…that's fantastic, Ardhi."

"And you? Now that we're face-to-face, tell me honestly what you think of this new North Carolina house. I've heard it's quite rural. Hillbilly horrors, Steve Gomez has been telling everyone."

"Oh, I don't know." I shrugged, while the faces of people I knew, my little house, the view from the overlook at Walt's forest flashed by in my mind. "I've enjoyed it."

He paused, head slanting, and sipped his wine. "You know, Erin, I think it's been quite good for you." He nodded enthusiastically. "Yes. It has been. You're much more relaxed. Softer."

"Softer? Was I hard—"

"No. Not hard." He considered it for a moment, swirling the remaining Merlot in his glass as he did. "Rigid, I'd say. Hmm, yes. Quite strict about things. Lots of expectations, lots of structure."

I knew my mouth was open and felt myself blink as I listened to him, speechless and completely off-guard. Ardhi had worked relentlessly while he was in Los Altos at the Main house, as I did. As every rising member of ThinkMine management was expected to do. His appetite and stamina for taking the company public was near mythic. And to be called rigid and structured by him and with that particular *tone* in his voice…

"But these aren't bad things. You love your work," he said, raising his shoulders genially like he was discussing a sports score or a movie he'd seen over the weekend.

"You do too," I muttered. Why was this a problem? Why had he noticed this and never mentioned it? And why was my hand fisting around itself, pressing into the sofa cushion behind me? "We all work hard and like what we do."

"Yes, of course."

I nearly heard the *yes, dear* in his voice. The near-physical sense of him patting my hand turned my rigid spine to glass. And almost as illogical as Ardhi's surprise assessment of old me—the me he had been happy to have dinner and sex with two or three times a month when we were both still at the Main house—I suddenly drained my wine and blurted, "I have a boyfriend."

"Do you? You're *dating*? Seriously?"

Was I? Walt and I had started to be considered a couple among the people he knew. We had a routine, had reached a place with each other. Right there, as Ardhi looked on, I realized what that was. Trust. More than anyone in my past life in California, I trusted Walt. Claire, too, and even Lucy, whose judgment I was certain of when I met her.

Finally, I replied, "I am," and heard my voice soften with it as I remembered what *dating* entailed.

"Oh, I see." Ardhi chuckled a little and suddenly the man who used to whisper raunchy Mumbaiya phrases in my ear when we had sex turned doting and almost…paternal. "Yes, you *are* quite infatuated, aren't you? So he's another Miner, then? Does he know about the douchebag sys admin who keeps dumping lines from your code? I should speak with him, Erin. I'm not convinced this Alan bugger won't cause a serious meltdown when the virtualization project rolls —"

"Wait, wait a second, there." I refreshed my glass of wine so I wouldn't pour the remains of the bottle in Ardhi's lap. "Let's correct some assumptions. He's not a Miner, he knows about the *dirtbag*, and he thinks I can handle him myself. And so does Steve, and so do I. Jesus, Ardhi, I've been watching his CenterTalk windows through the mirror site for months. How do you think I knew he was dumping my code? I won't let him crash my servers. I don't need help running QA on my people."

"No," he said with an unruffled smile. "Of course not. And I apologize for sounding patronizing, which I did. You can mind yourself. Forgive an old lover who only wants to see you safe from douchebags, eh?"

God, he was still ridiculously charming. I giggled, shaking my head, and took a long drink of wine. "Okay, Ardhi, turn down the suave a little. You're forgiven."

"And you're still a tigress under there, which is why I've always liked you. Now, tell me about your new love. Thank God he's not one of us. Techies are the fucking bores of the Earth."

We spent another hour catching up, discussing our new offices, and Ardhi's fiancée Urmila, who he described as earthy and practical, as I claimed Walt to be. It was good being around Ardhi again. As we talked, I realized just how much I'd missed my friend.

"I think I've been so focused on being a manager that I've missed out on developing peers at Callahan House."

"You know Steve," Ardhi said. "He's a good guy. I thought you two got on well."

"We do, yeah. Of course. He wouldn't have brought me to Callahan if we didn't get along." I tugged at my ponytail, flipping the ends around my fingers. "I need to get some face time with him about this admin, actually. I've done all I can. After that last botched patch job, I'm going to have to action plan him."

Ardhi winced. Action planning an employee was a serious step. ThinkMine management culture emphasized *problem-solving, not problem-stating*. Action planning was the equivalent of not only stating there was a problem but naming how it came to be and how it would be fixed. Effectively, it put me on notice as a manager as much as it warned Alan his job was in jeopardy.

"After what I've seen and heard from you, I don't think you have a choice." He shook his head and drained his wine. "I don't envy you. Kamal Gupta had to action plan one of his developers, and it nearly gave him a fucking ulcer." He stood, smoothing at the front of his shorts. "Well, my body hasn't a clue what time it is, and I've drank all your birthday wine, dear. I'm afraid I must be off for bed."

I paused by my open hotel room door as Ardhi passed into the hall. "Let's have lunch before I go home, okay?"

As we compared schedules, buzzed on wine and laughing over our conflicting cases of jetlag, a shadow passed behind Ardhi. A sharp cough echoed through the hall.

"Well, well, well," followed.

I peered past Ardhi's shoulder after the sound. Somehow, and thank God for it, I managed to stifle a gasp before it came out. But I couldn't squelch what I knew was definitive shock and awe reading all over my face.

"What is it?" Ardhi's hand fell on my elbow and he looked over his shoulder. I shook my head and stayed silent, waiting for the sound of a door *thunking* closed. Finally, it came. I looked back to Ardhi and let out the breath I'd been holding. "Erin, are you okay?"

"That was Alan. *Dirtbag?*" I shook my head. "No. I'm not okay."

CHAPTER FOURTEEN

The Tocheeostee River was full. Full of water, let down from Highlands Dam, and full of boats, early arrivals for the long July Fourth weekend. Walt could see both, just beyond a thicket full of tulip poplar saplings fighting it out for dominance with kudzu, the vine that ate the South.

And Lucy was full of attitude. Too much attitude for seven thirty in the morning.

"You know you're worse than an old biddy-hen lesbian, Wanda. A few dates with a new girl and suddenly you fell off the radar. So, you and the babysub picked out your kitchen curtains yet?"

Walt closed the passenger door of Tate's truck. "Gonna take the boats down to the put-in," he said over his shoulder. "Meet y'all down by the water."

"Oh, please. You can't carry Tate's boat and that battleship of yours, big girl." Lucy passed him before he could detach the first bungee cord from the side of the truck and swung herself into the bed between the two kayaks. After a few extra seconds of pointed silence, she sighed. "Okay, Walt. Shit...I'm sorry."

"All right. Fine."

Together they worked in silence, removing the boats and gear. Tate swung out of traffic, heading down the road to look for a place to park, shouting that he would meet them by the river.

A benefit of carrying close to nine feet of orange heavy-duty molded plastic over his head was the insulation from Lucy's watchful stare, which was a hell of a lot worse than her continuing commentary. And it wasn't Lucy, really. It was her questions, probable insinuations, and coming up with answers he didn't have the words for yet.

Once Tate found them, they scooted into the water and set off, Walt in front, Lucy in the middle, and Tate, the best paddler, in the back. As the morning went on, Walt shut down Lucy's attempts to make peace with sporadic grunts and huffs. After a couple of hours, she gave up, backtracking to smart-mouthing Tate and trash-talking Walt's paddling skills. Finally, Walt spoke up, reminding her who taught the debutante to run whitewater in the first place and the morning settled into a companionable silence.

Past two in the afternoon, Walt, Lucy, and Tate pulled their boats from the Tocheeostee River, having skipped a break for lunch riverside to get ahead of the slower July Fourth vacationers. After stowing their kayaks and gear in the back of Tate's truck, they crowded into the cab.

"Lunch? Crusts?" Lucy tucked her legs beside Tate's once he'd climbed in.

Tate moaned. "Yes. Dear Lord, yes. *Please.* And after you two had me on a forced march all morning, you're paying, Lu."

"Buy your own, Tatiana, you've got plenty of money. Come to think of it, it's time for second quarter dividends to roll out. You can buy mine and Wanda's too."

Their regular waitress, Ernestine, greeted them at the door.

"Afternoon, y'all. The usual?"

"Hey, gorgeous. No," Luce answered before either Walt or Tate could speak. "This one wants the double bacon burger and sweet potato fries—with extra bacon. Tall, dark, and handsome and his delicate constitution will have the grilled chicken with candied pecans on organic greens, balsamic vinaigrette on the side. I'll have the three-egg omelet with cheese and a double order of extra crispy homefries with onions and green pepper."

"No sausage?" Ernie asked, just beating Walt to the punch.

"Nope. Thanks, angel."

Lucy fixed her with a dazzling and respectfully flirtatious smile, given the woman was well into her grandmother years, and turned her attention to looking through her bag. The waitress and Walt looked at each other, at Tate, and back to each other.

"Lucy, the omelet comes with sausage. You always get extra."

"Sage, link, we've even got some of that extra spicy that you like so well, Lu," Ernie added helpfully, her eyes seeking out Walt's as she spoke. Of course, Miss Lucy Johns had only so much patience for helpful reminders of things she already knew. And she was busy looking busy with her phone.

Shrugging along with Tate, Walt shook his head and put on the happy face for Ernie. She'd been waiting on them since the three were transplants to Callahan twelve years before. After the first two years of trying to marry Lucy to Walt or Tate, a few sly attempts to couple up the men and introduce Lucy to her own grandson, Ernie settled into a familiar routine with them that didn't include their relationship status.

"I'll take the sausage, Miss Ernie. Would you care to bring Lucy some pancakes instead, please, ma'am?" Tate's down-South manners always got to her. The old-school, country girl waitress pretended she hated his thick servings of charm almost as much as Lu, but was much more susceptible to him.

"Sure thing, Tate. There's another pitcher of tea behind the cakes. Y'all help yourself."

Walt watched Ernie as she cleared the gleaming stainless steel pastry cases and headed for the kitchen, purposefully not noticing Lu glaring at him.

"So?"

"So what?" Walt looked at her over his glass of tea and gave her a blank stare.

"Wanda, obviously you've been with Erin every second you're not climbing trees or organizing your map stands in the visitor center. How are you doing? How are things going? How are you doing with how things are going?" She nudged at Tate's arm. "That *is* why we're here, right?"

Walt took a long drink of tea and gave her an equally long, considering tilt of the head just to piss her off more.

"Hang on, there." Tate's hand hovered between them, always the peacemaker when Claire wasn't available to smooth over the rifts and headbutting between Walt and Lucy. "We wanted to see you, too, Luce. It's been a while since we've gotten out. Just us. We'd like to know about how *you've* been too." Tate laid it on thick, using his best sensitive friend voice, earning a hearty snort from Lucy and a face full of wadded paper napkin.

"Bullshit. Okay, spill, Wanda. Facts first," Lucy countered, one square stub of a red nail tapping against her glass of tea. "So? Plans for the babysub?"

"Not sure." Walt picked up a straw and began knotting the wrapper — very, very focused on the white paper.

"Walt," Lucy groaned. "Really? Is this you?"

"I don't want to rush her." He shrugged and lifted the straw to his mouth, blowing the wrapper at Lucy. She batted it away easily, without a blink.

"She's not Holly. And you're not this guy, either. Either way, there's no reason to—" she lowered her voice like Walt had heard her grandmother, Percy Johns, do at numerous holiday dinners "—you know... *be afraid*."

"Luce, I swear you say *afraid* like it's a terminal illness." Tate finished his tea, stood and started across the dining room. "You two are wearing me out today. I need a refill."

"No, I'm well aware she's not Holly. As for *that guy*, well...sure."

Sure. Not afraid — responsible, pragmatic, respectful, reasonable. Not afraid.

"Look, Walt, you've always known what you wanted. When you start...I don't — it's like you headfuck yourself out of things when that therapy stuff of yours tells you to do something more reasonable."

Suddenly the back of his neck itched like hell, and he had to look anywhere but at Lucy. The case of Miss Ernie's cakes and tortes seemed like a good choice, and Walt began counting huge dollops of chocolate frosting on a hubcap-sized chocolate cake, until Tate crossed his field of vision.

"Here, Lucinda, stop talking and drink some more tea." Tate refilled their glasses and sat down. "And quit the judging while you're at it. I wouldn't be the well-adjusted, responsible man I am today without six or seven good therapists. Neither would you."

Lucy took a long drink, watching Walt all the while. He did the same in return.

"I fucking hate it when you two play Chicken." Tate sighed expansively. "Walt, have you talked to Erin about your grandparents asking you to leave home? About what happened to you and Brady?"

"Some of it. I told her about what happened back home with Mel and her parents."

Lucy's eyes narrowed. "And?"

"Didn't faze her," Walt said, shrugging. "I haven't really told her about taking off once everything came out about me and Mel. It was just for the summer, anyway."

"Okay, whatever. You left home a couple of months early before college. Fine, no big. And what about when you and Brady were at school? Did you mention you got kicked out of cadets? And why?"

"Lu," Walt said, his frustration stacking for the second time in a day. "We're at the line, okay? I don't want to talk about this any more."

Tate sat forward, his hand stretched across Lucy's. "I don't see a reason to worry as far as Erin's concerned anyway. Hell, if life hasn't jerked you around by the neck once or twice by the time you hit thirty-five, you haven't really been living."

"True," Lucy said, nodding. "But how many jerks has *she* had?"

"More than you realize." Uncertain, nebulous thoughts of Erin in danger, lonely, lost—all things he wanted to protect her from—made Walt harden his jaw. "But those are her stories to tell me when she's ready."

"Oh, you keep too much under your skirt, Wanda. Your female probably does too." Lucy's eyes twinkled as the terse line between her eyebrows softened. The tension dropped a few more degrees.

Finally, Tate chuckled and sat back in his chair. "Speaking of what's under a skirt, Lucinda, are you going to tell us about you and this mystery lady you're running off to Atlanta to court every chance you get?"

"Oh, we're talking about me now? Okay." She sipped at her tea and tossed a braid over her shoulder. "I love talking about me. Fabulous. What do you want to know?"

"He asked about the girl in Atlanta, not you, Barbie-dyke." Walt shook his head and laughed at her obvious deflecting, though he'd pretty much done the same thing.

The surprise, though, was Lucy's reaction. A smile, one Walt couldn't remember since her first serious college girlfriend, crept across

Lucy's face, too big to be confined just to her mouth. Her cheeks flushed; her eyes actually sparkled. Damned if she didn't look down and tuck a piece of hair behind her ear like a teenager with a crush.

"Oh, hell," Walt muttered, suddenly infected with the same grin. "You're shitting me."

"She's, um…" Lucy pressed her lips together, pushed at the tight line of them with her tongue a little, and actually giggled. "Well, she's pretty stellar."

"Yeah?"

"Fucking stellar." She actually hunched her shoulders over her coffee.

"No," Tate said, peering at her. "That isn't…"

Walt caught it too. "Louis, are you blushing?"

"It's the middle of summer and I've been in the sun, numbnuts! I do *not* blush. Ever."

Behind them, Miss Ernie approached, clearing her throat and scowling at Walt and Tate. "You two deviling my girl again?"

"No, ma'am." Tate twisted away from the table so she could place his burger before him, giving her a good look at his humbled face.

"So do we get the story on how you met and when? Any details on the lady in question?"

"Jesus, Walt, when did you become such a woman?" Lucy flushed again and looked up at Miss Ernie, sheepish. "Pardon, ma'am."

"Um-hum." The elderly waitress sat a mound of fresh salad greens and grilled chicken in front of Walt, fixing him with a no-nonsense look similar to the one she'd just given Lucy. "Now, it might be past lunch and they's nobody in here, but I won't have y'all gettin' loud and cursin' in my place of business."

"Sorry, ma'am." Walt dipped his head respectfully.

Lucy, always so tight-lipped about her own love life, had even piqued Miss Ernie's curiosity. "So, you finally meet you a decent lady?"

"All right, all right. She's great. Just…shi — shoot," Lucy said, deferring to Miss Ernie. "Would y'all let me figure this one out, okay?"

Lucy's voice drifted away and she turned to Walt, actually looking up through her eyelashes at him, suddenly beautiful and vulnerable and full of the newness of this woman none of them knew. All at once, Walt felt proud and scared and elated for his chosen sister.

"Okay, baby. No problem." He grabbed her fisted hand and smoothed it under his thumb, nudging her into letting the tension drop from her long fingers. "I'm glad." Tate made an encouraging sound as Miss Ernie patted Lucy's shoulder, once again cooing over *her girl.*

"Me too, Wanda." Lu laced her fingers through Walt's and sat up straight. "I'm glad for both of us. Maybe we're growing up. And maybe you might someday too, Tatiana."

They stared at each other for a beat, before giving in to the absurdity of it all and bursting into laughter that earned an indignant sigh from Miss Ernie as she walked back to the kitchen.

"Three of you are nothing but a mess," she said over her shoulder as the door whooshed closed behind her.

"You know, she's right," Tate said. "We should be mature enough at thirty-seven to be respectful of others and carry on an adult conversation without sending poor Ernie off to the back to pray for our blaspheming souls."

Walt settled against the back of his chair, drinking from his tea in his best mature-conversation pose. "So," he asked between sips, "how're her tits?"

Lucy's eyebrow shot high over a half-grin, and she mimed a pretty good-sized handful.

"Nicely done, Louis."

Despite feeling more and more distant from myself and the people around me, I knew I could survive the rest of my visit to Los Altos. I would, if I managed it with the familiar tactic I'd always used for survival: work and lots of it. I spent most of my last two days meeting with my counterparts at Main House, creating a schedule to test my portion of the memory virtualization project at Callahan House. With this new step in programming, ThinkMine would expand our data storage capabilities by more than fifty percent without adding a single piece of hardware. And once we completed that expansion, we could do it again and again.

"Once this stage goes live, I want to start considering taking more of our remote houses virtual." Steve Gomez, the site director at Callahan house, had joined Ardhi and me for a quick lunch in the Main lunch room.

"Dear God, Miner Chicken Tikka and tofu Pad Thai." Ardhi sniffed as we looked over the hot food offerings. "I can't. Bless our corporate directors and their altruistic catered lunches, but I need a salad. Meet you chaps in the courtyard, hm?"

I accepted a plate of Pad Thai, watching Ardhi's departure and wishing after him and his salad. All the long days on the back of spicy, oily lunchroom food was doing my stomach no favors. Once we were outside, Steve and I sat at one of the primary-colored free-form plastic picnic tables that were scattered between the two large, green glass buildings making up Main House.

"You know, I thought I saw one of your admins this morning in the hotel lobby."

"You did." Setting my untouched—and now unwanted—lunch aside, I cleared my throat. "He talked Connie Simpson into bringing him out here for an all-hands meeting on the census project."

Steve's eyebrows rose. "He could have called in for that. Did you approve it?"

"No. Connie did."

"Nice of her to approve travel from my site," he said. "This guy—?"

"Alan. Alan Richardson."

"Right. Alan Richardson. He's been with us for seven months? Second wave of admin new hires."

"Nearly seven. Closer to five on my team."

"Ah. Just seems like he's been there forever since I see him everywhere I go." His lips pursed a little and I had to do the same to catch a laugh. Snark was highly frowned upon at the Mine, especially when handling an associate's performance, but sometimes the situation asked for a little griping. And this was my in. Steve knew it, and I knew it.

"Steve, I need to action plan him."

"Oh? Hm." He chewed for some time, looking across the courtyard at a group of developers playing volleyball with a neon pink and orange Nerf ball. "I'm sorry, Erin. Based on the patch jobs he went solo on and this stunt, I'd terminate him if we were part of any other organization."

"But we're Miners."

"Oh yes, we are. And we *create solutions, not conflict.* I'm the worst mentor, Erin. I'm sorry you and Ardhi are saddled with me."

He shot me a rueful grin and pushed his chicken away. "At least ten percent of our associates at Main are from somewhere in India, and the lunchroom is still murdering Chicken Tikka. Fixing that would be a more beneficial solution than stringing people along who are a bad fit."

"The Pad Thai hasn't improved either, I'm afraid."

"Once we're back in Callahan, write up his plan and when I've looked over it, we'll meet with him together."

"Oh, I can…No, I want to handle it myself. If that's okay with you." I added hastily.

"I'm fine with that, but are you sure you don't want me there for backup? I know this isn't your favorite part of being a manager." He glanced around us for any unaccounted-for ears. "This guy doesn't play well with anyone, but I think women are a real issue, Erin."

I heard Walt's voice, from the night of our first date, in my head: *and doesn't it piss him off that he can't fuck you out of your power?*

"No." I shook my head. Ardhi was crossing the courtyard to us. "I can handle him."

"Okay, then. It's your call."

Discovering the Sensual World around You

The act of submission should be a pleasurable one, even if your experience of that pleasure comes from the most harsh discipline. For many submissives, embracing their own true nature opens a new sensual world to them. I don't mean sensual in expressly sexual terms but in the larger definition of the word. Because we are asked to reveal our true selves to our Dominants and answer so many questions to Them as well as ourselves about who we really are, I believe the way we experience the world is profoundly changed. Heightened. A Dominant, especially a sensual one, will use all of your senses to train you, make you more aware and responsive. If you're looking exclusively for a disciplinarian, you might elect to move to the next chapter, but I'd encourage you to give this exercise a try. Your ability as a submissive to surrender to your senses, rather than your rational mind, will enhance your experience — not to mention your poise and presence as a sub.

Of course, the five senses are taste, touch, smell, sight, sound. How often are you really aware of these senses? How often do you choose clothing for utility rather than its feel, the color, or even the scent of the fabric? Do you use your sense of taste exclusively for eating? Are you simply hearing music, the sounds of life around you, or truly listening?

No doubt you've heard the term "sub space." It is my belief, and that of my Master, that we can only find this space when we are willing to let go of the mundane, vanilla world and dare to visit the part of us that is pure pleasurable sensuality — and sensual pleasure! Finding this space inside you may be difficult at first, or you might wonder just what it has to do with a Dominant working you hard with His/Her toys. However, your Dominant will expect focus and discipline as you work toward reaching the goals He or She sets for you. Wouldn't it be easier if you were responding with your whole being?

Sensory Exploration: Senses.

Choose an item that appeals to each of your five senses and find some time alone to discover them all as one experience. Concentrate on the appeal of each item and then indulge all of your senses simultaneously. Be aware of how this exercise affects your mind and body: How does your body feel? Has your breath changed? Are you sleepy or hyper-alert?

Alert? Sleepy? Was it possible to be both?

Suspended between the two? Yes.

I shoved Claire's notebook and an empty vending machine bag of M&M's away from me and took off my glasses, blinking hard at dry eyes. After four days back in the arid environment of Los Altos, everything about me felt drier, especially my temper, which had turned to crispy after Alan's surprise arrival at the Main House. And I missed Walt. Terribly. So much. We kept missing each other's calls too, which added frustration to the ache. Even missing Walt, as ridiculous as it should have made me feel, was far better than worrying over Alan's appearance earlier that week. I felt low. Tired. Detached even from my own thoughts.

My phone was by the hotel room window, charging on the only available outlet. Crossing to it, I played Walt's latest message again, then twice more, gnawing at my thumb so I wouldn't smile too much at the wide-open vowels on his deep voice as he called me sweetheart.

I caught my reflection in the shaded glass, lit with a shaft of early evening sun, and despite flinching in surprise, I couldn't quite look away. I saw the angles of my face, the same camisole I'd put on once I stripped away my rumpled suit, the flyaway hair around my ears. My legs twined together as I huddled over my phone and smiled at the sound of his voice. And I saw the last shadowed traces of Walt's bite peeking from under the white cotton stretched across my breast. I heard my own gasps, the whine in my throat as his teeth closed over my skin there and he thrust his fingers into me.

Was this who Walt saw? And what would he think if he saw this new seam of neediness opened in me?

"Sir," I said, half-aware, a thin, thready sigh. The memory of his voice answered.

"...they'd want to remember how beautiful you were when they didn't have you with them. Because they'd want to see your skin all warmed up and pink from their hands. Because they'd want to have proof for themselves they got you to make that face you make when you come."

I turned my phone over in my hand, considering. Before I could consider too much, I snapped a picture.

I miss you.

"Miss you, too. Wish I could see you a little better in this picture."

Smiling to himself, Walt sent the message and thumbed over the smooth glass face of his new smartphone, pulling up Erin's picture again. It was exactly the kind of thing she'd do to him, sending a dim image of herself, reflected in a window. Nothing like any naked phone-pic he'd been sent before. Nothing more than outline hinting at the full curve of her breast, receding into a stretch of bright white. And very clear, just beneath it, a deep blue and purple bruise, just about the size and shape of a row of teeth. His teeth.

In the past, he'd had the most obvious reactions to the marks he left on the women he played with. Sometimes it was pure lust and want for the mind-blowing sex that followed a hot scene. Sometimes, he'd nod his head a little and smile, remembering how a bottom looked and sounded under his hand. Occasionally, he'd even gloated at the reactions he could bring out of a woman. But Erin…the slight hint of the mark he'd left on her clenched down deep into his gut. His teeth ground at the urge to leave his handprints over more of her, to haul her close to him by her messy ponytail and make her breath go shallow, her eyes turn wide and a little wild. There was a difference, though. He wanted all of those things because they were part of her, not because he'd made them happen.

"Don't you have any sort of short-term memory?" came Erin's text reply.

"Been four days since I saw you naked. Technically that's long-term memory."

Still grinning, he stretched across his bed and pulled down the picture. Once it was in view, Walt cupped his balls and tugged, grunting with satisfaction at the pleasant shift of pressure in his thighs. *Later*, he promised himself, and pushed back the urge to compare and contrast the way Erin affected him to his long-ago, horny teen-age guy self.

"Well, technically it's been five days since you've see me naked because I was dressed before you woke up to take me to the airport."

Should he tell her he'd watched her that morning as she wiggled that ass of hers into her jeans, muttering and sniffing over her luggage while he pretended to sleep?

"Too long then," he typed. "Send me a better picture of you."

Walt chuckled to himself, imagining his Type-A Miss Reboot on task, taking picture after picture with her phone, trying for the best angles and lighting. After a stretch of minutes, his erection began to wane. Her ass. Now, memories of that ass and what he'd done to it Saturday night would keep him hard until she got the picture together.

"Speaking of four days, how's your ass look?"

No answer.

"You there?"

Still nothing.

"Erin."

The reply was almost immediate. "Sorry. Here. Lighting conflicts."

Another apology. If he could make one rule for Erin, it would be the end of her sorrys. Rules.

She wanted to keep up the D/s while she was gone, had told him, right there in her bed after they finished.

So. Give it a shot.

He typed, "Try that again."

"Try?" After a few seconds another message from her appeared. "I'm here, Sir."

Walt sank into his pillows, grinning to himself. "Good girl."

She didn't reply again, at least with words. A picture followed, though, this one much clearer than the reflected shadows and shafts of light in a window she'd sent before. It was her. All of her, with no glasses and no prim ponytail, but still Erin, looking into the shot over her shoulder. Her eyes had dropped a half-hitch shut, framed with her pale hair falling to her shoulder. And down that long slope, past the deep curve of her waist, her ass. High, rounded, and still bearing the marks his hand left there four days before. Groaning, he dialed her number.

"Walt? I mean—"

"You sound sleepy," he said.

"Mmmm…I am. Have to be in at six tomorrow." She yawned, and the phone rustled against her. "Oh and hi, by the way. You didn't have to call. It's late for you."

He imagined her smiling as she said it and smiled too. "Hey yourself. And I wanted to."

"I'm glad you did."

"So how was your meeting?"

"It was fine. Long. Productive, though. I…" He could see her, slanting her eyes away under a raised right eyebrow, as she always did when she didn't want to say what she was thinking.

"Was your review okay?" He knew the answer already, but a simpler question would ease her open. It was a muddy area, between kinky play and coming closer to D/s, expecting answers to questions he knew she was skirting. When she didn't respond, he cleared his throat. "Erin, answer me."

She did, but only after several long, drawn exhales, a sniff or two, and the telltale rustle of her phone sliding under her chin. Finally, she took a short breath. "I miss you, Sir."

That forlorn note in her voice; it wasn't usual Erin. The revelation was hard for her, Walt knew, and took time to let it out. "I miss you too." He rolled to his side. "Have you been doing the drop care I told you to do?"

"Please, not now. I can't talk about this here. When I think about it, I miss being like that with you, so much I can't…" she said, her voice barely a whisper. "I had to quit reading Claire's notebook and am focusing entirely on work. But I'll be okay. I can make it until Thursday."

"Two more days?"

She laughed a little, quiet and a bit rueful. "I'll keep eating chocolate and drinking hot tea and taking deep breaths. I'll get outside when I can for some sun. I can't promise I will be able to sleep more than I have been. So…" Her voice quaked. "So I'll do all of those things, because you told me to and Claire wrote about it in her notebook. But…I wish you were here. Can I do that too? Can I miss you?"

"Of course you can — I told you I miss you too." The conversation was close to running off the rails and the first steps at modeling the formal D/s exchanges he'd watched over the years had evaporated in the face of Erin's distress. Being there for her was more important than acting like a kinder, gentler version of Paul Saldino anyway. "How was your day?"

"It's over. That's the best thing I can say about it. And you called, so it's ended better than it started." She sniffed and let out a long, ragged breath.

"Sweetheart, what's wrong?"

"Steve and I agreed to put Alan on an action plan this morning."

"Oh yeah?" Walt would have fired the asshole months ago. "How did Dirtbag handle his medicine?"

She sighed heavily. "I haven't done it yet. I'll meet with him once I'm back at Callahan House," she said, her voice falling off at the end. She went silent.

"Erin?" If the damn signal dropped now…"Hey, Erin, you still there?"

"I am. Let's—can we talk about something else?"

"Okay," he said. "I can let you go if you're—"

"No. No, I want to talk to you, Walt. Just…I want to not be that person right now. I don't want to be work Erin, either."

"All right. Who do you need to be?"

"Right now? Your girlfriend, I think? If that's what I—"

"Erin, yes. Girlfriend."

"Oh. Okay. Well, maybe you could tell me a story," she said softly. "Tell me something about you that I don't know. Or tell me something that happened to you today in your forest."

His forest. There she went with that *your forest* business again, making him grin to himself over this idea she'd always had of Poplar Branch being his domain or something crazy like that. Reaching past his shoulder, Walt tucked his pillow around his head again. "All right. You remember those retirees from the first day you came up to the park?"

"Oh? Estelle and the girls from Long Island?" Her laugh, a real one, bloomed and filled the airspace between them. There was something about making this girl let loose, remember to let go, let herself just relax.

"I think they sent a few more members of their bridge club down. And guess who led them around the Hemlock loop?"

"Sam?" She giggled again. "Sam and a tour group of retired ladies? What happened?"

"Well, it would seem my assistant ranger had a date this evening. With *four* ladies."

It felt good to hear the taut edge drop from Erin's voice as she speculated about Sam Cross's potential for polyamory. The knot of tension in his shoulder he'd been twisting and popping at all day had disappeared. And, he realized as he listened to her, he heard his own laughter again and again.

CHAPTER FIFTEEN

The final leg of my flight was three hours late, nearly grounded in Chicago due to weather. Our pilot made an announcement assuring the passengers he could skirt a break in the line of thunderstorms traveling north along the Appalachian Mountains from the Gulf of Mexico and still land in Charlotte close to the original arrival time.

So the captain engaged the *Fasten Seatbelts* sign somewhere between Nashville and…Ohio? Beneath the clouds was unknown country, one of the few regions Kathy never moved Dani and me to. The plane pitched a little, prompting another reassuring announcement from the cockpit. And I held on, crushing my hand around the cuff of an obscenely overpriced sweatshirt I'd purchased when I changed planes in Chicago. The lulling effects of the glass of wine I'd drunk before boarding in San Jose were long gone and, with the cabin crew restricted to their seats, so was my means of getting another.

There was so much lightning. Rain drove hard against the window beside me. I'd refused to trade the kindly-looking woman beside me for her aisle seat, earning a sour look and stony silence for the rest of the flight. The concave space between my seat and the window provided a sterile, silent cocoon where I could watch, my eyes fixed on the blinking red light perched on the wingtip outside my seat.

If I went down, at least I'd see it coming.

During the initial descent into Charlotte, the plane dropped, more than once. A violent, sudden surprise. Each time, the captain's voice reassured us all was well. *Just a bump…a little turbulence.*

But then an intense silence fell over the inhabitants of the plane, as though we were all just willing things to be okay. When the flight crew put wheels to the wet runway in Charlotte, more than one pair of hands came together, applauding our anonymous captains. I couldn't join them. Until I saw the plane anchored to the gate, I would keep one hand curled around the armrest, the other into the sleeve of my ninety-five-dollar sweatshirt.

Somewhere beneath the dimly lit atrium, spread past the wing that bounced and shook with the force of another wind gust, Walt was waiting. I shut my eyes hard at the thought of him sitting there, waiting so long for me.

Deplaning and the long, chilly march from jetway to concourse seemed to happen to someone else. I was a ghost traveler, hardly aware I passed shuttered stores and dimmed gates, merely following other bodies to the end of concourse. I stepped in time with them, depending on the rule of a crowd to steer me to baggage claim.

And there he was: blinking at me with heavy eyes and mouthing my name. Standing, his long legs pushing him to his feet from a seat that looked too narrow and too hard to have given him any kind of comfort. A paperback book tumbled from his thigh, the spine cracked midway through the pages.

He smiled the familiar half-grin I'd imagined so many times over the past week.

Two thirty a.m. Waiting for me.

"There you are. Hey," he said as I reached him. I felt him pause, waiting for my usual response — *Here I am. Hi* — but I couldn't make the words form. I disappointed him. It seeped from his skin immediately. This was not going how he'd imagined. "Hey, you okay?"

Still avoiding his eyes, I nodded and crouched down for his book. *Gavin McCloud, Esq.: Assassin, Plead the Fifth.* "Looks like a good one."

"It lags in the middle," he said and accepted the paperback from me. "You okay?"

"The flight was full. I had to check my bag." I turned for the carousel, already lurching along. Walt's fingers skimmed across my hand and I stopped, inhaling.

"Erin, look at me. I asked you if you're okay." His warm skin hovered near mine. I let myself reach for his index finger and no more.

My voice hung in my throat, thick after nine hours of silence. "I am now. The storm—" I wrapped my hand around his finger and didn't care how juvenile it was. I couldn't reach any farther. "Walt, I need to not be in an airport anymore."

He kissed the top of my head. "Stay here. I'll go get your bag."

"No," I said, too quickly, and flinched at it. "I mean, you don't know which—"

"It's black and has the ThinkMine hangtag, right? I carried it to the car when I brought you." His thumb found my wrist, stroked it twice. "You wait here. I'll be back. All right?"

I nodded silently and crossed my arms across my chest, resolute in my floor-watching. If I looked up, caught sight of him, of his back, walking away from me...

Damn you, Erin. No. Not like this, not in the middle of this place and not like some hysterical woman.

"Got it." His big hand, splayed wide in the center of my back, was a warm and solid living thing, so much more welcome than the stiff, narrow back of an airplane seat. A real anchor behind me. "I'm parked across the way."

To me, in the punch-drunk perception of my overstimulated shutdown, Walt said *across the way* like the traffic lanes outside baggage claim were a river we needed to traverse to get to some place that was his, and called up that phrase, his—our—words *I've got you.* Someone other than me making sure I'd cross to safety. Again, I nearly broke apart. Instead, I let my nerves sink into the heavy bundle of exhaustion, and let him ford the crosswalk.

The short-term parking garage was nearly empty and silent, except for the occasional bark from the wheels of my bag. When Walt finally stopped and stepped from my side, the chirp of a key fob made me jerk back to the present. Instead of his truck, or my car, which he had driven me in to the airport, was Lucy's sleek black Range Rover.

I stood behind it, watching as he slid my laptop bag and suitcase into the rear hatch. My purse dangled from my elbow, in danger of dropping to the concrete beneath me.

"Where's your..." I struggled to push the words from my mouth, too tired and too wary of what was churning inside me to make more than a whisper.

"Shhhh," Walt said into my forehead as he placed a kiss there and took my hand again, leading me to the passenger side. "Thought you'd be more comfortable riding home like this after that flight. C'mon and get in." He pulled the door open for me. When he took my hand in an attempt to steady me as I climbed in, I tensed. *He shouldn't have to...I don't need him to...*

Yes, I did. *So much.*

And with that, I wanted to collapse, sobbing, on his shoulder. I wanted Walt's arms circling me and needed to hear the familiar deep, comforting sounds rumbling from his chest.

I found my breath again and turned my head away, blinking at gritty eyes as I searched through my bag, pretending I needed to blow my nose. Walt shut the door behind me and walked to the driver's side. Seated behind the wheel, he turned to me, reaching across the console for my hand.

"Erin," he began.

"I'm sor—" Clearing my throat, I started again, this time with what I needed to say. "Thank you. For the late night and Lucy's car and...just thank you."

"You want to get a hotel room, stay here tonight?"

"No." I shook my head, enough to send my weary senses scrambling again. "I'd like to go home, please? If you are able to drive so late?"

"Sure. Why don't you try to get some rest?" The big SUV came to life. "We should be there in an hour or so."

Before we cleared the exit gate, I was asleep.

I opened my eyes again to the sound of his voice calling me sweetheart, his hand on mine.

"Walt?"

"Yeah, I'm here."

And he was, really was. Waking up to him as he leaned into the space where I slept, smelling him, feeling him, with no time to come alert and find mental space between needing him so much and the low-grade terror of the return flight sent me over the edge I'd been peering past since I saw him waiting for me in baggage claim.

"You're here," I said, reaching for him. "You're here."

"Yeah. Shhhh." His arms were around me, cradling me against his chest and I rose. "Got you. Shhhh."

"N—can't. Walt, you can't carry me." My eyes blurred with tears, burning my sandy eyes.

He laughed softly. "Well, better open your eyes then, sweetheart, because I am."

"Can't," I said, my head thumping against his shoulder.

"Hold on to my neck. I'm gonna put you down so I can open the door, okay?"

I felt a whoosh of cooled air and caught the scent of sun and wood and the new bamboo-lotus candle I'd bought the last time I was in Asheville with Claire. *Home.* I reached for the lights by the front door, but Walt's hand was already there, turning the switches on.

"Can you make it back to your room? I'm gonna go get your bags."

"Um…sure. Okay." I inhaled, heavy and somehow still sharp, and sagged into his arms again. "Hurry back."

Chuckling, he kissed the top of my head and was gone.

I shuffled through my bedtime routine, answering only the most important needs. Walt and I exchanged places in the bathroom.

Before I could rationalize it, I was on my knees, waiting. The bathroom door swung open and he was behind me.

"Hey, baby, I—" He went quiet for a stretch of seconds, then crossed my bedroom, coming to rest in front of me, dressed only in his navy boxer briefs. "What's this?"

"I need you." He was so far up there, from down at his feet, and the dim light from my bedside lamp didn't illuminate his face at all. Being on my knees in front of him, out of the blue, without invitation, and without his careful planning and negotiation from our first scene, was like flinging myself into a narrow, shadowy void.

"Erin," he began, his voice husky with something. Weariness, wariness, maybe both.

"Sir, please. I don't know how to explain. I need you to…" He sat at the edge of my bed, in front of me. A good sign, which was very helpful considering I had no idea just how to ask someone to spank me so hard I'd feel put back on the ground again. He reached toward me and tucked my chin into his palm.

"It's okay, Erin. Don't worry about right. Just tell me what's going on."

The pass of his thumb over my cheek settled me enough to speak again. "I need you."

"Hm. Need. Okay." He didn't sound convinced. Not reluctant; just not convinced.

"I've been so…like I've been floating all week, here—or there—but not?" The lack of precise words to explain what the ache for him was like frustrated me, and I shook my head at it, once again making my travel-weary self a bit dizzy for my efforts. "It was like being anchorless. It made me miss you more, but the only thing that helped me focus was thinking about this, between us. About calling you Sir and the way you talked to me when we played and what it feels like to…you know—to submit to you. About what it felt like to be yours, and knowing I'd let you be in control. Well, and the chocolate helped too, Sir."

At the sound of his deep chuckle, I relaxed, and sank further against my bent knees.

"Sub drop. I wondered about that," he said. "So, are you going to tell me what you need or are we going to bed?"

"You want me to say it, don't you?"

"No. I need you to say it." He lifted my chin again, turning my eyes to his. "And you need to ask for it. Exactly what you need."

I glanced past my shoulder at the dimmed hallway. The old needlepoint runner had moved again, wrinkling in front of the bathroom door.

Should tape that down or something before we hurt ourselves.

"Erin?"

"Sir?" I jerked my head back to him.

"Let's do this in the morning. You're too tired to—"

"Sir, please. I need a spanking." I pulled at the old polar bear print pajama pants I'd put on, tugging them over my knees as I stood. "Please?"

He watched, silent. The current between us was there, but spinier and somehow darker too. This wasn't teasing and playing with bodies and sweet, delirious emotion. This was something harder.

"Sir, it hurts when I can't feel your hands on me," I said. I could barely hear my own voice. I waited, though, and listened to my own pulse in my ears.

Finally, he spoke. "Panties, too."

I pulled them away, fumbling the loop of cotton in my tired fingers, and staggered into him a little. He caught my hips, steadying me in front of him. His fingers went into the soft flesh there, clenching as he dragged me closer. He lowered his head and pressed me into his face, inhaling.

Gasping, I wrenched at his hold on my hips. He was inhaling *me*, taking my scent in. No one had ever stood sentinel over me like he did, and no one had ever wanted me like he did. Liking it, the sensation of him filling his senses with something elementally feminine and intimate from me, turned my body limp in his hands. But as I stood threading my fingers through the dark curls at the base of his neck, aching and wanting his mouth closer to me, the distant, frosty judge in me screamed louder. Words like travel and sitting and smell. He cupped my backside in his hands, his forehead resting against my mons, and he inhaled again.

"Sir, I've been on a plane all…Oh God, Sir."

He looked up at me, jaw ground tight. "Quiet."

"I'm sorry, Sir."

One hand left, connecting again with my backside in a hard, cracking slap. "Don't tell me you're sorry. Be quiet."

And then I understood. I gave over to my need for him and admitted it, but I had to submit to him needing me too. The want and ache for him I'd managed all week turned physical. I put my hands on his shoulders for balance, waiting for his bidding.

Finally, after releasing me, he sat back and lifted his arms.

"Lay down."

Don't talk, just do.

I did, wobbling as I climbed to the bed beside him and stretched across his legs.

"I'm going to give you twenty-five. Count them out. Nothing but numbers." He threaded a hand through my hair.

Before I could nod in understanding or prepare myself, it started. There was no warm-up, no sensual build like the first time he'd spanked me. He wasn't provocative, didn't rouse me with his voice in my ear. He didn't linger over me, dipping and teasing between my legs.

It came fast and with no pattern, popping between each side. The sound echoed along with my own sniffling, hoarse cries through my room, as hard on my ears as his hands on my ass.

Twenty-two burned and lifted my hips from his. Twenty-three drove me against his thigh again. Orgasm hovered so close, mocking me but best ignored.

"Twenty-four," I gasped against his leg. The coarse hair there curled into my mouth and nose and as I winced away from it, I felt something wet and warm where my cheek had rested. His hand descended again before I could process it. "Twenty-five, Sir."

He bunched my hair in his hand and lowered me to the floor between his legs. My shoulders rose and fell, and the sounds still came—wheezy, heavy-breathed sobs.

They were from me. I'd cried through the entire spanking.

"Good girl," he said quietly, his hand stroking my hair away from my face. He settled my head against his knee and let me soak it with tears and snot and the remnants of my mascara. His hand never left my head.

He was the thing that righted me, even as I cried messy tears that racked my chest and turned his skin wet under my cheek. As off-kilter as I know I looked, inside I felt like a nearly capsized boat coming back over its keel again.

"It's okay," he said finally, like he'd been repeating it over and over as I cried. "Your feet are on the ground now. You're home."

I was. Calm. Soothed by the stinging, hot skin on my backside. At Sir's feet.

Somewhere between that first spanking and this one, I'd fallen in love with him. And how it felt was incongruous to what I thought love would be. Loving him wasn't just about the heady things between us, but about a place for them to happen. With him, I was finding a place where I belonged. I was finding my home.

I raised my head, looking at him with sleepy eyes. "Thank you, Sir."

"You're welcome." Standing, he tugged me to my feet beside him. I bent again, reaching for my panties, but he caught my arm. "Nope. Leave those there. Now, get in bed."

I crawled over my quilt and pulled it past my knees so I could slide between the sheets. "Mmmmm," I sighed, wiggling at the feeling of cool cotton on my aroused and scalded skin.

He climbed in beside me, turned out the lamp and gathered me to his chest. His lips brushed over my forehead. "G'night, sweetheart."

Oh.

No sex. No feel of Sir inside me. No coming under him and for him.

I didn't ask for it.

Pressed to his warm, solid body, heavy with need for him and denied—very purposefully—was one of the most erotic and baffling things I'd ever experienced.

I fell asleep against his shoulder, his hand resting across the curve of my hip.

The next morning we slept in. Or dozed in, really, our legs tangled together as we woke each other with trailing hands and nuzzling, half-awake kisses until we slept again. Eventually the sun rose over the trees in my front yard, sending slanting fingers of light across my bed.

My bed. My house. Walt's arms around me. I tugged at his hair, bringing him to me.

"Missed you," I said and kissed him, taking my time with it, tasting the curve of his lip with my tongue. And he waited, still and quiet, letting me stroke and lick and nibble at every part of him I found under my hands.

This was different. Without sharp-edged, insistent power crackling between us, the causeway still opened, the light soft-focus, filmy.

We touched each other, but simply to please each other with the feel of our hands rather than a studied means of drawing reactions and stoking a flame to incandescent. We were gentle with each other. And when Walt brought his body over mine, he entered me slowly, his eyes on mine and smiling down as he rocked into me. Making love.

"Missed you, too," he said and settled his forearms on either side of my head. Dipping to me, he paused for another long, lazy kiss, his hips still moving against mine, and on to the little hollow under my ear that always stole my breath when he passed his tongue over it.

I smoothed a dark curl from his temple and whispered his name against his lips. Needed more. Opening wider for him, my knees swishing over his hips, I rocked with him. Sighs and moans echoed around us. Without words he questioned, nodding with raised eyebrows, and he knew, as soon as I gasped, craning forward to see where our bodies met and moved together. Walt tipped his body to one thigh, nudging with his knee, opening me, getting closer to me. He slid a fraction deeper, and I tumbled into a long, undulating orgasm that didn't race, but rolled, a steady, deliberate path toward its end. He met me there, squeezing his eyes hard as he came into me and said my name in a hush against my temple.

I wanted to tell him then, but love was another word I didn't know how to say.

We dressed and went to the kitchen for food, making ridiculous jokes about *the world's latest brunch* and *world's earliest linner* as we kissed and puttered around the kitchen.

"You dropped pretty hard. More than I expected," he said as we sat at the table for the meal that could not be named.

I nodded. "I didn't realize until last night that it was connected. Or I was disconnected? That's what it felt like—being disconnected. But it was a stressful week as well."

"Hmmm. That'll make you drop worse, too." He brushed his thumb over my knuckles. "You talk to your mom again after you saw them last Sunday?"

"Phone tag. Just like you. I should call her today." Dani would require a cooling off period.

"I'm gonna run over to the cabin and pick up some clothes, take Lu's car back to her. That should give you some time to yourself to settle in."

Like the surprise of the comfortable ride home, his understanding—without me forced to find words for why I needed time alone after being around so many people—made my eyes cloud. I turned my head, blinking at it.

"Hey, it's okay." He grinned at me and took a sip of coffee. "Let me do this for you."

"I'm working on letting you do it."

We laughed quietly over a couple of meaningful glances.

"All right, you work on it." He clapped his hand against my thigh, breaking the stream of unvoiced thoughts between us. "You want to play a little tonight?"

"Again? It's like having two Christmases." I giggled. "Really?"

"Yeah, goofy, *really*. This lost, floating thing—I want to work on it."

"Um, okay? Work on it with what sort of…"

"Mostly sensation, no toys. Don't want you waiting in position or anything like that. But I'd like to pick up D/s with you again. You okay with that after last week and then last night?"

"Mmmm, yes." I leaned into him. "Yes, I am completely, very, very okay with that."

He shook his head, chuckling. "Damn, I've created a greedy little monster."

I pushed my plate aside and climbed into his lap so I could have him again.

"Rawr."

I spent the afternoon in silence, doing laundry, dusting and vacuuming. Sorting the mail Walt had retrieved for me from my neighbors, the Jensens, before he left with Lucy's SUV. With each purposeful, familiar task, I felt myself settling in again, more here than there. *Home.*

In the early evening, Walt sent me a text. He was on his way. I was to wait for him, in my bathrobe, on the living room sofa.

He let himself in with his own new key, pausing to kiss the top of my head before turning down the long hallway to my room, his overnight duffel in his hand. He came back with a bottle of water for each of us and sat beside me.

"Hey," he said.

"Hi. How was your afternoon?"

"Good. You?"

"Great. I cleaned." I smiled, lazy and happy over it.

"God, you and Lu and your chores." He shook his head, laughing. "You still want to do this?"

"Yes. I do."

"All right." He set his water aside, turning to me. "This time, we're going to try something different."

I tried to nod, hoping it would mask how disappointed the word *different* sounded to me. It didn't, of course. He caught the hesitation before I could cover it.

"What's going on?" His hand slid around mine—warm, strong. It connected me to him by more than flesh, and I forced myself not to cling to his fingers like I was lost, sitting on my own sofa, in my own home.

"It sounds…I don't know? Worrisome?"

"Why, Erin?" He tugged at my arm, and did it again when I resisted looking up at him. When I finally complied, the familiar feeling of blooming, a deep and secret place in me spread out before him, returned. In such a place, I could only tell the truth.

"I don't know. It's that word. *Different*. And *try*. Together they're scary."

He didn't shush over me or roll his eyes dismissively. "You can do it." And there was the unspoken, always there, still echoing through me from our first time: *Got you.*

This time the nod came easier, and there wasn't anything attached to it but agreement. *Ready. Yes. Yes, Sir.* I squeezed his hand and stood, careful to keep our fingers linked.

"Good," he said, rising from the sofa.

My will and body were already surrendered to him. Now, after three times settling into this mindframe, it felt like coming back to a favorite, secret island. To me, when we were like this, Walt changed, as apparent on his outside as I felt different inside. I wondered if it was the same for him internally—if he felt quieted inside, relaxed but so much more aware, too, as I did. But it wasn't time for questions. He was waiting for me.

"Come with me."

I followed him, still holding his hand in front of me as he navigated the dim hallway. I glanced toward my bedroom window as we passed and could see my back yard, beyond. Outside, fireflies climbed from the shadows around the big oak tree there. Crickets and frogs were warming up for their nighttime concert.

Walt turned me into the bathroom first, tucking himself behind me. He reached across my shoulder to pull the shades taut, and I shivered at the sensation of his sturdy body behind mine. He gave me an indulgent, soft, neck-nuzzling chuckle in reply. Turning my head, I inhaled the scent of his shampoo and the sun from his hair, moving enough to let the brown curls dance across my cheek. My new contacts bunched a little and I blinked at them.

"Take your robe off," he whispered against my skin.

It puddled around our feet with a quiet swish, a streak of grayed white in the nearly dark bathroom. His T-shirt followed.

Rounding the edges of my body, his hands rose from the shadows. Our reflections shone in the mirror in front of us, dim from the last, hazy light of the day. When his fingertips connected with my skin, I tensed and drew in my breath, hissing it across my teeth in time with the meandering descent he took as he traced over the outside curve of my breasts, waist, hips. He finished at the top of my thighs, slowly kneading the muscles there against the heels of his hands.

I squirmed against his chest, still watching him watching me. His fingers splayed, nearly dipping through the tuft of hair between my legs. It was impossible not to move my hips along with his hands; they were guiding me to tilt and sway along, anyway. The crush and roll stopped, and he rested one wide palm in the curved cleft between my thigh and mons.

"You stay right there, okay?" He stroked my hip as he leaned over my shoulder again, reaching. The same hands had made the fading bruises on my breasts and had stung me with a spanking so hard I'd cried against his thigh. His attention felt protective and affectionate, and I settled into it like a cocoon.

A candle flickered to life beside us, and then he was behind me again. Our eyes met in the mirror, reflection to real, and his arms circled me, chasing away the bare-skin chill.

"You all right?"

I nodded. "Yes, Sir. Fine."

"I've been thinking about something you told me last night." Behind me, he shifted a little, and my ear fell closer to his neck. Drawn closer by the salt and spice of his skin, I could hear the click of his jaw as he swallowed and sensed the faint drum of his pulse over my own. "You said you felt…" He paused and looked at me, waiting for me to continue.

"Anchorless. When you—when we played the first time, I'd built it up so much mentally and then I had you…had so much of you? You make me feel rooted to the ground, like I have somewhere solid under me. When you weren't there, I missed that feeling."

"What is it about me that makes you feel like the ground's underneath you?"

"Because you want me here, Sir." The revelation was huge, but so easy with him behind me, his arms around me. Sturdy. Still there. "Not just sexually—but I like that, of course."

"Of course," he said, chuckling, as he mounded one of my breasts against his palm and gave it a soft tug. "Yeah, I like that part a lot, too. But is there anything else?"

"Because you've seen so much of me. And you're still here. Especially now, after…um, last night. When I needed you like that again, and you made me ask you for it."

"For?" He grinned with raised eyebrows, catching me hiding in my vagueries again.

"For the spanking. And for knowing you had to give me enough to get me to cry. I never break, Sir. But I fell apart for you." I felt his eyes on me, and glanced back to his refection in the mirror. "You are—"

"—so beautiful," he said, his voice mingling with mine. We smiled at each other, a little self-conscious, and he tipped his head toward mine. "You are."

"You are, Sir."

"You…" He inhaled, deep, from behind my ear. "God. You, you, you."

His palms rode over me again. I looked on, watching the image of him touching my body and the attentive, deliberate way he took in each part of me his hands skated over. When his eyes rose and found mine, the sharp, focused stare was there again.

Sir.

I fought hard at the rational voice telling me I was standing in front of a mirror, in my bathroom, dark except for the flame of a single candle, and without a single stitch of clothing. And even if I'd been covered in enough layers to ward off a deep-winter wind, I would have been completely naked to him. He saw it, too. Like the night we met, and every time since, the recognition was instant and mutual. As always, he nodded a little, enough to show me he acknowledged it too.

With one hand seated on my hip, he reached toward my head and threaded his fingers through my hair. The pressure was steady, but not painful.

"Erin, what do I have in my hand?"

"My hair, Sir."

I knew this call and response. I'd been here before and could conjure the right words for him. The pull against my scalp intensified enough for me to notice the change. I flicked my eyes back to his.

"Whose hair is this?"

It wasn't a rhetorical question. It was a decision, just like Claire wrote about in her notebook, and it was one I'd made at some level weeks — months? — ago.

"Yours, Sir."

Hair was nothing, really. Something that was essentially dead. Something I hardly considered and never fussed over like other women seemed to do. But dominion over it, for this time, was no longer mine. And it became more than hair.

My thigh muscles shook and I jerked, unable to catch the tremble before it registered against his body. He pulled his hand from my hair and dragged his knuckles across my temple and down my cheek, his eyes still fixed on my reflection. His hand opened, and his index finger traced over the shape of my lips, my chin, across my jaw. It came to rest.

"What's this, Erin?"

I looked up at him, not in the mirror, but over my shoulder, and barely constrained a giggle.

"Um…" I turned to him. "That's my nose, Sir."

"Yep." He reached past me and returned with a tissue, passing it over my nose before tossing it theatrically over his shoulder. "And whose is it?"

"If you want it, my nose and everything in it is yours, Sir," I said, and I lost it. The absurdity of it all tipped me forward, laughing, against his chest.

Suddenly what was happening was lighter. We were his fingers digging into the spot below my behind that drove me to helpless giggles. We were the sound of our laughter mingling together as it filled the bathroom. Even the candlelight seemed to flicker in time with us.

"All right," he said once we'd regained our composure. "Don't forget, now. All mine."

"Okay. Got it."

"What about these?" He cupped my breasts in his hands and bent to them, grunting as his head bobbed in time with his mouth. He took one nipple, then the other, between his teeth. I squealed and swayed as he moved between them again and again, clutching at his shoulder to steady myself.

"Yours, Sir," I said on a gust of breath as his teeth sank deep into my skin.

"Hmm?" His head slanted and one wide-pupiled blue eye turned to me. His eyebrow rose and his teeth closed, so much harder. "Hmm?"

"My um…my breasts, Sir. *Your* breasts."

"No," he said, rising, and slapped his hand across the crest of one nipple. The sting of it sent me whimpering, arching toward him for more. "These are my tits, girl. Mine. Tell me."

"Your teeth…no, *tits*—your tits, Sir." God, if he'd do that to them again, I'd call them Bipsy and Buttons.

"They are." He bent and drew his tongue over the reddened skin he'd just made. "Mine."

In the mirror beyond us, I caught sight of a couple. Him, broad shouldered and tattooed, bent deep from his waist and moving his head from side to side over his partner. Her, arched back and cradled into his arms, her hand resting across his shoulder, fingers curled into his hair, her face flushed and heavy-lidded, so turned on by him and for him and by herself with him. She looked at me. And though I'd been unsure I'd recognize who she was when I finally looked there and saw her, I knew exactly who was looking at me.

"It's me," I whispered to that woman. "This is me. And us. This is *us*."

His head rose, and his reflection grinned at me.

"Yeah, it is."

Standing, he eased me back to the soles of my feet as his hand settled on my back and sent us scuttling toward the door behind me. His hips ground against mine, raising me to my toes again, and his lips dropped to my ear.

"You know who you belong to, don't you, girl? Now you won't feel like you're going to float away again." His fingers spanned the column of my neck, cupping my jaw into his hand. Just inches, and he could grasp my throat, crush his fingers into the delicate cartilage under them. He could, but he wouldn't. *But he could.* And that openness, balanced on a pin's point, made me and my reflection finally unite as one.

I trusted him. Trust was my aphrodisiac.

"No, Sir." I blinked hard, inhaling. Not the time to cry, no matter how strong the sense of joy surged in me from freedom and completion of something—*the something*—I'd been toying with for most of my adult life. "I can't be alone when I have so much of what's yours with me."

"That's right."

Sir smiled down at me with Walt's smile, the easy half-grin I always saw first when I thought of him. Two facets of him melded as I studied the gentle rises and weathered falls of his face. He leaned down and kissed me, then stood, dragging me along the length of his body as he rose until we were eye-to-eye.

"Wrap your legs around me, baby."

Once I'd convinced the muscles in my abdomen that they could really constrict like that, I struggled and finally managed—inelegantly—to lock my legs around his waist. He balanced me against one thigh.

Hand thrust between my legs, he said it again. "Mine."

I smiled, even laughed a little because of course that was his too and shook my head so emphatically, a few strands of hair tumbled across my face. "Yes. Oh my God, yes, that is absolutely yours."

He went still. I'd never felt a blatantly predatory intention from him before, his evaluation and consideration always a more sensual tease. This wasn't. It was Lucy, the cagey cat eyeing an unguarded bowl of cream. It was Tate skimming the tip of a cane over Gala's purpled backside, and finding that one deep plum stripe that sent her screaming for more. It was Paul's hands snapping a lock into place.

"It's not a *that*. It's my pussy. Don't call what's mine *that*."

He was waiting for me to say it. No *yes, Sir* would suffice. My breath turned to shallow pants and my lips turned dry under them.

"Not..."

"It's not a *that*." He repeated and pressed the heel of his hand against my mons. "It's my pussy."

"Can't…"

"Yes, you can. Tell me what this is and who it belongs to."

I needed to have my hands in front of my face and needed not to be naked and needed my feet on solid flooring. The light around us dimmed and I wobbled, grasping at his shoulder. "Can't."

"Erin."

"I need down. Now." Pushing against his arm and realizing too late it was the one he'd shattered, the one that had delivered him from the horrible months of hazing and assault he'd endured as a cadet. I squirmed against the door. "I can't."

His voice softened, and his touch did too. "You can do this. Tell me what this is."

Finally I gritted my teeth and shoved my shoulder against his. "Red. Put me down *now*."

He stepped back, lowering me to the floor. I heard him say "shit" under his breath and he stepped back. "Erin? What happened?"

"I need to get out of here." My breath came harder and faster. "Please, I need air." I fumbled behind me, grasping at the doorknob with shaking fingers.

"Here. Erin, here, let me. Baby, stay still and let me open the door."

"No! I can do it myself." I found a hold and wrenched the door open. Behind me was dim, cool space, expansive and familiar. I stumbled over the runner under my feet, fighting for footing all the way to my bedroom.

Walt nearly folded over my back, reaching for my arms, saying over and over in a stern, efficient tone, "What's going on, Erin? You gotta talk to me. What's happening?"

"I need—" I twisted away from him, turning for the bathroom.

"Hey, no, will you stop?" His hands closed around my arms and held me before him. "Now, take a breath and tell me what's happening."

I looked up at him and my teeth began to chatter, from adrenaline or the chill in my bedroom.

"Let me get your robe. Stay here."

When he came back, he held my bathrobe open to me as I reached for it. The acrid scent of a snuffed candle wafted behind him.

"I can do it," I said, grasping at the sleeve.

"Here, I've got it open for you. Just step into it."

I folded my arms across my stomach. "Walt, I can put on my own bathrobe."

He looked at me closely for a few seconds and, lifting his chin, handed it to me. Once I'd cinched it shut, I crawled across my bed and between the sheets where we'd been together just hours before.

"Can I join you?"

I pulled back the quilt for him and lay down facing his usual space, tucking the edge of my pillow under my chin. Once he was settled beside me, Walt reached for me.

"I'm so—"

"Don't—" he said over me.

"Okay." Without a *sorry* to offer, I was effectively lost for words. I looked up at him, silenced.

"What happened?"

I glanced down at my fingers, winding around the thick white belt holding my robe shut. "It's ridiculous."

"No, if it set you off like this, I'd say it isn't ridiculous at all. Did I hurt you?"

"Oh no," I rushed to say. "That was fine. All of it. I'm sturdy, you know?"

A corner of his mouth lifted a little. It was like manna from the heavens and the tension between us began to ebb.

Instead of paying attention to important things—to Walt, smiling again, chest bare and lying beside me—I closed my eyes at voices from the past, like old recordings looping over each other, cutting in at illogical junctures. A guy Ardhi knew at MIT, come to visit him in Los Altos, telling a joke about "*a Lebanese woman's gyno.*" My mother and Dani fighting in the single bedroom of our apartment in San Jose, the one from our junior year in high school.

"*Did you say no? Look at that skirt, Dani. No wonder he was pawing at you. You can't just throw your legs open and let any guy who shows interest in you get in your panties. Do you want them calling you an easy piece of pussy?*"

I rubbed at my face. "I have to tell you."

"I'd like for you to." Walt dug his body further into the bed so we were eye-to-eye. "But you don't have to."

"Your feet are going to go to sleep, hanging off the edge of the mattress like that," I said, unable to disguise a laugh.

"I'll be all right." He smiled again, broader this time, and pushed a strand of hair from my cheek.

I had to say something. It was ridiculous and illogical and very obviously some kind of tic I'd developed over the word—and it really was just a word.

"I hate that word, Walt."

"What word?" His eyebrows drew together and I knew he was cataloguing the scene. Finally he looked at me and scratched his earlobe. "You mean pussy?"

I flinched at it, drawing into my robe.

"Oh."

"It just…it sounds…"

"It's coarse." He grinned. "I admit it. I mean, I wouldn't have said it to my grandmother."

I giggled in spite of the awkward space we'd stumbled into. "That's a relief. But, after what you've said about your grandmother, she would have literally washed your mouth out with soap if you said something like that to her."

He laughed. "If she could've caught me." He held out his hand to me and I slid my fingers between his. "Sometimes I worry about you. I see how you are about your body on occasion. How covered up you keep yourself." His hand closed around mine and he dipped his lips to my knuckles. "Erin, did something happen to you? Someone hurt you?"

"Um…no. Not me." I wanted to protect him from this part of me. It was too close to his own deep fractures in Tennessee. "Dani."

"Someone hurt your sister?"

"I—it's that, yes. Or I think it is. It was when we were in high school. I only overheard her telling Mom and I wasn't sure what to ask. I think she might have been trying to tell Mom about a date rape or a really aggressive guy." I smoothed my hand over his bicep once, and then again. "I don't want to upset you by talking about this."

"Hey, I've heard plenty of shitty stories about people's pasts. They're not about me."

"Okay. Um…well, it is that word. Kathy—my mom? She…she yelled at Dani when she tried to tell her, and blamed her for what she was wearing and for being available or too easy, I guess. And I know it's irrational. But she said that word when she was yelling at Dani. I hear it and it makes me feel dirty."

"Bad dirty?"

"Yes." I dropped my hand to the belt on my robe. "I've never been convinced there is a good dirty, or at least one I could be."

He looked at me, considering something for a long stretch of seconds. "Can I hold you?"

"Yes," I said, nodding quickly. "I'd really like that a lot." There was so much more I needed to, and should tell him. But for the moment, everything I'd told him was enough.

CHAPTER SIXTEEN

On his way to Crusts, Walt turned memories of Brady over and over in his head. He would have liked Erin a lot. He knew in his gut, Brady would tell him to really try with this girl, that she fit with him, could even hear Brady's voice saying it to him.

"I'd say she's the smartest decision you'd ever made, Bubba."

Just like he'd been over Melissa and his grandparents, and the bullshit with Joyce and Zane during his time in cadets at Clemson, Erin was in the same predicament. Stuck, feeling ashamed of something she hadn't asked to be part of, and sure it was better to keep it to herself. The easier, softer way was dragging her down with it, smothering her.

Brady was the most bull-headed person he'd ever met. Worse than him, worse than Lu.

You have to fight back, Bubba.

It'll get worse that way. They're gone after this year, Brady, just fucking drop it.

When he sat down at Crusts and explained the plan to Claire and Lu, it still made sense to him. Lucy had other ideas.

"Are you out of your fucking mind?" She glared at him.

"Lucy!" Claire hissed, eyes darting toward the kitchen doors. "Miss Ernie will hear you!"

"You've been asking me that for close to twenty years, Louis. Haven't you figured it out for yourself already?"

"Walt, I'm serious. You don't fix emotional stuff with playing. Especially with a headfuck."

"It's not a headfuck. She'll have an idea of what she's going into." Before Lu could jump back at him again, he added, "*And* she'll know she can end it at any time. Not red out, but just end it. Different dynamic, no D/s."

"Oh, really? You so sure she knows the difference if you ask her to do this? Speaking of, you two just started trying D/s and the last time you did it, it went south. Now you're going to sit there and tell me you can take this woman up against a trauma — really knocking at the door of a public consensual non-consent scene in the middle of a bunch of vanillas, if you asked me — and do it in public, and it won't blow up in your face?"

Walt shrugged. "Yeah."

"Well, I'm not bailing you out of jail, you stupid fuck."

"Hey, there, watch it with the sass." He folded his arms across his chest. "May I remind you, you've done more in the middle of a Clemson homecoming game."

Lu's eyes flashed as she recalled the incident, and she grinned. "Well, that was youth and alcohol and a very hot brunette named Lauren." She shook her head and took a long sip of tea. "I don't see how you're going to pull this off, Wanda."

"I don't know, Lucy. I think this might be a good thing for Erin."

Lucy's head swiveled to Claire a second before Walt's. "Excuse me, honeybuns?"

"Erin's aversion isn't to the word, it's to what it means. It's to the baggage."

"Right," Walt said, gesturing toward Claire.

"She's such an overachiever, Lucy. Can't you see it? You're just like her, but you gave yourself permission to relax and play around with the dirty part of yourself."

Lu's eyebrow rose as she smirked. "Are you fucking kidding me? I wear it like Mrs. Astor's diamonds." She turned back to Walt. "I want nothing to do with Erin doing this big claiming-her-inner-dirty-girl, women's magazine-variety feminist exercise."

Jesus, she could be vicious—and pig-headed.

"She needs to face it." Walt ground his jaw and took a deep breath, tracing a finger across the tabletop. He pushed his lemon pie away from him, his taste for it gone. "Look, Luce, I know you think it's a long walk between doing something like this and Erin's…I don't know what to call it. Body problem?"

Lucy's eyebrow hovered. She'd been to therapy too, after the Johns family disowned her and cut her off, and was known to pay a return visit now and then. "Oh, I don't know? Repression? Her reaction to her sister's lifestyle by overcompensating with school and then work? Her mother denying a possible assault and calling her sister trashy in the same breath, while exhibiting the same behavior she both condemned and reinforced in that same daughter? Erin's inability to get past first when it comes to her sexuality? A head problem. Not a body problem."

"That's a good summary, Lucy." Claire nodded, giggling. "You should have been a therapist. Or an attorney."

"The hell. Most of the Virginia Johns are lawyers." Lu sneered, tossing her hair over her shoulder. "Sleazy fuckers."

"Yeah, well, it sounds worse when you put it like that." He pushed his lemon pie away, his taste for it gone. "She makes it past first. Makes it to all the bases. But part of her hates herself while she's doing it, or doesn't seem to think she has the right to be the one running bases in the first place."

Walt drained his tea but failed to dislodge the knot catching in his throat. "Look, she sees it too. Hell, if she hadn't connected the dots on her own, I never would have thought of this in the first place. The only way through a stretch of bad throws is another set of balls."

After a long stretch of seconds, Lucy inhaled and looked at him with soft eyes. "You sound like Brady. All of these stupid baseball analogies. Stupid fucker and his baseball."

Walt looked away from Lu, blinking hard. "As much as he loved that game, he sucked at it. Worst aim ever." The loss of their best friend—their brother—fell hard, out of nowhere. Another stage of their lives without Brady. He knew better, and recognized the heaviness of it for what it was, but the guilt still ground at him. It was the right thing to do, leaving cadets. But he would never stop regretting leaving Brady on his own in the Army.

"Your bad aim was what got you out of that brute squad and released from the Army. Thank goodness for it. Stop with the guilt trip you just started in your head."

"Was a fucking back-assed way to luck out of a war."

"Oh, Wally—" Claire reached for his hand.

"Thank goodness for that too. Don't stir up that survivor's guilt crap again. It would piss Brady off. Besides—" Lu wrapped her hand over Claire's, both of them holding his once-broken one, and lifted her chin with the haughty air of the debutante she'd been "—I needed you more. You couldn't have gone anyway."

"Me too," Claire said quietly.

Something about the catch in Lu's throat and the shine over her eyes caught Walt's attention and wouldn't let him get back to the conversation in play. This wasn't just Lucy riding his ass about a risk he was taking with Erin. He turned his hand over, palm up, and caught both their hands in his.

"Hey," he said. "I'm not going anywhere now either."

Lu paled a little and pulled away. "Of course you're not. Except jail if Erin bolts and somebody calls you in for public indecency."

"Lu, you know what I mean." Walt grasped at her hand again, urging her attention back to him. "Things with Erin. It doesn't change you and me. Won't change any of us."

Claire shook her head. "No, it won't. Of course it won't."

"Well, of course it *does*," Lucy said, rolling her eyes. "Or it should, if you're serious about her. And, that is just fine with me. In fact, I'll break your other arm if it doesn't. This is your only and forever one. Like Brady and Hailey."

"C'mon…it's not—"

"Stop being such a stupid boy, Wanda. You're in love with her."

They sat for a stretch of seconds, one eyeing the other, impasse reached.

"I think that's wonderful," Claire finally said, hardly louder than Miss Ernie's voice thundering behind the closed kitchen doors. Now her eyes were welling up, and damned if he hadn't made two women cry in one afternoon. "You're turning into such a good Sir, Wally. This is the right decision for your girl."

Hearing Claire go fuzzy and romantic about kink was uncomfortable to witness. But what was happening in her dynamic wasn't theirs to dissect. Right? Nobody offered unsolicited opinions on someone else's relationship.

Lu shunted her jaw, widening her eyes at him, and reached for her tea, obviously on purpose. "You have a contingency plan?"

"Nope. We can't go any further if she can't get past this."

"So, if she can't? It's over? Seriously? Your whole relationship is over? I've seen her look at you, you know."

"No, if she really can't get past it, we'll pull out of the lifestyle. Together."

"I don't get this at all. You'll shut yourself down for her? And she'll do the same for you, too." Lucy snorted, sitting the empty glass aside. "What did you just say about taking it on the chin, like a man, and shutting up? That's a setup for a real healthy marriage."

"Oh, don't bring up marriage, Lucy. You'll scare him to death."

"Look, we can talk this around in circles all afternoon, but I'm still doing it. I'd like your help so I do the woman things right. Y'all in or not?"

"I need to call Sir and ask—"

Lucy rolled her eyes for what was the sixth or seventh time over their lunch. "Dear Lord. Give me your phone, I'll talk to Paul. We have to go to Charlotte, and I'm driving." She stood, tossed three twenties on the table for Miss Ernie, and slung her bag over her shoulder. "*Woman things.* Jesus, Wanda, you're such a caveman. And don't try and tell me I didn't warn you, dipshit."

Lucy's voice trailed behind her as she sauntered toward the door, turning her attentions to Claire's phone.

"Promise me you'll choose what I pick out for Erin?" Claire tucked her arm through his.

"Yeah." Admittedly, Lu would have picked out some hot little scraps of nothing for Erin, but for the first time, it might be overboard. "Probably shouldn't blow her doors off, right?"

"I think that's already happened." The sweet, hopeful smile on Claire's face made him consider it. Maybe it could be a good thing, being the guy who could blow Erin's doors away.

In addition to being a talented artist, fabulous baker, and someone who seemingly bore no ill will to any other person or thing, Claire had powers of persuasion rivaling a televangelist. The week after I returned from Los Altos, she convinced me to do something out of character for me. It had become, apparently, a regular task of hers.

The request even surprised my boss, the data center director, Steve.

"This is it?" He glanced at me over his laptop. "You had to talk to me in person about taking the afternoon off?"

"I can make up the—"

"Make up? Nope." He pushed his desk chair away from his desk and glided toward a monitor behind him. At the bottom *utilization: 79%* flashed in perfect, grayscale letters. "Erin, take the whole day."

"But—"

"No buts. You worked at least seventy hours the week we were at Main. Go do something mindless. Go have a pedicure or something. Have you ever had one? Amazing."

"Um…well, actually…"

"Perfect. Have a massage too." He rolled back to his desk. "Brian raves about Greenleaf Body in Callahan. Have a facial while you're there. They do something with Ayurvedic acupressure and oil. Clary sage, I think. Maybe lavender. Anyway, go. Please. You're getting that stress wrinkle between your eyes again."

Stress? Walt had been in Tennessee for the past three days at his grandfather's nursing home, attending to some healthcare business. But missing him wouldn't cause that. "Wrinkle?"

"When you're stressing, you wrinkle. Right between the eyes." He peered at me again. When Steve paused and really took someone in, the cessation of his constant movement was unsettling. Being on the receiving end of that stare was like being under an electron microscope. He gestured to the sofa opposite him and instead of walking over, simply rolled his custom ergonomic chair around the perimeter of his desk to join. "Stress. See, I know my managers. How's that admin of yours?"

How and why did I allow Claire to persuade me to do this?

"I have him scheduled for another week of direct observation and then we'll try a weekend on the census project again."

"You know, he's got chutzpah." Steve laughed to himself as though we were discussing a wayward puppy. "The insubordination is not ideal, but I do like an admin who's willing to stick his ass out there to get noticed."

"I would prefer someone who does that within the parameters of appropriate conduct." Especially when Alan's parameters of appropriate included calling me a fucking cunt, which I hadn't relayed to Steve.

"No, and he's vulgar, which I can't bear." He looked at me again, and my stomach churned. "Where are your glasses?"

"I'm trying lenses."

"Have Lasik. Best thing I ever did. Glasses are tiresome."

"Steve, I can come in on Saturday to make up the afternoon."

"If I see you've swiped yourself into the building, I'll action plan *you.*" He waved his hand at me and glanced over his shoulder at the center monitor. "Take the day. I'll watch your admin's console."

I stood, smoothing over my skirt and in tandem, Steve pushed himself back to his desk. "Okay. I apprecia—"

"Nonsense." He was back at his laptop, answering an instant message. Before I could skim past his door, he looked up again. "You're happy here, right?"

"Happy?" No one ever asked a Miner if they were happy. Who wouldn't be happy with the stock options and catered lunches and nature trails and on-site daycare? "At the Mine?"

"No, Callahan."

"Oh," I said and immediately thought of all Callahan meant to me. Most of it had very little to do with the ThinkMine campus, and the smile all of those things called up was too instantaneous to hide. "Yeah. I am."

"Thought so. Good. I need you happy, Erin. I need someone here who's happy." His shoulders dropped, and the sharp, high-alert expression he always wore fell away. Steve, it seemed, was not happy. I closed the door and came back to his desk.

"Are you okay?"

"I'm fine. My center's up and running. You're going to have my capacity doubled by October with the virtualization project. I don't have to sit on the 5 for two hours every night to get home. I've quit sleeping in my office to avoid sitting on the 5 for two hours every night." He clicked around his laptop screen, swallowing heavily.

"Steve, fine isn't always okay." I pulled a chair to the side of his desk.

"Brian's not okay." He checked over his shoulder again. *Utilization: 79% capacity.* Humming along. "Brian's really not okay. I think he might divorce me."

"Oh," I said, muted. Afraid to ask for details of my boss's marital problems, I made a few empathetic sounds. A personal trainer and massage therapist, Steve's husband Brian was as much a stereotypical Northern California product as Danielle. "I'm sorry."

"He still hasn't found a job. He could stay home, you know. Money — we're fine. And he did, you know? He did. For a while." Steve took a deep breath. "Our friends at home think he's insane. They don't understand what it's like here, how hard it is for us. Especially Brian. He won't try to pass, and no one at home understands why that's even something he should consider."

I looked past his shoulder at the CentreView monitor, acclimated to his mental rhythm already. It was so similar to the one I usually moved to, but something felt a half step too fast. Maybe I didn't move to that beat anymore.

"He shouldn't. That's ridiculous, there's no reason to hide who —" Steve's expression stopped me cold. How would I know? "Have you met anyone here? I moved a lot when I was young, and the new places always were easier to handle once I had a routine and a friend or two." God, I sounded like my ever-chipper mother, each time we unpacked a U-Haul trailer.

Steve sighed and shook his head. "This is a very small town. In a very conservative state." He left the conclusions to me. "So Brian feels very isolated here. And when Brian's not happy...Well."

Lucy. If I could introduce Steve to Lucy, maybe she would help. But she would tell Brian every florid, cane-striped detail of her life. I could easily see them pitted in a lifestyle challenge, and I didn't know Steve and Brian's tolerance for kink. Unlike what Claire had done for me, I couldn't take the risk of exposure. I wasn't ready to.

"Try Charlotte," I offered instead.

"We should, I suppose." He sighed and turned away for a moment to answer another chime from his in-house private messenger. "I'm sorry I unloaded on you, Erin. I just needed to talk to someone who knew me there and knows me here. Does that make sense?"

"It does." I nodded, smiling. "It makes more sense than you know."

"Pedicure." He gestured toward his office door. Like most of us who had matured in ThinkMine culture, once a topic was finished, you moved to the next one without summation. "And massage. Don't worry about the facial. Honestly, I've never see you looking so alive, Erin."

I wanted to tell him I'd never felt that way either. But how to explain — to a mentor, a boss, and a man — it was because I'd met a man. I was the worst corporate cliché, a career-obsessed woman who was happier because of a man who brought regular — and very intense — sex coupled with lazy, comfortable evenings at home to my life. I wasn't supposed to be this easy.

I was, though. Walt made it that way.

I chose the coral pink Claire suggested for my pedicure. No massage, though Claire could have used one.

"I'm finished with your notebook," I told her over the sound of vibrating chairs and foot whirlpools. "Are there more chapters?"

"More?" She looked up at me, a little dazed. "Oh...I don't remember. I think I started the next lesson after I gave you the book. I'll print it off and bring it to you." She took her phone from her purse and swiped open a scheduling app.

"You can email it to me, that's fine. Oh, that's the new ProjectMe, isn't it?" I leaned toward her phone. "How do you like it?"

She sighed, swiping at pages as her brows knitted together. "I don't know, it's a Tessa thing. She's convinced Sir we all need to have a household calendar to manage when we're available for him, and she has all of their appointments and contacts mapped out, and I still can't figure out how to set the date."

At Claire's feet, the pedicurist's eyes rose slowly but bounced back to Claire's partially polished toes as she spoke to her coworker in hushed Vietnamese. I offered a weak smile to the woman stationed over my own toes, which was coolly ignored.

"Do you want me to show you?"

"Well...Sir wants me to figure it out." She shrugged. "I can do it. I just need some time with it."

"I don't mind," I said. She'd done so much for me and returning the favor — helping her not feel so self-punitive when she wasn't able to anticipate Paul's every expectation—seemed important. I nudged at her arm lightly. "C'mon, let me help. You're more comfortable with your pottery mud than my tech, Claire. It's no trouble."

"That's so kind. But I have to figure it out." She smiled gently and replaced her phone in her bag.

"Okay." For some reason, I couldn't let it go. "But don't forget, I'm here to help if you need me."

I let myself in the front door, feeling like a truant. It was four on a Friday afternoon, and I was at home. I looked down at my smoothed, polished pink toes and wiggled them up to myself, giggling.

"These people are turning me into Marie Antoinette," I said to my house.

A sheet of paper waited in the center of my otherwise bare coffee table, almost my house's answer to my queenly indulgence. I left my bags in their usual place on the painted-wood hall chair and walked across the living room, the soft slap of the salon's disposable flip-flops echoing in my ears.

It was a note from Walt.

I slid the little shoes off and padded toward my bedroom, reading. His handwriting was direct, in blocky capitals. He'd left a quantity of it on the single sheet of white paper: instructions I was to follow—if I chose. There was an address, the old Callahan Paper Mill's company store, which had been converted into a large bar and music hall.

"Not an expectation," he wrote. Twice. And made it clear I had the right of refusal at any time, at home or after I'd arrived at the bar. I wouldn't *need to call red*, I could simply say I wanted it to end.

"A request."

Laid in three neat stacks were clothes, shoes—black, in suede with a little sliver of a cutout to show my pedicure. There was a bra. There was a toiletry bag. None of what he'd left out was mine.

I lifted the clothes first. There wasn't enough of anything to cover most of me, certainly not enough to wear to a place called Merle Travis's Taproom. Setting the tiny pile of sheer fabric aside, I turned to the underwear. There was a bra made in taupe satin, covered in black net with pinpoints of tiny black dots, and a lace edge. Nothing more. The toiletry bag was equally Spartan. Black mascara and liner. Powder similar to my own. Glossy lipstick the color of a persimmon.

"This is not an expectation, it's a request. I want you to see yourself differently. I want you to see something in yourself that I see, and that you don't. The choice is yours."

For a long while, I sat in silence. At the edge of my bed. At the edge of what Walt had left there for me. I watched the dappled sunlight from my bedroom window trickle shadows and light across it all and listened to a lawn mower start, a distant dog's barking.

Walt's vision of me was something I couldn't ignore, and he was worth the risk I sensed around my own dim corners. Of course he was. I'd do anything he asked. He made me brave.

CHAPTER SEVENTEEN

After twelve minutes alone in Merle Travis's Taproom, a man approached me.

He wasn't leering or twisting an imaginary villain's mustache. I tried to return his smile and lifted my drink to my mouth.

"Hey there," he said. He smiled again, showing off dimples and a pair of honeyed-brown eyes. His pressed khaki shorts and summer blond hair completed the non-threatening picture. A nice guy. Based on his country-clubber-at-ease wardrobe and genial Southern accent, he could have easily been a distant cousin of Lucy's. "Finished? I'll get you another one."

"Oh, I'm—" Seeing something different: that was my assignment—at least in its motivation. So I answered accordingly. "Okay. It's coconut rum and diet."

"I'm Justin." Justin drank beer. He had a pint, stout I judged, from the color of it, in his hand.

"Erin." I forced another smile instead of wincing at the flare of worry. *Should I have told him my name? Should I have another drink?* Justin still smiled, waiting, while I tumbled past steps and scenarios in my head of how people just did this. "Hi."

Justin sat across from me, leaning on his elbows. "You're not from around here, are you?"

Newbie, again? *Still?*

"Not originally," I said, pushing the last ice cubes around the bottom of my glass, which must have been a bar signal of some sort. Justin waved across the room at a bartender and pointed to my drink, then his beer.

"Me neither. I'm from outside Asheville, but I hung around after I graduated from CNCU."

And from there, I was given a tour of Justin's life so far since graduating from Central North Carolina University. He was nice. He was attractive. He was employed as an accountant and was on good terms with his entire family, earning him a first round win in the *nonthreatening* sweepstakes. As he talked, I sipped the drink he bought for me, and nodded and tried to make sounds and expressions that looked like interest, which had to have been quite a farce for anyone watching.

Across the bar, the door swung wide, and like a vacuum had opened, everything around me — including Justin — disappeared. Walt stepped in, his head ducking a little as he always did when entering a room, even when the doors extended well past his head. He paused there to make a quick scan of the room. When he found me, he grinned and stepped to the bar where he stood for nearly seven minutes, watching me listen to Justin's account of his most recent trip to Myrtle Beach for a golf weekend. Walt's eyebrows rose and he inclined his head toward my tablemate.

What do you think?

I brought my empty glass to my mouth, glancing down at it as I shrugged my shoulders, and looked back to him.

After another stretch of observation by Walt and small talk from Justin, I cleared my throat lightly, because Dani and my mother always seemed to do that when they wanted to break into a lengthy stretch of talk.

"Damn, I'm just running at the mouth, aren't I?" Justin looked sweetly, gently embarrassed.

"I need to step away for a minute," I said, gesturing toward my empty glass. "Two drinks."

"Oh, yeah. Right." He nodded as if I'd imparted the wisdom of the ages.

"But...erm, Justin, I should be honest with you. I'm here on a mission."

"Excuse me?"

"Not really a mission. A task, actually." I was certain I heard Justin telling himself the crazy train had just arrived at his station. Disappointment pulled at his kind face and he began to gather his now-empty pint glass. "Wait, please." I gave him my most non-threatening, conciliatory smile.

"Uh, okay…"

"Justin, I'm dressed like this and by myself in this bar because my boyfriend told me to dress like this and come to this bar. By myself."

Justin picked up his glass.

"No, that didn't sound at all safe or sane. Please…let me try that again." He waited for me to continue, but kept his glass in his hand. "I can't believe I'm telling a stranger this. My boyfriend—no, this is really about me. I've not dated much. Mostly I've been friends with men I've worked with or, before that, men I went to school with. And we had sex occasionally. Not all of them, just a few."

"Uh huh," Justin said. "Well, Erin, I'm sorry to hear that but sounds like you were a good friend and a great coworker to those guys. So I'm going to head out—"

"Oh, no, please. Please give me a chance to say this right. Um… can I get you another pint? I owe you, after all."

"No. I'm good." He sat the glass to his side and crossed his arms over his chest. "Why didn't you date? You're h—I mean, you're attractive. Obviously very smart."

"Awkward."

"A little," he said, too fast for comfort, and shrugged apologetically when he realized it. "Sorry. I don't think you're really awkward, just maybe a little too nervous. You just need some social skills."

"I've heard that before."

"I don't get why you're by yourself in a place like this, though. You said you have a boyfriend."

"Oh, I do. He's—" I paused and decided to keep that information to the side. "I'm too nice."

His eyebrows crumpled. "What? I mean, yeah—you're nice. Why is that a problem?"

God, I was going to have to tell him. In detail. "It's not that my behavior or the way I treat people is a problem. There are words and um…things…I'm not good at saying—er, being them."

Justin went quiet, clearly piecing together what I'd babbled to him. And then, his head tipped back very slightly and something, an air or affect around him, went rigid. His voice dropped. "I see."

Tension knitted between my legs and I crossed them, shocked and loving the sensation of pressure at the sudden knot of arousal there. "You do?"

"You have always been the good girl, right?"

"No, not *good* in the puritanical sense," I said, pushing at my glasses. Which weren't there. "I'm not stunted or blocked about... things—"

"Sex."

"Yes, that."

"Don't you like fucking?"

"I...um, excuse me?"

"Do you like fucking?"

"Yes. Of course I do." A waitress appeared from the dark aisle with another pint of stout and a glass of water. Without a word, she set them on the table and was gone into the shadows again. I glanced across the bar and found Walt's stare waiting. "I like it."

"You like fucking."

"Yes." I squeezed my knees together and glanced to Walt again, finding him engaged in conversation with a tiny brunette in a tinier dress. His eyes flicked to mine. Tight, tingling heat surged down my thighs.

Justin took a long drink of his stout. "He's here, isn't he?"

"Yes. He's at the bar."

"Where? The guy in the Panthers hat?"

"No, the one in the blue shirt. Dark hair. Tall."

Justin's eyes went wide. "Shit. That's a big dude."

"Oh, don't worry. He's harmless." I shook my head at myself. "God, that sounded ridiculous."

"Hey, it's okay." He grinned at me. "You two looking for a third? I'm not sure I could take him, but I'd sure like to try while you sucked my cock."

I choked on my water. Before I'd regained my breath, Walt was at my side, introducing himself to Justin in a particularly low-pitched tone.

Walt leaned toward my ear. "You okay? He didn't—"

"No. No, I just surprised myself. Too much at once." I pointed to my half-empty water glass.

"Erin was just telling me about her assignment for the evening." Justin's eyes never moved from Walt's.

"Was she now?" I felt his chest expand. His arm slipped around my waist. "Right then, when she got all choked up? She was telling you about some kind of an assignment?"

The air between us all pricked and hummed, charged by them taking each other's measure. Justin's body shifted, so slightly I wasn't convinced I'd seen it happen. When he spoke, though, I knew. He'd enjoyed one, maybe two seconds of an illusion of holding the power between the three of us. But some insistent, elemental thing in Walt asserted itself and put it to an end.

"Yeah. Um…about being too upright in bed or something."

"Uptight?" Walt chuckled and raised a pint of deep amber beer to his lips. "She tell you that?"

"Not exactly. Something about words and not dating much." His eyes glinted. "But she did admit she likes to fuck."

"Well, I know that." Walt settled me closer to his body, resting his hand on my thigh. I wobbled a little at the pressure of his hand, so close to the throb that was increasing with each exchange between them. He looked down at me, sending me blooming, wide open and reeling, right there in a dark, loud bar. Right there in front of Justin. Walt pitched his voice lower so his words would be just between us. "You doing okay, sweetheart?"

I shifted my head so my hair fell across my cheek, screening my face. "Yes, Sir."

"This isn't about that. You're running the show."

"I'm okay."

"All right," he said and kissed the top of my head as his hand moved higher on my leg. His fingers were so maddeningly close, and I shivered at their nearness. "You look beautiful. I knew you would look amazing in that dress."

"Thank you, S—I…thank you. I like it. I've never worn this color." It was a filmy, deep coral fabric, accented with white and gray cabbage roses that managed to look retro without being a costume. The short skirt fell in a flippy circle above my knees—much shorter than I would have chosen, but not so short anyone would know Walt did not include panties in the stack of clothing he'd left on my bed. I leaned toward him and slid my hand over his. "I like all of it."

"It looks good on you," Justin added. "The dress is hot on you."

Walt smiled down at me. "You think so too, huh?"

"Yeah, she looks…" He swept his hand toward my chest, then toward my legs. "Well, you can see it, man. Right? She's totally fuckable."

Totally fuckable?

Never mind giving him a fake name, I should have checked his ID.

"Totally." Walt chuckled and inched his hand higher, bunching the layers of thin chiffon under his palm. So close now to the open, uncovered part of me he'd made wet and eager for his fingers. It must have registered against his fingertips because he made a low sound in his throat. His thumb crested over the bare flesh under it. When I looked down to my lap, I saw skin — his and mine. "You okay?"

He'd bared me to his hand and I didn't care, so much so that I let my knees fall apart enough to give him better access to me. "I'm fine," I said. Purred. That sultry purr was my voice, and those were *my* hips wiggling toward his hand while a stranger watched us. Justin's eyes caught mine from across the table.

"Is her pussy wet?"

Walt's index finger dipped along the inner ridge of my labia and I squirmed again. "Oh, God…"

"What do you think?"

"I'd like to find out for myself." Justin looked from me to Walt. "You want to go somewhere?"

"No." Walt dragged his finger along inside me again. "Not particularly. You good with that?"

"What? Just watch you? Here?"

"Sure," Walt said and circled — finally — my clitoris. I gripped his hand, whimpering. "She waxed her pussy for me."

Justin's eyes widened a little, and he sat back against his barstool, apparently settling in to enjoy the show. "I don't like bald pussy. I like hair on balls and pussy, both."

His hand tensed, minutely, for a second against my body. Clearly, Justin had surprised him. Walt's answer was his middle and index fingers sliding into a V around the tight flesh between them. Stroking, so slow. He drew them together a little, coaxing my clitoris between his rough knuckles, and I gasped again. "She left a little strip. I don't like girls waxed all the way bare either."

"She's gonna come if you keep doing what you're doing," Justin said. "I don't mind. I'd like to see her."

"She will." My hips agreed, pressing toward his hand. "Pretty soon, too."

"So what's her problem with words?"

"Erin, you want to tell him?"

I looked up at him. My breath was coming in quick pants across my open mouth and Walt's fingers kept teasing, stroking, tipping toward my center, and all around us people drank their beer and listened to the competing sounds of a baseball game from the television over the bar and the music blaring, and not one person besides Justin knew. I glanced around the cavernous space, squinting into the darkness. No one looked back.

"Um…okay," I said. "It's pussy."

"What? Really?" He wrinkled his brows at me. "Why?"

"It sounds—" I rolled against Walt's hand again, nearly moaning out loud. He knew where to touch, for how long and how much, just how to draw this out for Justin. For me. And for him. "It sounds dirty."

"The way you said it right then? It sounded hot. Really fucking hot."

"It did, didn't it?" Walt agreed. "Say it again, baby."

"Oh…" God, so close. "Pussy."

"Damn." Justin groaned softly. "Say it again."

"Go ahead," Walt whispered beside my ear, dragging his fingers in perfect, unrelenting circles around the hard, swollen crux of me. "Say it."

"Pussy."

"You sure you don't want to go somewhere, man?" The table bounced in time with his jittery legs. As loud as the music and crowd around us were, I could hear the empty glasses in front of us rattling.

"Nope. We're good here. Aren't we, sweetheart?" Walt looked down at me, again, smiling. He liked this. Liked seeing me like this and didn't care if Justin or the bartender or the little brunette he'd talked to before saw me falling down into an incoherent, whimpering mess, because he was the only person who mattered. And me. To-gether, the things we could do with his will and my body when it was his—dirty, filthy, fierce and hard, and animalistic, and so, so sweet with love—this was us, too.

"Yes." *Yes, Sir.* "I'm good." I shifted forward and swirled my hips for him. Them. I met Justin's gaze and ground against Walt's hand again. "So good."

Justin stared, unblinking, as his jaw clenched. "I bet you are."

He wanted me. He'd wanted me before, too, but that was in the context of social niceties and pleasant talk and maybe a night together that would lead to a few dates. This was about fucking me. Justin had ceased to care about my interests and thoughts and routines. The simplicity and unpretentiousness of it made me laugh a little. I sounded drunk.

Walt wiggled his finger against my clitoris, making me gasp and giggle and flinch far too much for discretion. He laughed too. "What's so funny?"

"It really is just about that, isn't it? For men? It's pussy."

"Yeah," he said, grinning. "It is, when it gets down to this. You ready?"

"Yes, please, Sir," I whispered. There was no one and nowhere else but us, and his hand working into me, a private universe within a crowd. Leaning close, he rubbed hard and fast.

"Say it and come for me."

Turning to his mouth, I whined hard and came into his hand. "Pussy."

I was still shuddering through my orgasm as Walt pulled me to my feet. There were a few words between him and Justin, and then we were moving toward the door. His hand was firm around mine, and sticky-wet musked with my arousal. I was all over his fingers. I could smell myself over the scents of beer and sun-warmed wood and old brick.

A concrete sidewalk, and then gravel sounded under our feet as we crossed under the hazy orange light of a few streetlamps, and then his hand was in my hair, clenching it in his fist at the base of my neck. Smooth, cool metal skimmed my cheek and I leaned forward into it. Around us, it was dark. We were at the distant corner of the city parking lot. Secluded.

"It's not always pretty, is it, baby?" His breath washed hot over my neck and I wiggled my ass into his hips, his thick, heavy cock pushing against me through his jeans.

"No, Sir. But I like it." I drew my skirt to my waist. "Please."

"Please? What, please?" He wrapped his arm over my hip, cupping between my legs and lifting me to my toes. "Please, what, in this parking lot, where anyone could catch you?"

"Sir, please fuck me." I swayed against his truck and whined in a voice that hardly resembled my own. "I can't wait until you take me home. Please, now. Here. Please." The final, throaty, sounds had barely echoed into the air when Sir pushed me forward, spreading my legs apart with his muscled thigh and pinning me against the cold metal door in front of me.

He was inside me, to his hilt, his balls swinging forward into my thighs, held where he wanted me with a fist full of my hair. A hard orgasm coursed through me, making me spasm around his cock, and a hoarse cry escaped from me before I could swallow it back.

"Someone might hear, huh? Tell me what this is," he growled into my ear. He thrust faster into me, his thigh still pressed against mine, and ground his palm against me in time with his hips.

"My pussy, Sir." Another orgasm began to flare, this one from somewhere deeper, calling me to strain toward it as warm, wet coursed over his hand and beneath us.

His fist tightened around my hair, bowing my neck. "Yours? Or is it mine?"

"Yours," I keened, twisting my mouth toward his. "Your pussy, Sir. Yours. Yours."

"Mine." His arms circled me and he crushed me against his chest, whispering into my ear. His thighs trembled behind my legs, and he came hard, deep into me. "Mine."

CHAPTER EIGHTEEN

August was good. Hot and humid, because it was August in North Carolina, and besieged with day-trippers from Charlotte, looking for cooler air than the frequent one-hundred-plus-degree days down south in the Piedmont. Sawtooth Falls was fed by cool spring water and under a thick tree canopy that shielded the forest floor from the stark sun. Many days, it looked like half of the state had finally discovered Poplar Branch State Park existed, decided to pack a picnic lunch and come visit. Walt even hired Tate as a seasonal employee, which made Lucy howl with laughter, but there weren't many other applicants he would consider trusting to guard Poplar Branch.

Despite busy, sweaty days and longer shifts taking care of his filled-to-capacity campground, Walt hadn't felt this good in a very long time. He didn't bother to pass it off as anything but her, and anyone who knew him knew anyway. Erin was the reason for his very improved mood, and platitudes for it shouldn't be set anywhere but in the sweet, soft lap of his girl.

It was sneaky and selfish, but a benefit of being the guy in charge was being the guy who decided who worked when. Walt scheduled himself and Tate to cover most of the first weeks of August's over-night duty, which bought him a couple of Sunday nights away from his cabin and down in Callahan in Erin's bed. But Sam still groused about being scheduled for a Saturday night.

"Sam Cross bitches and moans more than my Great Aunt Jeannie," Tate said as he took Walt's toybag from him. "In fact, he looks damn similar to old Jean. I'd nearly call him her drag king doppelgänger."

"I'm not sure who should be more offended, Sam or Aunt Jeannie."

Tate leaned into the truck's open window. "Well neither one could touch that picture. Hello again, Erin. Isn't that a pretty dress you're wearing."

Walt peered over Tate's shoulder at her, still sitting in the passenger side, wearing the same dress she'd worn to Travis's Taproom. He'd told her to put it on for him, and without a second's hesitation over his motives or what message he was sending her because she knew damn well what that dress did to him, especially when she grinned up at him and answered with that pursed-lipped "Yes, Sir" as she padded off to the bedroom to change into it. Those were the times it felt right to lead her.

"Hi, Tate," Erin said, waving.

He needed to thank Claire again for finding that dress, and for insisting Lu stop pushing the pleather and denim mini-skirt that should have never escaped a late eighties Mötley Crüe concert.

Just looking at her, pretty and soft and so unlike many of the women walking past them up to the house, bound up in their corsets and hard dungeon clothes, made the thing he'd sensed since she came back from California ring clear and true. This relationship with this woman — this one wasn't just a lifestyle thing for a season. Not play partners, not *see you at the next party* or *next time we're in the same city at the same time.* Everything around him felt more filled-in. When he caught someone taking notice of Erin, the filled-in edges become brighter and more defined. As Walt watched her begin to get to know people at the Enclave, he was proud of her for pushing herself to open up. Just proud of her, and being the one she chose to be with. His.

Shit, Lu was right. He was a fucking caveman.

"I'm going to find Claire," Erin said, grinning and pursing again as he opened the passenger door for her.

Opening doors and holding out chairs was the first stage of their protocol. Erin fussed like a wet cat every time she had to let him do anything that resembled what he'd been brought up to simply consider good manners. And Walt had made the decision to enforce those rules for that very reason. The actions wouldn't be noticed in public if they decided to take their D/s outside of home and Tate's house, but it underlined, for both of them, the power exchange growing between them.

She flicked her eyes to the open door and back to him, barely suppressing a laugh. The simple expectations and ground rules they'd agreed on were still new, and they both fumbled with them. For now, he'd give her a pass on the smirks and giggles. He occasionally screwed up at his own commitment to be constantly attuned to her direction, too.

Erin caught herself and tipped her chin down, inhaling to settle herself. Walt waited.

"Thank you, Sir," she said, finally, and raised her eyes to his.

Better. And fucking hot.

"Good girl," he whispered into her ear. He set a kiss on her cheek and stepped aside. "I'll text you before dinner."

As Erin passed her, Lu paused and blew a kiss in her direction. She came to his side, chuckling.

"Well, goodness. Aren't you two the picture of precious?"

"Down, killer," Tate said, elbowing her. "It's nice. They're happy. Let them be." He saw a couple from Knoxville struggling with their belongings and sauntered away to help.

Lucy hooked her arm through Walt's and they started for the house. "Are you?"

This was a voice he rarely heard from Lu. Quiet and free of the snarky tone she'd just used on him. Her hair was loose, curling into its natural waves, and she'd eased off the heavy Doma Lucia makeup. She wore a pretty summer dress too, one in her favorite black, long enough to brush the tops of her feet, and her shoulders were turning golden from afternoons in the summer sun. Lucy almost looked like that girl from his calculus class he'd wanted to go out with so many years ago.

"Yeah," Walt said. He tucked her closer to him and kissed the top of her head. "Yeah, I am. You too?"

She smiled. At this stage of the game, admitting to feelings in that voice would be too much for Lu.

He squeezed her shoulder and they paused at the steps under the *porte-cochère*. "When can I meet her?"

"This fall. Maybe?" She shrugged. "Let's see how it goes, okay?"

"All right. Ready when you are, baby." They stepped into the mud-room.

"Oh. Really?" Lu snarled.

So much for soft and personal Lucy.

She had good reason to be irked, though. Stationed by the powder room was Paul's secondary, waiting on him most likely, as she munched on a handful of chips. And she was wearing a heavy-gauge steel collar like the one Claire wore when she was away from her job at Paul's dentistry practice. It was, in fact, an exact replica, except for the rhinestone-covered kitten head hanging from it.

Leaning forward, Walt peered into the dim light. "Is that cat wearing a hairbow?"

"Stop squinting, PaPaw, she'll think you're checking out her tits. The last thing that piece needs is a pump to her ego." The piece started waving to them. "Great, she saw you. Now we have to go over there or Claire will never hear the end of it."

"Hey, guys." Powderpuff had this way of drawing every single syllable of a word to its breaking point. What was that girl's name? Tina? Tessa? She shook crumbs from her hands to the floor under her and sauntered toward them, smiling and hamming it up as she fluttered her eyelashes. She lifted her chin and shimmied her shoulders so the cat head attached to her collar sparkled in the dim interior light. "Look what I got."

"A collar. How sweet." Lu was the picture of herself at a sorority formal, twenty years ago. "Darling clip-on too. When? Tell us everything."

Walt didn't have the stomach to watch this. It was like looking down at a shark cage and pitying the chum. He stepped back, squeezing Lu's elbow and nodding to Powderpuff.

"Congratulations," he said.

"Oh no, Ranger, wait. Sir said I could have you play with me down in the whip room while he does a scene with his other girl."

"No thanks. I've got plans."

Four or five months ago, he might have done it, just to buy Claire some alone time with Paul, and because he rarely got to use the dedicated lane when Tommy and his wife Alex were around all night, throwing their homemade whips at everyone and anyone who asked. Then, but not today and never again, because Erin's presence at the Enclave colored every decision now. Even if she'd not been able to get away from the upgrade she had her team running at the data center, Walt still would have declined. Playing for the sake of playing just held no appeal. It wouldn't, never again.

And being granted permission, through his secondary, for a play session with one of Paul's girls like he was some kind of lackey with a toybag pissed Walt off. Fuck Paul Saldino's damn edicts and fuck him for leaving Claire in the kitchen helping everyone else while he strolled around with a collared girl young enough to be his daughter. Anger flared, surprising him, and forcing him to set his jaw as the sense of it escalating climbed over his skull.

"Oh, *please.*"

"No," he said again, his voice sharp enough to surprise Lu, who flinched a little at his arm and looked up at him with an arched eyebrow. "Thank you for the invitation. Excuse me."

Walt lifted his toybag and stepped back outside. There was an old foam core-covered tree stump at the far corner of the garden used by the mentoring classes for their first attempts at throwing a whip at another thing. It was the only place he trusted himself to be until he could cool off.

When I found her in the Enclave's kitchen, I noticed right away Claire didn't seem like herself, in any way. Though she was normally quite pale, her cheeks didn't have their usual healthy pink flush — something my mother would have called "roses in her cheeks." Her demeanor, though, was more troubling. As dulled as her appearance was, a more elemental part of Claire seemed scattered, or even panicked beneath her usual focus on preparing the house for the monthly play party.

"Oh, Erin, you're here," she said, breathy. "How are you? Oh, look at your dress, it's beautiful on you. Is Walt here? Did you come together?"

"Claire." I lifted a chafing dish from her arms. "Slow down."

"Tate brought a caterer in this time and they were two hours late dropping off the food." She tucked a damp strand of hair behind her ear. "We'll never get everything warmed and put in the serving pieces."

"Claire," I said again, reaching for her arms. "You *have* to slow down. Breathe. Have you eaten today? You look like my mother does when her blood sugar drops."

She waved me away and turned for the butler's pantry. "Oh, Tessa and I are doing a juice cleanse. It's all organic and—" She reached for the large island a second before her knees buckled.

"And you have to sit down." I lead her across the kitchen.

"I'm fine, really." Her hands vibrated in mine. "I need to check… something." She looked around us, dazed. "Where's Tate?"

"He's outside. Come with me and sit. I'll go find him."

She didn't protest again. I lead her past the dining room table, already filled with light appetizers, plated to make any lifestyle maven's chest swell with pride. I snatched a bottle of lemonade, a few cubes of cheese, and some grapes.

Pulling the door of Tate's reading room shut behind me, I pointed to the deep, leather sofa. "Over there."

Claire made a thready, distant sound resembling a laugh. "Wow, Erin. You can be bossy. Are you sure you're not a switch?"

Fine, call me bossy.

I switched to work Erin and leveled my eyes at her. "Claire."

She sat.

"I can't eat that," she said as I arranged a pair of tapestry-covered pillows behind her. "Sir…I'm doing this juice cleanse with Tessa."

"You told me that in the kitchen. I don't think Paul would begrudge you a little bit of protein and some fruit to keep you from fainting."

She shook her head. "I can't, Erin. I'm not allowed to break the cleanse."

This was completely absurd. "I'll talk to Paul. Or…if that's problematic, I'll ask Walt to talk to Paul. Or Lucy—*she'll* definitely explain it to Paul in a way he'll understand."

Claire accepted the bits of food and nibbled at a piece of cheese, watching me carefully over her hand.

I sat. Tate could wait until I was sure she'd actually eaten.

"Did you see Tessa?"

"I did, in the mudroom."

"Did you see her collar?"

The lost, wide-eyed look wasn't entirely from low blood sugar. Their dynamic, I reminded myself. None of my business, something I couldn't comment on.

"I thought I noticed something but I was more interested in finding you," I told her. Claire cast her gaze down like a scolded child, and that was that. My friend's breaking heart was more important than Paul's imperious rules. "Are you okay about the collar, Claire?"

"Oh, sure," she said, waving as she pulled at a grape stem. "It's not really something I can say yes or no to, but Tessa's very sweet and Sir loves her, so…"

Her shoulders shook a little and the grapes tumbled from her hand. I reached to her and she broke, heaving heavy, silent sobs against her curled fingers.

"Claire…sweetie," I whispered into her hair as I settled her against me. Her skin was icy, slick with sweat. There wasn't a throw behind us or a stray jacket nearby. Only me to get her warm. I wrapped both arms around her, and I did my best.

Minutes later, after several rounds of her sobbing and my *shhh*-ing, and many pointless whispers of how okay everything was against Claire's pallid temple, she sagged against me. Her hands lay heavy in her lap.

"I'm sorry about the grapes," she said, her voice hoarse and dull.

"They're grapes. I'll get more." I squeezed her shoulder again. "One of us will speak with Paul, Claire. I can't imagine he would want you to make yourself ill for a crash diet."

"I've put on a little weight." She stared into her lap again.

"I think you look wonderful."

"Tessa…she was a rope bunny before, you know? She's really athletic. She and Sir have been running and they just got this racing bicycle. It's a tandem…you know? For two."

"Hey," I said, picking up her hand. "You are talented and beautiful and the kindest person I know. You can't be Tessa, and you don't have to be."

Claire's shoulders fell and her eyes clouded again. "I know."

My phone buzzed in my pocket. "This might be work, I have to take this."

"It's okay." She turned a small smile toward me and shrugged. "I'm really fine."

I stepped into the hall. The number was local, but not a work exchange. "Hello?"

"Uh...Hello? This Miss Proctor?" *Miz Prua-ctuh.* It was the reedy, elderly voice of a man, accented like many of Callahan's older locals.

"Yes," I said, guarded.

"This is Bob Jensen from down on Sycamore Street. You know, your next door neighbor? You doing all right?"

"Yes, I'm..."

"Well, now, I wanted to give you a call about your house. I was cutting my grass and noticed a woman on your front porch and looked like she might of went inside. Thought it was you at first, but then I recalled you and your boyfriend taking off earlier." He cleared his throat and continued, "It ain't my business what you do, but I just noticed y'all leaving when I was doing the weedeatin'."

"No, that's fine. I'm glad you called."

"T'be honest, like I say, I thought it was you at the first, but then I remembered you and Mr. Easton headed out in his truck, and then I looked around the front and I noticed your car still in your driveway."

"Thought it was—" I sagged against the doorframe. "I see."

"Sorry to be any trouble. Just thought you'd like to know."

"Yes, I would. I'm glad you called." *Damn. Damn, damn, damn.* "Thank you very much for being such a good neighbor, Mr. Jensen. I'm on my way home now. Have a nice afternoon."

"You do the same, Miss Proctor."

Leaning to my side, I ducked my head in the room where Claire still sat, with tear-stained cheeks, gazing into space. "Claire?" I cleared my throat. "Honey?"

"Hmm?"

"I need to go to my...I need to go home for a few minutes. Will you stay—*yeeeoooww!*" A hand—too small to be Walt's—connected with my backside. I turned and found Lucy and her toybag.

"Whatssa happenin', haaatschtuff?" She wagged her eyebrows.

"Oh, Lucy, thank God."

"Yeah, I hear that all the time." She grinned, tossing her golden hair over one shoulder, and set her toybag against the wall. "What's up?"

I pulled the door closed behind me, tipping my head toward the room. "Claire." I dropped my voice further. "The collar."

Her face turned to thunder. "That fucker." She looked like a furious shieldmaiden, ready for battle. "I'm going to take that tacky fucking cat charm and shove it up his hairy shithole."

"Um, I hope you do, and that you do it exactly how you just…said. But right now, could you sit with Claire? I have an emergency at my house and need to go home. Oh, have you seen—" after watching Claire's breakdown, Sir felt like wet cotton on my tongue "—Walt? I didn't drive and need the keys to his truck."

Lucy's eyes darted over her shoulder. "Um…he's doing some practice with his singletail in the garden. Here, take mine."

"Lucy, I can't—"

"It's just a car. Shit, what is it with you and Walt and worrying about fucking cars?" She pressed a keyfob into my hand. "I'm parked by the guest house. Shut up and take it. You have my permission to drive like a bat out of hell, all the way to Callahan, okay?"

"Okay." Before I realized it, I had clenched Lucy to me. "Thank you, Lu."

"Hey," she said, patting my shoulder. "It's a stupid car. No big whoop." She stepped away and smiled softly at me. "Hurry back, okay?"

Twenty harried minutes later, I turned Lucy's Range Rover into my drive. Just as Mr. Jensen said, a compact gray sedan was parked behind my car. Nondescript, much like the rental I had in Los Altos the month before.

"Oh damn. No," I said to the cool, quiet interior. It smelled of Lucy's perfume, which was a surprising comfort. "Damn."

I removed the key from the ignition and stepped out from the big SUV.

My neck prickled with the intermittent twin ESP I shared with Danielle. She was in my house. I knew. I could almost feel her, hanging heavy in the air around me.

In fact, she was lounging across my sofa, her bare feet crossed over the coffee table. Drinking Walt's beer and eating what appeared to be my leftover chicken enchiladas. On my sofa.

"Dani?" The sister in front of me looked much, much more like the one I'd left in California when I'd moved to Callahan nine months ago. The carefully applied makeup and tailored clothing she'd worn when I saw her a month before was gone. Her hair was twisted on top of her head in a messy topknot. "Dani, what are you doing here? And *how* did you get in here?"

"You hid your spare key in that cheap-ass frog on the front porch. It's like *hi, look at me, I've got a spare key in my ass, burglars!*" She rolled her eyes at me. "And by the way, hello."

"Hi." I sank into the opposite sofa and took a deep breath. I knew she wasn't, but I had to ask. "Dani, are you okay? Isn't Saturday your big night at the restaurant?"

"Dante broke up with me, so I probably won't be having any more good Saturday night shifts." She made the same stony face she always made when she was trying to not cry.

"Oh," I said. I should have gone to her, reached for her hand, mirrored the same motions I'd made with Claire less than an hour before. I couldn't move. "I'm so sorry, Dani."

"Yeah, well…he's a guy, what do you expect?" She sighed heavily. "Why are you all dressed up?"

"I've been at a…a thing. For work."

"On a Saturday afternoon?" She squinted. "Nice dress. I've never seen anything so…um, colorful on you."

"Thank you, my—it's a favorite."

Her eyes narrowed and she sat the plate on the edge of the coffee table. "You're acting weird. What's wrong?"

"Nothing," I said and made a show of sisterly, compassionate smiles and sitting close to her on the sofa once I'd scooted the plate of sauce-soaked enchiladas across the coffee table. "Tell me what happened with Dante."

"It doesn't matter."

"Of course it does," I said.

"I'm not educated enough for him or something." She turned hardened eyes toward my front windows. "He wanted to send me to…I don't know, some kind of class."

"Class?" I was prepared for a drunken argument or one of Dani's intermittent spending sprees, but not this. "What kind of class?"

"I don't know, Erin. Like…you know, business classes. If I'm going to help him manage the vineyard, I have to go to business classes."

"So he offered to help you with your education, which will help you help him make his business more successful, and make the two of you more financially stable, and *then* broke up with you?"

Her chin lifted. "No."

"No?"

"No, he broke up with me after I told him to go fuck himself for trying to change me, and if I'm not good enough for him now, I'll never be."

"Dani, I don't think this sounds like—"

"No, that's exactly what it is. Mom's an embarrassment and I'm nothing but a waitress with a decent face and a nice pair of tits. Once that goes, he'll leave me anyway and find another ornament."

Wincing, I passed my hand over my face, sighing. "I think you missed the point, which, by the way, sounds like the opposite of what you think Dante is doing. Did you actually ask—"

"Look, Erin, I didn't come all this way to hear your judgment too. I have to be back at work on Tuesday morning. I just need to get my head together for a couple of days so I can figure out my next move and I'll be off your ass, okay?"

"Dani..."

"No, just...whatever!" She stood abruptly, pushing past me. "Do you have any more beer somewhere?"

I rose too, following her to the kitchen. "No, only what's in the fridge." Walt had brought a six-pack the previous Sunday evening to accompany our pizza and the remaining four had sat, unnoticed, since.

"When did you start drinking beer?"

My phone sounded an incoming text. Of course it was Walt. Of course it was.

Ready for dinner?

"Dani, I need to make a call. I'll be back."

I was going to hide from my sister in my own house to call him.

He answered right away. "Hey, where are you?"

"I'm sorry, I got a call and Lucy said you were doing something with a—" What did Lucy call it? A swinging tail? "I'm at home, but I'll be back."

"Are you okay?"

"Yes." I closed the bathroom door behind me. "Yes, Sir, I'm fine. My sister's here."

"In Callahan? At your house?"

"Believe me, I'm as shocked as you sound. She let herself in. I don't know…something happened with her fiancé."

"Shit, well…you stay there and take care of her. I'll get Lu to DM for me and come over there in a while."

"No," I said too quickly. "Um…I have Lucy's car. I'll bring it back. Danielle's been traveling all day and probably wants to sleep."

Mr. Jensen from next door knew Walt, but my sister didn't. I'd kept him a secret from Kathy and Danielle, too, covetous of him and everything that was growing between us to share with them.

I passed the kitchen, very purposefully not looking at the bottles and discarded take-out package abandoned on the table where Walt and I always had breakfast.

"Dani, I need to return my friend's car. I'll be back as soon as I can."

"Hey, wait—whose car?" Her footsteps echoed behind mine. "Are you going back to your party? Hang on, I want to go too. I could deal with some new people—"

"No," I said, again too fast. "I'm just going to return Lucy's car."

Dani walked past me to the front picture window. "Damn, some car. That's a new Range Rover. I should have been like you and went into computers. Those are fucking ninety grand, easy."

"*Ninety?*"

"Yeah, for a base model."

Lucy sent me off, down a narrow two-lane lake road in a ninety-thousand-dollar luxury steamship? I reached for the door. "I'll be back, Dani."

Before her protest could register, I pulled the front door closed and hurried down the steps. The front door swung open.

"I said I wanted to go too, give me a sec to change. I want to drive that thing."

"Need to get her car back," I called brightly over my shoulder. "I'll be back soon."

CHAPTER NINETEEN

Walt drained a couple of water bottles and tossed them into the recycle bin in the mudroom. In the distance, he saw a flutter of flowered reddish-orange fabric exiting the kitchen.

There she was.

The main floor rooms were still sparsely inhabited. Most people who had arrived for August's play party were downstairs in one of the playrooms or on the deep screened porch overlooking the lake, enjoying dinner. He passed Nerita's boys, one bobbing his head as he offered a tray of berries, followed by the other who held a tray of champagne flutes, half-filled with a sip of champagne to follow the fruit.

Down the long hallway past the formal dining room, Walt could make out Tate and Erin around the clusters of people. They turned into the small room Tate called his reading room. It was usually off limits during parties.

Walt followed, pausing to say hello to a guy from Charleston he'd mentored a few years ago, and his new wife. It was their last time for a while, he reported. His girl was expecting a baby, already gone soft and pink with it. Walt congratulated them sincerely, the ugliness of the past couple of hours vanishing as he grinned at their questions about Erin, and at his own errant thought of her, turning rosy and round with a baby they'd made together.

That thought worked better than anything to stir him out of his funk. He left his friends, promising to introduce them to her later.

Raised voices and a quick scream sounded from Tate's library. *She's in there.* Walt hurried to the room.

He found her, across the wide, oak floor, and went to her, aware he'd passed a cluster of people but too concerned with getting to Erin to notice the players. Her hand slid into his.

"Oh God," she whispered. "Walt…"

The room drew away from him. He could smell Erin's perfume beside him and hear Lu's voice in that same tone she used when her parents came down to Clemson to confront her about her girlfriend and he knew he saw Tate hustling that stupid secondary girl of Paul's away from Luce, but none of it — even Erin — punched through the sound of Claire's sobs. She sounded like a frail, wounded animal.

"Sir, please…" Kneeling at Paul's feet, she wailed it again and again as she reached over her head to Paul's arms. "Please, no. Please."

And the bastard clicked open the safety release on her collar. "Claire, we're through."

That simple. No explanation, no listening to Claire's broken-soul weeping, no consideration for what he'd done to this woman who'd loved him and served him and followed his every fucking rule for close to fourteen years. *Done.* Just turned his back on her.

Like Melissa turned her back on him.

Walt felt his feet moving under him, saw in periphery Tate kneeling beside Claire as he pulled her to him, knew Lucy was right behind him, headed for Paul, just like he was.

It felt good, heaving the guy's waspy body up and into the walnut bookcases, and the sounds of something rattling away and crashing a second later on the wood floor rounded out the angry concert of sound and emotion that had been playing out in his head all evening.

Behind Walt, Tommy hauled at his shoulder. "Hey, man, what the fuck?"

What the fuck was that Paul Saldino was about to need the services of a surgeon — and a dentist.

"Walt," Lu said, stepping between him and Tommy. Her low, even voice slaked off enough adrenaline to let Walt take a single, ragged breath. "Walt, stop."

Paul still grasped and clawed at Walt's arms. He wrenched his head in Lu's direction, hissing, "You stay out of this, you bitch."

Walt's hand twitched around the edge of Paul's leather vest, itching to curl into a fist. "*You* better watch your fucking mouth, asshole." He rattled Paul against the bookcase again, just so he knew things were about to get painful and ugly.

"Walt? Sir?"

Sir?

Erin. She could see all of it. The brutish, violent parts of him people had taunted out of him his entire life. And she saw it now too.

Oh, fuck…not her too. Not Erin.

He drew his hands away, not giving a single shit about Paul staggering to the floor or the sounds of a second casualty when a heavy book tumbled from the bookcase and sent a plume of yellowed pages into the air. Walt rubbed his hand over his face, stepping back enough to open a face to face audience for Lu with Paul. Her hand cracked hard across his face, opening a thin, red seam on his bottom lip.

"Don't you *ever* call me a bitch again. Now, you get your things from the mudroom, you take this girl, and you leave."

Standing, Paul wiped at his lip and coughed out a hollow laugh at her. "You can't tell me what to do. This isn't your house and I've paid to be here."

Tate rose from Claire's side, thrusting his hand into his pocket. Stopping at arm's length, Tate dropped a pile of hundreds at Paul's feet and glared at him. "That should more than cover your refunded dues for the remainder of the year—and for that matter, your gas back to town. You have twenty minutes to leave my property."

"Fine." Paul swung his hand wide, laughing as he shook his head. "Fine. This—all of you—you're all bullshit. All of you. You're no more BDSM than a dime-store wank book."

Walt took a step forward. "Believe the man said it's time to get out of his house, Paul."

Paul turned to Walt, sneering. "Little big Top, you touch me again, and I'll have you arrested."

Walt stepped back, shoving his hands into his pockets. The muscles in his jaws throbbed, sending sharp, crunching pain down his shoulder as he screwed down the need to strike out hard and without rest at something threatening the people he only wanted to protect. He couldn't move, couldn't look around the room for Erin, couldn't let her see him turned powerless and unable to take care of them. He didn't want to look into her eyes and see himself, debilitated, and reflected back to him.

The room fell into heavy silence. In the worst kind of encore, Paul's new girl stomped across the room on her candy-apple plastic boots, a rhinestone-crusted leash in her own hand, and picked up the cash at his feet.

"It's okay, whatever. This place *is* bullshit. We'll use this for a vacation together. *Alone*. While she packs up her stuff. Let's go, Sir." She hooked her hand through Paul's elbow and steered them to the doorway.

The room fell silent with their exit, stirred only with the sound of Claire's soft sobs.

Across the room, Erin cleared her throat. "Wa—Um…I'm sorry," she said and flinched, like she was scalded by the sound of her own voice.

The first expectation he'd given her. No more I'm sorry's.

He tipped his head toward her, hoping she'd get it. But rules didn't matter right now. There was more than her obedience to something he'd asked her to do and was meant to help her, anyway. After all, he wasn't Paul.

Erin looked away, her eyebrows drawn tight over her eyes as she twisted her fingers in the hem of her pretty, coral dress. "I need to go too. My sister is…she's in my house. I need to go home and check on things."

"Sure. Okay." He managed a small smile.

She knelt beside Claire and said a few words, and they hugged.

Walt gathered his toybag and stepped to the hallway, stood by the door, waiting to return Erin to her tidy little house for the evening. He felt like the big, bad wolf getting ready to drive Little Red Riding Hood back to her grandmother.

Once Walt closed the door behind me and crossed to the driver's side, I looked to his truck's steering column, silently willing it to start without shuddering and jumping. His temperamental clutch might be his last straw.

Until the moment he started across the small library where I'd left Claire in Lucy's care before I drove home to check on Dani, I'd not seen Walt angry. Really incensed-angry. And he was Walt, the man I'd always considered "Sir," but had come to think of as "my Sir," a mental and emotional shorthand for safety and consideration and care. His ability to threaten or even purposefully injure someone as a result of his size and strength was something I never considered.

But it was possible. I'd just watched it happen. He was close, really close to hurting Paul. In the abstract, I would have supported him, maybe even encouraged his defense of Claire. But the reality of a large, powerful man unfurling that kind of rage was something I'd never witnessed. The things we did together and called play only skewed different than the assertions of dominance and power I witnessed him unleash toward Paul because of intent and trust. Someone could make a the case that what we did together—what I agreed to, what I asked him for—made me just as wronged as Claire.

He sat beside me, closing the door with a soft thud after himself, clearly exhausted. After a few seconds' silence, he took a deep breath and leaned back, resting his head against the glass behind him. His hand turned over on the seat between us, palm open. I covered it with my own.

"You okay?" He opened one eye, glancing at me.

"I'm—" I began and swallowed at my dry throat. "I'm more concerned about you."

"Just need some quiet, to get out of here for a while." He squeezed my hand. "How do you think your sister would be with me at your place tonight?"

And Dani's surprise appearance in my living room, of course, added to the fallout from Paul and Claire. Our weekend had started so well, a whole two days together without interruption after the hectic early days of August at his forest that kept us snatching time together in brief hours rather than days.

My phone chimed. "You have to be kidding me."

Walt turned his key and mercifully his truck started. "Work?"

"Of course," I said. "I need to call in."

"Go ahead. I'm going to go through town for some dinner. I never ate. Want anything?"

"No, thanks."

I lifted my phone to my ear and waited for my admin to answer. It was a simple issue of a few dropped characters from the script I'd written for monthly maintenance to our center's first layer of network security, but took her several tries to stop the install and back my machines out, then start again. I nibbled at my thumb, listening to her executing commands, huffing over them, and restarting, over the entire drive back to my house. We turned on to Sycamore Street just as I ended the call.

It was the kind of predicament that turned me useless. Walt needed a calm place to have dinner, be quiet, possibly just sleep off the effects of the evening's high emotion. Despite what I witnessed happen to Claire after so many years taking care of others, and the events I observed in the months I'd known her, I wanted to give that to Walt. He made things better for me, so often. I wanted to do the same for him. Dani's presence would make that impossible. He wouldn't relax around her. She was going to be livid about him. She always rearranged things to suit her whims without a thought of what others wanted. Or, really, what I wanted.

Walt parked, not in my drive, but along the sidewalk in front of my house.

"I don't think you'll be comfortable, after…you know, um…everything, here tonight."

"Not sure I would be either, to be honest. Why don't I walk you to the door so you can introduce us, and I'll go on home?" He stretched over a deep yawn. "Don't think I'll make it much longer anyway."

I nodded and reached for the door handle, then let my hand drop. "Sor—I mean…hmm." Finally I tucked my hand in the fabric draped over my legs.

"Hey, it's okay. Open your door if you want, or wait for me if you want. Right now I don't care how you get out of the car." He gave me a tired, shallow smile and got out. I waited, my fingers on the metal handle, finally opening the door just as he reached my side, a semantic sleight of hand I promised myself was compromise.

As we crossed the narrow patch of grass in front of my house, Walt reached for my hand. I curled two fingers around his. Every step toward the front door screwed my throat tighter.

"Dani?" I called, stepping aside for Walt to enter. "Are you awake?"

After a rustle of sheets and the sound of what was likely the bedside table rattling against the wall, she stepped from my spare room, eyes blinking hard over blotchy cheeks. She'd fallen asleep crying. All the markers were there.

Walt stepped to my side.

"Rin-Rin?" She said her childhood name for me in a voice creaky with sleep as she shuffled down the hall. "I thought you were coming right—Who's this?"

Walt's hand rested on the center of my back, our arms touching. If the who was not obvious, then what surely was. But Dani had to. She just had to.

"Erin, *who* is this?"

"Hey there," Walt said, stepping forward. "I'm Erin's boyfriend. Walt Easton. Nice to meet you."

I was still turning my head to him, still sent gaping and fluttery-eyed over hearing him say *boyfriend* when he said what he was to me—because he didn't usually have to say it, our people just knew—and still feeling the heat of his hand on my skin as he squeezed my shoulder, when Dani did it. She never met a social cue she willingly picked up when she could just kick it to the moon.

"Boyfriend? I had no idea my sister was even dating anyone."

After twenty of the most awkward minutes of my recent adult life, Walt made his apologies to Dani and me. He'd *had a hellacious day*, he promised. Needed to *get into my own bed* where he said, solemnly, he belonged.

I followed him outside, pulling the front door shut behind me. The sight of his back moving away from me, going home alone to the tiny cabin at the edge of his forest, sparked a flare of fury in me. I turned to glare at Dani through the window.

Without me there, she'd started looking around again, moving to the bookcase that housed my small television and the few sentimental items I'd bought since moving to North Carolina. She picked up the amethyst formation Claire had insisted I buy that April Saturday, when we met outside of Paul's office for the first time. The day she confirmed to me who she was. The day she told me about the Enclave, about her friends who were people just like her—and, she promised—like me.

Dani's nose wrinkled as she considered the crystal in her hand. She set it down again—in the wrong place—and it shuddered on its jagged surface until it found a hesitant balance.

"Erin? I'm gonna go now."

I knew I needed to put together words to explain it to him, how Dani, and often my mother as well, took without pause, assumed consensus, and they never asked just what I wanted. But I went mute.

She'd come into my home without warning, invited herself right inside and took my chicken enchiladas and Walt's beer and was wearing my favorite headband and eating those saucy, messy damn enchiladas on a beige sofa I'd kept clean and neat because I had a kitchen table where eating was done. The living room wasn't a dining room and a bedroom and I didn't have to share anything with anyone I didn't want to give to. Except him.

Say something. Tell him.

I turned back to him. He'd started down the steps. Away.

"Walt?"

"Yeah?"

He stopped and turned, waiting for me at the edge of the porch.

After watching my mother and Dani do it so many times throughout my life, I should have known how to chase after a man who'd decided it was time to go. I'd heard the theatrical pleas, knew the timing of every wail and tear that should be coming. It should be easy.

They always walked away. The ones I liked, and the ones who terrified me too. They always left, no matter how loudly Mom or Dani called for them.

My legs went useless under me.

After a stretch of seconds watching each other, Walt nodded, a crisp efficient jerk of his head. Clearing his throat, he stepped forward and folded me into his arms.

"I'll talk to you later." He kissed the top of my head and took the stairs in one long stride. He didn't turn back to me as he usually did, walking backward as we continued to smile and laugh over our repeated good-byes.

He just walked away. Walt. My Walt. My friend, my lover, my Sir. My love.

Mine.

I moved forward, nearly stumbling over the worn wood underneath my bare feet, and managed one step before the others beneath it receded into twilight. My hand hovered at my side, reaching for something, for some manner of support that wasn't there.

"Walt?"

His hand rose in the night shadows, waving, and he disappeared into the darkness.

"Walt?" I called again, alerting the neighborhood dog and, based on the front porch light next door, Mr. Jensen too. I stepped off the porch, the dewy grass sick under my soles. "Walt? I…I'm —" I shuddered at the plaintive, pathetic squeak in my voice, and snapped my mouth shut. This time, the time it mattered most, I couldn't make myself say *I'm sorry.*

"Call me when you can. If you want."

I sank to the sun-rippled boards behind me and watched his truck's taillights disappear around the corner, heavy in the knowledge I'd hurt him more than he'd ever admit to me. He'd think I was ashamed of him, and think I'd deny our relationship to my sister, because that had already happened to him. Why couldn't it happen again?

The next morning, I did everything I could to keep Danielle away from the part of me that needed Walt. Polite redirection wouldn't stop her, so I offered an afternoon of shopping in either Asheville or Charlotte as a distraction. Calls to Lucy and Claire went unanswered, not a surprise after the scene the night before, and I left messages with both of them, inviting them to join.

I also called Walt, who was on duty for the day at Poplar Branch, but knew he wouldn't answer either. I disconnected without leaving a message.

"So, which one's better? Charlotte or Asheville?"

"Um, well, Charlotte is a large city that's had something of a business renaissance over the past few years, so there's a lot of little boutiques downtown. Restaurants. I've only been there a few times wi — for dinner with friends."

"Oh. I see." She pursed her lips and batted her eyelashes. "Dinner with Sugar Bear?"

"Asheville is in the mountains. It's very eclectic. There's a lot of galleries and new age stores. Oh, and this place that makes their own chocolate and a bookstore—"

"Charlotte. Definitely. The last thing I want to do today is follow you around a dusty hippie bookstore."

I stood, collecting our breakfast dishes, and took them to the dishwasher. "Okay. Charlotte it is, then."

As we passed through Callahan, Dani asked about the new businesses opening in the old mill town's restored Main Street.

"What's 'Merle Travis's Taproom'? Do they have their own brewery? Y'know I went to this workshop with Dante one weekend in Portland called Craft Brew U. I wonder if they've ever considered having a beer sommelier?"

"Portland? That sounds fun. What did you learn?" *Portland. Not Callahan, Dani.*

"Just stuff about flavor profiles and food pairings, how small breweries can expand to the wine-buying customer. Have you been in there?"

"Didn't that girl you know from Cupertino move up to Portland?" I was determined to keep her attention on her own coast—where our mother and Dante were.

"Okay, Erin, would you please just stop? Ugh—and don't call Linda a girl."

"Stop?" I forced myself to look at the side of the street opposite the tiny Trattoria Stella, home of Nonni Isolde and chicken piccata and Walt's hand in mine. This morning was supposed to be ours, a chance to sleep in and indulge ourselves with a few long, lazy hours in bed before he had to go to his forest. We had discussed trying canes at Tate's house, in one of the bedrooms upstairs. I was going to wake up with Walt's arm hooked over my hip, his hand resting on my thigh and his marks on me. "Stop what?"

"Stop ignoring me. I'm asking you about your life here and you're ignoring it."

"Dani, please. Let's focus on you, okay?" I smiled mildly at her. "This is your weekend to figure out how to talk to Dante about all of this. It's not about me."

"I don't have anything to say to him." She stared ahead, folding her arms over her chest.

"You should talk to him." I turned on to the highway. "You've never been so serious with a guy, Dani. You break up with them way before they gain traction in your life. I could see he was different when I had dinner with you and Mom last month."

"Was."

"Dani," I said. "Have you called him?"

"I called him plenty of things when I threw his ring back in his face." She snorted. "Look, I don't want to talk about him anymore. He wants a vintner's hostess-wife, that's fine. But that's not me."

I inhaled deeply, wishing I'd stopped at the Callahan biscuit shop for coffee. A Wine Country wife was exactly what Dani had always wanted to be, down to the imported Spanish espadrilles and Wednesday afternoon French manicures.

"I feel like shopping. Let's dump the museum and go look in those boutiques you were talking about, Pudge."

It was going to be a very long, very expensive day.

Well after lunchtime, I had simply had enough of standing beside changing rooms, waiting on Danielle.

"I'm going to go sit down," I said, rising on my toes so I could speak over the door. "Let's go have lunch after this, okay?"

Her head popped through the neckline of a small, sheer garment she identified as a *dress*. "I wanted to go to that jewelry place across the street."

"Dani, I need to have lunch. Soon."

She looked at me like I was speaking another language. "Fine. Okay. Whatever."

Once I found a place to sit, I dialed Claire, whose number went straight to voice mail, and then Lucy.

"Hi there. What's up?"

"I'm with my sister."

"Uh-huh, figured so. Well, that sigh says it all. They might be uptight WASPs, but I thank the heavens above every holiday season that I have brothers. Hang on," she said and jostled her hand over the speaker. "No…no, Alex, they're in the other bathroom. We can come back for her winter clothes. Just the stuff from the bathroom in the basement and her desk."

"Is Claire with you?"

"No, she's still over at Tate's. She's going to be there for a while."

"How…" I faltered. How were any of them? I'd missed being there for Claire, really all of them, in the aftermath of what happened. "So this is definite?"

"Done deal, Sugarbritches." She actually sounded breezy about the whole moving-Claire-from-her-house business, like she was really in Claire's house to hang a new painting or help with a casual dinner, not beginning demolition on a marriage of twelve years.

I gnawed at my lip, glancing around the shop for Dani. "Is she, you know…how is she?"

"Nerita and Tate are with her."

"I tried to call. I don't know, maybe she didn't want to—"

"Oh no, she wants to talk to you. She asked about you this morning. It's been a while since there was a grand-scale drama unfolding, so last night it was all of a sudden about the kinky telephone tag, people she's not heard from in months calling for the story. Fucking gossipy hens, every one of them. Tate finally had to turn off her phone when it wouldn't stop ringing."

"Will you tell her I'm thinking of her?" Like that would do anything to help Claire feel less of a spectacle and not abandoned in front of her friends at a party. Suddenly, Walt's solution to Dr. Paul Saldino made much more sense to me. "I can't really leave Dani today but once she's gone…" Unsure of a concrete thing I could do for Claire, I left it as an offer of my presence.

"Talked to Walt today?"

"No, I—" Wincing at the sound of Dani's voice, I tucked my phone closer to my mouth. "He's on duty at Poplar Branch today."

The line went silent for a moment. Finally, Lucy spoke again.

"Hey, you know…this is not really any of my business, Erin, but someone should say it to you because Walt won't. He doesn't like to let himself go like that easily, you know? Brings up stuff. It's hard on him."

"No, I get that. I…he shouldn't worry about it, though. Everyone was angry in their own way. And for good reasons, too." It was a cop-out statement. We both knew it, too. I didn't know how to say more to Lucy, how to explain what I'd done to him. And once she heard, she most likely wouldn't want to hear my flawed rationale anyway. "My sister's ready to go to lunch, Lucy. I should go."

"Sure thing," she said. "Chin up, buttercup."

CHAPTER TWENTY

After he lost his ROTC scholarship for injuring Joyce and Zane, one of the stipulations of Walt staying on campus as a student at Clemson was two semesters of weekly anger management sessions at the student counseling center. His assigned counselor, an older woman he only knew as Eva, didn't begin with talking about his feelings or getting him to cry or some other feely-weely shrink shit.

She asked him to start running. Not because a coach or a bat commander or a teacher told him he had to. He could go three or four times a week, over to Issaqueena Lake, and run on the trails there, just himself. No Brady, no Lucy. Just Walt and the big, silent forest. It was the one thing he'd admit to Eva he cared for besides his two friends.

It wasn't easy, with his arm still wrapped up in gauze and fiberglass, and he slid down more than one pine needle covered hill on his ass when his feet got tangled up under him, but eventually the cast and the sling came off. Eventually Walt found his stride.

Trail running was something that got him breathing fast enough to feel like he'd worked hard and got his feet pounding so heavy he couldn't hear old voices in his head. Once he found some peace from their near-constant chatter, he decided to give Eva and her weekly talks a chance. She had, after all, been right about the running.

And still from time to time, once the park was closed, he took to the Overlook Trail and just ran. It was his secret benefit of being an onsite ranger at one of the smallest parks in the state.

No matter how hard he pushed himself up the hills or how heavy his breath crashed in his ears, Walt couldn't get past what brought him out to the trail in the first place. Because Erin was here too. He'd brought her here, without a second thought, less than twenty-four hours after they met. Just opened everything up for her to look at and turn over and consider, if she wanted. So much for sitting out anything but the most superficial relationships.

How'd that work out for you?

Fucked. That's how it worked out.

He let momentum carry him down a steep incline, taking a narrow stream in one leap. As his feet came back to the trail, something small fluttered toward him and bounced away at a sharp angle. Walt made it two or three strides further before he realized what had happened.

He scared it. He hurt it. He broke it. That's what he always did, even when he'd never intended to, when he couldn't have on purpose. Things came close to him and he broke them.

If he could just get it to her, she could fix it. She always made it better.

"Mama, I hurt it. Help me fix it."

"Let's see here, Bub." She had blue eyes, blue like the lake out at Indian Path Park where they went for the swings. Her eyes looked sad today. More sad than usual. She turned away, coughing hard, and then sat it in the grass beside her. "Honey, it's not fixable. Sometimes things aren't. Butterflies are delicate creatures. I'm sorry."

He looked overhead, in the direction the Monarch flew. "I'm sorry."

She didn't answer. He wasn't sure if it was Erin or Holly or Mel or his mom but not one of them called back to tell him it was okay, that he hadn't broken them too.

A stitch coiled up his side and he walked in circles, hands on hips, trying to shake it off. Through pants of breath, he was saying something, rambling out gibberish to the oaks overhead as he scrabbled after air and once he knew he was talking and not just panting, he heard his own voice over the dusky stillness of the woods around him.

He roared out, into the tree canopy, sending birds squawking into the evening sky. A long-dead black walnut trunk listed over the stream and Walt charged it, shoving it to the ground with his shoulder. He staggered past the cracked wood and slammed his fist into a narrow dogwood, sending a shower of leaves down around his head.

"I'm sorry, all right? Fucking sorry. I'm sorry. I'm sorry. I'm sorry."

And there was no answer.

After so many years of saying sorry for just being himself, one more apology just wasn't going to help. He was what he was. Sorry wouldn't do a damn bit of good to fix it.

He sat down hard on a big rock, not bothering to look around and check what might be sitting there already. His breath was coming down, but still shuddered in his ears. Not winded. Crying. And this was as good a place as any to do it.

Alone, Walt bent his head into his hands and sobbed.

Dani and I drove back to Callahan in silence. In turns, I worried and seethed, sure she was wrecking a relationship over her own pride and certain she would take mine down along with hers if she knew more about Walt.

It was dusk when I signaled and turned off the interstate at the Callahan exit. Beneath the green sign was a matching brown one giving directions and the distance to Poplar Branch State Park. When the headlights swung over a graphic indicating hiking, I flinched, sending the car fishtailing.

"Please try not to kill me in North Carolina," Dani said, hoarse. She'd been sleeping.

"Sorry, I thought something ran across the road."

"In this wilderness wonderland, that could be any kind of man or beast." She laughed softly at her joke and turned to me. "I never would have put you in a place like this and with a guy like him."

"Please, Dani. Don't." I'd come to this. A bereft, weepy woman who believed even the road signs were emotionally attuned to her.

"Why won't you talk to me about him?" She shifted in the passenger seat, reminiscent of how Walt turned to me the night his truck broke down and I took him home. She shrugged. "He seemed like a nice guy. Not your type at all, but nice."

"I…"

"Dante calls guys like that '*non possono essere tenuti al guinzaglio,*' like the big Brunos from his town that work on the line."

"What does that mean?"

"Um, sort of like a big horse that can't be put on a lead? *Il grande stallone, non possono essere tenuti al guinzaglio.*"

"When did you learn Italian?"

"Dante." She let out a long breath. "He taught me. It's nothing special, just kitchen Italian."

As I turned down Main Street, I glanced her way. "So speaking his language is okay, but…?"

"Erin, it's different. That's…it's nothing. It's just learning slang a bunch of line cooks say to each other." She faced the road again, blinking. "It was nothing."

I parked the car. "You wouldn't spend your half of the rent to fly across the country for thirty-six hours if it was nothing."

She looked down at her hands and blinked again. Exactly like me when I tried not to cry. "Why did he have to expect so much from me?"

"I don't think he expected anything more than what he knew you were capable of." I took my keys from the ignition. "Sometimes it's better to listen to someone who loves you over the voices in your own head."

She chuckled softly. "You too?"

"All the time." I pointed to the restaurant in front of us. "So, feel like Italian?"

"Great, that's all I need. Red and white tablecloth Italian on a Sunday night in back-ass nowhere North Carolina? Erin, just feed me a frozen pizza and kill me."

"It's good. No, I promise, it's very good. They make the best chicken piccata I've ever had."

By the time we finished dinner, Dani still refused to call Dante, but she did agree our little Trattoria wasn't entirely hopeless. I was relaxed, too, thanks to the attention of the staff who knew me, and a few extra sips of a wine Dani chose to go with the meal. I suppose she sensed I had reached the limit of my patience with the Walt questions, and we had a pleasant time not discussing our respective relationships.

Nonni Isolde sent us home with an extra bottle of the Friulano that impressed Dani, and a take-out container filled with Limoncello-soaked lemon sponge cake. She didn't ask about Walt, but she wondered. Once again, I felt someone's eyes on me, silently questioning, and I knew why they were curious.

At home, we moved around each other in the bathroom as we got ready for bed, in an old and familiar dance we'd done nearly every night of our lives until I left home for my final two years of college. Laughing over the small, intimate piece of our shared history felt good. It didn't solve anything, and didn't erase so many years of a contentious relationship, but I did start for my bedroom without the same sense of dread from knowing my sister slept under the same roof as me.

"Hey, Rin?"

"Yeah?"

"That guy, Walt? It's serious, isn't it?"

I glanced down, watching as I smoothing my still-pink pedicure over the needlepoint rug. "It…I think so, Dani. But I may have made a mistake that hurt him too much to fix."

"I doubt it," she said and surprised me with a hug. "You can fix anything, Erin. You always could. I'm going to go call Dante. You should give Shady the Bear a call too."

"It's Smoky," I said, stifling a giggle. "Smokey the Bear."

"Whatever—the ranger guy, smartass. Just call him. Don't let your head get in the way."

I took my phone from the charger and began to close my bedroom door. "Oh, Dani, what time is your flight tomorrow night?"

"Nine fifteen from Charlotte. I'll be out of here by five. Want to grab some lunch before I leave?" Her head popped around my bedroom door and she smirked. "Does Smokey eat things he doesn't have to catch and kill first? He can come too, if you're up for it."

"I…no, I'm not sure he's going to want to." My lip started to tremble and I ground my jaw hard at it.

Dani pushed the door open and came in. "Rin?"

"I'm fine," I said, shaking my head as I thrust my hand in front of me. She couldn't come any closer. "I need to get ready for wor—"

"Shut up, you're crying. I bet you never cried over that Iranian dude."

"Indian!"

"What?"

"Ardhi. He's Indian. He's my friend, not my god damned boyfriend, Dani. He never was!" Turning from her, I threw my phone against my bed and then followed it, bouncing against the pillow that still smelled of Walt's shampoo and sobbing into it like a sixteen-year-old girl.

The mattress shifted a little. Dani sat beside me.

"Don't cry, Rin." I felt her hand on my shoulder, and then pushing my hair from my wet cheeks. "He loves you. It'll be okay."

I turned to her, sniffing. "He's never said that."

"I saw him look at you." She shrugged. "You don't have to get us together for lunch, but I'd like to meet him again. Anyway, you have to talk to him."

"I…yes, Dani," I sighed and pushed myself up to sit beside her. "I need to. I've made a huge mistake with him."

"You?" She snorted, shaking her head. "You don't make mistakes. What is that shit your company says? *We don't make mistakes, we make opportunities?*"

"Oh God, please don't spout Miner-speak at me right now." I covered my face, wincing.

"Fine. Then listen to your big sister. Who is flying home on your dime so she can embarrass the fuck out of herself when she grovels to her fiancé to take her back after she screamed at him in front of a kitchen full of Italian cooks. And pegged him in the head with a three-carat diamond ring."

"Three flawless carats," I added, grinning. "And you're only the big sister by fourteen minutes."

"Oh, screw you, Erin." Dani snickered. "I'm worth three flawless carats. So are you."

From nowhere, the trembling and tears started again. I cringed. "I don't care about those things. I just want him to know I'm proud to be his. I'm not hiding him."

Dani's eyebrows crumpled in confusion. "Um…well, of course you are. I mean, not like he owns you or anything, but you like being his girlfriend or…whatever."

"Yes, right," I said quickly. I forced a laugh. "I'm so strung-out over having a boyfriend, I can't assemble a sentence, huh?"

She drew me to her for a hug. "Sure. Why don't you call me around eleven tomorrow about lunch, okay? I'm going to go throw my stuff in my suitcase."

"Work this out with Dante, okay?"

"You too?" She surprised me, squeezing me again, so tight I swayed a little with the force of her. Dani wouldn't let me go, though. "Hang on, and listen to me. You deserve to be happy, Rin. I know you haven't been, a lot of the time, and I hope you can be with this guy. I'm sorry I'm such a pain in the ass."

"You're—" Inhaling, I sat. "Never mind. Yes, you are a pain in the backside. But it's usually okay."

"Thanks for putting up with me. And you—go call Walt," she said. "If you really did fuck up, admit it, and try to make it right. That's all you can do."

I sent a quick note to Steve, letting him know of Dani's unexpected visit and my late arrival the next morning.

Then, Walt.

His phone went directly to voice mail. After twenty minutes of mindless scrolling through a news site, I decided he wasn't going to respond to my text message either.

Blinking hard, I snapped off my bedside lamp and tucked the pillow he used under my chin.

Damn it, no. Damn.

While she slept in, I took the down-time from Dani to drive in to ThinkMine for a few hours. The stillness and hum of work would be a welcome calm after the past two days of upheaval. Simply navigating the precise aisles of gray cubicles made me feel better, and my private cube was as soothing as an ashram.

Quiet.

"Oh, good morning, Erin."

I stepped away from my darkened monitors, inhaling sharply.

"Morning, Alan." *Today? Are you kidding me?* "Can I help you with something?" I set my bags aside, connected my laptop, and booted up. "I didn't see any errors this morning on the patches you and Tasha and ran on Saturday night. Congratulations."

Dirtbag.

Of course there wasn't a problem. Tasha Alexander ran the same code she and I wrote together with no deviations.

"Yeah, about that. Tasha had a lot of trouble with those old Alpine servers. They hung up on her and she didn't seem to know what to do with them. I've worked on those boxes for years and know how to override the defaults."

"I know. I walked her through the override script Saturday night. The Alpines are phasing out when we roll out the first phase of virtualization this fall and I'm not going to upgrade them again next month. I think we'll be okay. But thanks, Alan."

My desk phone rang and I nearly lunged for it with the irrational hope it would be Walt calling on the center landline. "Excuse me."

"Hey, Erin," our front receptionist drawled. "Your sister is here with your phone. I can't believe how much y'all look alike. There was no question it was her, so I sent her on back, okay?"

The words were still on the air, currents tickling my ear, when I looked up and found Dani marching toward my desk, her face drawn and eyes fiery.

"Dani," I said, wary, and stood. Alan's impeccable talent for scenting blood in the water rousted him from his chair a half beat behind me. Whatever this was about, it did not need to happen in front of him.

"You want to tell me what this is?" She glanced at Alan over her shoulder and, stepping in front of him, thrust my phone in my face.

My phone. Oh my God, when I tripped this morning on that stupid runner and dropped my messenger bag and my lunch and my purse spilled everywhere...so much stuff. Like all that stuff Claire carries around...

I couldn't say anything.

What do you say to your sister when she's gone through your phone and discovered the seven pictures you've actually stored there? How do you explain why you're undressed in each of them and how do you explain the bruises and welts and bite marks on your body when she couldn't hear the voices and words and didn't understand how it happened because you kept him away from her like your own precious, perfect jewel? It didn't hurt; not like she believed it did.

Too much to explain. And not there, in my cube.

"How long has this been going on? Have you told someone?" She tossed my phone to my desk where it landed, thankfully, face down.

"Dani, I…we need to talk about this in private." Before she could begin again, I stepped around her, clasping her hand in mine and squeezing. "Alan, I need to speak with my sister. Would you please excuse us?"

"Sure, no problem," he replied as he turned a polite smile toward Dani. "Nice to meet you. Hope everything's okay, Erin."

I turned a stiff smile toward him and waited, with Dani's hand still clenched in mine, until I saw him disappear into his cubicle.

"What in the world were you doing snooping in my phone?" I hissed.

"You've got pictures like that on your phone and you're worried about me?"

"How did you get in there in the first place?" She had hacked into my house; why was my phone such a surprise?

"I can't believe you. You work on computers all day and you of all people used our birthday as your password. Are you fucking stupid?" Her voice carried over the staggered rows of moveable walls. Several heads popped up, turning in my direction. "Did he give you some kind of brain injury or something?"

"Dani, you can't do this here," I whispered, reaching for her again. "You can't show up at a place like this and start screaming. Everyone can hear you."

"Fine," she hissed. The concerned, encouraging, hugging-it-out sister of the night before was gone, replaced with someone who looked and sounded much more like our mother.

I led her through the aisles, shooting a furious glare over my shoulder every time she began to speak again. We passed reception and I waved, raising Dani's hand too.

"What a resemblance," our receptionist called after us.

Dani's rental was parked, hazard lights flashing, by the front door.

"You can't leave this here."

"I'm not doing one more goddamned thing until you explain to me why that guy has been hitting you. Are the pictures evidence or something?"

I gaped at her. She thought… "Dani, it's not what you think."

"How could that be anything other than your ass and your tits covered in bruises? Huh? I may not have my MBA, Erin, but I think

I know when someone is getting beaten up. I've had a little more experience with guys who like to shove a woman around than you."

"Dani…" Inhaling, I took her hand and marched her away from the entrance. "You shouldn't have been looking around in my phone."

"You kept getting texts. I was trying to shut it up."

"This isn't what you think it is. It's my private business, Dani." I glanced around the parking lot, distracted with the sound of people coming and going. "But I promise you it's not what you think it is."

"Are you telling me you, of all people, are doing this kinky sex thing? After everything you've said—how many times have you said women shouldn't be slaves to men, Erin? And your classes and those marches when you were in college. You're going to tell me now that *you're* into this?"

"I've never asked you to justify your personal life to me. Ever."

"So I'm going to let you stay with an abusive asshole because I was a little crazy when I was a kid? When it was okay and normal to be a little crazy? Are you out of your fucking mind?"

"He's not abusing me, Dani. I say it's okay, I'm the one who makes the decision to let him take over. I'm his submissive." I could hardly hear my own voice over the sounds of people coming and going around us and hoped above all else our voices weren't carrying.

"Submissive? Listen to what you're saying. This isn't a movie or something, Erin, this is a big guy with an excuse to hit you. What does this do for you? What, submissive, bullshit…are you waltzing around naked and on a leash?"

If he requested it of me, yes. I kept quiet. I shut my mouth, obviously. Purposefully. I knew, in that moment, though I might never be asked to wear a collar and leash by him, I would. Anything Sir asked. Just like Claire. It was a kind of freedom, seeing that part of me, right then as I watched Dani rail against me, because I knew he'd never ask me to be like Claire. I trusted him. And I trusted myself in his hands.

"But that kind of thing, Erin. Don't you have to live up to his rules? That's a kind of perfectionism you don't need."

"No, not like that. Si—Walt wouldn't expect anything of me that wasn't already part of who I am. Remember what I said last night about Dante asking you to take marketing classes and teaching you Italian?"

She rolled her eyes. I thought of Lucy, and nearly broke open.

"Okay, look, say I'm happy for you, because it's good you're dating someone for a change. You're actually letting people in and letting them get to know you. But how do you know he's not just forcing his vision of you onto you instead of seeing what's really there?"

"Because I trust him. And I love him." I blinked hard and had to turn away from her. It was too much, being forced to defend something that might have crumbled to nothing Saturday night.

"Great, now security's here." She groaned. In the distance past her shoulder, an old white SUV pulled up at the entrance.

"Not security, Dani. That's Walt." I watched his big shoulders clearing the doorframe and wound my fingers together. "Why is Walt here?"

She scowled, folding her arms across her chest, exactly like the time she let Kathy's kitten out during the summer between sixth and seventh grade because it was walking in front of the television while *VideoRequestLive!* was on, and it never came home.

He walked toward us, his jaw clenched.

"Dani, *why* is Walt here?"

"I called him on the way here."

Mentally, I staggered. For a long second or two, I gaped at her. After Saturday night, the next contact he had with my sister was a surprise interrogation about our relationship. The need to throttle her warred with relief of seeing him again, regardless of the circumstance, and the need to protect him from her judgments based on the lowest common denominators she knew.

"After last night? You actually said something not completely self-absorbed to me and then you do this?"

He stepped around Dani, to my side.

"Hey," he said quietly. No *there you are*, this time.

"I'm sorry."

"No need to apologize. Thought I'd come on over here and save the police the trip to the park."

"Police, Dani? Are you kidding me? Did you actually call them?"

"No," she said, chastised. "I wanted to see what you said first."

"You need to go."

"That's it. I have to go?"

"Yes," I said. "That's it. I'm not going to try again to explain this to you. You're an adult, and I'm certain I remember you were with me when I saw people in the city practicing kink for the first time during Folsom, and every time after it that we went together. Except I didn't look at it like a sideshow like you did. You dragged me along, but did you ever see me do something I didn't want to do? I went with you because I needed to see people like me. I needed to know there was a place for me, when I was ready to find them." I glanced up at Walt, but he didn't return my look. "Dani, it's time for you to go. And please apologize to him."

She looked from Walt to me, and to him again, gritting her teeth.

"Sorry if I offended you."

Walt, a credit to his grandmother's manners, shook his head. "I don't know what you saw, but it's okay. You want your sister looked after, same as me. Thank you."

"I'm going to go get my things and go home." I reached for his hand. "I'd like to talk. Can I come to the park?"

"I left Sam alone over in the visitor center. Why don't you come by once Dani's on her way, all right?"

"Okay, I..." I patted my pockets. "Dani, can I have my phone? I need to send the site director a note before I leave."

"I don't have it." She stared at me, eyes wide. "I gave it back to you."

"Oh God." I shook my head. "I'm sure it's fine. I mean...people leave their things out all the time, right?"

"Sure," Walt said. "I doubt anyone noticed." He squeezed my hand and stepped away. "See you in a bit. Dani, you have a safe trip home."

Once my sister and her suspicions drove away, I started for the entrance. The day had turned sweltering again and I was covered in a fine skim of perspiration from standing under the late morning August sun. A blast of cooled air was a profound relief once the center doors opened. The receptionist apparently had watched the entire argument and a beady-eyed kind of curiosity hung around her. Even with my skin still heated from the sun, a cold bolt of dread shot up my spine.

Nodding to her, I retrieved my badge from my skirt pocket and held it aloft at the scanner as I passed.

I passed row after row of cubicles, insisting to myself there was no need to scamper to my desk. Just as Walt said, people leave their belongings at their desks all the time.

Several of my admins were telecommuting for the day, and it looked as though a few others—including Alan—had gone to lunch. The pale gray walls of my cube looked the same. A fractal screensaver pulsed on the monitors I used with my laptop. And my phone sat, benign in its plain black protective case, on my keyboard.

I hurried to pack away my belongings before I was noticed. Once I was outside in my car, I keyed a quick note to Steve from my work phone citing a "personal emergency" and letting him know I would be at home but telecommuting for the rest of the day.

CHAPTER TWENTY-ONE

Walt was occupied with a small group of day hikers when I reached the park. I caught his eye, waving, and crossed the open space to the visitor center. Sam Cross was behind the desk as usual, arms crossed over his stomach and nodding toward his afternoon nap.

"Well if it isn't the prettiest computer repairwoman in Grayson County." He came to me, chuckling, and offered his hand. Such an old flirt, Sam. After the accusations and horror of Dani flipping through the first and only pictures I'd ever taken with my phone, it was a relief to be looked at with favorable eyes.

"Hi, Sam," I said. "How was your weekend?"

"Well now, I've got to be honest with you. I'm ready for these kids to get back to school and let an old man get back to cutting the grass once a week and nappin' in the afternoons when Walt ain't looking."

My phone chimed in my pocket. I reached in and turned it to vibrate.

"Tell you what, Sam. I'm going to distract him for a little while, just so you can get your nap this afternoon, okay?"

As he laughed along with me, I felt normal — even comfortable — again in my skin. I'd learned the skill of talking like this from Walt, not a management class developed by forward-thinking human capital experts.

We chatted about the upcoming fall season, which would bring a final surge of weekend visitors and then the park would fall mostly silent through the winter, giving Sam, a seasonal employee, the opportunity to visit his grandchildren in Arizona for the holiday season.

Holidays. I looked out to the lawn and found Walt helping a father adjust an infant's hiking carrier on his back.

We could take a few days, maybe visit somewhere he's always wanted to go...

My phone continued to buzz, almost incessantly.

"Sam, I'm getting hit with a lot of work emails and should check them."

"I'll see you later, darlin'." He grinned and shuffled back to his lookout over the glass display cases.

Outside, I checked my work phone. Twenty-three new emails since I'd arrived at the park. I keyed in my password—and rolled my eyes over the much more secure one on the phone that, until I met Walt, was the one I most often used.

For the second time in as many hours, my heart plummeted into my stomach.

I'd sent a mass email to all of ThinkMine, with an attachment.

"Oh my God no, no, no..." I muttered, waiting for the message to load.

It was me. Naked, looking over my shoulder at my bruised backside.

I didn't consider looking like a hysterical woman and didn't bother to cover up the horrified sobs shaking my body so much I stumbled as I ran to my car.

"Erin?"

He was behind me. He'd see, too. The picture was for him, but he'd not seen me humiliated by it. How fucking careless could I be?

"Hey, what's wrong?"

I couldn't take relief from the easier tone in his voice, compared to what I'd heard in the ThinkMine parking lot. Just minutes before I'd been comfortable, hopeful about us.

"Sweetheart, what is it?"

I shoved my phone at him.

"What the hell..." Brows drawn, he scrolled through the email. "Did this go to everyone?"

"Every name in the company directory," I told him dully. The phone rang, and he handed it back to me. It flashed an international exchange and a Mumbai number. "Ardhi? Oh thank God." I stepped away from Walt.

"Your douchebag has been at work, dear."

"How do you know it's him?"

"He has a remote link to your laptop from his desk. The proxy has been sitting out there since mid-July but inactive, so we didn't notice any resources going from the location where he buried it. It was on one of your Alpine machines."

"Ardhi, what…can you fix it?" Behind me, Walt cleared his throat.

"Yes, I recalled the email as soon as I caught it. It's bloody lucky I'm here this evening, dear. You never send corporate-wide email and it caught my eye."

"Oh, Ardhi, thank you so much." Tears rolled over my cheeks and I raised a shaking hand to wipe at them.

"Anyone who opened the original email will have seen it. Steve is wiping the image from all of the locations that opened it, but sadly, we can't unsee it from anyone who opened the email and looked." He sniffed. "I'm a good security engineer, Erin, but not that good. *Yet.*"

"Are you sure it was Alan?"

Walt's hand covered my elbow. "Alan? That guy?"

"Quite sure. Who's that with you?"

"Er…my…um no one from work."

"Damn it, that's it. I'm going over there." Walt turned on his heel and started for his park SUV.

"No, Walt." I jogged after him. "Walt, you can't do that."

"The hell I can't."

"Walt, you have to let us—let *me* handle this."

He stopped by the Blazer's door, and his hand grasped the wide view mirror housing so hard his knuckles immediately went white.

"Erin, I don't give a fuck about how y'all plan on handling this inside your company. I do, however, have a very big say in how that son of a bitch treats you."

"Walt, no!" A couple walking toward the Hemlock Loop trailhead paused and looked at us. I tugged at his hand. "Please don't. Let me take care of this myself before it gets so big I lose my job, not just my credibility."

"I can take care of it and make sure it's in a way this guy gets the message to leave you alone. Until his warning — or whatever you all call it — is over and he's gone. But I will not stand for you being pushed around anymore."

"Walt, you can't do that. Those are my coworkers, my team. Do you understand? Alan isn't your problem, he's mine to manage. I have to fix this."

"I just told you, if he's hurting you, he's my problem. That's how this thing we're doing — what you asked to do — works. It's how I work, Erin. I don't stop looking out for you once you go off into the vanilla world. You're still mine to watch out for."

"You can't. This isn't The Enclave, Walt. This is my work. My career, which he's incinerated. He's ended me at ThinkMine and you're worried about…playtime?"

"It's not playtime for me." He put his hands on his hips. "Erin, haven't you paid attention for the past three months?"

I looked away, silenced, and before I could take my centering breath, as he'd taught me, and look back, Walt turned from me and walked across the grass. Away from me.

"Fuck this."

"Walt!"

Shaking his head, he stepped into the visitor center and pulled the door closed hard enough to make the windows bounce.

"Erin?"

Ardhi. I'd never disconnected the call.

"I'm sorry, Ardhi."

"No. Not at all. I have to tell you, though, I agree with your friend."

"That's not going to help." I sat inside my car and started it. "As much as it seems like a good idea, it still won't take—" I paused looking over the grass wrapping around the visitor center and Walt's forest beyond. I needed to say it. "It won't take back every comment I've heard about being a girl coder. About IT ass and how I'm getting it. I manage nine other men besides Alan, Ardhi, and they will never forget they've seen me naked."

"No," he said finally. "No, dear. I don't suppose they will."

Back at the house on Sycamore Street, it was Monday afternoon. The neighborhood dog barked. Mr. Jensen waved amiably from his weedeating. Two white butterflies flitted across the grass, a never-ceasing dance, just between them.

Not the artificial calm of the Mine. Comfortable and familiar, all the same.

I swallowed hard and crossed the front porch.

Dani's bags were by the front door. She had curled up on one of the sofas with a home magazine I'd never taken from the mailing sleeve during the past few busy, Walt-filled months after it arrived. Beside her was a glass of the iced tea he'd made Friday night.

And she'd used a coaster.

I let my bags slide from my arm and stay where they landed.

"Hi."

"How's Walt?" She patted a cushion beside her.

I shook my head. Too much. I sank beside her.

"Erin, if this—" she started. "If I've ruined things for you at your job…I'm so sorry."

"It's not your fault."

"It was on the floor by the bathroom. I should have ignored it, but it kept ringing and when I picked it up it saw it was him. I…I was curious. I've never seen you like—" she waved her hands between us "—this. In love, I guess. And then the pictures."

"Yes, the pictures." I arched an eyebrow at her. Though she was contrite—and should have been—I couldn't let one more opportunity to remind her she'd invaded my privacy pass.

"I mean…Rin? Really?" A small smile threatened at her lips. "You're into kinky sex?"

My cheeks heated and I looked away. "C'mon, Dani. This is private."

"But you're my sister," she said, her voice going soft.

"That still doesn't mean you need every detail of my life."

"No, you're right. It doesn't. But you don't need to shut me out completely, either." Taking my hand in hers, she moved closer to me and rested her head against mine, like she'd done when we were children, sleeping together on our ancient pull-out sofa. "I hated it when you left, but I'm glad you did, Rin. I think you belong here. I hope I didn't mess that up."

As I got older, I was careful to keep my feelings to myself. Dani and Kathy had so many, all the time. There was so much chaos around them. It had been years, maybe twenty-five or more, since I'd let her see me so hurt. But for the second time in just under a day, I turned and cried, without any hesitancy, on my sister's shoulder.

We spent the afternoon sitting, mostly silent, on my sofa, watching the trees spill light and dark across the golden oak floors. Two, maybe three hours of sitting. I didn't bother to change from my work clothes, and never booted my laptop. Eventually the chimes from my phone stopped. Ardhi had erased the replies as well. Someone else took care of it, after all.

I loved this place. The house, the town that held it. Mr. Jensen and Nonni Isolde and the night shift at Crusts. Callahan's quaint Main Street, coming back to life again, and ThinkMine being part of its revival. It was the first place I'd been at home. Even before I knew Walt and Claire and Lucy and Tate, before I'd gone through the stone pillars with the copper lanterns at Tate's house, a fundamental part of me felt right here. Almost at home. And then I found them...

A knock at my door shook me from my shadow and light staring.

"Sit," Dani said, standing. "I'll get it."

Steve was there. My mentor, the data center manager. A new wave of humiliation washed over me. Steve Gomez knew what I looked like naked.

Dani showed him in.

"Before I say anything," he said, crossing to me, "This is a personal visit."

Oh my God. I was going to be fired tomorrow morning.

"Erin, relax and take a deep breath. I'm not here to fire you."

I stared at him for a few seconds, willing my adrenaline to creep down to a manageable level. Not firing meant I had my job, but now also had to look people in the eye every day who had looked at me naked. With fading, purple-welted handprints on a good part of me.

"By the way, I'm Danielle Proctor, Erin's sister." Dani offered her hand, and they shook.

"Judy from reception was right. The resemblance is amazing."

"Well…" I began.

"We never see it," Dani added. After a polite laugh we all looked at each other. "Please, won't you sit down?"

He sat and motioned to her to join us.

"It's fine, Dani. He said this is personal, not official." I turned to Steve. "How do I handle this?"

"I'm surprised at you, Erin. There isn't anything to *handle*. You will come back to work tomorrow or Wednesday if you need and you'll keep planning your virtualization roll-out."

"But…the pictures and Alan and—" I winced. "Alan. He's still there."

"No, I walked him out personally just past three p.m. All of your updates on his action plan and Ardhi's logs were all we needed to close his file."

"But—"

"There's no need to go global over this, Erin. He crossed the line for the last time. You didn't have to give it any more of your attention. This was a business decision. Which I am speaking to you about off the record. Personally."

"But I should have taken care of it. How does it look if another man fixes it for me?"

"Rin, it sounds like a couple of guys who respect you took care of business. Let them," Dani said.

"In this case, Erin, it's more appropriate for me to handle it. And Arch Norman out at Main."

ThinkMine's CEO. I groaned and folded over my knees.

Dani cleared her throat. "It sets a tone, Erin. Dante does it in the kitchen. No disrespect. If it happens, he addresses it. Otherwise, *Il pesce pulla dalla testa.*"

Steve snorted, shaking his head. "Indeed."

"Fish stinks from the head." Dani winked at me. "He's taking responsibility for it."

"And wants to address it company-wide. At all houses. He's putting together a board to address harassment at the Mine. And he'd like to talk to you about it, Erin. Once you're back at work."

I sat back against the sofa pillows. He was gone. No more arguments and no more dumped code and no more barely-concealed comments to his two lunch partners. No more being called a fucking cunt any time I asked him to do his job.

Steve leaned toward me a little. "Erin, was there more than just the botched patches and star-fucking other managers? You look very, very shaken."

"I…" I took a long deep breath. "I am. He…it was difficult. I'm glad he's gone."

"Was there more? Something you didn't mention in your notes on his plan?"

I nodded and despite the horror of it, batted my eyelashes at tears. I'd cried more in the past month than the past five years.

"There were a lot of comments. It felt pretty hostile."

"Christ, Erin, you shouldn't have kept that to yourself."

"I didn't know what to say. It's not always been easy, being a woman there."

He looked at me with such sympathy and patted my arm. "I know. Try being a geek with a stereotypically twink husband and no gay snark skills to speak of. I miss the days when you could go to your desk as an admin and not speak to a soul and know no one wanted to talk to you either unless it was about a game you were running or a con you'd gone to."

"I'm sorry, Steve. That was incredibly self-centered of me."

"Poo. Stop." He rolled his eyes. "ThinkMine can try to position us as evolved and associate-centered until the ends of forever and it won't change it, inherently. Corporate places are big, messy engines that need a lot of us to make them work. Women, especially the ones who are doing male-identified roles, have a hard time in tech. We all know this. You read *Information Today*, just like I do."

I nodded, letting out a rush of air I didn't know I was holding. "Do you think the fallout would be more manageable if I went back to Los Altos?"

"I don't know. Offices don't have walls now." He shrugged. "After this, you're not just a girl admin and catching shade for that. People won't forget this, but Arch's actions and this workgroup could make a difference. And it's your private life, just like what I do in mine is my life. It won't affect your job and won't affect your leadership once you've processed this and quit apologizing for being who you are. So you like kinky sex and—from what I saw outside the center this morning—you have a very hot boyfriend who does too. As long as you have one hand free to code when I need you, you are free to play like a grown-up in private when you work in my center. You can't say sorry for who you are forever."

My chin trembled again. *Pedicures and contacts and stupid flowered dresses and all of this crying.*

"I don't know if he's going to be my boyfriend much longer." I sniffed. "I think I hurt him by trying to keep him—or really, us—to myself."

Steve's eyebrows rose and he smiled. "That man? In that uniform? Dear God, I would keep that to myself too if he were mine."

Dani snorted. "Right?"

"But if you're hiding him out of shame for what you do, that's not good."

"No. Not that, really. Mostly it was from—" I glanced at Dani sheepishly "—my mom and sister and he found out and that pushed a few buttons."

"We are all minefields." He shook his head. "You can't survive your twenties without leaving a minefield behind you."

"Yeah." I said, quiet. "Thank you for coming over here. I know it's not…typical for you."

"I like you, Erin. I always have. There aren't many people on this planet who could tolerate what you have to get here and still excelled professionally, no matter their gender. What are you going to do about Woodsy the Dom?"

"I don't know. He was so angry about Alan." I grinned a little. "I thought he was going to pull him apart. Over me."

"Oh my God…a white kinght! Stop, I might come over with the vapors. Give me a hankie to wave." We laughed together.

Something Lady Nerita said to me the first time we met echoed in my head and I laughed again over it.

A white knight. My white knight. My Sir.

"I'm going to go see him." I stood, smoothing over my skirt. "I'm going to need some armor and a blazing standard, though. And a white horse."

"You go on, Erin." He laughed with me and followed me to the front door with a grand flourish. "Go on and talk your man down from his tower of solitude."

After I'd shown Dani how to replace my spare key in the frog where she found it, I drew her to me for a final hug.

"Thanks, Rin. For everything." She whispered into my ear as she squeezed me tighter. Stepping back, she looked at me, her eyes narrowing. "Always."

"Dani?" I caught her hand as she turned from me. "I'm glad you were here. Thanks…you know, for helping me get through this."

"I didn't do anything but try to help my sister."

"I know. That was exactly what I needed."

The park was closed when I pulled up. I parked outside the brown access gate and stepped around, looking up at his cabin in the distance.

How to storm a castle?

Fortunately, the castle path, at least, was paved. I was, after all, still dressed for work in my gray pencil skirt and heels.

As I walked to his cabin, I didn't hear the commentary of my mother and sister, the items on an endless tide of to-do lists, or the voice of my own judgment. I heard birds chattering. The rustle of leaves as a small animal scampered away from me. Wind threaded through the tall hardwoods over my head in a long, sinuous sigh. No straight, perfect lines. The world—the natural one—was big, beautiful, random, and older, more real than anything we could ever build. Its many ages were more truth than things we created to distract us. I was more than thought and mental processes and pulses of electronic intentions. I was this too. I was of the earth too. His world.

The screen door creaked open. He'd changed into his favorite, battered cargo shorts and a T-shirt.

"Hey," he said, clearing his throat.

"Steve—the site director? He came to my house earlier. Alan's gone."

"Well, that's good. Should've fired him months ago."

"There's going to be a company-wide workgroup on workplace harassment. So maybe it will change." I twisted my fingers around my skirt and then forced the fabric from my hand like it was on fire. "I could have handled that better."

"Erin, you did fine handling it. The guy was—"

"No," I said and shrugged with a weak smile. "I meant you. I could have handled us better."

His eyebrows rose and walked to the end of the porch. "Thought you were handling it fine."

"Sir, I'm—"

"Can you not say the *Sir* shit right now? Just tell me what you have to say, Erin."

Swallowing, I took a step forward. "I wasn't hiding you. Well, I was. But it wasn't because I was ashamed of you or us. I wasn't ready to share you."

"Share me?"

"I've never felt like this. I wanted it to be mine as long as I could keep it that way."

"How would your mom and sister knowing about us take it away from you?"

"I don't trust them with you. They…they break things, they don't understand how delicate people can be. I don't want anything to hurt you."

"Delicate?" He thumped his bare heel against the edge of stone steps beneath him. "I'm strong, Erin."

"I know you are. But I don't want you to *have* to be any more. Not because of me."

He shoved his hands deep into his pockets and leaned against a wooden pillar. "I don't want you to feel afraid because of me."

"I don't. I've never been afraid of you when we played, Walt."

"Not talking about playing. I'm talking about you and me."

"Okay," I said. My fingers fidgeted over the fabric covering my thigh, searching for something to grasp and twist. "I've not considered those things as distinct entities, Walt. I can't separate belonging to you out here—" I gestured to the tall, green trees around us "—with what happens inside. At my house or Tate's, or in a dungeon, or even inside your cabin."

"I'm not sure I'm ready for all the time. I don't know that I want to be like that with you 24/7. I know you don't want the divide, but I don't want to lose us."

"Why does *us* have to be what someone says it's supposed to be? Let's just be us. Have our thing, the way it works for us. No titles or collars. We don't have to be like Paul and Claire. We only have to be us."

He cleared his throat and stayed silent.

We were going to follow each other in circles over this point. There was only one way to storm a castle. Right through the thickest wall.

"Walt, I love you."

His fingers hovered toward his ear but he folded his arms across his chest instead and a grin slowly spread across his face, lifting his cheeks, crinkling beside his eyes. "I swear, I never know what's going to come out of that head of yours."

I took another step, finding worn stone instead of a gravel path under my foot. First line, passed. "You know, I've never been inside your cabin."

"There's not much to see. It's an old park service cabin, Erin. Just a place to sleep and stay dry."

"But it's your place." I took another step. "It's where you've slept and lived and been Walt for twelve years. It's where you've been waiting for me."

He stepped aside. "You going back to California?"

"No. I'm not leaving. I like it here and I like being with you here."

"It's okay if you need to go. There's gotta be a forest or two left in California that needs looking after. I love you, Erin. We'll figure it out."

I threw myself over the highest wall, reaching for him.

And he caught me. I knew he would.

"Hey, whoa. Got you." He chuckled and held my arms. "Erin, wait. It's…you just need to know that. If you don't want to stay—"

"Don't? How could I leave you? You're my home."

"Home? Nobody's ever called me something like that."

"I said it because *you're* where I belong. I need you, Walt. I need to be where I belong. Please let me stay."

He drew me into him, settling his forehead against mine, and scooped me up into his arms. It made me squeal and giggle and sound ridiculous, like a girl.

"What are you doing?" I laughed as he shifted me against his chest.

"What do you think I'm doing?" He grinned down at me as he crossed the porch. "I'm acting like a caveman."

"Oh, I like cavemen." I trailed my fingers over his shoulder and followed them with my mouth, tasting the skin behind his ear. "Let's go inside, Ugg."

"All right, then." He pushed the screen door open and stepped inside his cabin. "Let's do that now."

THE END

ACKNOWLEDGMENTS

Without question, my words wouldn't feel complete without the eyes and hearts and minds of a special group of people who open their inboxes on occasion to find all kinds of ravings and word stew from me. They have the kindness and grace to read, mull, and respond to me. If not for them, I'd still be stirring and making mush. With profound gratitude and love for Gilly Wright, Kari Haines, M.V. Freeman, Jennifer Grizzard Ekzarkhov and Alexandra Sevilla, my beta readers. You're all blessings to me. Thank you. So very much.

To the forces of nature known as Kendall Gray, Rie Warren, Heather Savage, and Aaron Michael Ritchey: Let's just meet in the lobby.

Thank you to Eric Lohmeier who was there in times when I needed an adult, a warrior on my side, and a cooler head.

I'll always be grateful to Heather Hall, Janice Pauls Crampton, Bec Pishkin, Mer and Jess, Miss Patsy, and always dear Jilly who encouraged me to take this leap. Em girls always!

Early on, I engaged in a number of brain-storming sessions with Venessa Guinta about the structure and POV of The Enclave series. I'll always be thankful for her suggestions and encouragement to go my own way in finding the voices of this series.

I can't quite describe the moment of shock and awe I experienced when I received an email from Lisa O'Hara telling me Omnific wanted this series. I've admired this company and what they've accomplished for a long time. It has been my sincere pleasure to come to know Lisa, Elizabeth Andrews, Micha Stone, and Traci Olsen. I'm beyond thrilled to have my first book birthday with all of you. Thank you for your patience and your wisdom.

Michelle Grajkowski, my agent, has already talked me down from a number of high branches. I'm so glad to have her on my side and still surprised I've been so lucky to find her there.

Kasi Alexander, you are the editor I needed and I'm so glad I got you. Thank you for your calm, your insight, and your patience.

To the PRGs. Always.

ABOUT THE AUTHOR

After many years spent onstage mouthing the words of other writ-
ers, Jenna Barton found her own voice while playing with an online
community of mouthy broads. Writing down her own stories proved
to be far more satisfying than dodging the human and inanimate
hazards that come with backstage life, as well as alleviating the need
to walk and talk and gesture while inhabiting 89.37% of someone
else's reality.

Mostly settled into a life of carpool lanes and checkout lines,
Jenna happily resides in suburbia with her husband and their two
children. Sadly there are no drooly, furry, corpulent lapdogs at Chez
Barton. For now. For. Now.

check out these titles from
OMNIFIC PUBLISHING

◄ ⟶Contemporary Romance◄ ⟶

Keeping the Peace by Linda Cunningham
Stitches and Scars by Elizabeth A. Vincent
Pieces of Us by Hannah Downing
The Way That You Play It by BJ Thornton
The Poughkeepsie Brotherhood series: *Poughkeepsie, Return to Poughkeepsie* &
Saving Poughkeepsie by Debra Anastasia
Recaptured Dreams and *All-American Girl* and *Until Next Time* by Justine Dell
Once Upon a Second Chance by Marian Vere
The Englishman by Nina Lewis
16 Marsden Place by Rachel Brimble
Sleepers, Awake by Eden Barber
The Runaway series: *The Runaway Year* & *The Runaway Ex* by Shani Struthers
The Hydraulic series: *Hydraulic Level Five* & *Skygods* by Sarah Latchaw
Fix You and *The Jeweler* by Beck Anderson
Just Once & *Going the Distance* by Julianna Keyes
The WORDS series: *The Weight of Words, Better Deeds Than Words* & *The Truest of Words*
by Georgina Guthrie
The Brit Out of Water series: *Theatricks* & *Jazz Hands* by Eleanor Gwyn-Jones
The Sacrificial Lamb & *Let's Get Physical* by Elle Fiore
The Plan by Qwen Salsbury
The Kiss Me series: *Kiss Me Goodnight* & *Kiss Me By Moonlight* by Michele Zurlo
Saint Kate of the Cupcake: The Dangers of Lust and Baking by LC Fenton
Exposure by Morgan & Jennifer Locklear
Playing All the Angles by Nicole Lane
Redemption by Kathryn Barrett
The Playboy's Princess by Joy Fulcher
The Forever series: *Forever Autumn* (book 1) by Christopher Scott Wagner

◄ ⟶Young Adult Romance◄ ⟶

The Ember series: *Ember* & *Iridescent* by Carol Oates
Breaking Point by Jess Bowen
Life, Liberty, and Pursuit by Susan Kaye Quinn
The Embrace series: *Embrace* & *Hold Tight* by Cherie Colyer
Destiny's Fire by Trisha Wolfe
The Reaper series: *Reaping Me Softly* & *UnReap My Heart* by Kate Evangelista
The Legendary Saga: *Legendary* & *Claiming Excalibur* by LH Nicole
The Fatal series: *Fatal* & *Brutal* (novella 1.5) by T.A. Brock
The Prometheus Order series: *Byronic* by Sandi Beth Jones
One Smart Cookie by Kym Brunner
Variables of Love by MK Schiller

←···→New Adult Romance←···→

Three Daves by Nicki Elson

Streamline by Jennifer Lane

The Shades series: *Shades of Atlantis* & *Shades of Avalon* by Carol Oates

The Heart series: *Beside Your Heart, Disclosure of the Heart* & *Forever Your Heart*
by Mary Whitney

Romancing the Bookworm by Kate Evangelista

Flirting with Chaos by Kenya Wright

The Vice, Virtue & Video series: *Revealed, Captured, Desired* & *Devoted*
by Bianca Giovanni

Granton University series: *Loving Lies* by Linda Kage

←···→Paranormal Romance←···→

The Light series: *Seers of Light, Whisper of Light* & *Circle of Light* by Jennifer DeLucy

The Hanaford Park series: *Eve of Samhain* & *Pleasures Untold* by Lisa Sanchez

Immortal Awakening by KC Randall

The Seraphim series: *Crushed Seraphim* & *Bittersweet Seraphim* by Debra Anastasia

The Guardian's Wild Child by Feather Stone

Grave Refrain by Sarah M. Glover

The Divinity series: *Divinity* & *Entity* by Patricia Leever

The Blood Vine series: *Blood Vine, Blood Entangled* & *Blood Reunited*
by Amber Belldene

Divine Temptation by Nicki Elson

The Dead Rapture series: *Love in the Time of the Dead* & *Love at the End of Days* by
Tera Shanley

The Hidden Races series: *Incandescent* (book 1) by M.V. Freeman

Something Wicked by Carol Oates

←···→Romantic Suspense←···→

Whirlwind by Robin DeJarnett

The CONduct series: *With Good Behavior, Bad Behavior* & *On Best Behavior*
by Jennifer Lane

Indivisible by Jessica McQuinn

Between the Lies by Alison Oburia

Blind Man's Bargain by Tracy Winegar

←···→Erotic Romance←···→

The Keyhole series: *Becoming sage* (book 1) by Kasi Alexander

The Keyhole series: *Saving sunni* (book 2) by Kasi & Reggie Alexander

The Winemaker's Dinner: *Appetizers* & *Entrée* by Dr. Ivan Rusilko & Everly Drummond

The Winemaker's Dinner: *Dessert* by Dr. Ivan Rusilko

Client N° 5 by Joy Fulcher

The Enclave series: *Closer and Closer* (book 1) by Jenna Barton

Shackled by Debra Anastasia
Swim Recruit by Jennifer Lane
Sway by Nicki Elson
Full Speed Ahead by Susan Kaye Quinn
The Second Sunrise by Hannah Downing
The Summer Prince by Carol Oates
Whatever it Takes by Sarah M. Glover
Clarity (A *Divinity* prequel single) by Patricia Leever
A Christmas Wish (A *Cocktails & Dreams* single) by Autumn Markus
Late Night with Andres by Debra Anastasia
Poughkeepsie (enhanced iPad app collector's edition) by Debra Anastasia
Poughkeepsie (audio book edition) by Debra Anastasia
Blood Eternal (A Blood Vine series single, epilogue to series) by Amber Belldene
Carnaval de Amor (*The Winemaker's Dinner*, Spanish edition)
by Dr. Ivan Rusilko & Everly Drummond

coming soon from
OMNIFIC PUBLISHING

The Dead Rapture series: *Love Starts with Z* (book 3) by Tera Shanley
Missing Pieces by Meredith Tate
The Way to Go series: *Way to Go* (book 1) by Mandy Colton
Command the Tides by Wren Handman
The Hidden Races series: *Illumination* (book 2) by M.V. Freeman
The Record of My Heart by Georgina Guthrie
The Counterfeit by Tracy Winegar
The Embrace series: *Entwined* (book 3) by Cherie Colyer